SEAN WILLIAMS

saturn returns

ASTROPOLIS BOOK ONE

www.orbitbooks.net

ORBIT

First published in the United States in 2007 by Ace,
Penguin Group (USA) Inc.
First published in Great Britain in 2007 by Orbit

Copyright © 2007 by Sean Williams

The moral right of the author has been asserted.

A CIP catalogue record for this book is available
from the British Library.

ISBN 978-1-84149-518-7

Typeset in Garamond by M Rules
Printed and bound in Great Britain by
Clays Ltd, St Ives plc

Orbit
An imprint of
Little, Brown Book Group
Brettenham House
Lancaster Place
London WC2E 7EN

A Member of the Hachette Livre Group of Companies

www.orbitbooks.net

For Shane Dix, brother of the art.

And my dreams are strange dreams, are day dreams, are grey dreams,
And my dreams are wild dreams, and old dreams and new;
They haunt me and daunt me with fears of the morrow . . .
I wander forever and dream as I go.

Henry Lawson, 'The Wander-Light'

CONTENTS

THIS WRECKAGE   1

THIS ELEGANT BITCH   51

THIS DYING MACHINE   91

THIS HUMAN CORROSION   139

THIS PRISON MOON   198

THAT TACITURN AND INVISIBLE GOD   266

Map of the Milky Way   282

Appendix A: Absolute Calendar   283

Appendix B: Glossary   285

Appendix C: 'My Confession'   288

All quotes attributed to Robert Charles Maturin are taken from the first edition of *Melmoth the Wanderer* (1820), edited by Victor Sage (Penguin Books, 2000).

The planet Saturn takes 29.46 years to circle the sun and, according to Astrological traditions, to return to the House it occupied at the moment of an individual's birth. During a 'Saturn Return,' the light of this cold and distant world shines on our lives, encouraging us to examine our choices, our aspirations, and our disappointments. It is a time of endings as well as beginnings, and will be dreaded by those whose path through life has been ill-chosen.

THIS WRECKAGE

The relics of art for ever decaying,
— the productions of nature for ever renewed.

Robert Charles Maturin

'I am not a decent man.'

The words were spoken in response to a question Imre Bergamasc couldn't hear. Although he knew they came from his own mouth, he knew also that the utterance was a memory, not something occurring in his present. He wasn't talking to anyone. He appeared, rather, to be lying on his back with his eyes closed, as though he had just woken from a deep sleep, but fully dressed in a soft jumpsuit made of material that whispered softly as he raised his hands to touch his chest and explore his face.

Something was wrong, or at least very different. He had breasts.

His eyes opened wide. A grey bulkhead greeted him, less than a meter from his face. He raised his head and looked down along his foreign, curved body. A coffinlike space enclosed him on all sides except his left, where it opened onto a larger chamber. The surface beneath him was padded: a bed of some kind, yes, but one of spartan proportions. There was room for just one person, and no space to sit up. Two narrow striplights provided the sole illumination, cold and characterless. The chamber beyond his bunk was dark and sounded empty.

His breathing became more rapid. He had no recollection at all of how he had arrived in such a place, or become female into the bargain. He was profoundly out of his depth. He was—

'Who are you?' asked a voice.

He jumped. The words came from a speaker built into the wall to his right that didn't seem to be functioning with perfect clarity, for the voice came with more than a hint of static.

'What's your name?' it asked him.

'Don't you know?' His own voice – real, not remembered – could have been a man's, contralto and throaty from disuse. He cleared his throat. The timbre didn't change. 'You brought me here, didn't you?'

Instead of answering him, the voice asked, 'Who do you think you are?'

'We could ask each other questions all day.' He lowered his head back onto the thin mattress, already drained by the short exchange. 'Tell me who you are, first. Then we can talk.'

'We are the Jinc, fifth ganglion of the Noh exploratory arm. Perhaps you have heard of us.' The voice addressing him sounded faintly hopeful but not expectant. 'We trawl the outer edge of the galaxy for clues to the nature of God.'

He suppressed a momentary discomfort on finding that he was addressing a group mind. He didn't know why that should bother him. 'God? Why?'

'We have reasons. In the course of our explorations, we found you.'

'What do you mean, you found me?'

'Your body, in a manner of speaking, drifting. We will provide full details shortly. You need know for now only that we spared no effort in restoring you to consciousness and, we hope, full physical fitness.'

He flexed his fingers. Despite the odd alteration in gender, he did feel fine enough. 'I'm well, I suppose. What happened to me? What was I doing so far from the Continuum?'

'Is that the last thing you remember, the Continuum?'

'Why would that be unusual?'

'We will explain. Your situation is unique, and we do expect there to be some injury to your memory. It would help us to know your name, if you do in fact know it.'

'Some injury . . .' He rubbed his forehead. An alarming

dizziness threatened to consume him as he tried to recall what had brought him to such a strait. His body, drifting on the galactic fringes; rescued by deep-space scavengers and turned into a woman; his memory impaired. 'My name is Imre Bergamasc,' he said. 'That I'm sure of. The rest . . .' He rubbed harder. His brain was as heavy and sluggish as lead. 'I don't know. I do have memories, but – I – they won't fall into place.' He kicked out suddenly, flailing his legs in an ill-advised attempt to swing out of his bunk and into the chamber beyond, there to stand and seek out his questioner, the voice known only through a speaker thus far, buzzing and removed.

Nausea overwhelmed him before he came close to succeeding. A flock of memories, beating at his mind like a storm of crows, drove him back into the bunk.

'I don't know,' he moaned into the speaker. 'I don't know who I am.'

'You said your name is Imre Bergamasc. Isn't that who you are?'

'I suppose it must be. It has to be.' He placed both hands over his eyes and felt cool wetness on his cheeks. 'Who is Imre Bergamasc? Do you know who he's supposed to be? I don't know, and I don't know how to find out.'

'Are you saying now that you're not Imre Bergamasc?' The speaker sounded puzzled and cautious – perhaps, even, oddly fearful.

'That's my name,' he said, 'so I must be. Right?'

The speaker fell silent. Imre wept softly to himself, seeing no way out of the terrible conundrum. He knew his name but didn't know who he was. Something in his mind wasn't working correctly. The uncertainty cut like acid deep into his thoughts. He couldn't think through that terrible block, now that he had confronted it. He was stuck, frozen, damaged.

A door in the chamber outside his bunk hissed open. Air shifted minutely as pressures equalized. He wiped his face and blinked his sight clear of tears. A hunched, monklike figure had entered the room.

'We, the Jinc, will explain,' it said, coming to his side. Its voice was the same as the one before: thin and dusted with static. The speaker had been working perfectly. 'Please let us.'

He looked up into a face that seemed composed of nothing but gristle and grey skin, as animated as a corpse. Its eyes were shut, but its hands moved with all the purpose and certainty of the sighted. He reflexively recoiled when it reached for him with long, flexing fingers, but again he reined in that instinct. The Noh was a group mind distributed through the skulls of numerous willing hosts. The creature before him had no more individual will than his own foot, being the instrument through which the gestalt mind acted. It was a mouthpiece, not the mouth.

He nodded to his strange host and let himself be eased out of the bunk.

The Noh vessel was cramped and torturous to navigate. Corridors little wider than the bunk in which he had woken snaked between sepulchral chambers that doubled or tripled functions in order to utilize the volumes they occupied with maximum efficiency. The room in which he had woken was, it transpired, normally reserved for medicinal purposes as well as bunking space for the mouth-pieces roughly equating to doctors or nurses within the Jinc. The dispersed entity – who took its name as a parenthesis around a single parcel of the greater culture or creature known as the Noh – needed such functionaries just as an individual human needed an immune system. When components fell ill, repair was easier than replacement. Voyages through deep space demanded such careful use of resources, since the next stop might be hundreds of years Absolute away.

Imre could not have retraced the route he followed through the Jinc's vessel. He hoped he would not need to. Along the way he noted clues as to the physical nature of the ship: a spinning habi-tat providing centripetal gravity in a low-thrust environment; decentralized life support capable of isolating one segment of the vessel from another in case of a major catastrophe; numerous signs of age and wear indicating that the vessel had been in service for a considerable time, even by the standards of deep space. His guide

negotiated the tight tunnels by application of well-practiced taps
and kicks to anchor points and solid bulkheads. The sounds and
smells of humanity were everywhere, even among the Jinc, where
all notions of individuality had been subsumed. He smelled food
and spices and sweat, and a faint stink of corruption, as though
from a faulty water reclamation plant. The scents triggered memories he couldn't pin down: faces and feelings that were, for the
moment, fragmentary and nothing less than frustrating. Somehow,
he knew everything about centripetal gravity and water reclamation plants but failed to piece together anything more substantial
about himself than his name. That struck him as grossly unfair,
and he hoped the Jinc would soon explain why that might be.

His guide brought him to an observation port at the very edge
of the spinning habitat, where gravity approached half Earth
Standard. Unfamiliar details made themselves felt as he stepped
into the center of the port: the weight of his breasts; the width of
his hips; the narrowness of his feet. He had no hair at all and no
obvious markings on his skin. He had, as yet, not seen his own
face, so couldn't tell how much it resembled the one glimpsed in
his memory. That his new body possessed a suite of implants and
cognitive modifications came as no surprise; such were standard in
the Continuum. Only the most recalcitrant of people, Primes,
rejected such technology and lived more or less as humans had
hundreds of thousands of years ago.

A name drifted across his thoughts – Emlee Copas – and with it
an image of a wiry, blond-haired woman with jade green eyes.
Before he could pursue the recollection, the reflective black bulkheads of the port faded to transparency, and the full glory of the
galaxy at close range confronted him.

He gasped. One hundred billion stars filled the view to his
right, shining across all frequencies of the spectrum. To his left was
mottled darkness, lit only by globular clusters and more distant
aggregations of galaxies. The Noh vessel was still too close to discern the true shape of the Milky Way – the barred spiral that
humanity had long ago spanned from end to end – but the central
bulge was clearly visible, as was the thick, curving arc of one arm.

'Behold,' said the Jinc's mouthpiece, rather unnecessarily Bergamasc thought, until he realized that the wizened creature pointed not at the galaxy but at an object much closer to hand. 'This is your origin,' it said, indicating a long, grey cylinder with the rough proportions of an old-fashioned flashlight, hanging immobile with respect to the Jinc's vessel. Its size was impossible to determine without points of reference. 'Do you recognize it?'

Imre could only shake his head. 'What's it made of?' he asked, taking stock of starlight gleaming dully from undecorated metal. 'It looks like iron.'

The creature bowed its cowled head. 'The most stable element in the universe. This artifact was built to endure the ages.'

'How long has it been drifting out here?'

'Many centuries Absolute, at least. Its rest was disturbed, making a more precise date difficult to ascertain.'

'Disturbed how?'

'The Drum, as we call it, was discovered in pieces. Two crude but effective nuclear explosions had reduced it to little more than dust, which we gathered, mote by mote, from within the blast radius. Our painstaking reconstruction of the original artifact took longer than we anticipated, for much has been lost forever – including, we thought at first, its contents, for the Drum proved to be hollow.'

'What makes you sure there were contents at all? It could have been empty when destroyed.'

'That was our second thought. Someone built this artifact and set it adrift on the outer limits of human space in a stable orbit that would have seen it neither escape the Milky Way nor return to habitable regions. Then someone else, for unknown reasons, came along to steal its contents and eliminate the evidence.'

'A long way to come for a heist.'

'Indeed, and just as far for murder.'

Imre studied the expressionless face of the Jinc mouthpiece even though he knew it would reveal nothing. 'What do you mean, murder?'

'We have ascertained that the Drum was always empty of

matter, but not information. Its interior wall was inscribed with a single groove, looping around and around like copper wire in a crude electric motor. The groove contained notches spaced at irregular intervals. When we examined those notches – played them, if you like, as one would once have played a record with a diamond needle – we quickly ascertained that they contained information. The Drum was a data storage device, strange and magnificent in its own way, and intended to last forever. That it might have done but for its deliberate destruction.'

'You managed to recover and decode the data,' he said, guessing ahead. The feeling of dizziness returned, and it had nothing to do with the vertiginous view. 'This must be where I come in.'

'Yes. The Drum preserved the life of a single person in hard-storage. We have reconstructed a large proportion of that person from what remained of the Drum. Who that person was, exactly, we couldn't tell. Now you are awake, we know.'

'How much do you know, really? The record preserved my name, but it got my gender wrong.'

'Gender is a matter of choice not biology, as it should be. It is one data point among trillions. We only had your genes to rely on for your physiognomy. They allow the possibility of a masculine form, but also several species of late-onset cancer as well. Would you have had us retain those tendencies too?'

'Of course not.'

'Then we can only apologize for assuming incorrectly regarding your gender. We had a one in two chance of getting it right. The mistake can be rectified, in time.'

'I'll think about it.' If reclaiming his past self and finding out who he had been was to become his priority – as seemed logical, given the lack of an alternative proposition – then adopting his prior physical form could be an important first step. In none of the memories clamoring for his attention was he female or any other gender but male. 'In the meantime, what should I do?'

'You may remain our guest, if you wish.'

Imre took a deep breath. So many thoughts ran through his brain at a time that it was hard to concentrate on just one. From the collision between them, he picked out several key notions. The Jinc was a long way from anywhere, so leaving might be difficult, perhaps even impossible, given that he had no vessel of his own or any belongings that he knew of. He had to assume that the Jinc was genuinely willing to keep him around, since it had gone to so much trouble to re-create him from the splinters of his outlandish personality backup. Only when that willingness ran out, perhaps in conjunction with its curiosity about his identity and past, would he have to make other plans. Until then, it seemed simplest to take the Jinc at its word and accept its hospitality.

Part of him, though, hated the thought. He had only the Jinc's word that any of this was true. There were other ways to edit memory, and only some of them were benign.

'You said that you were able to reconstruct "a large proportion" of the person I had once been,' he said. 'What about the rest? Where did that come from?'

'Extrapolation accounts for much of the missing genetic code,' said the Jinc, not flinching from the question at all. 'The rest came from a standard human template. Several neurological modules required direct intervention – functions of the brain, in other words, that simply did not work until we intervened – but we did everything we could to ensure that such alterations were kept to a minimum. Memory could not be repaired. Only you can put those pieces back together.'

'There's no single answer, then,' he said. 'I'm me plus some bits you made up. I'm not me mixed with someone else, though. You're definitely saying that.'

'Yes. It was not our intention to create a new persona. You are as close to the record of the Drum as we could make you.'

That was something, Imre supposed, even though intention was a guarantee of nothing.

'I'll stay until I can sort myself out,' he said. 'You've wasted enough resources on me already.'

'We do not think so.'

Imre studied the expressionless face of his guide, sensing a meaning hidden but unable to tease it free. He resolved then to spend as much time studying the Jinc as himself. If he could discover why it had gone to so much trouble to resurrect him from the dust of intergalactic space, that would go some way to revealing who it thought he might be.

And then, possessed with that knowledge, he could begin to wonder who had tried to kill him.

He had no plan of attack. Who had ever been in such a situation before? Not he, if the incomplete reminiscences at his disposal were anything to go by. There were uncountable such fractions, each needing to be lifted out of obscurity, examined, then rewritten in both the neurological and narrative senses back into his mind. He chose to let instinct be his sole guide, taking him where it willed throughout the Noh vessel, and beyond, to the Drum itself, where someone – his former self, presumably – had gone to painstaking effort to preserve him for posterity, only to see it blown to smithereens.

Moving around the Drum was easier than expected. The Jinc gave him a cowl and robe identical to the ones worn by its mouthpieces. A translucent microfilm provided him with air and maintained a comfortable temperature. It also adjusted the magnetic properties of the soles of his feet, enabling them to stick to the iron of the Drum's curving wall. It was easily thirty meters across and well over one hundred long. He walked for hours along the thin spiral decorating its wide interior. Less than a millimeter wide, they formed the single helix that had preserved the data comprising him and his body. The magnitude of the venture startled and shocked him. This was information engineering on a massive, hubristic scale. The Drum had been built to withstand everything the void threw at it. Only intelligence, deliberate and malicious, had ultimately done it in.

He could see places where the Jinc had failed to reassemble the Drum from its multitudinous bits. Tiny black dots marred its metallic grey surface where a resinous material filled in for the missing parts, offending a deep-seated need in him for neatness and order. He felt as though he were walking across a starscape in

negative, one that arced up and around him in a powerful repre-
sentation of the curvature of space. The real stars shone down
either end of the Drum, where the Jinc had left open the construct's massive caps. Naked vacuum bathed the cylinder and its
contents. The sound of his magnetic footsteps propagated through
the metal in silent waves.

When he was done, he walked to where the short-range shuttle
scoop waited to take him back to the Noh vessel. The Jinc's home
looked like a giant neuron, all curves and distended spines with a
semitransparent outer hull that gleamed liquidly in the light of
the Milky Way. Imre could discern no front or rear. Similarly with
the shuttle scoop, which was a large, seed-shaped vessel pock-
marked with thirteen mouths that could, at will, distend vast
magnetic vanes. The purpose of the vanes was simple: to suck up
the dust and debris the Jinc encountered in its long, destination-
less voyage. The remains of the Drum had been gathered in just
such a fashion, the mouthpiece of the Jinc had told him. What the
Jinc did with its normal harvest, Imre hadn't yet ascertained.

The mouthpiece awaited him in the scoop, as lifeless as ever.
Perhaps it was the same one who had greeted him on his awakening, perhaps not. The distinction was meaningless. He told
himself to stop thinking about it as an individual and treat it, in
both his mind and every aspect of his behavior, as the Jinc itself.

'Did that trigger any memories?' the Jinc asked him, as he
reached the edge of the Drum and prepared to cross.

'I'm afraid not. I've never seen anything like it before.' He
stepped carefully into the belly of the scoop, disengaging his magnetic feet with relief. Fleeting g forces gripped him as the scoop
accelerated away. 'I suppose it was worth a try.'

'You sound disappointed.'

He was, but saw no point in dwelling on the fact. Although the
data had been encoded in the Drum with a fair degree of redun-
dancy, nuclear blasts and wide dispersal were huge hurdles to
overcome. The Jinc had done an amazing job to recover anything.
'The way I see it, I'm lucky to be here at all. Wherever we are,
exactly.'

The hunched figure beside him made no move to offer any information on that score, so he took it upon himself to ask.

'Show me where you've come from.'

A series of three-dimensional maps appeared around him. He waved them away.

'No. Pointing will be fine, while we're out here.'

The mouthpiece looked up at him. A long, wrinkled finger pointed through the transparent hull of the scoop at the splendid starscape ahead of them, tracing a line around the extremities of the galaxy. There was no clear purpose to the Jinc's past movements just as there was no obvious 'captain' aboard the ship. It was driven by collective will in directions unknown.

Imre's gaze slid from the outstretched finger outward to the galaxy, truly grasping its immensity for the first time. It filled one-half of his view, a tilted, glowing waterfall looming over the shuttle scoop and its passengers. Every speck was a star — one of a hundred thousand million, large and small, dead and alive, and none of them overlooked by humanity. The Continuum connected them all, whether by arcane quantum loops, stately webs of electromagnetic radiation, or sluggish bullets of matter. The minds inhabiting the Milky Way ranged from as small as his, via gestalts as complex as the Jinc, to intelligences as large as the galaxy itself. Layer upon layer of sentience and civilization stretched upward from the individual to heights he could barely imagine, and all of it had originated in one remarkable system, on one tiny world.

He staggered, not under the influence of acceleration or the immensity of the view, but from a flashback that burst in his skull like a Roman candle.

'What about the individual?' said Alphin Freer, an angular, high-cheeked man with iron grey eyes and neat black hair. 'Are we supposed to forget everything you told us — that we fought for?'

'The Forts are the big players in the galaxy now.' His own voice again, ringing in his ears. The disorientation was profound. He was undoubtedly in the scoop, but at the same time he was on the bridge of a burning ship. 'They may have had the Aces all along.'

'No shit,' said a big, scar-pitted soldier looming like a small mountain to one side, combat suit open to the waist. The green-eyed blonde beside him looked ready to cry.

'If you do this,' said Freer, 'you're as much a traitor to the human race as they are.'

'Listen to me.' Imre's reminiscence was full of anger, resentment, and frustration, but his voice conveyed nothing but entreaty. 'Whatever it takes to get us out of this – isn't that worth pursuing?'

'You really think we're getting out of this?'

The new voice came from behind him, silky and subtle like a stiletto blade. Imre turned – or remembered turning – and the recollection suddenly dissolved, leaving him with fleeting impressions of snakeskins and stab wounds.

He shook his head. The stars were making him feel light-headed.

'Are you unwell?' asked the Jinc. One cool, skeletal hand fell on his shoulder.

'I don't know,' Imre said. 'I think I'd like to lie down.'

'That can easily be arranged. You have been assigned a private berth. We will show you there now.'

'Thank you.' The Jinc's statement took a moment to sink in. 'A private berth, really?'

'We made it especially for you.'

It was, he supposed, somewhat less involved than plucking his pieces out of the void and putting them together again, but the thought still made him uncomfortable. 'I'd be happy enough in the sickbay.'

The Jinc didn't reply. As the scoop rolled into a new course, Imre held on and kept his eyes averted from the view.

Incoherent memories trickled down the crater wall of his mind, threatening an avalanche of incapacitating proportions.

The burning ship was called *Pelorus*, and it had been the flagship of an armada vast enough to cast a shadow across a solar system. Like many ships of the day, it had endured the ravages of interstellar space by sloughing away layers of hull in much the same fashion that humans shed dead skin cells. Across a voyage of several hundred light-years, every external surface might be completely replaced many times over while everything within remained pristine.

'In the same way,' a voice from his memory said, 'the Forts replace frags. But are they skin cells? I don't think so. A skin cell doesn't feel pain or loss. It doesn't feel anything at all. The comparison, and the practice, is odious.'

Humans had evolved vastly and without check across the galaxy. People came in all shapes and sizes and communicated by every imaginable means. No reliable method had been found to cross the light-speed barrier, but that was no deterrent. Where space would not break, time would happily bend. If a journey was to take a thousand years by the 'natural' tick of the clock, why not make the subjective ticks longer so the journey seemed to last only a decade, or a year, or a day, or even a minute? Indefinite life extension had been in common practice since before humanity left Earth. To grow old and die while visiting a neighbor – for anything less than a thousand light-years away was practically on one's doorstep – would be considered wasteful, even obscene. People shook hands across the constellations. They made conversations, and love, and war.

'This machine runs down.' That was the big, scarred man again. His accent was untraceable, wooden only in the sense that a forest was made of wood. 'So few of us are left.'

'That's a bleak outlook.' Imre's face hurt as though he had recently been laughing uproariously. Or screaming.

'Only gods walk on water.'

'Only idiots or fools would try. 'We're neither, right?'

'Amen. We're the new religion.'

An acrid wave of ozone swept that memory from the stage. A name took its place: the Corps. Just as humans in ancient times had formed friendships, allegiances, and armies, so too did affiliations spring up across the intergalactic gulfs. Some were necessarily loose; others were as tight as they had ever been. Some were between numerous discrete, different individuals; some

consisted of multiple copies of one individual, propagated across
the starscape like seeds, meeting up every millennium or so to
exchange memories. Such singletons were themselves an ambigu-
ous blend of individual and multiplicity. Novel pronouns and
neologisms abounded as language struggled to keep up with
numerous new ways to be. All were human, since they had sprung
from the same ancient home as all known intelligent life, but not
all were the same.

The Corps was just one of many affiliations caught in the
middle. Imre Bergamasc – the man who had amassed the memories preserved in the Drum – had seen through many sets of eyes
and lived in many bodies. He had none of the smeared awareness
of the Jinc, however; each body had a keen sense of himself – and
that, gradually, was how the revived Imre was coming to think of
his former incarnation: Himself, the being that had preceded him
in life's great adventure. There were bound to be more of him out
there somewhere, unless whoever had destroyed the Drum had
finished them off too. There were also, most likely, other members
of the Corps.

Alphin Freer was definitely one of them: cool, remote, and
knife-sharp. The big man whose name and origins wouldn't quite
come, another; also the reticent blonde, Emlee Copas, with eyes of
green stone. The fourth of his former companions was the woman
whose voice had crawled down him like oil on a ship's hull. The
five of them had been a team, he gradually surmised; soldiers of
both kinds, war- and peacemakers, as circumstances demanded.
Had they been friends? That he couldn't quite unpack. Certainly,
they had been close; perhaps even codependent. At least one of
them had been his lover, if the complex knot of emotional associations was anything to go by. Flesh and blood and pain and
fucking, all wound up in one vicious tangle. If he pulled at it too
hard, he feared he might strangle himself.

His own voice formed the backdrop to many of the memories –
demanding, cajoling, commanding, ranting – but the words
weren't always comprehensible. So many speeches: when had he
ever found so much to say? Now, all he wanted was to close his ears

and think. If he opened his mouth to answer the Jinc's questions, he feared the dusty, disconnected pieces of his mind might fall out.

Sloughing hulls and singletons in rows demanded that he keep it together as best he could. Whether he was divine or merely decent, or not even that, he owed it to himself to piece Himself together. Then he could stand back and decide who or what he had been. Soldier? Victim? Leader? Man?

He was in a bar. Three glasses of a pinkish liquid rested on the table before him. The big man glanced over his shoulder as though at a sudden sound. 'Something is wrong.'

Imre reached into the pocket of his uniform jacket for the Henschke Sloan sidearm he kept there, fully loaded. Before he could draw, a single shot discharged into the ceiling behind them, and a voice barked that they should stay seated.

He remembered nothing after that point.

But her name, the name of his lover, did eventually come to him: covert ops specialist Helwise MacPhedron, she of the liquid voice and thin, soft ribs that went down her waist like those of a snake.

Just thinking of her sent a shudder along his spine, but once again he didn't know why.

The quarters assigned to him were as cramped as the sickbay, containing a coffinlike bunk identical to the one in which he had awoken and barely large enough to crouch in. At least the door locked behind him. From the other side of the bulkhead came the sound of machinery and people moving about. Never voices. The Jinc ship was empty of language, unless he was part of the conversation.

Sleep was a long time coming. Getting undressed and slipping into the elastic coverlet didn't help. His body felt both pleasantly and unpleasantly unfamiliar. It was in perfect condition, but the differences between it and the one he remembered irked him, making him irritable and suspicious of his hosts when on the face of it he had no good reason to be either. His skin was healthy, pliable and soft, even where body hair was making its presence newly

felt. There were no visible scars. Nerve endings responded as he
ran his slender fingers down both arms and across his stomach. His
eyelids blinked smoothly in the eternal gloom of the Noh vessel.

He wondered if he was being watched – and, then, whether he
should pursue a faint and not entirely erotic impulse to mastur-
bate. That would help him sleep, if nothing else. It always had in
his old body.

His nipples hardened at the thought, but fear of failing stayed
his hand. He told himself that he was unwilling to embrace this
body that he had not chosen. It would be like screwing a stranger.
There was a time and a place.

Earlier, the Jinc had asked him, 'What is the last date you
remember?'

He had considered the question a long time before answering.
Little linear sense came with the memories assembling in his
mind. The feeling that some were more recent than others was
therefore hard to justify.

'What date is it now?' he had asked in return.

'We are nearing the end of the nine hundredth millennium.'

'Absolute?'

'Yes.'

That had told him nothing. 'Is the war over?'

'Which war?'

'People were calling it the Mad Times even before it had finished.'

'Yes, that war finished 150,000 years ago. Is that the last thing
you remember?'

That figure still bothered him hours later, as he lay on his bunk
and contemplated the arousal states of his new body. So many
years – yet they had passed in the blink of a cosmic eye, as they
might have for one of his enemies in the Mad Times. Humanity
had gone from savagery to the stars in such a time.

His right moved down to cup his pubic mound. The lack of
penis and testes gave him no comfort at all.

'I don't know,' he had said. 'Why the interrogation? I'll tell you
when I remember something important.'

The Jinc mouthpiece had bowed in apology. 'Perhaps you would like to know who won.'

'I can guess. It was a stupid war fought over meaningless ideals. Sol Invictus was never going to come out the other side. The only question was how many of the Forts we took down with us.' The intensity with which he spoke surprised him. Clearly, this had once mattered deeply to him. 'Am I right?'

'You are,' the Jinc had told him. 'Sol Invictus did fall in the end.'

'Could that have been when my record was destroyed? The Drum, I mean.'

'No. Over such a long time, your remains would have dispersed too far for us to gather. You would have become one with the Holy Background.'

He had immediately thought of the cosmic microwave background radiation, on which were imprinted the ripples of creation. Was that what the Jinc worshipped? The fiery Original State from which the universe had emerged?

'Well, that'd be some funeral pyre.'

'You misunderstand us. We pursue the ExoGenesis, the ultimate source of life in the galaxy – perhaps the universe. Life on one world can seed life on another, but science cannot tell us where life started in the first place. We seek that place on the galactic outskirts, where expeditions only infrequently come and where your remains might have been lost forever.'

'Mixed up with anything else you found,' he said, remembering the Jinc telling him that it had been looking for the nature of God. 'Now I understand why you went to so much trouble. I was a contaminant that would've screwed up the Background.'

'This is undoubtedly true. Our motives are not entirely self-serving, however. We are curious. We wanted to give you the possibility of rescue if you desired it.'

'If I—' He paused, realizing only after a second what the Jinc meant. 'I would never commit suicide, if that's what you're suggesting.'

'We did not know that then. We take your word for it now.'

There was moisture under his fingertips. He moved his hand experimentally, remembering times he had touched Helwise the same way. Was this how she had felt? Was this?

'Have you found anything else apart from me?' he had asked the Jinc, feeling the stirrings of curiosity. Nebulous notions of God meant far less to him than the possibility of artifacts of ancient human, or possibly even alien, origin.

'Our discoveries have been few but significant. We will show you when you have rested.'

Almost, then, he had changed his mind about wanting to lie down. Sleep was a luxury, not a necessity; he really only wanted a moment in which to process everything he had learned. Couldn't it wait for him to see what the Jinc had discovered? Wasn't that potentially more important than himself?

He didn't know. Over 150,000 years had passed in the galaxy since he had last gazed upon it. Even for those accompanying the Forts on their slow journey through time, much could have happened. Aliens might have been discovered and exhaustively cataloged, and more besides. What he considered a mystery might now be common knowledge.

His own mental and physical state bothered him more, at that moment. So did the state of the Continuum as a whole. The Mad Times had been a pivotal conflict. He couldn't remember how it had ended, and the Jinc were no help on what had come afterward.

'Our quest has occupied many millennia, far longer than the gaps in your knowledge. Our contact with the Continuum has therefore been infrequent and incomplete. For much of the time, as now, we are totally disconnected.'

That didn't seem to faze the Jinc. It bothered him profoundly. He couldn't contact home, wherever that was. He couldn't call for help. He couldn't let anyone know that he was alive, if anyone still cared.

His pulse began to race as it did when panicked. He was sweating under the synthetic coverlet. The hand between his legs moved more confidently now, without his conscious direction. A flush spread up his chest to his throat. He could feel the blood surging through all the tissues of his body – his muscles, his organs, his skin. His back arched.

It wasn't his. None of it was. The hand, the body, even the orgasm that rose up like an invisible wave and crashed over him in the darkness. It was longer and deeper than any he had experienced before, that he could remember, but even in the midst of it he felt untouched. Nerve endings dutifully conveyed their message to mind, but the message didn't connect to the essence of him. The homunculus in the seat of his skull remained determinedly male and unmoved. Dispassionate and dispossessed, he buried his new face into the mattress when it was over and thrust his legs straight and closed toward the far end of the bed.

When he awoke, his right hand was brown with dried blood. His gut ached with cramps. He dressed, knowing that the jumpsuit would clean him while he wore it, and wrenched open the door to his tiny room. Grabbing the first mouthpiece he saw, he dragged it inside, pulled its hatchet nose against his.

'I want to go back. Make me male again. Now.'

'That will take time,' said the Jinc, unfazed by his sudden assault on its person. 'The process is not one we regularly employ out here. We can start it, yes, but your body will have to do the rest itself, at its own pace.'

'How long?'

'One month.'

Imre slapped a palm against the nearest bulkhead. The sound it made was much louder than he expected in the close confines of his quarters, startling him. His anger surprised and unnerved him.

'Can you turn off menses and libido sooner than that?'

'Yes. A simple hormone regulation will take care of both.'

'Well, good.' He exhaled through his nose. 'That's something.'

'Are you experiencing discomfort?'

'That depends entirely on your definition.'

He let the Jinc go and shut the door behind it. The smell of old paper filled his nostrils as he pulled his legs underneath him and sat with stubbled head brushing the ceiling. None of the erotic

sensations he had entertained before sleeping remained. His coun-
terfeit flesh felt wrung out and tired. A persistent ache in his left
eye made him want to squint. He felt no hunger or thirst, or any
need to defecate. The designers of his body had provided it with
considerable self-sufficiency. That sexual and reproductive capacities should accompany gender he supposed wasn't entirely
unreasonable. He just wished to be free of them while he worked
out who he had been, and who he now was.

He wondered what he looked like. In his memory, he was a
slender man with a triangular face framed by perfectly white hair.
His skin had only slightly more color, and his eyes were bright
blue. He had been described as birdlike, for both his movements
and the slim lines of his limbs and hands, but he didn't feel
remotely like a bird. He wasn't flighty or weightless, but patient
and determined. He pictured himself as a large white cat, poised to
pounce.

Did that hold any more? He didn't know, and he didn't know
what would be more alarming – to have the same face he'd always
had or one he didn't recognize at all.

He opened the door and eased into the crawl space outside. A
mouthpiece was waiting for him, its features ghoulishly lifeless.

'Would you like to see our discoveries?' it asked him.

'I, uh, yes.' He had no reason to say no, unless taking the tour
would interfere with his gender reassignment. For all he knew,
that was happening to him as he spoke, put into motion by an
undetected command and cascading through his cells in their
thousands.

'Follow.' The hooded figure turned like a spider in a pipe and
led him through the convoluted corridors of the ship. Strange
hissing noises and creaks grew louder as they traversed one particular sector – something to do with life support or maintenance, he
guessed – but that soon fell behind. They passed rooms containing
dozens of identical mouthpieces stacked up in bunks like components of some vast, organic machine. Imre remembered the Forts –
the galactic overminds that had evolved so far from their origins as
to seem utterly alien – and wondered how close the Jinc had

become to being one of his enemies in the Mad Times. That it had showed him, a singleton, no hostility meant nothing. To be ignored was the fate worse than death those fighting under the banner of Sol Invictus had feared.

They came to a bloodred pressure hatch, the first that hadn't automatically slid aside as they approached. The Jinc paused a moment there, with a hand on Imre's arm, firmly gripping him as though in warning.

'Is something wrong?' he asked it.

'Nothing. We are merely adjusting your tempo. What lies beyond this door is more precious than I can convey. A sudden disturbance could undo centuries of work. I'm sure you will understand.'

He nodded, even as he wondered just how far his metabolic and cognitive clocks were being slowed. He felt no different. The inflation of his lungs, the shifting of his limbs, the blinking of his eyes – every biological process might have changed in a dozen small ways, but to him they still seemed natural and normal. To feel otherwise would have been distracting.

Finally, the red – now blue – door opened, allowing them access to the largest chamber he had seen in the sprawling Noh vessel. It was easily thirty meters across and ten high, with curved walls crisscrossed with tapering spars. Affixed to the spars like insects in a web were legions of strange and unidentifiable shapes, some large and bulking, others small and frangible, all perhaps incomplete or unfinished, having been pulled out of the void in bits like him or grown in vats from scraps of genetic material. At least two dozen mouthpieces moved among them, tending the Jinc's collection with the patient intensity of mortuary attendants. The air was icily cold.

His particular mouthpiece led him inside, drifting from point to point like a slow-motion moth. The ambient gravity was much lower in the chamber than he had expected, either because of the tempo shift or because they were close to the center of the spinning portion of the ship. He felt ungraceful and awkward, as though he should be tethered to the spars too or even bottled up like some of the strange shapes he saw confined to gleaming tanks. He studied them warily, the twisted limbs and jagged forms, thinking as he went: there but for the grace of someone else's God . . .

The Jinc kept up a running commentary as they went, describing the origins — confirmed or suspected — of each item they passed. No matter how remarkable they were, little mystery remained. The entire collection, he was assured, could be explained in terms of the remains of lost travelers, ejecta from planetary impacts or collisions, known panspermic strains evolving and combining in the heart of molecular clouds, and the like. The origins of life remained as elusive as Imre's memories, despite the extensive museum collected before him.

The largest exhibit by far penetrated the back wall of the chamber like a finger through the skin of a balloon.

'Is that what I think it is?' he asked, pointing.

'A starship,' the Jinc confirmed. 'The remains of one, anyway.'

Imre regarded it with interest and some concern. He had seen such vessels before, camouflaged to look dead when in fact they were very much alive. It had no obvious windows or doors, no external jets or exhausts, no antennae or dishes, and no visible insignia. Its blackened hull was quite inactive, deeply pitted by energetic particles, as no living ship's skin would have been. Yet inexperienced pilots had been fooled by similar camouflages during the Mad Times and other conflicts. Once taken aboard for salvage, the zombie awoke and wreaked havoc from within.

'Are you sure it's dead?'

'Quite sure. It hasn't moved for forty-three thousand years.'

'But—'

'We have examined it quite thoroughly.' The Jinc took his arm and tugged him away from the blackened relic. 'Here, Imre Bergamasc, is our most significant find.'

Despite his misgivings, Imre let himself be guided through the entrance of a spherical containment vessel several meters across. They passed through layer upon layer of esoteric insulation, each adding its own peculiar effect to the vessel's interior. By the time they reached its heart, the air felt stifled and desiccated. All light was extinguished, except for that emanating from the object the Jinc had recovered or re-created from the void.

A silver sphere no wider across than Imre's head hung in the exact center of its arcane container, shielded from touch by a curved, transparent window. The Jinc waved him forward, and he placed his nose right up against the window in order to see more clearly. A distorted image of his own face loomed back at him, as unrecognizable as a melted rubber doll.

The silver sphere rippled, as though it could sense him watching. He went to ask the Jinc what it was, but something dipped into his mind and eradicated the intention from his thoughts.

Further thought vanished next, subsumed by a Babel of identical voices all whispering at once. They spoke of oxygen

of a broken aluminum sheet

of matter/antimatter imbalance

of hunger

of physical exhaustion

of acceleration

of a mislaid container

of wounds

of stars

and of him:

'He is with the Artifact. >I stand behind him. He is looking at >me with an odd expression on his face.'

The shock of hearing himself discussed wrenched him out of the strange dialogue. He was, he suddenly understood, somehow hearing the cross talk between the mouthpieces of the Jinc. That they continued to talk about him suggested that they didn't know he was listening.

'. . . breathing . . .'

'. . . mending . . .'

'. . . balancing . . .'

'. . . eating . . .'

'. . . resting . . .'

'. . . overseeing . . .'

'. . . seeking . . .'

'. . . healing . . .'

'. . . navigating . . .'

'There is no sign of recognition,' said one voice.

'No. He is still looking at >me. >I will ask him what is wrong.'

The mouthpiece beside him stirred. 'Are you well, Imre Bergamasc? You seem unsettled.'

He opened his mouth to reply.

'Do not answer,' said a new voice into his mind, one quite different in tone and timbre to the others. This voice was smoother, almost melodious, and came to him not through words but out of his thoughts. 'If the Jinc realizes that you can hear it, it will make you a prisoner too.'

Imre blinked, feeling a return of the discomfiture that had struck him in the shuttle scoop after examining the Drum. Was the possibility that the voice belonged to the silver sphere so strange, after everything else revealed to him the previous day?

'His lack of reaction could hide recognition,' whispered the Jinc components among themselves.

'It could. Silence is the first and most primitive mode of dissent.'

'He is more than a primitive.'

'He is an anomaly, like the Artifact.'

'That does not necessarily make him Holy.'

'No, it does not. >I will press him further.'

'I – I'm confused,' Imre said before the mouthpiece could act on its statement. 'What is this thing? Some kind of machine?'

'We do not know,' said the mouthpiece, still watching him intently. 'The reflective surface is not its true appearance, but we have been able neither to penetrate its outer layers nor to discern how they are sustained. It is clearly the product of technology quite different from ours. We have come to no firm conclusions regarding either its origin or nature.'

Gooseflesh rose up on his arms. 'What does it do, then? Why do you keep it so tightly shielded?'

'It does nothing, inasmuch as we can tell. The containment bubble protects our many instruments from external influences that might corrupt the data they collect.'

The surface of the silver sphere rippled again. 'The Jinc keeps me here against my will,' said the mellifluous voice. 'But I am not powerless. I can help you.'

Imre glanced from the sphere to the mouthpiece. The latter seemed completely ignorant of the one-sided conversation taking place right under the Jinc's nose.

'He can tell us nothing.'

'>I do not concur. Our knowledge of him is still growing. >I will allow him to interrogate >me further. Perhaps he will let something slip.'

'Nod if you wish to pursue the possibility of an alliance,' said the voice to him.

Imre did so without hesitation.

The Jinc's mouthpiece froze like a statue, poised with its mouth open on the cusp of speaking. The air in the containment bubble, already dense and stifled, became as thick as glue. Colors shifted down to the red end of the spectrum, indicating that he was over-clocking, that his tempo had risen to an extremely fast rate, accelerated by the thing in the silver sphere. Shadows consumed him; the silver sphere became a black hole yawning hungrily on the far side of the window.

'We can talk now,' said the voice, 'for a brief moment. The Jinc will not notice.'

'Who are you?' he asked, voice sounding too loud in the close confines. 'What are you?'

'In many ways, I am your ally. That is all you need know. The Jinc is your immediate concern. It is lying to or concealing the truth from you on three particular counts.'

'I presume you're about to tell me what those are. Or are you intending to offer them as payment for helping you escape?'

'I will tell you for free. One: the Jinc didn't stumble across your remains by accident. The blasts that destroyed the Drum were visible from a great distance. They are what led the Jinc to this location, not pure chance.'

'So it hasn't been a hundred and fifty thousand years since the Drum was destroyed?'

'That figure remains accurate. The Jinc is capable of spotting single stands of DNA from very great distances, but its vessel is not as fleet as the ones you might have been used to. It doesn't need to be. There is no competition out here. Not normally, anyway.'

'What do you mean by that?'

The sphere ignored the question. 'Two: the Continuum is not merely out of range. The data halo dissolved a long time ago. Transmissions have been erratic since. The Jinc has made no effort to investigate this phenomenon.'

That was more worrying than how long exactly his remains had been drifting on the edge of the galaxy. 'What's happened?' He thought of the Mad Times, the terrible conflict that had pitted new and old of all forms of humanity against each other. 'Another war?'

Again, the sphere ignored him. 'The third thing the Jinc isn't telling you is this: the ship you asked about moments ago is not completely dead. It has been neutralized, yes, and its malevolence contained, but its drives and reactors remain functional. Its AI and hull can be revived. It can, in short, be flown.'

'Why are you telling me this?'

'Because should you need a means to escape the Jinc, this will be it.'

'Why would I need to escape?' he asked, even as the misgivings he had felt upon his awakening returned. 'Why should I trust you over the Jinc? You might not even be human in origin.'

'What does that mean to you, Imre Bergamasc? Is trust merely a matter of genes?'

'That's all I have to go on at the moment.'

'Nothing could be further from the truth. You have your own senses and judgment. I urge you to make up your own mind.

Decide who is lying to whom, then reach your own conclusions. When you have, come talk to me again. Or call for me.'

'How do I do that?' he asked.

'Simply speak this code word: "luminous." I will answer, no matter the circumstances.'

Imre caught a flash of humor in the bizarreness of the situation. 'This is all very cloak-and-dagger.'

'Yes. For good reason. You are more important than you realize.'

'Me,' he asked, 'or who I used to be?'

'Is there a difference?'

With an abrupt lurch, the light changed back to normal. The oppressive heaviness of the air relaxed a measure. Silence fell — complete silence, for his ability to eavesdrop on the Jinc's internal conversations ceased as suddenly as it had begun. The Jinc mouthpiece spoke as it had always intended to, uninterrupted by the strange fugue moment Imre had experienced. The entire conversation with the sphere had taken barely an instant.

'We found this object,' said the Jinc, 'not long before you were discovered. For a time we wondered if this was more than a coincidence.'

Imre suppressed a flash of anger. 'I've never seen anything like it before,' he told the gestalt with utter truthfulness. If he had, that knowledge was still locked in his skull. 'How on Earth did you find it, way out here?'

'Our detection systems are excellent,' the Jinc told him, echoing the silver sphere's claims.

'Sensitive enough to see the explosions that destroyed the Drum?'

'Yes, as a matter of fact. Our sensors examine every quarter of the starscape for anomalies. The two nuclear explosions that destroyed the Drum were noticed. However, the echoes of war still propagated through the vacuum even then. Your death-signature was archived and not closely examined for some time, hence our delay in attending the scene.'

That loosely accorded with what the sphere had said. It didn't, however, make his circumstances any clearer than they had been.

That the Jinc had not acted immediately didn't make it his enemy, even if prompt action might have spared some of his present complications. Nuclear explosions weren't the objects of its long quest. Life, not death, was its objective.

Still, that made one out of three, he thought. If he could verify the second of the silver sphere's claims, that would convince him of the third, and of the certainty that he would take advantage of the sphere's offer, if it, in turn, was genuine. That something might have happened to the Continuum in his absence was a matter of considerable concern. Shielding himself from that possibility was not in his best interest.

He indicated the sphere. 'Have you asked anyone else about this? It might be an important find.'

'We are in no doubt about that,' the Jinc told him, 'but neither are we in any hurry to relinquish it. Our examination continues. Should every attempt fail, then we will call for assistance and advice.'

'From whom?'

'Another ganglion of the Noh, or from the Continuum itself.'

'That makes sense.'

'We think so.'

They stared at each other for a long moment, Imre sensing the combined attention of all the individual Jinc mouthpieces focused on him. What were they saying about him now? Did the Jinc still suspect a connection between him and the sphere, or had it abandoned that thought for the moment – ironically just as a connection had been formed?

'I've seen enough,' he said. 'Whatever it is, congratulations on finding it, but I can't help you open it.'

The Jinc mouthpiece backed out of the containment vessel, and he followed. The long, black nose of the starship loomed over him. He avoided looking at it as they passed through the museum of relics. What was the point of escaping, he asked himself, if he didn't know where to go? As he passed through the bloodred door, he banged his widened hip against the seal and cursed in a language he hadn't known he spoke until that moment.

*

His guide took him to the observation port, where he sat looking out at the stars until fatigue sent him back to bed. The Jinc adhered to no strict diurnal cycle, and his body lacked the physical need to sleep that ancient humans had been enslaved by. Yet part of him yearned for rest every eighteen hours or so, and he had no real reason to fight that impulse. Neuronal rewiring continued apace whether he was awake or asleep, and as many revelations waited in dreams as waking recollections.

The Corps walked and talked with him through numerous adventures. Real or imagined, he didn't know for certain, but their familiarity — or the supposition that he should find them familiar — was not unwelcome. Those four people might be dead now, expunged from the galaxy just as violently as the Drum had been; but they had lived, he had known them, and he clung to them now as links to who he had once been.

Alphin Freer, Emlee Copas, Helwise MacPhedron, and the big soldier whose name he still couldn't place — walked large against a backdrop that was at times unimaginably exotic. Humanity occupied not just the surfaces and atmospheres of planets annexed during their extensive travels, but every possible niche between. With viruslike mutability, colonies had sprung up around dead stars, red dwarfs, even black holes. Habitats accreted in the hearts of dense molecular clouds, drifting with the tides between stars. Even stars themselves proved hospitable to hardier, high-energy types, those who chose to speed up rather than slow down their metabolic rates. Whole civilizations rose and fell in the hearts of some stellar furnaces, unseen for the most part by the rest of the universe. One such civilization so disrupted the inner workings of their home that they caused it to go nova prematurely, destroying everything within. Another deliberately collapsed the entire mass of their blue variable into a supermassive, rotating cylinder longer than the diameter of the Earth's orbit but less than an atom's-width wide, which promptly disappeared, triggering gravitational ripples felt half the galaxy away.

Experiments in biology and high-energy physics occasionally struck alchemical gold. The Continuum's inhabitants wrought in forms from the very large to the very small with equal aplomb. Their failures were just as impressive. Sometimes it was difficult to tell them apart.

Imre dreamed of shattered moons, poisoned planets, and tattered rings left in the wake of the Mad Times, or simply in the ordinary course of business. He saw hollowed-out worlds swimming through the outer atmospheres of old, diffuse stars. He remembered navigating oceans, skies, and crusts made from every possible substance: diamond spires, hydrocarbon seas, acid clouds, rivers of molten metal; the possibilities were endless. All were sources of conflict when the Corps came to visit.

Finally, he saw a star born fat and vital, more than a hundred times larger than Sol and swollen to red corpulence in its middle age. Once part of a dense cluster some small distance from the galactic plane, it had drifted free millions of years ago and dragged several companion stars with it. These eight stars circled the central superstar like planets in an ordinary system, occupying orbits tipped at all angles to the ecliptic: two golden, two small and red, one bright blue, one white, one green and fitful, and one dark and dangerous. Some of those stars had spawned worlds of their own, deep in the heart of the original cluster, and they came along for the ride too, forming a supersystem made stable and inhabited by humanity in several waves down the millennia.

One such habitation had grown voracious, fueled by a combination of resource acquisition and political fervor. A technarchy founded on principles of extreme rationalism and intolerance, it had boiled out of its corner of the supersystem and threatened all of its neighbors in a manner both subtle and devastating. Even at the best of times, the supersystem was a navigational nightmare, with asteroids swinging from companion star to companion star along orbits almost too complex for Forts to chart. Simple nudges were enough to divert dozens of such bodies into missiles massive enough to wipe out whole worlds. Such nudges were the first shots fired in the conflict that came to be known as the Chaos War. Patient, ruthless, resourceful, the Alienist Technarchy set the Continuum against it in a fight it could not possibly win.

Imre dreamed of long gun battles through the tunnels of the Scathe, the enemy's primary habitat. The conflict had been long, complex, and wearing, with numerous fronts and significant losses on both sides. Exotic weaponry played a major role, as it rarely did so close to inhabited worlds. The technarchy dreamed and built big, employing the largest field-effect generators Imre had ever seen and wielding asteroid-shearing lasers like chopsticks. After bombardments failed, less subtle techniques of warplay came to the fore.

At the technarchy's heart was a massive, crystalline intelligence. Scaling one face of this central edifice, placing exotic matter charges with timers every ten meters, he had endured the badgering of the technarch with silent certitude. It couldn't kill him without harming itself, so instead of force, it had tried persuasion, blackmail, and coercion, without response. Imre hadn't come for a conversation. He had a job to do, and the window of opportunity was narrowing.

In the end, it had resorted to flattery. .

'You won't do this,' the technarch had told him as he had kicked himself free and primed the detonators. 'You are a civilized man.'

With his left thumb on the manual detonator, he had paused to reply. 'Is that what you think?' he had told the technocrat, hanging before him like a faint shimmer in the heart of the habitat, eighteen stories high. 'You clearly don't know me at all.'

The button descended. The shimmer cracked. He had felt nothing – no shock wave, no tempest, not even a sigh – as the mind of his enemy shattered. Just satisfaction of a grim and resolute kind. Another job completed. Another enemy slain.

That feeling lingered when he woke. Satisfaction, but not without a measure of doubt. He couldn't quite pinpoint the source of the latter. His previous self had felt no remorse while eradicating his foe; neither had he doubted the necessity of that goal, nor the methods with which he had pursued it. He didn't question the minds that had brought him into play, shuffling him across the board of the galaxy as a chess player might move a knight in for the kill. Not at first, anyway. The events of the Chaos War had taken place long before the Mad Times; the Corps had obeyed its masters absolutely, then.

Perhaps, he thought, the doubt existed outside the memoir, originating in him and his present circumstances. Were the words his past self had spoken to the technarch a genuine anamnesis, or were they more dream than reality? He couldn't tell.

Certainty and doubt curdled through his mind. In the clutches of the Jinc gestalt, he couldn't tell what was real and what wasn't. With no external point of reference, he had nothing to go on but words and patchy memories. He needed much more than that if he was ever to find himself.

Without turning on the light, he rolled over and spoke into the small speaker grille next to his bed.

'Do you have an encyclopedia I can browse through?' he asked. 'There are some details I need to check.'

'Of course,' came the buzzing reply. 'To gain virtual access, all you need to do is—'

'Not virtual. Hands-on.' Until he completely trusted the Jinc, he didn't want to interface with its systems any more than he had to.

The Jinc took several seconds to consider his question. Maybe, he thought, the gestalt's mouthpieces were arguing again. How much more time and energy would it waste on its moody passenger? New bodies, individual quarters, jaunts outside, sex changes — and now this. He braced himself for a flat rejection.

He was surprised. 'Your wish can be accommodated,' the Jinc told him. 'We will come for you when the facility is enabled.'

'Thank you.'

He rolled back and stared upward into nothing. His breasts spread and flattened across his chest, heavy and disconcerting, as though the darkness was trying to suffocate him. His period had ceased, and all physical desire had vanished with it. That was something. It didn't, however, change the fact that he wasn't as he expected to be. He felt weighed down all over, under the influence of many gravities.

At the climax of the latest dream-memory, the nameless soldier had loomed over him, a dark shadow whose features were barely visible.

'Picture the man,' he had said, 'when the heartbeat stops.'

A feeling of deep, indefinable apprehension was not shaken by the tapping of his guide at the entrance to his quarters.

It took him more than a single relative day to locate the supersystem he remembered. That frustrated him, since the search would have taken seconds on the kind of smart databases to which he had once had access. The Jinc, however, placed little store in either search engines or up-to-date data. The encyclopedia it gave him access to was an ancient, cumbersome thing, containing the combined knowledge of the human race – frozen in time like layers of geological strata, since data had been accumulating at ever-increasing rate since the twentieth century – but hopelessly out-of-date after a certain point. A simple search on the parameters he recalled gave him nothing, so he was forced to trawl through the data himself.

He eventually found it in atlas cross-linked to the Jinc's navigational charts. The atlas was, perversely, a cognitive mirror image of every other one he had ever used. More detailed around the galactic fringes, where Noh vessels mainly traveled, its data became fuzzier and less relevant the deeper inward he browsed. Names and allegiances had changed in hundreds of places, sometimes more than once, but at least it was a living document, unlike the stone-dead encyclopedia.

As he searched, he was startled sometimes by just how much factual data was locked inside his skull, awaiting the right trigger to bring it forth. That was perfectly reasonable, he supposed, given that he was the summation of all the many different versions of Himself, the original him, who had existed prior to storage in the Drum. Names and dates were easier to remember than conversations.

There were four supersystems in the Milky Way, but only one matched his remembrance. He stared at its name for a good while before opening the file containing more detail. 'Mandala Supersystem,' he breathed to himself. 'I found you.'

What, exactly, had he found? The names of Mandala's eight suns were the same – Di-Zang, Chugai Zhang, Manjushri, Sakra, Jampa, Kuntuzangpo, Chenresi, and Akasagarbha – but almost everything else was different. The Alienist Technarchy was missing, as it should have been, but not because it had been wiped from the maps of the Continuum by the Corps' hard work, but because it hadn't even existed yet. What use was an atlas half a million years out-of-date?

At least he had a name, he told himself. That was somewhere to start. He had several names. In his mind, he arranged them in as many ways as he could conceive: shuffled like a deck of cards, in alphabetical order, sorted into branching categories:

- ▶ The Corps
  - ▶ Alphin Freer, Emlee Copas,
    Helwise MacPhedron, ???
- ▶ Mandala
  - ▶ The Chaos War
    - › The Scathe
- ▶ The Mad Times
  - ▶ *Pelorus*
  - ▶ Sol Invictus

Once upon a time, long ago in human prehistory, women of privilege had whiled away the hours stitching pictures into fabric, one loop at a time. That was how he felt: each name was a stitch. Surrounding each stitch was a vast expanse of empty fabric waiting to be filled. A list, no matter how long it might get, was not a picture.

Plugging 'Mandala System' into the dead encyclopedia gave him a little more information. The Chaos War had begun when the Jinc's data had last been updated. And he had been alive.

With a superstitious frisson, Imre put his own name into the encyclopedia. He had been afraid to do so earlier in case he received a negative result. Now, at least some detail of his memory had been independently verified. He had that much to protect him from the negation of his fragile identity.

The encyclopedia produced a match almost instantly, which surprised him given the many trillions of names that must have been in its dusty records. 'Sternsknecht Imre Bergamasc' was all it said, with a three-dimensional image that perfectly matched his recollection. He stared at the information for a good minute, slightly stunned by its stark existence – and therefore, by inference, his own – before deleting it from the screen.

'Picture the man,' came the voice of the big soldier again, echoing from the past like a voice out of a well.

Caught in a waking dream, the destruction of the Alienist Technarchy replayed over and over in his mind until it almost seemed something that had happened to him. He smelt the chemical tang of explosive gases not quite scrubbed by his skin-suit filters; he heard the reports and requests of the people under his command through a variety of senses; he felt the pain of several wounds, even as they were healed over by the powerful forces contained within his singleton body. At the end of the conflict, he had lost an eye and half a leg to close fire. Both had grown back within a day.

He was in no hurry to test if his present body possessed the same capacity.

'I want to contact the Continuum,' he told the Jinc when he was certain he had wrung every last drop of data from the encyclopedia.

'That is impossible.'

'Why is it impossible?'

'We are at too great a remove to detect the data halo.'

'You won't consider moving closer?'

'Our energy budget is not infinitely flexible.'

There, at last, was the constraint he had expected earlier. 'Just how flexible is it? Are you intending to keep me as an exhibit in your zoo while you meander around the galaxy? Or are you going to take me in deeper, so I can make contact?'

'It is not, at present, feasible to do the latter.'

'That leaves me in an uncomfortable position.'

'Not permanently. We can reduce your tempo until circumstances change, making the time pass more quickly for you.'

'But how long could it take Absolute? If there's something wrong' – he caught his tongue – 'something I've left undone, then the sooner it's addressed, the better.'

'We understand and apologize.'

'An apology fixes nothing. There simply must be another way.'

'There is not.'

He locked eyes with the mouthpiece, searching for any sign of duplicity in its dead stare. This was the point around which his rebellion would turn if it came to that.

'Supposing I could leave by my own means, would you let me?'

'Of course.'

'Why? You made me. You have something invested in my existence. Would you let me go so easily?'

'We have no reason to keep you here against your will.'

'What if God demanded it?'

'God does not make demands of us. God simply is, and we pursue its nature with all our being.'

'Except when you're rescuing drifting castaways.'

'A good deed needs no justification.'

'It does if it distracts your from your mission.'

'Our mission leads us in unusual directions. Be assured, Imre Bergamasc, that you are part of God's creation.'

His lips tightened. God was on his side, huh? There were no walls or bars around him. Few doors were locked. Yet he was as trapped as he would have been in any cell: unable to leave, unable to call for help, completely dependent on his jailers. A prisoner in all but name.

That struck him as brazenly ironic, since he was the one who had been murdered. He was the victim, not the criminal.

'I understand,' he lied, turning back to the encyclopedia screen, the better to hide his expression. 'If I am constrained, it is by circumstance not ill will.'

'Thank you, Imre Bergamasc. We are glad you see it from our perspective.' The mouthpiece bowed deeply, then straightened. 'Perhaps our sweeps will detect a passerby,' the Jinc said more magnanimously. 'That has happened before. If such can be

contacted, they may take you aboard and return you to the
Continuum.'

'Yes, perhaps.' He tapped at the keyboard. 'Rather than hope for
what might never eventuate, however, I will concentrate on the
matter at hand: regaining my memories and working out who I
was.'

'Have you made progress in that regard?'

'Some. I was a soldier of fortune, apparently.' He called up the
record. 'I can only wonder if I still look remotely like this,' he said,
summoning the image of the white-haired man back onto the
screen.

'Wonder no longer.'

The image changed to show a high-cheeked woman with bright
blue eyes and scalp dusted ash grey. Imre stared in alarm. Her
cheeks and lips were fuller than they ought to be, her lashes longer.
Her skin was smoother, her nose straighter. No trace of his Adam's
apple remained. One earlobe, so thin as to be almost transparent,
caught his eye and held it tight. He couldn't look away.

'That's –' Not me, he wanted to say. The obvious didn't need
stating. 'Take it back,' he said instead, his voice so soft and strained
that he barely heard it himself. 'I don't want to see it!'

The image vanished, and he fell back into his seat as though his
spinal column had been severed. He raised a hand and touched his
brow. A fine layer of sweat covered every inch of him.

'Are you unwell?' The mouthpiece came up behind him. He
waved it away with one hand.

'I am Imre Bergamasc,' he said. If the Jinc touched him, he
would scream or worse. 'You must have known it from the very
start – my name, at least. It would have been on the Drum somewhere. You must have wondered about the rest, just as I'm now
wondering. What kind of soldier goes to such lengths to avoid
being erased? What kind of man?'

The Jinc said nothing. Its mouthpiece simply bowed again and
backed out of the tiny room, leaving him perspiring and alone.

He fought the urge to chase it and pin it against the wall of the
corridor outside. Thrust hard against the tubes and conduits of the

crawl space, it would experience some of the pain he felt at that moment. Physical rather than mental, but real nonetheless. Moreover, it would be felt by all of the mouthpieces as one. All of them: all the Jinc.

The urge faded. His hands lay on his thighs, clenched so tightly they shook. He forced his fingers to unfold. They too were more feminine in design than any he had previously possessed. They too belonged to someone else.

He was becoming mortally tired – of not knowing, of suspecting, of trying to feel his way through a maze of uncertainties. In his former life, he had pursued campaigns with surety and confidence. Where were those attributes now? He felt weak and powerless. He was lessened.

A stupider, more primitive person might have assigned blame for those feelings to his new gender. He was under no such illusions. Even in the grip of his dissatisfaction, he knew that its source lay in his psyche, not his physical form. Modern humanity was no more victim to hormones than it was to saber-toothed tigers. His female body might not be his, but it was not betraying him.

He wondered, feverishly, if something had been done to him, if the Jinc had deliberately tampered with his mind in order to make him more compliant or at least less able to resist. What would be the point? What possible end could that achieve?

'You are as close to the record of the Drum as we could make you,' the Jinc had told him, shortly after his awakening. 'It was not our intention to create a new persona.'

He was less and less certain of that, the more he thought about it. Being cooped up with nothing else to do was driving him even further out of his mind than he already was.

Impulsively, he pushed himself up and away from the keyboard. The acrid stink of smoke and charred metal struck his nose like a physical blow. The bridge of the burning ship rose up around him, taking him back into a past that was as real and immediate as a full-immersion recording.

'We're fucked,' stated Helwise, holding the shredded remains of one arm across her chest. Blood ran down her stomach and thighs to drip unnoticed onto the floor. 'We're so fucked we don't even care any more. What's the point of bending over so they can do it to us again? I say we go down with the ship and end it at last.'

'She's right,' said Freer. 'Who are we fighting for, anyway? The Forts own the Continuum now. You said it yourself on Uraniborg: there's some utility in dying if it stops your enemy getting what they want.'

'What do they want?' Imre's former self asked. He could almost taste the bitterness through the smoke. 'They certainly don't care about us.'

'So why are we arguing?' Freer's hands were on his hips. His brows came together. 'Are you afraid to give a suicide order all of a sudden? Did you want us to ask you for permission?'

'You misunderstand me, Alphin. The Forts don't care about us, and that's why we can't let this end here. They should care. We'll have to make them.'

Helwise issued a sound like a kettle boiling dry. 'Isn't that what this was all about? Haven't we completely outworn that argument?'

'Maybe,' he conceded. 'Or maybe we've been going about it completely the wrong way.'

A distant concussion rocked the bridge from side to side. Imre put out a hand to steady himself—

—and found himself back on the Jinc ship, breathing air that stank of human, not fire, with two new names at the forefront in his mind. One was Uraniborg, the capital system of a Sol Invictus mainstay that had been flattened by the Fort juggernaut during a long Mad Times campaign. He remembered remembering his conversation with Alphin Freer in Uraniborg, remembered the events that had led up to it. They weren't relevant.

The other name came with an image of space so warped and twisted that it hurt him to visualize it. Looking through its moon-sized volume, as one might hold up a cube of ice, stars became red- and blue-shifted streaks, distorted far from true. A nearby golden sun shone like rings of precious metal against the black, repeated so many times it was impossible to tell which image was true. Deep in its heart, almost invisible against ragged sheets of molecular wreckage that had yet to clump into more than clouds and protorings, was a solid, dense speck.

Imre had never been a mapmaker. Of that, he was certain. He had, however, studied the art in his early years. He remembered warping a two-dimensional, rectangular image around a sphere and struggling to deal with the distinct pinching of the image at each pole. The name for that pinching, inherited from the ancient days of electronic cartography, was a 'cat's arse' – and that was the name given to the warp in space left by the Alienist Technarchy at the end of the Chaos War. Discovered during the dissolution of its territories in one of the plundered regions of Mandala Supersystem, its purpose was mysterious. That it actually had a purpose in its present form, and wasn't either an intermediate stage of some greater, interrupted project or self-sabotaged wreckage, remained uncertain. It simply was: the Cat's Arse. There was only one like it in all of the galaxy.

Why had that name popped into his head?

He didn't know.

'Damn you,' he growled, addressing the absent figure of his murderer – the person who destroyed the Drum and left him doubting every tiny fact about himself. 'Damn you to hell for all eternity!'

On all fours like a big cat, he prowled the cramped corridors of the ship, physically burning off the energy accumulating in him. He didn't know how much longer he could stand it. The word 'luminous' sat on his tongue like hot stone, burning him, but he would not spit it out, not until he had exhausted every last possibility of escaping the trap on his own.

The fear of exchanging one cage for another was very real, since the silver sphere could yet turn out to be as untrustworthy as the Jinc. It could even be another manifestation of the Jinc itself, cleverly playing both sides against him. That thought dismayed him. How could he ever tell the difference between being paranoid and maintaining a sensible degree of caution?

Perhaps, he decided, it would be better to remain cautious, no matter how much his emotions railed against it. Without any overt threat made against him, he had no real reason to run. The Jinc, surely, would threaten before making a move. Group minds rarely made snap decisions, in his experience. They were fractious entities, much given to long, methodical musings and arguing among themselves, just like any human – and he knew nothing at all about the sphere.

When he slept after his session with the encyclopedia, his dreams were full of unresolved confrontations from his past. The Corps had not always been a happy collaboration, judging by the memories his present experiences stirred up. Arguments and disputes abounded, over issues both minor and major. His original self had not been immune to such tensions, although it was his job to earth them, somehow, to keep the group together. He was occasionally even the cause of it, if the confrontation on *Pelorus* was anything to go by.

As the night progressed, interrupted by frequent half awakenings and much tossing and turning, Imre's dreams progressed beyond the arguments themselves, to their aftermaths, to nursing egos and restoring the dynamic that had existed previously. Long, intellectual discussions with Alphin Freer; wordless emotional reinforcement for Emlee Copas; urgent physical tussles with Helwise MacPhedron. Nostalgic desire disturbed him more than the actual arguments, or the lies he had to tell in order to knit the group back together. Each time he and Helwise made up – fucking as violently as though fighting each other, then lying beside one another for hours, speaking of times past in the manner of soldiers drunk on glory – he came away bruised, psychically and physically. There were no limits to their depredations. Together, they fed on each other's capacity for rapaciousness. They were always hungry.

'I'm old. So old.' The big soldier whose name Imre couldn't remember sat with knees apart and hands dangling from them like limp, dead fish. 'Cold and old.'

Imre's former self adopted a more relaxed pose on the bench

beside him: fingers laced behind head, right leg making a bold diagonal upward to the wall opposite, left leg crossed over it; black dress boots shining in a distant streetlight. It was nighttime; they were on a planet. He could hear the sound of a distant party. His bloodstream buzzed with alcohol or some other soft drug.

'You just need to unwind a little.'

Hard, empty eyes looked up at him. 'I don't need saving.'

'My friend, I never said you did. Never. In fact, you've saved my life more times than I can remember. Is that right?'

'So I'm told.'

'There, then. I'm not going break the habit of a lifetime now.' He glanced at his moody companion from under hooded eyelids. 'I'll buy you a drink.'

'I don't understand how you smile and pretend it's fun.'

'I know, mate. I know. I don't understand it either. Just get up, will you?' Suddenly irritable, he unfolded and stood in one smooth motion. 'I'm not leaving you here alone. Who knows what you'll do?'

'These quiet nights will slowly kill me.'

'Gah.' Imre tugged at the soldier's broad shoulders. It was like trying to move a mountain. In the end, he raised his hands and gave up. 'Okay, be like that. I'm tired of watching. See you.'

He felt watched every step he took down the narrow alley. Although he feigned dispassion, a heavy sense of responsibility dragged him like lead weights behind his ankles. The party was to celebrate the liberation of the world from the clutches of an enemy he could barely remember the name of, less than a day after victory. It was all meaningless – the party and the victory both – but he should be there for the sake of appearances. Helwise was waiting.

Only when he reached the corner and stopped to straighten his coat, on the brink again of light and movement and sound, did he realize that the fifth member of the Corps was standing directly behind him.

'You young things never stay young for long.' Despite his size and his mood – or perhaps because of the latter – the soldier moved as silently as a sigh. 'Come on.'

The soldier pushed into the crowd, and Imre followed with a sour look spreading across his narrow features.

He half woke in the grip of total paralysis. When he tried to move, nothing happened. He couldn't cry out or even open his eyes. He felt as though someone was sitting on his chest. Trapped within his body, he could only, silently, scream.

'. . . lambda-cold dark matter?'

The whisper came out of the darkness in his skull. He clutched at it, desperate for anything that might break his strange, hypnagogic state, but it darted away with eel-like slipperiness.

'. . . noncommutative inflation?'

He forced himself to think without panicking, without fearing for the sanity of his reengineered mind. It was most likely a nightmare, not some ghostly visitation. Earth and its legends were half a galaxy away – and since when had the Old Hag been interested in the physics of Genesis?

'. . . trans-Planckian imprint?'

Definitely a dream, he decided. His heartbeat began to subside. The urge to scream faded. He felt the darkness embrace him as sleep returned.

The whispers took on more substance, as though an aural lens had turned, bringing them into focus, and he became privy to a conversation taking place about him.

'He knows nothing. This exercise is pointless.'

'>I must continue to probe. Absence of evidence is not evidence of absence.'

'His reassembly takes too long. He grows suspicious.'

'Nonetheless. Nonetheless.'

Imre was instantly alert again. Those were the voices of the Jinc in his ears. What was going on? Why had the silver sphere – if that was what lay behind this strange nocturnal apparition – woken him to witness the strife-torn deliberations of his host?

Had he really heard the word 'probe'?

The whisper came again, different in tone from the Jinc's and much more insidious:

'. . . superhorizon curvator amplitude?'

So much for erring on the side of caution. He understood the Jinc's intent now: to ply his subconscious with phrases in order to see which ones generated a reaction. There was no possibility of lying; such stimulus completely bypassed his conscious mind. It also completely ignored it – which was how, he supposed, he could go unnoticed while the Jinc worked.

The whisper persisted, giving him a new phrase every ten relative seconds. He wondered how long this had been going on: minutes, hours, or even whole nights. When it came to—

'. . . persistent luminous archaeoglyphs?'

—the response of the Jinc was immediate and triumphant, and as startling as it was unexpected.

'He reacts! See? He reacts!'

Imre had indeed reacted to the familiar word: 'luminous.' The rest of the phrase was meaningless to him, but he couldn't open his mouth to tell the Jinc that.

'There is a connection. >I knew it!'

'The probe has been vindicated!'

'It vindicates nothing. This is just one word out of many. It may correlate to something completely unrelated.'

'That was no ordinary attention spike. It was fresh and meaningful, relevant to the present.'

'>You see what >you want to find. We need more than one match to be sure.'

'Sure? >You would call for a thermometer standing on the surface of a sun!'

'We must follow the Core Precepts. The course >you suggest is too costly. Keeping him in the dark was one thing, but this . . .?'

'There is more at stake here than one life. We owe it to the Continuum to find out what happened.'

'Agreed. We have no choice but to immediately assimilate him. The knowledge he contains will be ours forever, Holy and unclouded by uncertainty!'

Imre felt the return of panic. 'Assimilate' could only mean one thing: that the Jinc would forcibly merge his mind with the gestalt's in order to unlock the secrets it suspected him of keeping. In doing so, it would eradicate what few shreds of identity he had regained. He couldn't let that happen. That he had nothing to hide was irrelevant. He had nothing but himself.

The Jinc component calling for patience was methodically outtalked and outvoted. As Imre struggled fruitlessly against the paralysis, the Jinc as a whole decided that it would begin preparations to induct its guest into the group mind. Argument fell away, forgotten, as discussions of methodology rose to take the floor. The Jinc wasn't an aggressive assimilator, as some gestalts were. Imre had fought several in his former life. They were as bad as cancer, and the tools of predatory expansion were latent in every group mind. The human will didn't easily succumb to the greater good, even in volunteers. Millions of years of social programming weren't conquered in a day.

'He is exhibiting abnormally high activity in the cingulate cortex,' one component stated.

That's me yelling at you, Imre tried to say. You can't do this!

'A dream,' said another matter-of-factly. 'Quash it immediately. We don't want him waking up in the middle of the procedure.'

'Of course not. >I will—'

Darkness fell like the flicking of a switch, and all awareness went with it. Although he knew absolutely that his one chance lay in remaining conscious and thinking his way free, somehow – or at least pleading his case, if he could just make himself heard – there was no time for despair. Oblivion took him as surely as an ax chop. For a moment, there was nothing at all.

Then he jerked awake with a cry – an audible cry, and a whole-body spasm that brought his head up in painful contact with the low ceiling above his mattress. Stars flashed. He clutched at his temple, wondering if it was too late, if he had already been assimilated, if even now the tapering roots of the gestalt were winding their way through the crevices of his mind and strangling what remained of his self-will.

'Restrain him!'

The voice came through his ears in the distinctive, staticky buzz of the Jinc. The gestalt sounded alarmed and angry. Three of its withered components, ghastly in the half-light, loomed over him, hands extended like claws.

'Luminous!'

The word escaped his lips without conscious intent and burst like a curse in the faces of his captors.

The darkness deepened, became as red as blood. The three components froze in midlunge, their mouths wide and eyes gleaming hungrily. They looked like vampires, and he noted only then, when he was safe from immediate harm, that he was backed up against the wall behind him with hands upraised.

'Thank you,' he gasped, knowing the silver sphere could hear him.

'You are welcome, Imre Bergamasc.' The mellifluous voice came from the air itself, all around him. 'It had to be your decision. I could only inform, not direct.'

'I understand.' His heartbeat was slowing, but only relatively speaking. 'How long do I have?'

'You have until the Jinc becomes aware of your change in tempo. There will be an inevitable lag as its own tempo adjusts. You are overclocking so much right now that a second Absolute will seem like hours to you. Still, I suggest you start moving. This is the only chance I can give you.'

'Yes.' He swung his legs off the bed and crept between two of the components. He brushed against their robes and winced, feeling the heat of his superfast passage much more strongly than he would ordinary friction. Their faces didn't move as he rushed by. They didn't even blink.

He was out of the room before a single eyelid began to fall. The crawl space outside was blocked by a fourth component, wooden and corpselike as he pushed it aside, burning his hands in the process. He ignored the sting and hurried along the cramped tube.

'Take the first left,' the sphere instructed him. 'Then the second right.' A pressure hatch slid lazily open as he approached. He imagined himself leaving a hurricane of superheated air in his wake.

'Go down the ladder and across the chamber to the door on the far side.'

Another component crouched frozen in midmotion ahead of him. He went to edge past it when suddenly it moved, clutching at him with one clawlike hand. He flinched away, much more quickly than he needed to, and in the process jarred his right shoulder against the wall. The Jinc was moving sluggishly, its speed not yet a match for his. It was, however, accelerating. He hurried through the door, breath hissing through his teeth.

'I think I've broken my shoulder,' he said. 'Does the starship have medical facilities fit for this kind of body?'

'It does, and they are fully provisioned. Do not delay. The Jinc is reacting much more quickly than I anticipated.'

Imre shut the pain out of his mind and followed the directions with determined speed. Twice more components stirred as he passed, reaching for him like ghosts in slow motion. Each time he evaded them easily. But from behind him, growing louder and nearer with every minute, he heard the sound of pursuit. Rustling, scrabbling, desperate, the Jinc was not going to relinquish its prize without a fight.

'Left. Right. Right. Down.' The sphere's instructions came more rapidly as they entered a torturous section of the vessel that Imre had never visited. His exposed skin was hot with friction. He had to blink constantly to keep his eyes watered. When he breathed, the air seared his lungs.

'How much farther?'

'Nearly there.' A pressure door glided shut behind them, cutting off pursuit. One bony hand protruded from the jamb, caught there like a dying spider. It wriggled at him, then dropped away in slow motion, leaving a smear of blood on the dark metal. 'Hurry, hurry!'

He swallowed his horror and did as instructed. The pain from his broken clavicle was making him nauseous, but there wasn't time to adjust his internal chemistry to compensate. It was having enough trouble coping with the other demands he was placing on it. He didn't know how much longer it could keep up the pace.

'Wait,' said the sphere. 'Stop right where you are.'

Imre skidded to a halt. His skin sizzled. He was in a reinforced antechamber that could have squeezed in a dozen people at a pinch. Pipes lined one wall. Five entrances converged on the space through all three remaining walls, plus the floor and ceiling. The hatch behind him slid shut.

He backed up against a wall, feeling a trap closing around him. 'What is this? What's going on?'

'Don't move. Trust me.'

'Why should I?'

'Because the Jinc has you cornered, and I am your only hope of escape.'

'What about you? Why aren't you escaping with me?'

'My path is different from yours.'

Two of the hatches opened simultaneously. No less than seven components inched through, menacing and methodical. Their arms were outstretched, their expressions inhumanly blank. Imre didn't need to read the Jinc's mind to know its thoughts: the components would rush him as one and pin him down. Then the gestalt would assimilate him.

He looked around in desperation, lacking weapons to drive the Jinc back. 'Which way do I run?' he asked the sphere.

'You don't. Stand right there.'

He pressed his back against the hatch behind him. Bone grated against bone in his shoulder. 'I should never have listened to you. Look where it's got me! Talking to you only confirmed the Jinc's suspicions. It thought there was a connection between us – but there never would have been if you'd only let me be!'

'There always has been a connection between us,' the sphere told him. 'But it's not what you think.'

The Jinc closed in. Imre braced himself to fight it off as best he could. A red light flashed once out of the corner of his eyes, and the opening wail of a Klaxon reached his ears.

Then the hatch behind him burst open and he was sucked out into space on a wave of air. The Jinc looked as surprised as he was. Its mouthpieces scrabbled for grip on the floor and walls, anything to stop them being swept to their deaths. For Imre, it was already too late. The sides of the air lock were well out of reach. He was drifting backward with strange slowness, reflexes confused by the mismatch between his relative tempo and that of the Absolute universe. He had time only to flail before the glassy, outer hull of the Jinc vessel came into view. Then he was lost. Once outside the ship there was nothing to arrest his fall except the galaxy itself.

Something hard struck him in the back, sending pain shooting up his spine, shoulder, and neck. He slid helplessly along a rough, black surface before dropping into a deep pit. Bright orange walls enclosed him. The roof of the pit shut over him, blocking off the view.

A shuttle scoop, he thought, as air hissed into the chamber surrounding him. *The Jinc had a shuttle scoop ready to collect me, the moment I dropped out the air lock. It built this body, so it knew it would survive the vacuum.*

The look of surprise on the faces of the Jinc components testified to the false nature of that theory.

Acceleration gripped him, gave him weight. Groggily, painfully, he sat upright. The world's colors had returned to normal although they remained unreasonably bright.

'I am *The Cauld Lad*,' said the ship. 'The instructions I have been given will expire in forty seconds, whereupon I will need further directives.'

'I – I understand. Give me access to your navigational data.' There was no time for caution as virtual displays poured smoothly across his vision. Glowing arrows indicated vectors; smoothly curling tubes and sheets represented low-energy trajectories from which he could choose. The chart was relatively simple, with just two ships to accommodate and no other nearby mass. Even as he watched, four smaller dots launched from the sprawling shape that had to be the Jinc vessel.

'Away,' he said. 'Just take me away from here.'

'I require a destination.'

'The Continuum – anywhere.'

'That instruction is insufficiently specific. I am not rated for self-direction.'

He put a hand to his forehead, seeing stars creeping forward
from the corners of his vision. 'Mandala Supersystem.' That would
do. His fractured mind had produced no obvious alternatives.

'Destination confirmed.'

Weight increased. A wash of radiation obscured the Jinc ships
from view. When the static had cleared, all traces of the other
vessels were far behind. The gestalt's ageing tech was no match for
the starship's fiery delta-v. He didn't waste a second wishing it
farewell.

'How long?' Imre asked *The Cauld Lad*.

'One thousand, two hundred seventeen years Absolute.'

Imre nodded. He could accept that. In fact, he was lucky the
Drum hadn't been stationed by one of the galaxy's outer arms, in
which case his journey could have been tens of thousands of years
long.

'Good,' he said. 'I'll need medical attention in a moment.
There's one more thing I want you to start doing immediately. I
want you to gain access to the Continuum. I don't care what grade
connection or how you manage it. Just get me an outside data line
so I can see what's going on. Make that your first priority, after
navigation and maintenance.'

'I understand.' The ship's AI hesitated, or seemed to. Most
likely, its attention had been diverted to one or more of the many
subsystems it supervised. 'You will find the medical suite on the
aft deck.'

The air lock's interior door slid open, revealing a lime green corridor on the far side. Imre lurched to his feet. There were no gestalt
components to help him about now. He was on his own, at the
mercy of the silver sphere's intentions and the ship's well-being.
Where they would lead him, only time would tell.

'Thank you,' he said. 'It's good to be on my own.'

If anyone heard him, they played it safe and remained silent.

THIS ELEGANT BITCH

We may hate each other, torment each other,
— worst of all, we may be weary of each other,
(for hatred itself would be a relief, compared to
the tedium of our inseparability),
but separate we must never.

Robert Charles Maturin

Eight hundred and eight years into its journey, *The Cauld Lad* picked up its first recognizable signal from the remains of the Continuum. It was a distress call piggybacking on a pulsar's flickering polar beam like a shutter opening and closing in front of a bright light. Such beams were properly used as navigational and chronological aids, with many of the galaxy's two-hundred-thousand-odd pulsars conscripted to the task. Those pulsars that pointed across the galaxy's flattened disk, where most of the traffic went, were particularly prized, since shifting the orientation of a spinning stellar corpse into a more convenient direction was a job considered difficult even by the Forts.

This pulsar was situated in the Crux Arm, tens of thousand of light-years away. Imre was less surprised that *The Cauld Lad* had detected such a distant beacon than by the message. Decoding it took no time at all.

'The Slow Wave has ruined us. One by one, we fell. What have we done to deserve this end?'

That was the entirety of the message. Imre read it many times over, as though that alone might reveal some hidden subtext, some subtle clue that might otherwise have eluded him. There was nothing. He took the transmission's raw data and analyzed every 1 and 0, noting increasingly tinier arrhythmias, the slightest shift in frequency. There had to be more, but he couldn't find it.

The Cauld Lad raced on, tearing energy out of the vacuum and doing its small bit to delay the explosive expansion of the universe. It seemed unconcerned by the strange portent, but it wasn't designed to wonder about such things. It was a poor companion, one of reactions and reflexes, never initiating a conversation that wasn't about navigation or maintenance. Its encyclopedia was the original from which the Jinc's had been copied, so it had no new data to offer. Imre was alone with his doubts and found no succor among them. He slowed his tempo further and further until decades passed in just an hour, but still time seemed to drag.

A century went by before they finally encountered the data halo of the Continuum. He expected a torrent of information clogging every band of the electromagnetic spectrum. That was how it had been in his former life, a dense, infinitely complex web connecting every far-flung member of humanity, all across the galaxy's broad disk. Instead, whole bands were empty, or contained little but distant transmissions, broken up into static by dust and faulty relays. Other bands squawked with conflicting protocols, interfering signals, and active jamming. It was hard to make out anything beyond detached words or castaway clauses. This only deepened his puzzlement. Communication was what had bound the Continuum together, not trade. For what perverse reason would humanity have dismantled its greatest work?

'. . . the Slow Wave . . .'

The recurrence of that phrase chilled him. People spoke of seeking its origins and nature, of trying to elude it or turn it back, of damage done and ruination left in its wake. Imre was still too distant to see for himself what the mysterious, terrible phenomenon had wrought on humanity's home; part of him was afraid to see. But he had to know. He had to understand. What had the Jinc hidden from him, and why?

Another century passed. *The Cauld Lad* dove deeper into the dusty Sagittarius Arm that was home to Mandala Supersystem, wending its way through glowing nebulae and past fiery blue giants. Disjointed transmissions went from a trickle to a flood. Isolated packets seemed to be bouncing without purpose from relay to relay, long disconnected from their senders or the rest of the message they belonged to. There was no possible way to reassemble them all; Imre could only trawl through the most promising pieces, hoping without real hope for a match elsewhere. He found dollops of conversations, of stories, of scientific treatises, of political speeches, of thoughts, of artworks — none of which would ever reach its intended audience, none of which would ever be complete.

That thought more than any other filled him with unutterable sadness. If the Continuum had been a crystal of precise and unfathomable complexity, then someone had struck it with a very large hammer. The pieces lay all around him, gleaming and strangely beautiful in their own way, but heartbreaking in their randomness, their disconnection, their unbearable limitedness. Who would have destroyed such a tremendous achievement?

Revulsion filled him. He was a flea crawling across the galactic corpse. A flea with no purpose, no destiny, no past. What had been lost by humanity completely dwarfed his own personal crisis — but if there was any difference he could make, any sacrifice or surrender, he would offer it unhesitatingly. The ruin of humanity's work was awful and terrible. He could not go on.

Two things kept him moving. One: the Slow Wave. Without knowing what that had been, how could he decide what exactly had befallen the Continuum and whether it could be undone? And two: the galaxy had been shattered, but not all of the pieces would have been destroyed. Some must have been overlooked, somewhere. The thought that such isolated remnants might be hiding, waiting for the right moment to emerge, gave him some small hope. That was all he needed.

He raised his tempo closer to Absolute as *The Cauld Lad* approached Mandala Supersystem. All of the ship's sensors were set at their highest resolution, peering past the glowing cone of his deceleration to what lay ahead. Transmissions from that sector, like

every other, were garbled and incomplete. The Line relays leading
to neighboring systems and beyond were full of gibberish, those
that were still working at all. Imre began to despair of finding anything at his destination but dissolution, desolation.

Then, as he passed through the system's enormous bow shock
and officially left intergalactic space, he found in the central sun's
heliosphere that older and less pervasive means of communication
had been revived. Echoes of maser and radio communications grew
louder the closer he approached the system's heart, and he trawled
through numerous different archives to find codes that would
unlock the primitive signals before he arrived, in order to know
who they came from, what they meant.

The Cauld Lad's course took it on a long, curving parabola past
two of the system's secondary suns. This enabled it to triangulate
many of the transmission sources. The most powerful orbited Di-
Zang and Chenresi, two stars that had not possessed dominant
civilizations in his day. The sources he had expected to be lighting
up the sky were deathly quiet.

The transmissions, when he decoded them, contained news
reports, sportscasts, entertainment shows, and scientific data – too
much for one person to filter through in the short time available to
him. They were, in miniature, everything he had expected to see
across the whole galaxy. Where previously there had been no information to mull over, now he had too much.

Some light-hours out of Chenresi, the closest star, he prepared a
statement to send to the authority in charge of the major colony,
Hyperabad. He introduced himself and briefly outlined his circumstances. He requested an explanation for the state of the
Continuum, and offered his help, should it be needed. He asked
that his existence be kept secret, should the Jinc come looking for
him.

The white star loomed closer, freckled with sunspots.
Prominences waved like cosmic hair. Chenresi's siblings burned
brightly against the galactic backdrop. He thought of mourners
holding candles surrounding the body of a loved one, their faces
shrouded with shadow.

Doubt filled him. Who were these people who had taken over Mandala Supersystem in the wake of its previous inhabitants? They could be survivors of the terrible tragedy that had befallen the galaxy, or they could be collaborators living high on the spoils. Every instinct screamed at him to gain more information before declaring himself to anyone. He didn't want to end up a captive again.

The Cauld Lad baffled its drives and changed course at his command. He deleted the message unsent and considered alternate destinations. Di-zang was just as busy as Chenresi; Sakra was dark and forbidding, showing a lot of silent traffic in and out; Chugai Zhang's five gas giants and numerous moons were crowded with mercantile transports babbling on about wares and exchange rates. In the end, he chose the quietest, emptiest corner of the supersystem: Kuntuzangpo, a golden star with no major planets and no obvious transmission sources. There he could sit and listen without fear of discovery or interference. There he could consider what to do next.

Memories of the Alienist Technarchy swamped him as *The Cauld Lad* powered along its new trajectory. Decision made, he retired to his room to sleep them off.

He dreamed not of the technarch's demise but of giant breakers, of curling, green walls falling in slow motion over cities of glass. Worlds with naturally liquid oceans comprised only a small percentage of those found across the galaxy; many such $H2O$ reserves had frozen solid or evaporated away before humanity had discovered them. The thunderous power of water was therefore unknown to most people. Imre had experienced the real thing on several worlds; he had even learned to surf, once, on a brief R&R break between campaigns.

He was under no illusions, however, that the Slow Wave spoken of in tones of such terror and dread by the former citizens of the Continuum was made of water, or anything remotely like water. Something had propagated through the galaxy in the fashion of a wave, sweeping all that was civilized before it. What could it have

been? A natural phenomenon? An army? A virus, biological or software? He feared for his own safety and that of the ship. If he exposed
himself without proper protection, he might be corrupted too.

'I'm the disease,' he remembered the big soldier saying in a
lifter bay, waiting for a drop. 'Looking for a cure.'

'You're so full of shit,' Helwise had sneered. Imre had thought
that he understood, although that understanding wasn't part of the
recollection and sadly escaped him now.

The tide of the past was strong. It had ebbed during his escape
from the Jinc, with so many other issues to worry about along the
way. Now it rose again, stirred up by the gravity of settings both
familiar and unfamiliar. The supersystem's elaborate constellation
possessed a reassuring congruency with his memories; the activity
of its inhabitants did not. The fear of what he might find under
every unturned stone had not decreased. Oceans held more than
water. There were monsters too.

'I have detected a distress beacon,' the ship announced, when
they were still half a light-day from Kuntuzangpo.

He struggled out of his low-gee hammock and up to the brilliant, yellow plastic bridge. Every room in *The Cauld Lad* was
decorated in a different color: the orange air lock; the blue corridor;
his green bedroom; the purple head that he hadn't used yet. He felt
like turning out the lights sometimes to deflect the barrage of primary and secondary colors. That the ship had a bridge at all spoke
of anachronistic designers or idiosyncratic owners, somewhere in
its past, but it had nothing to say to him about that.

The bridge was circular, entered via a hatch from below, with a
wraparound display offering half a sphere's worth of visual information, as though his head were sticking out the hull. Ever-changing
instrumentation and contact pads occupied a sweeping bank below
the display, making a rainbow of flashing lights in still more bright
colors.

'Show me,' he said.

A window appeared in the display allowing him access to the
raw data and various treatments of the same. Waveforms glided by,
looping every half a minute or so.

'Give me audio as well.'

The transmission was sharp-edged and painful on his ears. He winced, even at the same time as he recognized it.

'That's a Corps transmission.' He could barely believe it, but his memories left no room for doubt. 'Are you sure it's an SOS?'

'The content is unambiguous.' A translation appeared in one of the windows: brief, brutal code requesting immediate assistance, but no name, no details of the emergency, no time or date. It could have been broadcasting for centuries, long after the reason for its existence became irrelevant.

He couldn't take that chance, though. If the transmission was recent, it might lead him to one of his former companions. They could help him stabilize his sense of self and perhaps offer a lead to the person who had tried to erase his existence from the galaxy.

'Where's it coming from? Have you pinned down the source?'

'I have.' A map of Kuntuzangpo's immediate surrounds ballooned outward from a point. The only navigational hazards consisted of dust clouds and a single, straggling asteroid belt, cleaned out long ago by the Alienist Technarchy. There was just one red marker, but it was a big one: the Cat's Arse, the virulent welt in space-time left behind after the Chaos War. The transmission's source lay in the very heart of it.

'Take us closer,' he ordered the ship. 'When reply times are below three seconds, send an acknowledgment. If you receive a response to that, ask for more information. Use your standard protocols if you're not familiar with Corps handshakes.'

'I am not.' The shipboard AI offered no further elaboration on what it was in fact familiar with.

Imre suppressed a growing restlessness as the ship swooped closer to its destination. The spatial anomaly was difficult to see from a distance, looking like perfectly empty space until it occluded a distant star, which crinkled and sparkled unpredictably. The ship carefully tracked such occlusions, projecting them on the display so Imre could view them in turn. He paced the interior of the bridge; seventeen steps took him once around the instrumentation panels. The images turned with him, always presenting the best possible angle to their sole viewer.

When, finally, the ship detected a hard image among the distortions, he was ready to see it. The picture swayed ever so slightly – the only indication that the ship was currently decelerating at hundreds of gravities – and he found it difficult to decipher at first. Flashed up in negative, he made out straight lines, half circles, and sharp angles: geometric figures that had to be artificial but didn't coalesce into anything recognizable. The ship threw up further enhancements, steadily refining the images until a kind of sense emerged.

'Ships,' Imre said. 'Lots of them. What are they doing there?' The forms visible in the images were jumbled, with no clear sense of order. 'It doesn't look like a dock.'

'Ambient radiation is minimal,' said *The Cauld Lad*, confirming his opinion. 'There are no navigational beacons or automatic hails.'

'A graveyard, then. And/or a trap. Take it slowly and carefully. I don't want to be hit by whatever hit them.'

The ship didn't state the obvious: that the crews of the previous ships might have thought exactly that, to no avail.

He stopped pacing and rested his hands on the edge of the instrumentation panel. With fixed intensity, he studied the new images as they came in. Each ship was a different shape and hanging at a different orientation in the anomaly. Some overlapped, as though they had suffered a collision. One, a slender liner more than ten kilometers long, skewered an inflatable habitat like a needle. Debris surrounded them both, hanging in thick tendrils where the spatial deformation was stickiest.

In the center of the anomaly, lurking like a black spider at the heart of its web, was a dense object he didn't remember from the Chaos Wars but had glimpsed in his memories. No more than a hundred meters across, it seemed completely inactive, but he assumed nothing. If a malign intelligence was behind the destruction of the ships, his money was on a remnant of the Alienist Technarchy – some lingering weapon brought back into service by accident, chance, or time itself. There was no expiration date on revenge.

'Do you think we should just leave this alone and go somewhere else?' he asked the ship.

The reply came, exactly as he had expected it: 'That question is insufficiently specific.'

He knew the answer to his question anyway: the anomaly, like Mandala Supersystem itself, was proof positive that his memory was accurate. The coincidence of a Corps transmission from the heart of it could not be ignored. Like a man peeling back the layers of an onion, he felt that he was at last getting close to a truth. It might be bitter, but he didn't care.

The Cauld Lad coasted the last million kilometers, engines at the ready for a hasty retreat. It possessed no weapons or military shielding. If it had in fact been a zombie derelict, all evidence had been stripped by the Jinc. Its reflexes, however, were fast, and Imre had no doubt of its instinct for self-preservation. Instructed to flee at the slightest threat, it would do so to the best of its abilities.

'I am broadcasting acknowledgment of our receipt of the distress beacon.'

He waited, barely breathing, for five minutes. 'No reply?'

'No.'

'Broadcast it again,' he told the ship, drumming his fingers on bright yellow plastic. His skin looked sickly in the harsh, artificial light. He slowed his tempo so an hour flew fly by in a matter of heartbeats. The ship seemed to shoot forward like a bullet during that time, then slam to a halt afterward. Still no reply had come.

'There's no evidence that it's a trap,' he said, speaking more to himself than to the ship. 'If it was, they would have given us a reason to come closer. Someone from the Corps would have done so, anyway.' He was sure about that. His colleagues might have been assembled from a myriad of disconnected pieces in his mind, but he had no doubt about their ability to set a successful ambush. 'We've come too far to turn back. Keep going in. Can you find a way through the anomaly?'

'I require a destination.'

'Oh, the thing in the middle. There.' He pointed at the dense object he had seen before. 'Is that the source of the transmission?'

'No.'

'Okay. Then take us to wherever that is.'

A red circle delineated the nose of the needlelike liner, and the ship began to accelerate.

Half an hour later, Imre instructed the ship to reduce the display to a small window on the far side of the bridge. He couldn't endure the light-twisting effects of the anomaly without such mitigation, but he couldn't cease watching entirely either. There was too much to see.

It became clear almost immediately that the tangle of ships definitely was a graveyard, judging by the number of blast craters, laser scars, and shrapnel everywhere he looked. Peeled-back metal mixed with shattered ceramics, melted plastics, and more exotic materials, all in a state of profound distress. The forces that had gutted the ships were long gone, however. The wreckage was cold and dead, and had been for centuries at least.

Among the pieces of dead ships and machines, he saw pieces of dead people too. Sad, broken figures drifted endlessly in vacuum, radiation-scarred and frozen. He couldn't tell without autopsies if they were Primes, singletons, or frags, but the distinction seemed irrelevant. Part of him that had been a soldier recognized distinctive signs of small-weapons fire and suggestions of a gun battle among the ruins. That bothered him. The dead crews weren't all victims of vacuum and the anomaly's obfuscations, then. Someone or something else had killed them.

The Cauld Lad edged nearer the stricken liner. Its curved hull looked intact, but all its air locks were open and dusted with frozen atmosphere. Two were clogged with bodies, spread-eagled and stiff. The source of the beacon was in the battered nose, a kilometer from their present location, and Imre watched nervously as the white hull slid by. Rows of windows occasionally broke its smooth, curving surface, revealing glimpses of the cabins within.

'Still no change?'

'None.'

'I'm going EV if nothing happens soon.'

'I can offer you that capability.'

'I know.' He had investigated the ship's resources during the long journey, and knew already that it carried three environmental skin suits in its extravehicular locker. Aboard the ship, he still wore the jumpsuit he had woken in but had fed the Jinc's jumpsuit into the recyclers at the first opportunity. 'Prep one of the suits and ready the air lock. I'll be down in a moment.'

He waited until *The Cauld Lad* had reached the nose of the liner and come to a halt relative to it. The display revealed no sign of foul play beyond the damage to the liner itself. Its nose was battered and blackened, probably by its passage through the inflatable habitat hanging in ribbons near its aft end. Nothing moved, except in the sky beyond. Every slight movement set the distorted starscape rippling and twisting.

'Is that suit ready?'

'Yes.'

There was no point delaying. Hurrying to the air lock, he stood motionless as the suit's black membrane spread up his legs and across his entire body. He looked down at the slick, ebony surface as the suit performed its final checks, turning his hands front and back to catch the light. Apart from two translucent eyeholes, he could have been made of gleaming oil. He had used such things many times before, but not in this new life. Never in such strange circumstances. The reflective surface only made the curve of his hips and breasts stand out even more.

The ship cycled the air lock open, exposing him to vacuum and the bedevilment of the anomaly. He focused his attention on the hull of liner, some five meters away, and jetted outside. Reflexes took over the moment he was in the void. Orienting by *The Cauld Lad*, not the stars, he flew across the short distance to the liner and crouched on the white hull. He had no weapon and no defenses; he was completely exposed, and he felt it. The one thing he could do was adjust the skin suit's color to blend more with the background. This he did the moment he touched down.

His heart thudded like a frenetic axman. The liner's white

needle was a complete contrast to the hollow darkness of the Drum. The only visible text was a single word writ large a kilometer back from the nose: DEODATI, in giant letters, which Imre assumed to be the name of the ship. No identification apart from that; no registration numbers, no home port, and no flag.

After a moment's stillness, he stood and ran on magnetized feet for the nearest air lock, forgoing jets in order to make himself less visible. In his mind's eye, he saw sniper fire stitching a line behind him, but nothing interfered with him. He made it to the air lock unimpeded.

The ship was dead. He could feel its morbidity through the hand he placed on the sterile, white wall. No vibrations rang through the frame: no engines thrumming, no reactor boiling, no life support whispering. Something, however, was active. The source of the transmission wasn't far away, judging by the information given to him by *The Cauld Lad*. There was a map of the liner's interior on the wall next to the inner lock, and he traced a route along the relatively broad corridors with a finger before moving off.

The liner's many levels were stacked like pancakes to provide an illusion of gravity while under thrust. Imre turned his suit back to black and kicked himself through the vacuum like a deep-sea diver, seeing in infrared, his jets at the ready should he need to change course quickly. Two levels down, in what appeared to be an administrative nexus for the liner's foresection, he found the device, a boxy structure with a cobbled-together look squatting in the center of a cleared space. Cables snaked through each of the room's four doorways to carry the transmission to the hull, which acted as a very large resonator, giving the signal enough oomph to be heard by someone passing Kuntuzangpo. Imre floated motionlessly in the entrance for a full minute, looking for booby traps. The power supply didn't appear to be rigged, and none of the cables looked live. There were no bodies slumped over the data-entry point. The transmitter might have been abandoned as soon as it was switched on.

He was too late. That was the only conclusion he could come to.

Someone from the Corps had planted the beacon long ago, probably when the liner crashed into the anomaly, and it had sounded out into the void ever since. Kuntuzangpo, being an empty corner of Mandala Supersystem, had too little traffic for rescue to come soon enough. The beacon was a memorial now, not a sign of hope.

As though afraid of disturbing ghosts, he gingerly nudged himself forward to the data-entry point and placed his right hand against the smooth plastic. The skin suit opened a channel between him and the transmitter's software and he brought a command screen into view, pasted across the silent cenotaph that was the *Deodati*.

He selected end transmission from a menu. The silence seemed deeper when he had done that, even though stopping the machine made no audible difference. He pulled away, the newly grown hairs on the back of his neck tingling.

'Take two steps back,' said a voice from behind him. 'Don't turn around until I tell you, or I'll shoot you where you stand.'

He did as he was told, unable to pinpoint the source of the voice. It was faint, communicated through the floor in the absence of air, and barely audible even after enhancement. A shadow moved in the corner of his eye.

'Put your hands where I can see them. Now.'

'I followed the transmission.' He talked while obeying, hoping that compliance would earn him an answer. 'Where's the emergency?'

'It'll be in your back if you don't turn around. Do it slowly so I can see you.'

He half turned to his right, just far enough to see the figure in heavy combat armor standing against one wall below an open ceiling hatch. That was enough. Setting his suit to mirror finish and flashing its jets full thrust at his assailant, he let the recoil propel him away and around the transmitter. Lines of energy followed him – a Birmingham X-ray laser, scintillating through dust and jet exhaust. He careened around the room like a deranged blowfly, his tempo rising steadily until the time between each laser burst seemed to take an age. The person shooting at him had a good aim and unequivocally meant him harm. Even overclocking, he was hard-pressed to get closer without being shot. His jets might have dazzled the shooter for an instant, but that small surprise didn't last long.

He kicked a chair at the laser, which burned it neatly in two. Pressure hatches had come down with the first shot, cutting the cables and sealing him inside the room. He had to take out the person firing at him quickly, or else he would inevitably die. That knowledge welled up in him from the same place that had made him move, once he had located the person threatening him. It was part of him, this soldier's instinct, and he trusted it without examination. It would keep him alive if it could.

Thick, acrid fumes filled the room. His attacker was moving, coming around to keep the transmitter between them. That made no sense until the laser started firing again, slicing the blocky construct into pieces. He couldn't stand by and watch his only significant cover being reduced, bit by bit. He dropped to the floor and thrust flat along it, reaching for the shooter's feet. They lifted as he approached and the laser came down toward him. He kicked off the wall with a grunt of effort and ricocheted away, imagining the target reticule gliding across his back. Even at full thrust, the suit was too slow – too fucking slow—

A bright red flash threw sharp-edged shadows across the room. He didn't know what had caused it, but he took advantage of the distraction, changing course for another section of the room. The laser skidded away from him, its beam slicing a wavy line up one wall and across the ceiling. Then it cut out. He rolled as he traveled in order to look behind him. The bulky figure holding the laser had itself been shot. Bright red edges limned a hole in its armor wide enough to see through. Flesh burned within the hole, stricken as much by the suit's destruction as by whatever had damaged it. As he watched, a second red beam struck the figure, blowing it backward into the wall and sending the laser flying. The suit's stored energy discharged in a brilliant crack, powerful enough to send the disintegrated remains of the transmitter bouncing around the room. Burning black soot billowed everywhere.

Imre followed the trajectory of the laser, even though he could no longer see it. One outstretched hand reached it just as the room's hatches opened, venting the obscuring atmosphere into the vacuum. The laser swung into his arms as though designed to fit there. His right index finger instantly found the trigger. Suddenly he felt whole.

The room was empty, apart from wreckage. His attacker's body had been burned completely away. His rescuer was nowhere visible.

'Thank you,' he said aloud and over several electromagnetic bands. His voice wavered only slightly. 'I owe you one.'

'We owe each other a favor,' came back an immediate reply, masked as his was by layers of distortion. 'She was trying to kill me too.'

'Who are you?'

'You're the one holding the gun. You tell me.'

'Imre Bergamasc,' he said, tightening his grip on the stock with his left hand.

'Impossible. He's male.'

'Maybe he was.' He responded to the challenge by putting a harder edge on his voice. 'Now he's not. Is that a problem for you?'

A silhouette appeared in the entrance to his right, a female figure clad only in a skin suit similar to his. He recognized the heavy cannon it held in both arms as an Acitak two-shooter, requiring recharge or battery replacement every other pulse.

'You're so not who I was expecting,' the woman said, dropping the vocal camouflage. Further connections flooded him – voice, posture, even the way the spent cannon drooped to point at the floor – as the blackness of her suit dissolved, revealing a face he had seen in this life only from memory. 'The last time you walked into a trap as lame as that one, Render didn't talk to you for a month.'

'Helwise?' The name felt wrong on his lips. He tried again, abbreviating it in a way that felt more natural. 'Hel?'

'The one and only.' She strode forward. Her hair swept back in a tight, black skullcap, throwing her features into sharp relief.

Her nose was strong and proud; her lips were full and curling up into a smile. She swayed when she walked, placing one long, slender leg in front of the other with fluid precision. Only she could go from killer to mankiller so quickly.

The laser swung aside without him thinking of it. The cannon drifted behind her, forgotten. One hand came up to cup the back of his head while the other slid around his waist. He froze for an instant at the feel of her suited body against his. He could feel her breathing, her body trembling with reaction to their fast-tempo, combative dance.

Her voice, physically conducted through the suits from her lips to his ear, made his skin tingle.

'Since when did you have bigger tits than me?'

He held her in return, then, and knew that by some strange measure he had at last come home. 'That's a long story.'

She pulled back from him. 'It'd better be a good one, you son of a bitch.' With a powerful, full-muscled sweep of her right arm, she punched him in the face.

They were in a maintenance closet off the main bunker's access corridor. She had stripped off her boots and camouflage pants, and her body armor hung open down her front. Imre's right hand was under her singlet, cupping her breast. His left hand gripped her buttocks, pulling her closer to him. He worked quickly inside her, captured by her slickness, her heat. Her hollow bones gave her a deceptive lightness. That he could pick her up in one arm if he wanted to made it easy to assume that she was weak. But her musculature was corded and powerful, and her limbs were long for better leverage. She bent like a whip, and snapped rope-tight. She could move as silently as a shadow, when she wanted to.

They were interrupted by a blast so powerful dust rained on them from the ceiling.

She laughed. 'Better hurry, or our asses will be blown off.'

'It's not my ass I'm worried about.'

'You and me both.'

His communicator buzzed on the floor, where he'd discarded it along with his pack and rifle. He ignored it. The urgency of the situation, the need for haste, the concern over what was happening elsewhere, the sheer irresponsibility of their behavior – all of it combined in a powerful, physical rush that swept him away, just for a moment, more completely than combat ever did.

Another subterranean concussion shook the floor beneath them. She lowered her legs and eased him out of her. 'Fuck.'

'We'll pick this up later.'

She grabbed his neck and pulled his face down to hers. They kissed hard, briefly. 'If you're lucky.' She bit his upper lip and pushed him away.

He staggered, off-balance, and put out one hand to touch the nearest wall.

'I didn't hit you that hard, did I?'

'No, I—' His head spun one way, then another. 'I told you. Things are only slowly coming together for me. Input provokes output. Being with you again – but here, like this – makes me . . .'

For a moment, he couldn't speak.

'Those Jinc cocksuckers should've left you where you were.' Her voice was hard in *The Cauld Lad*'s plastic corridors, ringing with upper harmonics. 'Look at you: you'd be dead if it wasn't for me. I could kill you now as easily as look at you. How you lasted this long is a miracle itself.'

The mazement slowly passed. He didn't know how to tell her that in his dreams he was male, thoroughly male, while in real life his female form remained as substantive as ever. Whatever changes the Jinc had initiated, they had yet to manifest.

'You're right,' he said. 'But I am still here. You obviously don't want to kill me, and I obviously don't want to die. The Jinc might not be to blame for the rest. Let's move on. What are you doing here? Who was that back there?'

'Her? She's irrelevant now. Forget about her.'

'She tried to kill me.'

'She'd been trying to kill me a lot longer. Don't take it personally.'

He let go of the wall, remembering the signs of small-arms fire he'd seen all through the graveyard. 'How long had you two been sniping at each other before I showed up?'

'Longer than I care to remember.' Her dark eyes watched him, revealing nothing. 'Come on. This old ship of yours is a sitting duck. We should get moving.'

She had said that earlier, while crossing the gap from the liner to *The Cauld Lad*. In the lock, they had removed their suits, noses crinkling at the acrid dust they had carried from the fight scene. Under her suit, she wore a light, insulated garment covered with zips. He remembered that kind of garb from his previous life, but he couldn't remember what she kept in the pockets.

'Where do you suggest we go?' He had brought her up to date on his situation – briefly, covering all the salient points – but she had yet to reveal anything about hers.

'The habitat,' she said. 'The Cat's Arse. That's why we're here, right?'

'I came here because of the distress call.'

'That's all?'

He felt her puzzled stare on him as he led the way to the bridge. 'Tell me what you think I've forgotten.'

'What's the last thing you remember? The Slow Wave?'

'Further back. *Pelorus*, the Mad Times.'

'Jesus. You should still remember. We'd agreed by then that this is where we'd meet if things ever went sour. We built a safe house here. You designed it. Are you telling me you knew nothing about this when you came here?'

He didn't say anything, unsure exactly what he did or didn't know. He might as well have forgotten the safe house for all the conscious knowledge he possessed of it. The Cat's Arse had meant nothing to him until the name had popped into his head, and even then it had seemed little more than a curiosity. Yet here he was, with Helwise, at the end of a chain of coincidence and luck. He marveled at the way his subconscious had crept him crabwise to where he needed to be.

'What happened on *Pelorus*?' he asked. 'I know we lost the war.'

'You surrendered on our behalf. The Forts rescued the survivors, junked the ship. It was all over. The Corps should have been tried and convicted as traitors. The Forts should have killed us. But you talked to them. They let us go.'

'Why?'

'I don't know for sure. I wasn't part of that conversation; this version of me wasn't there. But I can guess.'

He stopped at the base of the ladder leading to the bridge and turned to her, waiting.

'You really don't know?' she asked him.

'Give me one reason why I'd lie about that.'

'I gave up trying to work you out long ago, Imre. It wasn't something you encouraged. If it was, maybe we wouldn't be where we are right now.'

'What do you mean by that?'

She sighed. 'I don't know. Let's just get on with it, into the habitat. I'll feel better without imagining *her* everywhere I turn.'

'She had allies?'

'Well, there are more like her out there. That's close enough.'

Her nervousness was both uncharacteristic and contagious. 'You've been hiding too long, Hel,' he said as he ascended, hand over hand.

'Is that any different from being out of the picture?' she called up after him.

'You know it is. Neither's easy.'

'I'm not saying that. Not saying that at all.'

From the bridge, they put *The Cauld Lad* into motion, easing it away from the liner and deeper into the Space Age Sargasso. Firm nudges shouldered the hulks aside where no clear passage lay. The creaks and grumbles of reluctant metal came through the walls of the starship like the laments of dying cetaceans.

Helwise took manual control of *The Cauld Lad*'s navigation with efficient and easy familiarity. Imre had had no interest in doing so before; the AI could do the job better than he could. He indulged her, knowing that her wish didn't stem from her belief that she was a superior pilot to the AI but from a need to be in control. There was a stretched quality to her, a tightness around her mouth that spoke of a long proximity to murder and death. He had yet to ask her about the Slow Wave. It played, he presumed, a starring role in her recent history.

'Things were quiet after the Mad Times,' she said, her eyes on the wraparound display and her hands pressed firmly against contact points. The view shifted restlessly at her silent instruction. She didn't look at him. 'You disappeared for a while, but that's not unusual. Maybe you remember that much. Every century or two you'd hold your little wank-fests where every single one of you got together and swapped memories. A big fucking thought orgy, with no one else invited. Well, I just assumed it was another one of those. But you were gone longer this time and you didn't send word. People began to wonder. The war had shaken all of us one way or another. Maybe you'd gone to ground for good. Maybe surrendering had been the finish of you.'

Imre leaned against the instrumentation panels and listened to her words, to the unfolding tale of Himself in other times and other places. He felt as though she was talking about a stranger, and he had to remind himself that he and the Imre Bergamasc she had known were one and the same, separated only by circumstance.

While she spoke, he never once looked away from her proud profile, yet his eyes saw only what she had seen; his heart felt what she had felt. A past he had not known enfolded him. For a time without seconds, minutes or hours, he was utterly no one.

I was in Chimeleon (she said) when the Slow Wave hit. It had never been much of a system to start with, and that didn't look likely to change anytime soon. But it was somewhere, and its people called it home. There'd been an incursion from one of the Untitled States, and we'd been sent in to clean things up. You were there when we arrived, with no explanation as to where you'd been or how you'd found out about the gig. The powers that be told us to liaise with you, and we did just that. Just like old times.

I tried to get you to talk, but you wouldn't. Not at first. I could tell you had something to spill. Some big fucking secret or other. Let him sit on it, I told myself. Let him keep it to himself until it won't be kept any longer. Then he'll come around, and I'll listen if it suits me.

So we go through the motions. (She paused briefly to adjust the starship's trim.) US jobs were always untidy. Not any more, since I think they've fallen apart like everything else, and that's something I won't miss. The Mad Times only made them madder. We were hard-pressed to keep the cap on Chimeleon. Ground fights were breaking out all over the place, in a dozen big cities. We took a couple of tours ourselves, to get our feet dirty. You seemed pre-occupied and jittery. Maybe you could tell I wanted to ask you about it. Maybe that's why you took us out of orbit, to give me something else to think about. I don't know. But it seemed strange, you wanting to be in the thick of it again.

Don't get me wrong. You could still walk the walk, even if you were just going through the motions. I reckon I was the only one who could tell your mind was elsewhere. Everyone else was just glad to have you on our side.

('Wait. Are you telling me that nothing changed?' he interrupted her to ask. 'After the Mad Times, I mean. We went to war with the Forts over just this kind of stuff – us fighting their battles for them. Was that all forgotten?'

'You tell me, lover. You weren't there to offer an opinion at the time, having bugged out and left us to take up the slack. It was a weird kinda slack, let me tell you. The Forts weren't treating us any different, like the war never happened. *Pelorus* had barely burned out, and they were offering us assignments. None of us had the balls to ask the important questions, then or afterward. It was simplest to go back to doing what we knew best.'

'That's your explanation? You fell to pieces just because I wasn't holding your hands?'

'Believe it was that simple if you like, Imre. You weren't there. You'll never know.'

'I'm trying to find out.'

'Well, let me tell the story,' she said, 'and maybe you'll get the picture.')

It didn't go all our way (she continued). The Untitled States had their roots in deep. There was the usual collateral damage. There were the usual fuck-ups. We lost a million Primes in one badly timed counterstrike. The Chimeleon government considered surrender at one point, simply because they were tired. We talked them out of that, and in the end I think they were glad. When you're running at Tempo Absolute, you can't see the big picture. That's what we were there for – to tell them that the Untitled States were a bad deal for their planet, no matter how prettily it was dressed up. They had to trust us, just like we trusted the Forts. It made about as much sense for us to fuck over the Primes as it did for the Forts to fuck us. As long as no one starts a war they can't win, the system works, right?

We did our job as instructed, including you. We scoured Chimeleon clean of that particular poison – in less than 180 years too, significantly ahead of schedule. Noncombatant losses were below estimates. The Continuum meme prevailed, in the approved form. Yes to humanity at all stages of development; no to predatory regimes that robbed anyone of choice. Never mind the frag situation; never mind your big secret. We got it done. That made us heroes and sorely in need of a holiday.

I remember wondering if you'd let your guard down once the pressure was off. With your first gig after retirement behind you, and with all of peacetime Chimeleon before us, I planned to get under your skin and see what I found.

What I found was this: you'd discovered something new about the Forts. Specifically, how they communicate with each other and within themselves. They don't use the same means we do, which is why it never seemed to hurt them no matter how many communications relays we blew up. They use something new, something they call Q looping. It's not FTL, but it's very cheap, energy-wise, and very long-range. A single frag can be halfway across the galaxy and still plugged into the Fort it belongs to. No worries. They also call it the Loop.

('I remember that,' Imre said. 'I remember knowing about the Loop.'

'You do?' She frowned. 'That means you knew about it before *Pelorus*. How did you find out? Why didn't you tell us?'

The rear of his skull ached as though about to shatter. 'That I don't remember.'

'Sure, you fucker.'

'No, really. I don't know how it works or who invented it. I just know that it exists.'

'Existed,' she corrected him. 'The Forts are all dead now, and whatever secrets they had went with them.'

He opened his mouth, but no words came out. The greatest human minds that ever evolved – all dead? He could barely conceive it.)

The Forts had their Loop, and we were out of it. Ha-fucking-ha. That's the way I saw it, anyway, and you didn't rush to contradict me. That you were their pet again seemed pretty incontrovertible. Perhaps I should have worried less about that and more about the Loop, but you were doing your best to distract me, dropping hints about some secret project you were involved in, some mission a bunch of you had elsewhere that not even you knew the full story about.

I've never known anyone quite so paranoid as to keep secrets from themselves. That's what really gets me. While half of you were doing the Forts' grisly business, the rest of you were up to something so mysterious even you didn't want to think about it. Or maybe you were thinking about it, but you managed to convince me you weren't. I don't know. Layers upon layers upon layers of steaming horseshit until I feel like I drowned in it – and now here we are again, with you knowing fuck-all about anything, and me next to useless, trying to piece it all back together. You and the Forts, the Forts and their Loop, you and your secret mission . . . I'm as much in the dark as you are, and that's not a good place to be.

Are you getting this, Imre? Are you taking all this in? Because this is just the beginning. This is how it was before the Slow

Wave hit. We were in a spaceport over Chimeleon, waiting for a
ride out of the system. We were heading to Mandala, to regroup
with the others. There was only one ship ready to launch, and
that was a Fort liner, the *Deodati*. You pulled some strings and got
us aboard, tucked in tight with all the frags. You'd traveled this
way before, you said. In fact, you knew one of the Fort passengers.
There were just three: your friend Factotem and two others, or
parts of them, in a ship built to hold a thousand people. We were
the only singletons aboard; the rest were frags, linked by the Loop
to the rest of their selves. It was creepy as fuck. The ship was full
of things that looked like people, that ate, shat, and slept like
people, but they were just cells in a giant organism. I'd been fighting the Forts for so long, but that was the first time I'd been right
up close to one. They surrounded us but didn't even seem to notice
us. Just like the Forts themselves.

Factotem was a shit: he liked playing poker but kept cheating by
sending a frag behind you to look at your cards. I learned not to
take him on pretty fast, but he was good company despite that.
Not slow at all. I thought the Forts worked on a galactic scale, with
their tempos dropped right down low. I thought that was what
made them Forts, and why they hired people like us to do their
dirty work. But these dudes were quick. You could ask Factotem a
question, and he would respond almost instantly, sometimes
through interface software, other times through the frag itself. I
thought talking through a frag would be like us talking through
our skins, or out of our asses, but go figure. Factotem's main awareness was housed elsewhere, in the Orion Arm somewhere, you said,
so the frags ran the ship, those particular extensions of Factotem
and the other Forts. They were crew and passengers both. It was a
neat system that should have been completely foolproof.

We were halfway to Mandala at full throttle when the Slow
Wave passed us. I didn't know what the fuck had happened. The
noise was what hit me first. A thousand people screaming – that's
what it sounded like. The racket filled the liner, getting louder and
louder. I was in our cabin, and you burst in like the devil himself
was behind you.

'They're dead!' you shouted. 'Factotem and the others – something's killed them!'

I tried to calm you down, but I couldn't. You ran from the room and I followed you. That's when I saw what was making the noise. Or who, I should say. The frags had burst out of their usual torpor and were running amok through the ship, banging their heads against walls and tearing at their hair. I grabbed one of them as it went past – a woman, or would've been if she hadn't been born a frag. She didn't resist. She didn't even know I was there. Her pupils were pinpoints. Tears were streaming down her face. Her hands flapped about, repeating the same gestures without stopping. She wasn't really screaming; she was just making a whine that only stopped when she had to take a breath. I shook her, yelled at her, but she wouldn't shut up.

You told me to leave her alone. I didn't want to; she looked so helpless, so pathetic. Not remotely dead, as you had claimed.

'The frags aren't really dead,' you explained, looking a little calmer. 'The links to the rest of their minds connecting have been cut somehow. If someone opened up your skull and tipped out all your neurons, what do you think would happen to you?'

I got it then. That's why they were running around like chickens with their heads cut off. 'So who's flying the ship?' I asked.

We hurried forward to the nexus where I found you earlier. The *Deodati* didn't have a bridge per se, since the Forts were everywhere through the ship, but it could be run from a couple of key places. We found nothing but chaos all through the corridors, and the nexus was no better. There were five frags there. Two were fighting each other; one was sprinting in circles; the others seemed to be trying to make a difference, but they didn't know how to use the controls, and they weren't helping each other. It was like watching kids – big, stupid, cranky kids who were only going to make things worse if we left them to it.

You did something then that I hated you for, just for a while – until I had something much more specific to hate you for, later. You took out a gun and shot the frags dead. You didn't try to talk to them or calm them down. You didn't threaten them or give them a chance to get out of the way. You just killed them where they stood, and stepped over their bodies to get at the controls.

'Get in here, Hel,' you said. 'I'm going to need your help.'

I told you to go fuck yourself, but you weren't listening. Do you know how insufferable you are when you know you're right? The ship had no AI and no one at the helm. To Factotem and the other Forts, piloting the ship would have been less than a reflex. They didn't worry about automated systems because they never needed them. They were patched into the *Deodati* just as they were patched into the frags. One big happy family, until the rug was pulled out from under us all.

The drive was already feathering. It only seemed like minutes since the Slow Wave hit, but outside it had been days Absolute. The hull had begun to degrade. If at least a dozen basic systems weren't looked at soon, we were as good as dead.

I scrolled through the liner's manifest. 'There's a bailout pod,' I told you. 'It's rated for a relative century of life support. Let's take it while our momentum's up.'

'It only holds ten,' you told me. 'So it'd just be you and me. Now who's the callous one?'

'There's a big fucking difference,' I said, 'between killing someone and dying with them.'

You told me to shut up and get the reactor shielding back in the black.

I didn't want to die any more than anyone, but you were up to your eyeballs in the liner's software, jacked in via two contact points at once. There was no point arguing. The first thing you did was kill the drive and set us coasting. We were still moving at a fair chunk of C, but the interstellar medium was going to brake us sooner than later if we didn't start pushing again. Forgetting about the drive gave us some time to focus on shielding and getting the other networks stabilized. The ship was as bad as the frags, all spasms and seizures without the Forts in control.

Little did I know then that it wasn't just the ship. It was everyone, everywhere. I've pieced it together since, listening in to people talking about it, after the fact. The Slow Wave came from a point near the center of the Milky Way and swept outward across it at the speed of light. It wasn't a weapon in the conventional sense. Maybe it was something natural; I don't know. It sure was specific. The only thing it did was cut the Loops all across the Continuum. In the process, it killed the Forts. It broke their minds apart. There was nothing they could do; they didn't even know it was coming, since nothing travels faster than light. It tore everything to pieces without warning, without notice, in a wave that took fifty thousand years to cover the galaxy from end to end.

('Looks like we won after all,' Imre said, feeling emotionally and physically numb.

'Won what?'

'The war. The Slow Wave targeted the Forts. It affected no one else. Doesn't sound like coincidence to me.'

'You think that's a good thing?' She looked up from the wraparound display with eyes like pits. 'Look around you. Remember how the Forts always claimed we needed them? How if they relinquished control, the galaxy would collapse into chaos? Well, maybe they were right. The Slow Wave destroyed the Continuum, but not the wave itself. The aftereffects. Civil wars, infighting, and slaughters. Mass starvation and disease and natural disasters. You name it, we've had it, everywhere. If the Forts were the main target, we were caught in the cross fire.'

He could believe it. The Continuum was without doubt in ruins. Nothing simple or ordinary could have accomplished that. No mere war. The galaxy had collapsed in on itself once the supporting walls were removed. The Forts – slow, sluggish, pompous, unbearable – had been necessary after all.

'If you think about it,' she said, 'really think about it, the Slow Wave probably killed just a few hundred people. That's how many Forts there were in the galaxy, all up. Maybe even less. That's a tiny head count compared to the one we inflicted on ourselves. The thought that it might have been an accident, or a natural event, is too much for most people. They're looking for a guilty party. Whoever they are, if they exist, they're keeping their heads down.'

He thrust aside a flashback to the bridge of *Pelorus* – something about Alphin Freer waving a gun in his face – and focused all his attention on Helwise. If he hadn't seen the destruction left in the wake of the Slow Wave for himself, her story would have been incredible, unbelievable. But he had seen. There was no point doubting her. He had to get his head around the truth, whatever it took.)

Anyway, we didn't know any of this then. We thought the problem was purely local. We were stuck in interstellar space, gradually losing speed. You were tinkering with network settings deep in the liner's guts. Your big idea was to link the frags into an ad hoc network. Nothing anywhere near as sophisticated as what they'd known before, but enough to allow them to pool their talents. The shouting was dying down, but being calm wasn't going to get us anywhere. They were like autistic geniuses. Unless you could patch them together, they wouldn't be able to talk to each other, let alone get the ship on its feet again.

It took us a month. Half of them starved before they could take care of themselves. We did our best, but it certainly wasn't our specialty. We were better at taking Forts apart than putting them together from scratch. The first time one of them spoke, we held a small party. You, me, and a ship full of frags. It was like singing in a morgue. The survivors had formed a single gestalt that I called Headless, because it wasn't a real identity, just a frame that stopped them from flying apart again. You couldn't converse with it in anything but machine code, let alone play poker. It did the job, barely. The screaming had stopped for the most part.

By the time Headless was ready to work the ship for real, a full year had passed. There were no parties then. We were exhausted. All we wanted to do was get accelerating again, to reconnect the frags to the rest of themselves and us to the Continuum. We still didn't know what had happened to the rest of the galaxy. A year was less than a quarter of the distance to the nearest system. I wouldn't find out until we got within range of Mandala's light cone, and even then that was only local news. To get the full picture would take centuries. More.

The really weird thing was that the Slow Wave was still happening somewhere right then. We just didn't know it yet, since it took thousands of years for the information to reach us. There was no way, either, to warn the Forts left of what was heading in their direction. Nothing can go faster than the speed of light, not even the Forts themselves. All we could do was imagine them sitting there, oblivious, as their death approached.

Some fate, huh? Still, it's better than seeing it coming and knowing there's nothing you can do. That would really suck.

(Disconnection.)

They were at a political reception, surrounded by dignitaries and functionaries. Imre wore a black spider-silk tuxedo with a white bow tie to match his hair. Helwise's lithe form was barely contained by a purple velvet dress from neck to buttocks. He could easily discern the shape of her skeletal structure through the fabric, able to navigate each narrow rib from long familiarity. Her long legs didn't need high heels, but she wore them anyway. Her jet-black hair, piled high in a bun, only confirmed her place at the top of the most-striking list. They moved through the crowed like assassins looking for a target.

For once, however, they were off duty – or on duty only in the sense of needing to be seen, not needing to kill. The reception was not specifically in their honor, since their role in the world's recent conflict was not commonly known, but their affiliations with certain influential Forts had drawn them some attention, perhaps even notoriety, among some social circles. Their hosts hoped, perhaps, that their presence might stir up the sort of mild controversy that guaranteed the party would be remembered.

Among the singletons and Primes moved a number of frags, identifiable by their self-imposed isolation. They tended to stand in corners or to one side, away from the action, as befitted their roles as observers and data-gatherers. Every now and again one would stir and move to a different vantage point, prompted by a higher level of mind. Very rarely did one speak.

Imre drained a crystal flute of champagne and turned to get

another. Helwise had moved off to talk to a decorated old general with an antique Surflen Systems sidearm hanging from a holster at his hip. As Imre raised the scintillating liquid to his lips, a frag walked up to him, held out its hand, and introduced itself.

'Factotem-174. That's spelt with an E-M, if you're wondering.'

'Imre Bergamasc.' He took the hand and shook, displaying no reaction to the name. He hadn't been wondering, but he had suspected something along those lines. Forts liked their word games and puns. 'That's M-A-S-C.'

'Yes, I know. Your reputation precedes you. We're grateful for the function you perform on our behalf. It's hard work and not always appreciated.'

The frag's voice was deep and cultured, its thick hair grey and long. The robe it wore hung right down to its ankles, glittering as though covered in diamond dust. When the frag moved, the fabric swayed, sending gleams of light dancing across the room.

'I'm feeling appreciated tonight,' Imre said. 'This makes a welcome change.'

'Yes indeed. Change is not just welcome, but critical. To be unchanging is to stagnate and to die. Yet to you it must seem that my kind adopts a very different policy. At your tempo, the status quo must feel eternal, a bootheel crushing all deviation. I would show you, one day, how wrong that impression is. From where I stand, the galaxy is a vibrant and vital place, and it will remain so as long as we remain in charge.'

'That's one status quo you intend to maintain, then.'

'For now.'

Imre sipped at his champagne, watching Helwise with the old general. She had convinced him to unholster and give her the gun, which she was turning over in her hand as though appraising it for purchase. He knew part of her would be tempted to turn it on its owner and fire, just to see the reaction she would get.

'I didn't come here to discuss politics,' Imre told the Fort. 'I came to get very drunk before falling soundly asleep.'

'Both worthy aspirations, my friend. We will talk another time.'

The elegant frag weaved away through the crowd, long ponytail swaying. Imre wondered when the Fort called Factotem slept, and whether it dreamed when it did. What strange fantasies stemmed from the unconscious portion of a mind as large as a galaxy? What nightmares?

He had, just that morning, been approached by a representative from an organization calling itself 'Sol Invictus' – the invincible sun – whose aspiration was to topple the Forts from power. Too long, they said, had humanity languished under the yoke of their overevolved masters. Primes, singletons, and even frags deserved a greater say in how the galaxy was run. If the Forts wouldn't allow that truth to be recognized, they would be made to.

Now a Fort had offered to discuss just that very topic with him. An unrelated event? He couldn't tell, and he didn't want to. His head was overflowing with local politics. He needed to scour himself clean of that before taking on any more.

'Who was that?' asked Helwise, returning unarmed from her conversation with the old general.

'No one,' he told her, and moved away to get more champagne.

'This is really starting to piss me off,' she said.

He blinked and found himself back on the bridge of *The Cauld Lad*. 'What?'

'You drifted again. Where do you go when you do that? Am I really so boring?'

'You're triggering flashbacks,' he admitted. 'There's too much buried back here . . .' He tapped the side of his skull with his right index finger. 'It doesn't come free easily. Not at the right time, anyway. You're doing me a favor.'

'Well, I'm no Good Samaritan. Remember that, and try to pay fucking attention.'

He peered out the screen. Spatial distortions painted the sky a bewildering array of colors and shapes. Ahead loomed the blocky, functional form of the habitat. *The Cauld Lad* was stationary with respect to both it and the starship graveyard surrounding them. 'What's happening?'

'Nothing at the moment. I'm hoping you can tell me why.'

'How would I know?'

'You designed this place.'

'So you say.'

'Well, I've no reason to lie on that score, and you've no reason to disbelieve me. Shall we move on?' She pointed at an image on the display. 'That's the main lock. It's not opening.'

The lock was a stubby cylinder sticking out of the side of the habitat with a circle delineated on one side: the outer door was closed. 'I can't see any sign of damage,' he said.

'That's because there isn't any. You'll have to think harder than that.'

He came to stand beside her, wondering at his unsettled feeling toward her. Had they always behaved so aggressively toward each other? 'You say we all agreed to meet here. We must have agreed on an entry code or series of codes.'

'That's right, but they're not working.'

'I don't see how I can help, then. This place wasn't even on the horizon when my record was taken.'

'Are you sure? Couldn't this just be another thing you've forgotten?'

'Of course it could be. But seeing it now isn't triggering anything. That seems to be the way it works. I saw you and got a flashback about you. You talked about Factotem, and I remembered something about him. And so on. The only thing that came with here was the Chaos War and the Alienist Technarchy. Nothing about habitats and codes. Sorry.'

She looked downcast and frustrated. 'What did you remember about me?'

'It doesn't matter,' he said, thinking of them screwing in a closet during a heavy artillery barrage.

'I think it does.'

He shook his head. 'Not now.'

'Indulge me.'

'There's a time and place for indulgence,' he said, feeling a sharp spike of anger, 'and this isn't it.'

Her face tilted up so she could look at him. They were standing closer than he had realized. Her face was only centimeters from his. Her eyes glittered, heavy with unshed tears.

'Fuck you, Imre,' she said. 'We had an agreement.' She moved for him. He instinctively recoiled, but her hand was under his chin before he could pull away, as fast as a snake and gripping with brutal strength. She leaned closer, mouth opening, then her lips were against his, pressing hard. Their teeth clashed. The fingers of her free hand thrust forcefully between his legs.

He gripped her shoulders with all his strength and pushed her away. She didn't go easily, emitting a soft cry that turned almost instantly into a snarl. Her right hand came up to strike him again. This time he was ready for it and deflected the blow with his forearm. He caught her next blow and pinned her arm between them.

'I don't want to fuck you,' he said, 'or fight you.'

'Too late for either.' She wrenched free and headed for the hatch. Her angry footfalls faded down the ladder and into the distance.

When he was alone on the bridge, he sagged and put a hand across his eyes. He was shaking all over and breathing heavily. His skin burned. The Jinc had succeeded in reducing the desire he didn't want to feel. There was no physical arousal, in a sexual sense. In every other sense, his flesh simmered. He felt as slick as an eel.

Once, for a year, his former self had reverted to being a Prime, just to see what it felt like. Primes didn't allow themselves the physical edge singletons took for granted. Every modification to the natural human form had to be weighed up against remaining faithful to that mythical ideal. To remain truly pristine in a world of extended life spans and perfect physical fitness would have been stupid by anyone's standards, but Primes rejected heightened physical and sensory capacities on the grounds that they weren't needed to be human. Imre had never had such qualms, especially when such capacities had saved his life on the battlefield many times, but he could respect those that did.

In the end, though, he hadn't enjoyed the experience. Without the most recent cognitive implants, his body had felt heavy and useless, always at a remove from the world around him. The

natural visual and auditory spectra were ridiculously narrow slits
to peer through. His fingers had felt permanently gloved. And
sex — he couldn't believe it when he had tried. The limitations of
his primitive male form had seemed absurd. To be so spent so
quickly and with so little control had been novel the first couple
of tries, but it had soon grown to seem a futile exercise. With little
regret, he had abandoned the vagaries of unreconstructed biology
and returned to his status as a fully enabled singleton, one among
many comprising the being he called Himself.

In the present, his body shook like an anxious, adrenaline-
charged Prime. He fought the feeling. It wasn't a good time to be
distracted. Helwise hadn't reached the end of her story; he didn't
know how many more of her attackers might be out there, somewhere. While she was absent, he would have to tackle the habitat's
air lock on his own in an attempt to work out what codes his
former self might have installed in the security system.

'Tell me,' he told *The Cauld Lad*, 'if she tries to leave the ship.'

'Your companion has engaged the port passenger air lock.'

'Show me.'

A window opened in the display. She was standing in the
middle of the cylindrical, orange space with her arms by her sides.
Her black skin suit rose like a tarry tide up her chest and throat,
and soundlessly enveloped her head. Her eyes became translucent
ovals on an otherwise featureless face. He waited for her to activate
the air lock cycle and wondered if he would say something to call
her back.

Narrow and statuesque in ebony, she didn't move.

'Notify me of any change in her situation.'

'I will do that.'

'Thank you.'

He turned his attention to the problem at hand.

The habitat's security system proved to be as obstinate as Helwise
had described. No amount of argument convinced it that he was
who he claimed to be. Its intelligence was little greater than that
of *The Cauld Lad*, providing semantic obstacles more problematic

than mere physical walls. He could debate with it for centuries and get nowhere. In desperation, he tried every name he had recovered from his memory – and even resorted to 'luminous' when nothing else worked.

Fatigue and frustration had thoroughly supplanted anger by the time Helwise finally broke her lonely vigil.

'Your passenger has spoken,' said the ship.

'Can I hear what she said? I'll probably want to reply.'

'Both wishes will be accommodated.'

'I'm angry with you,' her image in the display said.

'I figured as much,' he replied.

She turned her head slightly, triangulating on the source of his voice. Her gaze fixed on a point slightly to the right of where the air lock camera was actually situated. 'Do you think I'm being unreasonable?'

'Do you think you're being unreasonable?'

'As a matter of fact . . . I guess I do. It pains me to admit it.'

'I can imagine.'

'Don't be an asshole, Imre. This is supposed to be an apology.' Her whole body moved this time, turning and dropping to a crouch with her back against the outer door. 'I'm angry at you when I should be angry at someone else entirely.'

'Yourself?'

'No, you idiot. The version of you in Chimeleon. I didn't finish telling you what happened on the *Deodati*. If I do that, you'll understand.'

'First, tell me what you meant about us having an agreement. You're not talking about you and me, here and now, are you?'

'No. This is old history, about staying male and female. The two of us, always. That's all.'

'Do you think I changed just to betray you?'

She shrugged and said nothing.

'Go on, then. Tell me the rest of your story, while I'm listening.'

She put her arms around her shins. Her expression was difficult to read through the skin suit. 'I slowed my tempo down as soon as Headless was in control of the ship, and we were back up to speed.

Then I slept for what felt like a week. I was tempted to put myself in hard-storage for the rest of the trip, but that wasn't really an option. Someone needed to put in an appearance every now and again, just to make sure everything was running smoothly. Headless was stable but not robust. Fights broke out among the frags, particularly between those who had come from different Forts. So much for them retaining no sense of individuality, eh? I didn't want *Deodati* to plow into something because a cog had broken and jammed the whole machine.

'You agreed, so we established a rolling timetable, where at least one of us would be on deck one day a week. That suited everyone. Headless didn't need both of us looking over its shoulder all the time – and the truth is, we were getting on each other's nerves by then. Keeping the ship alive and solving the Headless problem had given us something to concentrate on. Without it, even at the slower tempo, we had nothing to do but fight. That, in turn, upset the frags more. Headless was like a child – our big baby, you called it once – and it could tell when we were arguing.

'All this time we'd been heading into Mandala's light cone. The Fort low-frequency bands were empty, and every other transmission was bloody hard to decipher that close to C. Still, we managed to filter out some snippets of information. Whatever had hit us had hit Mandala too. In the absence of the local Forts, government had gone crazy. Primes were fighting each other; singletons were fighting Primes; frags were caught in the middle, as hopeless as Headless had been before we'd jury-rigged its brain. Occasionally we strayed across other transmissions, leaking from malfunctioning Line relays. A bigger picture began to emerge.

'"It's everyone," you told me on your last day with me. "It's everywhere. They're all dead."'

'"Who?"' I asked.

'"The Forts. All of them." You looked terrible. The truth was only just starting to sink in. It would be days before I really accepted it. I was the last on the ship who did.

'Not long after we talked about it, while I was in slow mo, you escaped in the bailout pod. It was gone before I registered the launch. I was taken completely by surprise. We were just a light-year from Mandala at that point. You wouldn't get there any faster than the *Deodati* would. But that wasn't where you were headed. You took the momentum we had and peeled away on another course.'

'I just left you?' Imre asked, surprised. 'That doesn't sound like me.'

'Well, it was. Get used to it. I hailed you, but you didn't respond. I wanted to follow, but Headless made it impossible for me to do that – not by refusing permission or actively standing in my way, but by committing suicide. It opened all the air locks at once and vented the air into space, killing its frags. I barely survived myself, and I was by no means certain I should be glad about that. One moment I'd been cruising, uncomfortable for sure but in control of my destiny; the next I was trapped in a ten-kilo-meter-long arrow aimed at the heart of Mandala Supersystem.

'The next year was an uncomfortable one, as you can probably imagine. I was living in a skin suit in order to recycle what air was left. I had no AI, no crew, no one to help me run the fucking ship. My aspirations were small. Going into orbit around any of the major settlements was likely to be too difficult, given the chaos I'd learned lay ahead. One of the governments was enforcing a traffic embargo that would've seen me shot out of the sky if I so much as asked for help.

'I chose to come in quiet and fast and use what resources I felt I could rely on. The Cat's Arse wasn't a big target from so far away – like hitting a fly with a dart from the other side of a city – but at least I knew it'd be a soft landing. Relatively speaking, of course. The final weeks of deceleration were pretty rough, and I hadn't counted on all the wrecks that would be waiting for me here. It worked anyway. I made it alive and in one piece, despite the odds.

'And here we are. After the way you and fucking Headless dropped the ball, do you blame me for having an attitude?'

Imre supposed he didn't, but he hadn't heard the full extent of the story yet. 'Why did Headless kill itself, do you suppose?'

'Out of despair. The more data we picked up from neighboring systems, the more certain it became that there was no hope of reconnection – with its original selves or any Fort at all. The Slow Wave had cut the Loop and wiped them out. Its only hope was gone.'

'Your companion, my other self – why do you think he left the way he did? Without you, without telling you where he was going, without even saying good-bye?'

'How the fuck should I know? You've got a better chance of working it out than I do.'

'He didn't leave any messages, any clues—?'

'If he had, I would've told you. It's been weighing on my mind. I'd like an answer too, one day.'

He nodded. She seemed hurt enough to be telling the truth. 'What happened here? Who was that woman hunting you? What did you do to deserve that?'

'Just being my normal, charming self, I guess.' She sighed. 'I came in hot, Imre. I attracted some attention from looters who'd been staking out the anomaly and picking the best scraps from the wreckage. I dealt with most of them in the first days, but a couple were more persistent. Obstinate, even. I was locked in a stalemate with the last one for longer than I care to think about. I managed to rig the SOS in the hope of either flushing her out or attracting help. In the end, I got both wishes.'

'Why didn't you call for help from elsewhere in the system?'

'Where do you think she came from?' Helwise unfolded her hands and leaned her head back against the bulkhead. 'Things have been crazy since the Forts went away. I told you that.'

Imre leaned his weight on the instrumentation panels and watched her 2-D image in silence as he considered everything she had told him. His head swam with so much information from his past and from recent galactic history. The chronology of events he was slowly piecing together included disasters on a scale he could barely conceive. He pictured the Slow Wave rolling across the galaxy like a dark tsunami, chaos and rumor riding in its wake, but his mind balked at the death of every Fort who had ever lived. Be they allies or enemies, they were as much a part of the landscape as the stars themselves. Take them away, and the walls of humanity's domain began to seem eggshell-thin.

'What are you thinking?' she asked him. 'You've gone very quiet.'

'I understand now why you're so highly strung,' he said. 'More than usual, I mean.'

She barked half a laugh. 'Does that mean I can come back inside?'

'I never said you couldn't.'

'Regardless, I'd like to hear your opinion on the subject. Am I welcome here, or would you rather I went away?'

'You're welcome. Just keep the theater to a minimum. I'm having enough trouble coping with the workings of my own head without worrying about yours as well.'

'I don't know, Imre. Histrionics and me kinda go together. Do you remember that time—?'

'Wait.' Movement in another window had caught his eye. 'Something's happening.' *The Cauld Lad* had noticed it too. The wraparound display became crowded with images take from numerous vantage points and at many different frequencies.

The habitat air lock was opening, turning with stately ponderousness until a dark, featureless maw gaped where the outer hatch had been. Imre tensed with his hands on contact pads, waiting to see what would emerge. Another would-be assassin such as the one that had tried to kill him and Helwise? Something even more sinister?

A minute Absolute passed. Nothing emerged. No other signs of life came from the habitat – no transmissions or signals. Just the open air lock.

'What did you do that I didn't?' asked Helwise from the air lock, still patched in to the ship's navigational system.

'I don't know. It just opened.'

'Do we take it as invitation?'

'Would you?'

'Well, it's not an obvious threat.'

'What did you say earlier about walking into traps?'

'Render isn't here. If you don't tell him, I won't.'

That was the second time she had talked about someone by that name. 'Render' didn't connect to anyone he remembered, although it itched at him as though it should.

'After you, then,' he said.

'Only if you've got my back.' Her chin came up. 'Have you got my back, Imre?'

He didn't reply immediately. The X-ray laser and 2-shooter cannon were in one of the ship's lockers, fully charged. They were the least of his concerns. He had no idea what lay on the other side of the lock. She could be lying, or circumstances could have changed. Someone else apart from the Corps might claim the Cat's Arse as its own now. The two of them might walk into the middle of a territorial war, or start one.

He considered arguing that someone should stay with the ship in case more hostiles arrived. That someone should be him, since the ship's AI had been configured by the silver sphere to accept his commands – but offering that up as an excuse would sound cowardly or untrusting. He didn't want to present that face to Helwise, or to start his new life on those terms. He had been a prisoner, then an observer. Now he needed to act, to take control. To become.

'I've got your back,' he said.

Her head rose again, as though surprised, then she nodded, once.

THIS DYING MACHINE

The secret of silence is the only secret.
Words are a blasphemy against that taciturn and invisible
God, whose presence enshrouds us in our last extremity.
                                    Robert Charles Maturin

The air of the habitat, gingerly sampled through the skin suit's ultrathin membrane, tasted of nothing at all. Imre floated three meters behind Helwise, with the X-ray laser at the ready. Just minutes ago, the circular air lock had cycled smoothly to let them into the pressurized sections of the habitat. No other activity had greeted them. No lights, no sounds, no life at all. By infrared, the smooth walls showed a uniform, grey temperature. Helwise burned purple-hot and trailed an orange wake.

'Ring any bells?' she asked. Her voice sounded tight and fuzzy across their skin suits' encrypted comms.

'None at all.'

'Well, it looks exactly the same to me.'

The habitat's lines were classical and clean, with functionality hidden behind flush panels and sliding doors. They traveled the length of three internal corridors, testing locked doors and exploring every chamber they could get into. None of them showed signs of recent occupation: no personal effects; no customization of the clothes fabricators; no disarray. There wasn't a single dust ball or scratch to be found, anywhere they looked.

The exploration they undertook wasn't completely fruitless. Imre found himself understanding the architecture barely without having to think about it. The interlocking panels, clearly designed for modular manufacture; the angled intersections between 'wall,' 'floor,' and 'ceiling' – all meaningless concepts in zero gee – that gave the eye clear reference points; the manifold but muted colors barely registered by senses that would have been quickly dulled by uniform, utilitarian white; and the corridors themselves, broad enough for two to travel abreast so people didn't have to crawl about as he had in the Jinc vessel . . . Neat, symmetrical, and perfectly habitable. The aesthetic sensibility of his former self was obviously something he had inherited intact.

They turned a corner and entered another long corridor.

'Do you have a destination in mind?'

'I'm heading for the center in a roundabout way. Going straight there would be too predictable, right?'

'What's at the center?'

'Food. Clean clothes. Weapons.'

'Assuming no one else got here before us.'

'Assuming that, yes.'

'The people who opened the air lock, for instance, could have cleared everything out centuries ago.'

'No sign of them yet. Maybe it was an automatic response.'

'Triggered by what?'

'I don't know, Imre. You're asking so many goddamned questions, perhaps. Are you going to shut up and let me concentrate?'

They proceeded down the corridor, finding it as empty as the other was. The habitat might have been undisturbed for thousands of years but for the breathable air and modestly clement ambient temperature, hovering around the freezing point of water. Imre wondered who had lived here in times past, and why they had needed so much space. He pictured dozens of versions of himself kicking their way along the corridors in the free-fall version of jogging, training up before bursting out on an unsuspecting galaxy.

A faint noise became audible as they neared the habitat's center. Something soft was hitting something hard, gently but loud enough to echo through the hard-walled, empty corridors. Not footsteps, not in zero gee, but not dissimilar either. Tap tap. Tap tap tap tap. Tap tap tap.

Helwise slowed and Imre drew closer to her.

'A distraction,' he said, turning the laser on the dark spaces behind them. 'We should ignore it.'

'If we were walking into a trap,' she said, 'wouldn't it have sprung on us already?'

'Perhaps that's just what we're supposed to think.'

'To what end? We're not much of a fucking army, you and me.'

'It's all relative, Hel. You know that.'

'True. They didn't have to let us in. They could've just kept the air lock shut if they were really worried.'

Tap tap tap. Delicate sensors in the skin suit's external surface caught the sound and magnified it until it seemed to fill the corridor around him.

'Are we nearly there?'

'That corner ahead is the last. From there it's all mess, head, bunks, and the like. Common area.'

'Open space?'

'Mostly. There are three entrances.'

'I'll take the nearest while you hook around the far side. Will that take long?'

'A few minutes. Imre—'

'Just do it. Click me when you're in position and we'll move in.'

Hefting the considerable momentum of the cannon with both hands, she shouldered past him and headed back the way they had come, her feet softly kicking off the walls. The noise she made faded slowly into the distance. The tapping sound ahead remained the same.

He inched closer to the corner, looking forward and behind with equal frequency. The tapping paused for a second when he was in position, then resumed a moment later. He held his breath and kept the laser close to his center of gravity, waiting for the signal from Helwise.

Tap tap.

The click came four and half minutes after she had left him. He didn't reply, just took a breath and kicked himself around the corner. The space beyond was exactly as she had described, a broad and low-ceilinged room with numerous hammocks and straps for anchoring bodies in various attitudes, spaces for food preparation, entertainment facilities, and several closed toilet modules against the opposite wall. Helwise issued from an entranceway to Imre's left, moving fast. He covered her with the laser's barrel, then kept it moving, sweeping across the room.

A lanky man with black hair hung suspended between two horizontal metal partitions, anchored by his feet and one outstretched hand as though standing upright in ordinary gravity. His other hand rested on the stock of an old-fashioned Sparks projectile rifle that hung securely at his side. He was tapping his foot, making the sound that had echoed up the hallway. It stopped the moment they were both in view.

'You took your time,' said Alphin Freer, his voice calm and measured. 'Forget the way?'

'What game are you playing, Al?' Helwise kept the cannon up between them, her expression distrustful. 'Did you keep me waiting for a reason?'

'You can talk about games. I saw you out there, right enough.'

A look passed between them that Imre didn't understand. Her lips tightened.

'Who's your friend?' Freer cocked his nose at Imre, then turned his attention back to Helwise.

'Use your eyes.'

'I am. Use your mouth and tell me. I want to hear the lie from your lips.'

'No lie. It's him.'

'It's not.' The denial came flat and unemphatic, but with a weight of certainty nonetheless. 'It can't be.'

'That's what I said. So he's a woman now. Big fucking deal, Al. It had to happen eventually.'

'It did not. It's more likely the other way around: a woman pretending to be him, looking to take us for advantage.' Freer's cold grey gaze turned back onto Imre. Appraising, not threatening, it made his skin crawl. 'I'm going to require some convincing.'

'There are two guns pointing at you,' Imre said. 'Is that not con-vincing enough?'

'Not while you're outgunned, no.' Freer's gaze flicked over Imre's shoulder. 'Hand over your weapons without a fuss, please. A shoot-out benefits no one.'

Imre turned to see another Alphin Freer gliding smoothly out of the entrance behind him. A third appeared in Helwise's wake. They were both armed with eight-pulse Balzac handguns, per-fectly safe in a pressurized habitat but deadly to humans.

Imre raised the X-ray laser and pushed it away from him. It floated smoothly to the nearest Alphin Freer. 'Fighting each other is pointless,' he told the identical trio. 'I'll trust you if it'll help you trust me.'

'I agree about the pointless part. The rest will take much more than words, whoever you turn out to be.'

Helwise gave up her cannon after a token tug-of-war. 'This is bullshit, Al. You know who *I* am.'

'Exactly.' Freer visibly relaxed once they were disarmed. Imre couldn't tell exactly how he knew; to all appearances, Freer looked no different than before. But something had dissipated, some mus-cular tension barely hidden by skin and body armor. 'The hab is fully stocked. Plenty of freshwater. Take a shower; rest if you need to. There's something I've got to do right now, then we'll talk.'

'Wait,' said Imre, as the three Freers headed for the room's third exit. 'That's it? You're giving us the run of the place?'

'Why not?' The first Freer stopped in the doorway, with a hand holding him steady on the lintel. 'I've got your guns. There's nothing here you can damage, and you can't get out. I've recali-brated the security system. I feel quite safe.'

'Why did you change the codes, Al?' Helwise looked as angry as ever. 'What are you hiding?'

'I'm hiding me, Helwise. That should be perfectly obvious.' Again Freer's gaze danced over Imre, then moved on. 'I'll see you in an hour Absolute. Be here, or I'll come find you.'

With that, he left, and Helwise exploded.

'I'll have his asshole for an earring.' She punched the nearest

wall, sending herself moving at speed in the opposite direction.
'The patronizing dick!'

Imre was suddenly weary. Of her aggression, of subtle threats, of
knowing nothing about his situation – of people. Ignoring the
deadly, sharklike way Helwise darted to and fro across the room –
the zero-gee equivalent of pacing – and the relentless tirade she
yelled after Alphin Freer, he turned and kicked himself through an
exit. He didn't care where he was going. He just wanted to be
alone.

Helwise didn't seem to notice or care that he had left. Her voice
echoed through the habitat, becoming ghostly but no less indig-
nant with distance.

He found a row of individual quarters whose doors opened at his
command. Choosing the third on the right, he slipped inside and
sealed the hatch behind him. There was no lock, but the illusion
of privacy was sufficient. His mind echoed with words and names
and things he was supposed to have done but had no memory of
ever doing. Killing frags and building Forts from nothing.
Abandoning Helwise in the *Deodati* without explanation . . .

There was a zero-gee shower at the back of the room, an airtight
tube with nozzles at one end and suction at the other. He stripped
off the skin suit and folded the collapsible screen behind him.
Fine particles of water abraded him, stripping away the oil and
dead skin cells that accumulated despite the suit's best efforts. He
gripped a handle in each hand and floated with his eyes shut,
enjoying the play of water across his skin. Breathing would have
been difficult, had he needed to. He enjoyed the suspension of
every physical function, apart from the beating of his heart. For a
timeless moment, he was at peace.

Then his mind started working again. Helwise, the Slow Wave,
Alphin Freer, the mysterious Render, who once hadn't talked to
him for a month . . . There was too much to absorb, on top of the
Jinc and his strange resurrection. Was this what the silver sphere
had intended him to find when it had sent him out in *The Cauld
Lad*? Did it have an agenda of its own he was yet to discover?

One thing was certain: his old self hadn't believed in random acts of kindness.

With a soft rattle, the shower screen slid aside. He blinked his eyes open and saw Helwise floating in the entrance. She slid in with him before he could offer an invitation – or a refusal, if that was what he intended. He was in two minds.

There was room for two, just. She shook her hair loose of its bindings and let it fly about like Medusa's coils, black and sinuous. Her skin suit retreated to a single white sock on her left foot. Her hands scrubbed at her face, and he sensed her awareness of him watching her, even though she had in no way acknowledged his presence as yet. Her breasts were high and small, with dark nipples; her underarm and pubic hair matched that atop her head. She twisted to catch the water down both sides, and her thin, flexible ribs moved beneath her skin. The performance was eerily sensual.

With her eyes still shut, she reached for him. He didn't fight her off. Her hands caressed his face and head, scratching lightly at where his hair was growing out. The lightness of her fingers triggered a sense-memory as they ran down his arms and jumped lightly to his waist: this was a familiar feeling, one that had excited him, once. She pulled him closer to her. His breasts flattened against hers. Her ankles entwined with his. Their skin met like warm, wet glass.

Her eyes were open. 'Nothing, huh?'

He shook his head. 'Sorry.'

'The Jinc did too good a job of making you frigid.' She inhaled deeply. 'Still, I didn't come here to get laid. This is enough, isn't it?'

'Enough for what?'

'To reconnect. With you. I know I'm a bitch sometimes, but I still have feelings.'

'I—' Imre thought hard to find the right words. 'I don't know what I have, Hel. The last thing I remember about us, we were on *Pelorus*. You were telling me you'd rather die than surrender.'

'Not very romantic.' She sighed into him and rested her head on his shoulder. Her arms tightened around his waist. 'That's such old news. It feels strange to talk about it now.'

'I need to. Not this second, necessarily, but I have to work through it in order to decide who I am. Me – this snapshot of Imre Bergamasc – was made just after the Mad Times. I'm that person, not the one you remember from Chimeleon and the *Deodati*. But I could be him if I wanted to. I just have to work out who he was.'

'And what he did.'

'Exactly.' Their skulls touched through her wet hair. 'I can't apologize for treating you badly, since it wasn't me, but still—'

'Don't say it. You don't need to. I'll find that cunt one day and make him pay for ditching me. In the meantime, it's nice just to be held. I've been alone such a long, long time.'

'You're not alone now. Neither of us is.'

They embraced without words, breathing in gentle synchrony, until she said, 'You're the only woman I know who needs to shave her stomach.'

'What?' He pulled away from her and ran a hand across his belly. Sure enough, stubble was sprouting there, as rough as very fine sandpaper. 'I'm changing back. Finally.' He reached lower. His clitoris was longer than he remembered and his labia were retreating. There was no pleasure to be had in touching them, so he withdrew his hand.

'You'll be writing your name in the snow before you know it,' Helwise said with a grin. 'I, for one, will be glad.'

'Don't count your chickens. Having the right plumbing is one thing, turning the tap on another entirely.'

'Cock jokes abound.' She pushed him away. 'I want to get out. Does this thing have an air dryer built in?'

He found the switch. Hot air buffeted them like parachutists. They held hands in a free fall that would have lasted forever, had they let it. He left the cubicle with skin tingling all over, and a feeling that life had taken a step in the right direction.

'I didn't have to let you in.'

Alphin Freer – just one of him now – sought them out in the

mess hall, where Helwise and Imre, dressed in comfortable outfits of real fabric, were eating real food and drinking real coffee from tubes. It tasted glorious, and for an instant Imre was unable to suppress of a flash of irritation at the interruption.

'If you're going to explain yourself, I'd prefer you just got on with it. This is the first meal I've had in a lifetime.'

Freer moved from handhold to handhold until he was stationed at one end of their low-gee table. 'I wanted to open the air lock. You should understand that. I wasn't going to open it without a reason. Not for Helwise, and not for someone claiming to be Imre Bergamasc.'

'You don't trust us?' asked Helwise through a mouthful.

'Trust has nothing to do with it.' He cast her a cold glance. 'I needed a reason to be interested.'

'You got it,' Imre said. 'How?'

Freer's grey eyes swung back. 'What do you know about "luminous"?'

Imre didn't move except to adjust one of the spent food packets so it was in line with the others. 'Why do you ask?'

'You used that word when you were trying to get in. It means something to you. I want to know why.'

'What does it mean to you?'

'I'm asking the questions.

'Come on.' Helwise looked from Freer to Imre with growing annoyance. 'Will one of you morons actually say something? Why is "luminous" important?'

'It's no big secret, Hel,' Imre explained, not taking his attention off Freer as he spoke. 'When I was imprisoned, that was the code word my rescuer gave me for when the time came to escape. I tried it here on the off chance it'd work a second time.' He shrugged. 'Seems it did.'

Freer looked disappointed. 'That's all?'

'Do you believe that's all?'

His narrow eyebrows came together. One hand worried at his brow. 'I don't know. You could be lying or concealing something else.'

'I tell you, Alphin, my head is full of holes. There could be all manner of things concealed in there that I myself don't know about. Why don't you tell me what you know, and we'll see what emerges?'

'Let me ask you one more thing first. Have you heard from Emlee Copas?'

'No,' said Helwise. 'Why?'

'That's why I'm here. I'm waiting for her, or for word to come from her. She says she needs our help.'

Blond hair and jade green eyes; slight but strong. An image of Emlee Copas swam through Imre's memory. 'Is she in trouble?'

'I don't know. I've been waiting a long time. The Slow Wave could have caught her too.'

Freer looked grim, and understanding struck Imre at that moment: Copas was a Prime. There was only one of her. If she died, she would no longer exist. Resurrection in a new body wasn't an option for her. She would be lost forever.

'Tell us,' Imre said.

I was on a troop carrier when the Slow Wave hit (Freer began). The usual deal: data only, in hard-storage. I'd signed up in Goolunmurru after the Mad Times. You'd disappeared, and Forts were being suspiciously friendly. I didn't want any of it. I figured serving with ordinary grunts would clear my head, and there were plenty of offers. The Mad Times might have officially ended, but craziness still abounded. Brush fires were flaring up everywhere. Someone with my experience could pick and choose.

I cruised for . . . I don't know how long. A good while, jumping from hot spot to hot spot, doing what I was paid for and bugging out afterward. It didn't worry me who I was working for. Ethics weren't the issue. I just needed some time to work out what had happened to us. We were caught up in that damned war, all of us, and I'd really thought we had a chance. The Forts were big, but they were seriously outnumbered. We could've taken them eventually – I still think that. We surrendered because . . . why, again? We got tired? We didn't want the responsibility of running things afterward? We changed our minds?

(Imre went to speak, but Freer waved him silent.)

No, that's not what this is about. The Mad Times were old news by the time the Slow Wave hit. I was heading for Morwedd, for some minor scrap I barely remember now. The carrier didn't notice anything until we hit the fringes of the system. We were running on silent, slipping in through the bow shock, and kept our connection to the Continuum to a minimum. It wasn't until the carrier hit the inner system that it realized the kind of trouble we were in.

Morwedd was a free-for-all. The collapse of the Continuum had hit it hard. Its civil administration had folded almost instantly, leaving a power vacuum the military tried to fill, of course. That had folded too, under commercial pressure, leaving chaos everywhere. Armed industrial complexes kidnapped asteroid mines from each other. Colonies were stripped or burned to the foundations. Someone had dropped an orbital tower onto one of the settled worlds a century earlier, and the fires were still burning. Od knows how many people died there before we blundered in.

The carrier knew it was heading into trouble long before it reached the rendezvous point. I was chief grunt, so it decanted me first. By the time I was embodied and awake, we were already under attack. A fleet of armored asset-strippers had spotted us and were moving in for the kill. We were bigger, slower, and taken off guard. I did the best I could, but in the end I had no choice. I ejected from the carrier just as the strippers reached the AI core and gutted it, killing all seven thousand of my hard-stored troops in an instant.

My trials were only beginning. I won't bore you with the details, but I will say this: I left the carrier with thirty soldiers. Five died avoiding the strippers, another five when we ran afoul of mines in one of the low-energy trade lanes. We lost ten stealing a long-haul ship out of the system, and six more during a drive blowout. The four remaining opted for hard-storage again when we finally hit near-C on the way back home. I was the only one awake, thinking at Tempo Absolute about what had happened to us and what it meant.

The Continuum was dead. That seemed obvious even then. It would take thousands of years, but if what I heard was true – that the Forts had really bought it – then the galaxy wasn't a safe place to be. Maybe it never would be again. If I stayed on the course we had chosen, I'd likely run into the same situation as existed in Morwedd, but with more time to stew over it, really build up momentum. I'd been lucky once and wouldn't be again; that was the way I saw it. Until I had sure knowledge of what lay ahead, I would be an idiot to barge right in. The best thing I could do was jump ship midway and take my chances.

('Cold logic,' said Helwise, with a slow shake of her head. 'You're as fucked-up as ever.'

'Coming from a hothead like you, I take that as a compliment,' he said, affably enough but without backing down from his position. 'Hot and dead. I'd rather be cold and old like Render, any day.'

Imre physically twitched as memories reconnected, sparking associations like two live wires touching. 'Cold and old' was a phrase he knew from previous retrospection: the big, scarred soldier had said it to him on the night Imre had tried to convince him to celebrate their victory over someone, somewhere.

'Are you all right?' asked Freer, staring at him with his face aslant.

'Fine. Just putting some pieces back together.'

'In a good way?'

He remembered the big soldier called Render saying, 'Picture the man when the heartbeat stops.' 'I hope so,' he told Freer. 'Go on, Al. Sorry to interrupt.')

I jumped ship near one of the Line stations between Morwedd and a neighbor called X03733. X03733 had been settled by some machine intelligence or other way back when, before the Forts cleared them out. Population was less than a couple of million. Lowlifes, mostly. Lots of gestalts looking for Primes to assimilate: a volatile mix. I didn't know any of this when I arrived, but it would cause problems later. I would've done my research better if the Continuum had still been working.

There were five Line relay stations between X03733 and Morwedd. One of them was a junction where one Line crossed another. I didn't know much about this stuff before I arrived. It's taken for granted, or at least it was before the Slow Wave. Sending signals directly from one system to another takes a lot of energy and is prone to errors. Dust, ships, gas clouds, even planets can break the link. Using repeaters is a lot safer and much more efficient, but the repeaters and stations need to be maintained. That's where the Line workers come in. They repair breaks, tune lasers, clear the lanes of dust, and so on, all so the signals are unimpeded and pure.

So I land in this junction. It's little better than an outpost, with a staff of ten, most of them hard-stored or at very low tempo. The place stinks; it hasn't been flushed or scrubbed for thousands of years, and its air filters are home to an ecosystem all of their own. I'd like to think that I caused a huge sensation, but that would be an exaggeration. Sure, not many people ever came physically down the line – most are hard-cast as data and decanted in situ – but they get the odd traveler. Some stations are equipped with shuttles and rescue craft. The big ones even have security forces. They see some action.

The real news wasn't me. It was the Slow Wave. The thing about being on a Line is that you're privy to all sorts of information while it's in transit. A lot of the Line workers are code crackers and decrypters in their spare time, so not much gets by them. News of the Slow Wave was filling the Line to capacity. One of them played me a recording of a Fort dying in midtransmission. It didn't sound like anything to me, just a chirped signal suddenly falling silent. But it was a signal that had been running unchecked for forty thousand years. Stopped dead in its tracks as though someone had pulled a switch.

The Line workers of Relay Station 642053 took me in and gave me a job. It was either that or go back into hard-storage. I wasn't about to do that, not with so much going on around me, and it seemed a fair trade. That decision saved my life. Not long after I settled in, gutting and realigning systems that hadn't been maintained for centuries, a raiding party came out of Morwedd, followed by a demolition crew from X03733.

It was a crazy time. None of the Line workers had combat experience. They officially had no weapons. That didn't mean they were sitting ducks, though. They had me, for one, and I was no keener than them on dying at the hands of rapists and thieves. I mean, I wasn't one of them, but the alternative was so much worse. I had to fight.

The other thing they had was the array of a half dozen monster beamers that formed the backbone of the Line relay. All I had to do was convince them to break the Line long enough to fight off the attackers. That wasn't easy. The cardinal rule of Line workers is: the Line must stay open, no matter what. A split second's break could see terabytes of data lost forever. That was the trade-off they had to face: a split-second downtime versus the Line broken forever or in the hands of a corrupt regime that would filter or distort what came through.

The short version is: I talked them into it. If I'd been in hard-storage, we all would've died. We fought off the attackers, but only just, and we knew there'd be more to come. Gone were the gentle days of the Continuum, where the Line was common property, shared equally by all and defended by the Forts. Now new regimes were springing up from the ruins, and information was power. They wanted control over all communications into and out of their systems – or, in extreme cases, they just wanted the resources the stations contained. The Battle of the Lines had begun.

At first, it looked like everything would hold on its own, that sheer stubbornness on the part of the Line workers would keep the channels open. It soon became apparent that this optimism wasn't warranted. Signals started to flicker and fade. Some dropped out altogether. Light-speed delays and false echoes meant that we could still be hearing transmissions from stations destroyed ages ago. The number of Line SOS calls went steadily up. Even with the equipment we had salvaged from the people who had attacked us, I knew the station was going to be lucky to last much longer.

It wasn't my fight, ultimately. Sticking around longer than I needed would have been suicide. Once I'd done everything I could for the workers on Relay Station 642053, I left them behind and got under way for Mandala Supersystem.

('Skip to the good bits, Al,' said Helwise, over the remains of her small meal. 'When did you get here? When did you hear from Emlee? What does all this goddamn Line stuff have to do with anything?')

Everything, Hel. I've come to realize that the Continuum would never have existed but for the Line and its workers. Forget colonies and Forts and the like: without a secure means of communication connecting them, shuffling signals from light-year to light-year, we'd still be sitting in the dark waiting for the lights to come on. The Slow Wave may have killed the Forts, but we're killing the Line. If the Line goes, we're back in the stone ages. Maybe we are already and just don't realize it yet.

It took me much longer than I expected to reach Mandala. I didn't actually reach it for even longer. I stopped at a relay junction a light-year out – Mandala 2, it was called – one of three major nexuses through which the bulk of the traffic flowed in and out of the supersystem. The other two had been destroyed by raiders long before I arrived. The remaining Line workers had pooled their resources and made a stand at Mandala 2. The junction had become a major station by anyone's standards, much expanded from its original design. No less than five habitats had been fabricated and cobbled together into one, sprawling structure. They had around fifty workers, a security force of about the same number, more than a dozen Vespula fighters, and six spare beamers that could wipe just about anything from sky.

They didn't stand alone either. At least one of the Mandalan governments recognized the importance of maintaining the Line out to other systems. It sent supplies and staff when it could, when its own problems weren't getting in the way. Mandala was as much a dog's breakfast as anywhere else.

I took stock at Mandala 2. My options were limited. Another version of me was there, fresh in from Fredolfo. Pooling memories gave me a larger perspective. Perspective told me one sure thing: the Line wasn't just the victim of exploitation and war. It was also suffering deliberate sabotage. Someone — a very large group of someones — was seeking out places of resistance and knocking them down, specifically to encourage the collapse of communications across the galaxy. They moved in disguise and never acted openly. Where they went, systems failed and morale plummeted, signal strength dropped and data was corrupted. If the Slow Wave was a knife to the galaxy's heart, the saboteurs were a disease spreading insidiously through the Line, poisoning everything we were trying to keep pure.

How did I know this? Through inference and deduction, and from the experiences of others. Everyone had a tale of disaster following a new arrival. Saboteurs came disguised as castaways and desperadoes, refugees and volunteers. I had seen a couple myself without realizing that they formed part of a larger pattern: a software editor whose systems became chaotic for no reason at all, and a mining expert who accidentally — supposedly — blew himself up, taking a large chunk of beamer with him. It took two of me to piece these rumors together into a bigger picture. I didn't like what I saw. I think I still hoped that the Slow Wave could have been an accident, an Act of Od or just plain dumb luck. Systematic disruption of the Line suggested otherwise.

The manager of Mandala 2 was a Prime called BB. She was respected by those under her and had done a good job of keeping the station afloat. Rumors said she was old. Very old. Some claimed she went right back to the twentieth century, uninterrupted, but I didn't give that kind of talk much credence at first. What would an Old-Timer like her be doing on the Line? It didn't sound very likely to me.

I changed my mind the first time I spoke with her. You know how people talk about being able to recognize an Old-Timer from the way they move, even if they're not moving at all? I've always thought that was crap. I mean, look at Render. But I'm not so sure now. BB wasn't much to look at — rugged, like most Line workers, with brown hair and eyes to match — but the moment she came in the room I knew her for what she was. She has some of what you have, Imre: she can take in a crowd at a glance and put everyone in their places; she knows where everything is, all the time; she doesn't waste energy on fools. But there was more to her than that. She didn't think the way we do. Sizing up a situation is one thing. Knowing how that situation will evolve is quite another. Her brain had been building neural networks for so long that she could recognize a pattern from the tiniest hint, and extrapolate outward in any number of directions. I'm still not sure if I was in love with her or terrified of her.

The first words she said to me were, 'You must be the pirate I've been hearing about. Tell me if I should waste my time getting to know you before you leave.'

We were in the main flight deck. I was getting into a suit while my Vespula was being prepped. I told her I was in no hurry to go anywhere.

'That's not what I asked,' she said. 'Deal with that singleship sniffing out the range of our senses, then come see me.'

'Yes, ma'am.'

'That's "BB," pirate. I'm no one's "ma'am."'

When I came back from patrol, she took me to bed.

('Al, you dog,' said Helwise, leaning backward with one stiff arm holding her braced against the table.

'Dog nothing. It was her decision. She'd pegged me as a type she liked, and who would like her in return. She knew how to get what she wanted, because she knew how to make me want it too. That was how she worked people. She never manipulated or lied; she never cheated; she never took what wasn't offered. She simply recognized, asked, received. After so much time and practice, I suppose it gets easy.'

'You said it yourself: look at Render. It's not easy for everyone.'

'It depends what you want, I guess. I've never had the impression that Render wants to be a better person, or that Render much cares what sort of people he surrounds himself with.'

Helwise pouted. 'Right enough, I suppose. Is your confession almost done? If I have to listen to your sexploits I just might vomit.'

'BB is important, and you need to know why I was in the right place to find that out.'

'Why?' asked Imre.

Freer turned his cool, grey eyes on him. 'You're involved.')

In my second year on Mandala 2, I was off duty in BB's quarters. The entry buzzer to her hatch sounded, and she took the summons.

'Wait here,' she told me, slipping on a skin suit and heading for her second room, where she worked after her official shift ended. Hers was the only cabin in the station possessing such a luxury. 'This won't take long. Don't interrupt.'

I stayed in her hammock, listening through the curtained entranceway. Secrecy obviously wasn't an issue or she would've kicked me out quite happily. I was more surprised that she intended to answer the buzz at all; her private time was sacrosanct.

The hatch opened. Someone came in.

'I've been expecting you,' she told her visitor.

'You're hard to find,' was the reply.

I almost fell out of the hammock. It was you speaking, Imre. I wanted to call out, but BB's instruction to keep quiet stayed my tongue. She didn't often issue orders so boldly. She didn't need to.

'Why do you think that might be?' she asked you.

'You're hiding,' you said. 'But that doesn't mean you're keeping your head down all the way. Here you sit, plugged into one of the galaxy's collapsing veins. One of the few who still is, I might add.'

'I know how it is out there. I see it every day, courtesy of the Line. It's like looking the wrong way down a telescope pointing out of Hell.'

'What can you tell me?'

'I can tell you you've got a bloody nerve coming to me like this. You dropped the ball. I can't help you pick it up again. My hands are full enough already. Spies, saboteurs, assassins – you name it. We've had it.'

'Is it going to get worse?'

'Is that what you came here to ask? The traitor of *Pelorus*, the architect of Domgard – are you so fallen now that you can't see what lies before you?'

'I haven't fallen. You'd be mistaken to think that, Bianca.'

'I'm never mistaken, Imre. Why else would you have come here?'

('Wait,' said Imre, holding up a hand. It was shaking. He couldn't stop it. 'Did you same her name was Bianca?'

Freer nodded with heavy solemnity. 'I did.'

'That's Bianca Biancotti you're talking about.'

Freer nodded again. 'I know.'

'Bianca who?' Helwise leaned in closer. 'She's not so famous that I've heard of her.'

'You wouldn't have,' Imre told her. 'Not in this form. You'd know her better as "2B."'

Now Helwise got it. 'The Butcher of Bresland?'

He could only nod, wondering why his original self had come to some obscure outpost seeking a woman who might have been one of the most vicious enemies of Sol Invictus.

'I thought you said she was a Prime, Al,' Helwise said in an impatient tone. 'If any of this is true, what was she doing on the Line? Why wasn't she dead with the other Forts? What was Imre doing there, talking to her?'

'I never asked about her origins directly,' Freer said, 'but I think this is the reason: yes, she became a Fort, and a very powerful one, a long time ago. She fought us in the Mad Times, and killed millions of Primes and singletons. But she never absorbed or disposed of her original self. BB existed alongside her Fort version, either completely independent or linked somehow – but capable either way of withstanding the Slow Wave when the rest of her could not. She wasn't a frag. She was as whole as you and I. And she of anyone had the best chance of knowing what the Slow Wave had been.'

'What did she say?' Helwise said, her eyes wide. 'What did she tell Imre?')

I remember every word the two of them said to each other.

'You came here for answers,' BB said. 'There are none. You've wasted your time.'

'Domgard did something. It must've done. The timing is too stark, too evident. If we trace the Slow Wave back—'

'You've not done that yet?'

'I'm trying to. The data is difficult to trace. Not enough time has passed. You're in a better position to do that than me.'

'There are more of you.'

'Quality not quantity, eh? Isn't that the Forts' motto?'

'It was. Here's another: strength in diversity. We have been beheaded. It's hard to bounce back from that.'

'Come on, Bianca. You've heard something – or at least you hope that you will. Tell me what that is, and I'll get out of your hair.'

She didn't say anything for a minute. Her stillness, her silence, was a palpable thing. It had a presence all its own that filled her quarters, like the air, or the smell of jasmine incense, which she burned despite station regulations.

'All right,' she said. 'The word you're waiting to hear is "luminous."'

'"Luminous"?' you repeated. 'This is what you're hearing on the Line?'

'A whisper on the edge of hearing. Barely there, but there beyond doubt. I hear it when I sleep, with the raw data of the Line flowing through my dreams. I dream of angels and burning swords. I dream of Lucifer, the morning star. I dream of Jerusalem when the bomb fell, the white flash like a second dawn. I dream of Apocalypse.'

I had never heard BB talk like that. It was deeply unsettling. She sounded like a prophet, a madwoman – a Fort.

'What does it mean?' You sounded as nervous as I felt, Imre.

'It means you're on the right track. I don't know where it'll take you. Follow it and find out for yourself. Report back to me, if you've a mind to. If I'm still here.'

'Where else would you be?'

She didn't answer. A moment later, I heard the hatch open and you leave. The hatch clanged shut and sealed with a hiss. Then she came back into the bedroom, undressed, and lay down next to me.

'Who was that?' I asked.

She didn't say anything. She just looked at me with her bottomless brown eyes, and I knew at that moment that everything had changed. I had known who her visitor was, and she knew I knew. She had always known. I shouldn't have tried to play her. If I'd really wanted to know, I should've asked her outright. But I didn't want just to know; I wanted her to tell me, and that wasn't the way things worked between us.

Still nothing was said. She didn't ask me to leave or tell me it was over. She didn't tell me the topic of you was out of bounds; I simply never brought it up again. Life went on, fighting an endless battle against breakdowns, sabotage, and anyone bold enough to tackle us head-on. A couple of me came through from different quarters of the galaxy, bearing similar news: dissolution, decay, despair. We pooled our knowledge and lived on, no stronger for knowing but no worse off either.

('It still freaks the fuck out of me, the way you do that,' Helwise, pulling a face. 'How many of you are there in your head now?'

'Just one,' Freer said. 'The same as always.'

A flash of memory went through Imre's brain: a long layover between targets with nothing to do but talk. Freer had described his pattern of meeting other versions of himself and joining into one in a way Imre had never heard before.

'I'm a tree with many roots but only one trunk,' Freer had said, 'or a river with many sources but one mouth. Where's the conceptual difficulty in that?'

'There were lots of you, and now there's just one.' Helwise had pulled the same face she was wearing now: nostrils high and mouth pursed, eyes squinting like dark, puckered pits. 'Isn't that some kind of murder?'

'I can't tell you they're still alive since there's no "they" at all. There's just me, with all of my memories. It's not an uncommon practice, and no less strange than letting lots of versions of you wander around freely, with no intentions of assimilating into one person, like you do. You should try it yourself, or at least get used to the idea, and get off my case about it.'

Time had obviously not made Helwise any more comfortable than before. Nor more accommodating of different views.

'Where are your two little buddies?' she asked. 'Are they still walking?'

'I'm right here,' Freer said. 'Can we get back to the subject? I would've thought you'd be keen to.'

She shot him a warning look. 'Why, sure. Fire away.')

I saw you on Mandala 2, Imre, a couple of times after that, but never again in BB's quarters. Once I bumped into you on the flight deck. I was going out; you were coming in. I caught your eye. You didn't seem surprised to see me, but you weren't too excited about it either. When I tried to draw you into a conversation, you were focused on one thing only.

'I'm looking for BB,' you told me. 'Do you know how I can get to talk with her?'

You obviously weren't the same one who had come through before. 'Just buzz her door,' I told you. 'She'll let you in.'

'Thanks, Al.'

You went to move away. 'Wait,' I said. 'Tell me about Domgard.'

'Never heard of it.'

I caught your arm and held you back. 'What does it have to do with the Slow Wave?'

You stared at me. I'd never seen you look like that before. You were guilty of plenty of things in your time, but being caught out wasn't one of them.

'Whatever you've heard, Al, you're better off not knowing.'

With that, you pulled away. I considered following, but I knew where you'd go and what you'd be told. I was caught in the middle of some ghastly loop involving you and BB and whatever happened to the galaxy. I didn't have the same access to the Line or the pattern-matching ability as BB and the other code crackers. I was just a grunt, a lay, a fool. I was sick of it.

That night, after my shift on patrol, I went to BB intending to ask her outright. Whatever that led to, at least it would be a change.

I buzzed. The hatch opened and she was standing in the entrance.

'There's a message for you,' she said before I could even open my mouth. 'It came down the Line last night.'

'Addressed to me?'

'One you'll want to hear, anyway.' She held my gaze and made no move to let me in. 'I've encrypted it and put it in your Inbox. The file header is "Emlee Copas." Talk to me afterward, if there's anything left to say.'

The hatch slid shut, with me still outside and my questions unasked. I opened the file right there, without stepping a pace back from BB's rooms. It wasn't large, just a few lines of text, calling for all surviving members of the Corps to meet at the Cat's Arse for an urgent recon and recovery mission. One of us had been arrested by a new Mandalan regime and was facing execution. Which one of us, exactly, she didn't say. She was going to try to talk the sentence down to imprisonment but didn't fancy her chances. If any of us were alive, she could use our help.

That was all, but it was enough. It set a whole procession of questions running through my head. Was the message authentic, and if so how old was it? Had BB been holding on to that message until she needed to distract me from pursuing her? Where did my loyalties lie – in finding out the truth about the Continuum's fate or helping an old friend out of trouble?

I didn't buzz BB again. Instead, I turned and headed for my own room, where I stewed over everything I had learned until my next shift came up. Even then, in the Vespula, I couldn't clear my head. The hash of the galaxy was out of my league; what difference would one nosy man make when better minds than mine were already on the case? Having aspirations beyond myself was the surest way to get myself killed, or at least permanently sidelined by BB. But could I let it go so easily, turn my back on the greatest catastrophe humanity has ever experienced in exchange for short-term personal gain? If we all did that, it would only prove that the Forts' low opinions of us had been completely justified.

It would've been much easier for me if Mandala 2 had been attacked that day, destroyed despite my best efforts. If I'd died with it, that would have been simplest of all – although I'm sure that somewhere another version of me would have received that same message and faced the same dilemma. I'd like to say that, in the absence of such an attack, I reasoned my way through a logical, emotional, satisfying argument, one that I could relate to you now, which led to the conclusion you have certainly guessed.

I did leave Mandala 2, but not because I had good reason to. I left because I had no reason to stay. It wasn't my fight. Their loyalties weren't the same as mine. They had taken me in, yes, but I had earned back the privilege a dozen times over on the front line.

I didn't return from my patrol. I didn't transmit a reason or a farewell. I simply vanished off the station's scopes and was never seen again.

Is that cold, Helwise? I don't think so. It wasn't an easy decision, but I think BB knew which one I would make when she gave me the note. 'Talk to me afterward,' she'd said, 'if there's anything left to say.' There was never going to be. She saw it coming long before I did.

When I arrived here, the hab was empty. No sign of Emlee or anyone else. No messages. I considered turning back, but what would have been the point? The only thing I owed Mandala 2 was the Vespula, which I put on autopilot and sent home, without me in it.

And here I am. Two more of me did come, lured by the same message. There was some other traffic; you've seen the wrecked ships, Imre. Not my doing, but that's unimportant, I guess. Just one more snafu left in the wake of the Slow Wave.

Then you came along. At first I ignored you, remembering the way you'd ignored me in Mandala 2. You didn't raise Emlee and the message, so I figured we weren't on the same page any more. Then you mentioned 'luminous' and my curiosity stirred. What was the point of sitting here doing nothing with the galaxy falling apart around me? Even with myself for company, I couldn't take the isolation forever. What would I do when the food ran out or something broke that couldn't be repaired? I would die here if I didn't take a chance.

I opened the lock in the hope that you might be able to give what happened to the Continuum some meaning – so you can show us how to fight back. I served under you in more places than I'll ever know, in more lives than I can count. I don't care if 'luminous' is a person, a government, a weapon, a natural event, or even an idea. Just point me at it and give me something to do. I'm better off dead than moldering here any longer. There's nothing more useless than a soldier without a fight.

'Is that it?' asked Helwise.

'That's all.' Freer looked as shaken as Imre felt. His eyes were red and his skin sallow. His cheeks were shadow-filled hollows. Now Imre could see it: the loneliness and tension etched in every line. Freer had been abandoned too long – how long exactly, he had not said, but it could not have been a brief period, given his condition – stewing over his mistakes and his failed aspirations. He had abandoned Mandala 2 to help Emlee, and when that had gone nowhere, he had been left purposeless. Perhaps Freer would have considered tracking down Imre and asking him for help; perhaps not, since Imre's former self had shown no interest in Freer on Mandala 2. Then he and Helwise had come right to Freer's doorstep, giving him an opportunity he couldn't turn down.

Something nagged at Imre then, a subconscious thought started but not yet finished. He put it aside for one moment, already congested by partial revelations and unclear glimpses of a past he had never possessed. The chain of discovery he was following became longer every time he pulled at it: from the Chaos War to Mandala Supersystem and the Cat's Arse; from the Slow Wave to Domgard; from 'luminous' to Alphin Freer and the missing Emlee Copas – and one of the Corps who, some unknown time in the past, had been facing execution.

And his original self . . . what was he up to? Traveling the Line looking for Bianca Biancotti, one of no more than a hundred or so survivors from the twentieth century, in search of information only she might have gleaned from the torrent of incomplete data spreading from relay to relay . . . Making dark connections between the mysterious Domgard and the Slow Wave, and receiving the word 'luminous' in reply . . . How could such activity connect to a silver sphere recovered from the edge of the galaxy, where the view was so beautiful only because civilization could not be farther away?

An upwelling of giddiness reminded him of the moment in the Jinc's shuttle scoop when he had first remembered *Pelorus*. That this recognition of remembering belonged to him, not the man who had bequeathed his existence to the void, was no consolation. Everything was touched by the actions of his former self, yet he felt as far away as ever from knowing what those actions were and what they meant – and how he should respond in turn. Should he take up the quest that might have resulted in the destruction the Drum? Was he qualified, yet, to investigate his own murder?

'I need to think about this,' he said, pushing himself away from the table.

'Imre—' Freer looked startled.

'Don't rush me, Al.' He suppressed a flash of annoyance. What was Freer thinking? That he would start issuing orders by reflex, without need for deliberation or debate? 'I know as much as you do about what we're fighting here. Going off half-cocked helps no one, no matter how long you feel you've been waiting.'

'You could at least tell me your side of the story.'

That was a good point. 'All right. Talk to Helwise. She'll fill you in on what I've told her. If you have any questions after that, we can talk some more. For now . . .' He looked at both of them in turn. They were waiting expectantly, and that irritated him. 'I need to be alone.'

'All right.' Freer nodded. 'Just tell me if you remember anything about BB and Mandala 2. Did you come through there on the way here? Is the Line still intact?'

Imre wished he could reassure his old friend on any of those scores. 'I'm sorry. I didn't come that way, and I – this version of me – didn't exist between *Pelorus* and now. That leaves me more in the dark than you.'

'Until we can find another version of you, I guess,' Freer said. 'He'll talk to you, at least. Then we'll get some answers.'

Imre wasn't sure how he felt about that. He had no evidence yet that any other versions of him still existed, just glimpses here and there since the Slow Wave: an enigmatic, transient figure drifting through Bianca Biancotti's strange outpost. He felt like a ghost in waiting, a resurrection in search of a corpse.

'Looking like that,' said Helwise, 'he's as likely to want to fuck you as help you.'

Imre bit down on an angry retort. I'm right here, he wanted to say. That's me you're talking about. The words sounded hollow even in his mind. He swallowed them like bile and turned and kicked away.

He didn't sleep. He couldn't. His veins were full of energy, a restless, fitful kind of energy that came from too many uncertainties, too few complete answers. The habitat was a kind of memorial to Himself: every line accorded with his own sense of aesthetics, from elegant but sturdy zero-gee tables to the sweeping curves of its hangar bays. The more he saw of it, the more he felt that he could navigate its deceptively wide corridors with eyes closed, moving from place to place by instinct alone. Every time he turned a corner, he was greeted by a sight that was at the same time new and familiar. He had patently never been here before, but the man whose memories he claimed had once dreamed of it.

This déjà vu, he thought, was perfectly understandable; it would have been strange for it to be otherwise. That, however, didn't make it any less perturbing.

Rather than return to the quarters he had chosen, he let his instincts guide him, seeking the heart of the complicated structure. He passed storerooms and empty fighter launch tubes, all safely locked under Freer's new security regime. He drifted through cylindrical gardens, green and rich with the smell of pollen. There were chambers that had clearly been decorated by others. He recognized spare, abstract metalwork that Freer would have liked, a whole wing in muted browns that made him think of

Emlee Copas, and a room devoted entirely to rare energy weapons that could only have been Render's contribution: functional, brutal, and with a strangely filtered appreciation of history.

('I don't remember our secrets,' the big soldier said from his memory. 'I won't remember. Did God retire?')

Nowhere did Imre see anything that might have belonged to Helwise MacPhedron.

The heart of the habitat wasn't in the physical center, or its center of gravity. It was, in fact, some distance from either, situated behind a closed door at the end of a short corridor with no other exit. He floated in front of the door, wondering what he might find on the far side. There was a biometric lock in the center of the sliding panel. It hadn't opened as he approached, so he put his left palm on the lock and waited to see what would happen.

The lock hummed against his skin, barely audible, then clicked. He withdrew his hand, and the hatch slid aside. Red light bathed him from the space beyond, and he kicked himself forward with eyes widening in wonder.

The room was spherical, approximately three meters across. The light came from the walls themselves, but wasn't naturally red. It shone pure white around the edges of hundreds of glass shards that covered the walls, each one a different shape and shade of red, like jagged petals seen from inside a crystal flower. Imre arrested his motion against the far side of the chamber, and gently nudged himself back toward the hatch, which had shut automatically behind him. The glass didn't shift even a millimeter under his weight; the relics were anchored against the walls by invisible molecular bonds, their surfaces oily and irregular to the touch. They were clearly very, very old.

Stained glass, he thought, taken from old windows. He saw petals, an apple, and a shoe amid uncountable geometric shapes. The crimson shards might once have belonged in old Earth cathedrals, stately homes, and parliament buildings. If they were original, the collection was beyond value.

To whom, he wondered. What was such a unique and precious

collection doing at the heart of a secret habitat hidden in Mandala Supersystem's spatial anomaly?

He could think of only one answer, even though it dismayed him to contemplate it. The collection had to be his, situated where it would go unnoticed and be defended if necessary. He imagined Himself passing through the Cat's Arse after one of his many long journeys, detouring only slightly to deposit another rare and delicate relic in his secret repository. Had Helwise known about it? Had anyone else? How strange to think that they might have full and complete knowledge of his past obsession when he himself, until that moment, had had none.

A strange urge swept over him: to smash the glass into millions of pieces. That he understood the urge's origins in no way diminished its destructive strength. The rosy heart of the habitat was a symbol of something he lacked, a key difference between him and the man he had once been. So long as it existed, he would always be reminded of it.

His fists balled. His knees came up, ready to kick out. An image of himself floating in a sea of red particles came to him, startlingly vivid, but in the fantasy the particles were of blood, not shattered glass.

He hugged himself. So much death and destruction. Perhaps he was better off not knowing everything his original had done, both before and after the Slow Wave. The latter worried him most: first abandoning Helwise to her fate, then appearing and disappearing in the obsessive pursuit of information only he and Bianca Biancotti seemed to fathom. What remained to be revealed? What dark secret might the next unveiling expose to the light?

Reaching out, he grasped a single, red shard — a curved, tapering shape that might once have represented a ribbon — and firmly pulled it toward him. With just a slight, momentary resistance, it came away from the wall. He let it float in the cage of his fingers, admiring the imperfections of antiquity, then tucked it into the breast pocket of his top and zipped it shut.

The empty space he had made in the display berated him as he

left the room behind him, otherwise untouched, and resolved to
look elsewhere.

The habitat's encyclopedias were considerably more up-to-date
than that of the Jinc, and their entries more substantial. Imre
immersed himself in the extra data for a full day, skipping from
record to record in search of anything familiar. The exploits of his
former self had taken him far and wide across the galaxy, if not as
a single individual, then as many whose memories were subse-
quently combined in reunions Helwise had described as 'thought
orgies.' He had pursued campaigns along all of the major galactic
arms, from the serene outer wisps to the frenetic fringes of the central bulge, where overclocking was the norm and the rest of the
Continuum was regarded as a dumping ground for laggardly do-
gooders. He had led armies of thousands and tactical squads of two
or three. He had toppled despots and advised beneficent leaders.
He had dismantled predatory AIs and infiltrated aggressive
gestalts. He had killed in cold blood and in the heat of passion. He
had pursued a lengthy and costly campaign against the Forts that
came to be known as the Mad Times.

Under his entry of 'Sternsknecht Imre Bergamasc' was a long
list of awards and commendations, plus the conclusions of several
investigations into his conduct. He had twice been censured for
'unnecessary measures' in the pursuit of his duty, charges to which
he had once pleaded guilty and once offered no defense. Imre
remembered just one of these incidents, and could see no way in
which it differed from the many others slowly coming back to
him. It was all death and violent change, however he looked at it,
in the service of making the galaxy a tidier place for the Forts to
inhabit.

His family's origin was listed as New Ireland, a small system
within the hundred-light-year bubble surrounding Sol still known
to some as the Round. It had been a traditional terrestrial colony,
with cities situated near rivers and a bluish sky not so different
from Earth's. He wondered if people related to him still lived
there, or if the Slow Wave had overtaken them too. He could

remember none of their names, however, or the names of his family. They might have died or simply been expunged from his recollections, erased more by the passage of years than by deliberate, dismissive act.

The encyclopedia entry went on to say that he had taken up permanent residence in Mandala Supersystem following the Chaos War, and was thought to have returned there after the Mad Times.

That was where his entry ended. There was no mention of the campaigns Helwise had told him about, in Chimeleon and elsewhere. There was, also, no reference to the Slow Wave. Presumably, the Continuum's automatic maintenance of such databases had ceased with the cutting of the Forts' Q loop communications system. Just one of many things the galaxy now found hard to do without.

He pictured himself – many different versions of Himself – converging on the Cat's Arse habitat after the Mad Times. Beaten on a thousand fronts, forced to surrender rather than see his friends and allies destroyed, haunted by images of war – what had gone through his many minds afterward? What plans had he made after that bittersweet merging of memories? Where had the many parts of him gone next?

'I see you found the room,' Freer said to him over the habitat's intercom.

'I did.' Imre was floating fully dressed in his hammock with his hands folded behind his head, all appetite for discovery temporarily spent. 'What's it to you?'

'It wouldn't open for me, that's all. It's protected by its own security system. I've been curious about the contents. Care to tell?'

Imre thought about it. The biometric lock must have been programmed by Himself to respond only to Imre Bergamasc's fingerprints, genetic code, or some other deep-etched detail. That it had recognized him was reassurance of a kind. He hoped it would put Freer's suspicions at ease.

'No,' he said in the end. 'It's private.'

'Understood.' Freer didn't sound especially disappointed. 'Hel has brought me up to date on your situation. I can accept that it's difficult.'

Well, thanks, Imre thought to himself. 'Tell me something, Al. It's been worrying me ever since we talked, but I only just worked out what it was. You've been here for ages, right? Before the ship graveyard formed, before Helwise arrived. You must have seen her. You must have seen the people attacking her. You didn't mention them. More importantly, you didn't help her.'

'It's complicated.'

'I can understand complicated things, Al. Try me.'

'I changed the codes for a reason, and that reason still held.'

'Until I came along.'

'That's right. Until you came along. I told you why that makes a difference.'

'Couldn't you and Helwise have worked together? I don't understand why I'm so critical.'

There was a small silence. 'She understands.'

'Does she?'

'We've stopped pointing guns at each other, haven't we? That's about the best we've ever got along.'

'True, Al. But I don't like it, and it doesn't really answer my question. She was broadcasting a distress call, for pity's sake, using Corps protocols. You ignored it. That's pretty hard to forgive.'

'I'm not asking for your forgiveness. Not ahead of her, anyway.'

'What's that supposed to mean?'

'That we've all done things others might find hard to understand. Me, her, and you.'

'Yes,' Imre said, unfolding his hands and letting them float at his sides. 'I assumed you were including me in that statement.'

The empty line hummed between them.

'There's a full medical suite here,' Freer told him. 'It can see to your condition, if you want.'

'My what?'

'It can make the process the Jinc started proceed more quickly.'

'You know, Al, for a lot of people being female isn't exactly a "condition."'

'I'm not talking about a lot of people. I'm talking about you.'

'Anyway, I'm not really female any more. I'm something in between.' He considered the suggestion, taking it in the spirit it had been offered. 'I'll think about it.'

'That's assuming we're not in a hurry to go anywhere, of course.'

He could clearly read the implication in Freer's voice. 'Where would we go?'

'Emlee's message originated in Hyperabad. We could try to find her there.'

'Did she say specifically that that's where she was?'

'No.'

'Then I think it would be a leap to assume she was still there. Take it easy, Al. When we go after Render, we'll do it the right way. Okay?'

That seemed to be enough for now. 'Okay, Imre. I'll reprogram the hab security to take your instructions.'

'You do that.' So saying, he closed the line. He didn't want to nursemaid Freer through a crisis of confidence when he had his own to deal with. Freer didn't want a fight; he wanted a commanding officer. Who was Imre to give out commands – this half man, half self, existing constantly on the brink of dissolution?

When he slept, he dreamed of the ghosts of the Forts looming like giant headstones on the brink of falling over and flattening him. Their last thoughts curled around him like dank, midnight mist. 'Luminous,' they intoned. 'All is luminous.' But it was dark in the boneyard, and darker still at the bottom of the grave Imre had dug for himself. When the first of the mighty headstones tipped over him, grating like the lid of a granite tomb, he saw his name written on it in block letters, chiseled there by the heavy hand of fate.

The halls of the habitat were nearly silent, the rooms all empty apart from three. Occasionally he heard Freer exercising, anachronistically pulling weights and swinging his legs in zero-gee treadmills. Sometimes he saw Helwise gliding smoothly through the halls, conducting an inventory of the habitat's contents. He avoided them for the most part as he went about putting the pieces of himself together. Only when he felt whole enough to stand on his own would he consider trying to put the Corps, then the galaxy, back together again.

Freer understood, but he was not so patient. With Imre's permission, he put *The Cauld Lad* into a permanent dock. He and the AI worked together to refit the starship after its long journey – on the assumption that it would one day be needed again.

'Better prepared for something that never comes,' Freer told Imre when queried, 'than dead.'

'I couldn't agree more.' The activity was good for Freer. 'Let me know when it's kitted out, and keep it ready to launch on a five-minute countdown.'

If Freer felt patronized, he didn't let it show. He did, however, send Imre the full text of Emlee Copas's message, as though to remind him of their ultimate goal. Imre refrained from pointing out that he hadn't forgotten, that his goal was the same as Freer's. They were simply operating on different timetables.

Guilt prompted him to overclock just a little, to hasten his deliberations and bring any conclusion he might reach steadily closer. The heightened stress on his body brought a new ache to his attention: a deep throbbing in his hips and spine that was certainly another symptom of his slowly changing sex. He took himself to the medical suite and had himself checked over, just to make sure the Jinc knew what they were doing. Building a body from scratch was one thing; ensuring it stayed healthy in the long term was quite another.

The suite gave him a general all clear. He didn't want to ignore a sign that might turn out to be bone cancer or something equally insidious, but at the same time he didn't want to dwell overmuch on the differences between him and his former self. In the mirror, he imagined that he looked more like the picture in the habitat's encyclopedia than he had with the Jinc. The nose was the same, and so was the mouth; his eyes were unchanged regardless of his gender. Fortunately, singleton bodies were complex and mysterious machines; he felt justified in taking the suite at its word for anything below skin-deep.

Before he left the suite, he thoroughly depilated his skin, stomach and all, leaving only the thick, if short, mat of white hair on his head untouched.

Next, he took on the task of unpicking the message Emlee Copas had broadcast, taking it apart as he had the first message he had received after escaping the Jinc. Starting with the route it had followed to the Mandala 2 relay junction, he soon realized that simply obtaining it had not been an easy feat. It had bounced for decades between dead ends in the Line, seeking a sympathetic listener. Some had copied it and sent it farther abroad; that was clearly indicated in the file's transmission history. Others, presumably, had deleted it on receipt, unwilling to clog up the Line with old cries for help. This single copy must have been preserved and propagated by a chain of people sympathetic to, or at least familiar with, the Corps and its members.

The essence of the message was much as Freer had summarized it. One of the Corps was in trouble, having been arrested on charges of sedition, sabotage, and conspiracy to overthrow the government. Which government, exactly, she didn't say; neither did she specify which of her colleagues was in danger. If the sentence couldn't be commuted, execution was inevitable. Unsaid was the detail of guilt or innocence. It was quite possible that Copas and any number of Corps members could indeed have been conspiring against a sovereign state, particularly if the Forts had anything to do with their being there in the first place. After the Slow Wave, however, all assumptions were thrown out. There were no more Forts, so how could the mission be a legitimate one? The charges could have been completely deserved or completely manufactured. There was no way at present to tell.

Copas concluded with a plea to congregate in 'the usual venue' and from there mount an extraction. Her avoidance of details was frustrating but necessary, Imre supposed. Anything too detailed might be intercepted and lead to a trap.

There was no way, either, to tell exactly when it was sent. Light-speed delays and the vast size of the Continuum had forced the abandonment of a contemporary calendar long ago. Dates and times were purely relative, as was the flow of time itself. Three people could occupy a room for an hour and experience that time in three very different ways. One moving at Tempo Fort could barely notice it pass while another severely overclocking could grow old and die. The third could experience it in the way natural humans had for millennia, at Tempo Absolute, but who was to say that that was the more correct version? So it was with even something as broad as the calendar year. What did it matter if two points on opposite sides of the galaxy recorded the same date when tens of thousands of years separated their every communication? Except on a moment-to-moment level, all discussions of time were conducted in the broadest and most flexible terms, in relation to events the participants had in common.

Emlee Copas's message might have been sent immediately after the Slow Wave struck Mandala Supersystem. It might have been sent much later. Either way, he told himself, there was no hurry. Unless Copas sent another message directly to the Cat's Arse, he had time to think about what to do next.

That, in a galaxy torn apart, seemed too precious a commodity to ignore, no matter how it was measured.

He was asleep when Freer alerted him to the incoming vessels. It took him a disturbingly long time to wake up. His dreams had become no less vivid with time. If anything, the constant input of information, present and past, stimulated his imagination to new heights. He saw himself in a thousand guises, as galactic master, slave to the Forts, rampaging destroyer, gallant hero, swashbuckling lover. He didn't know if any of them was true, but in every one of them he was male. His desire and the ability to act on that desire was very active. Sometimes he woke panting for breath and covered with sweat, clutching at the vestiges of an orgasm he could no longer feel. The feelings inevitably dissolved, leaving him with a keen sense of loss that could not be assuaged. The sabotaging of this aspect of his being became gradually and inextricably linked with the loss of the Continuum. When he grieved for one, he also grieved for the other.

'So do as Al suggested,' Helwise told him at one point, when he had come to her with his problem. She had taken a room up the corridor from his, one that remained identical in every respect to the others, apart from the smell of her. 'Make a man of yourself, literally. At least one your problems will be solved then.'

'Fiddling while Rome burns,' he said.

She hadn't laughed. 'You're not the Continuum. Why suffer any more bullshit than you need to?'

'I don't think I have a martyr complex, if that's what you're worried about.'

That did prompt a guffaw. 'If you did, that'd definitely mark you as a fake.'

('I'll give you nothing but lies,' he remembered Render saying once. The memory came to him in a flash, like a split-second migraine. 'I'll give you nothing but lies or nothing at all.')

'What if it is all fake?' he asked her, shrugging off the sense of double-time. 'What if none of this is me?'

She had patted him lightly on the cheek. 'Honey, the Jinc don't sound like practical jokers. There's no other reason I can think of to burden us with you.'

'I'm a burden to you now, am I?'

'You will be if you keep asking stupid questions. Now shut up and get undressed.'

'What?'

'You may not feel desire, but I do. Either join in or get out.'

He had stayed out of a sense of duty for what they had once had, and for what she claimed still to feel. More than mere desire, a complicated entanglement that had had as many good moments as bad. Was this a good moment? He couldn't tell. Holding her and touching her as he once had encouraged a sense of intimacy he wasn't certain he wanted. Without knowing who he was, how could he begin to love someone else? Without desire urging him on, he felt removed from the proceedings. Where once her naked body might have inspired lust, he felt only curiosity and awkwardness. He went through the motions, experiencing no arousal to match hers, no release. When she came, she reached for the wall behind her, not him. Afterward he felt tired.

They slept tangled in the sheet that stopped them drifting around the room. He dreamed of a headless golden statue on a very tall mountain, so tall that from its summit he could see the edge of the world. A tidal wave was building, growing steadily in mass and power. Sunlight gleamed off the top of it and the edge of his notched sword in exactly the same fashion. As the wave finally broke and began to rush forward, his sword melted into water and slipped through his fingers to the gold beneath his feet.

He woke to the sound of Alphin Freer's voice in his ears.

'Get up, you two. There's someone coming our way.'

'Who?' asked Helwise, pushing herself from Imre and reaching for her clothes.

'I don't know. They're not broadcasting, and neither am I.'

'Keep it that way.' She was dressed and gone before Imre had fully shrugged off the dream.

'Is this necessarily an emergency?' he asked Freer. 'Couldn't this just be a patrol of some kind?'

'Unlikely. There's nothing around Kuntuzangpo but us, and no reason to come looking. Mandala is full of dead ships and space junk. The Hypers have more important things to worry about.'

'The who?'

'Hyperabad is the seat the civilian government now, around Chenresi.'

'Yes, I remember. I just hadn't heard you call them that before.' He suppressed his irritation. 'Do these ships bear any resemblance to ships you've seen before?'

'Yes,' Freer admitted. 'They look like Vespulas.'

Imre was through the door and hurrying to the common area. Vespulas were a common enough fighter; their presence didn't necessarily implicate Mandala 2, where Freer had flown them for Bianca Biancotti.

'How many are there?'

'Five.'

Imre patched in to the habitat's telemetry as he hurried to the communal area. The deceleration cones preceding the ships were clearly visible as triangular distortions in the space-time surrounding Kuntuzangpo. Traveling well apart to avoid interfering with each other, they were decelerating at a massive rate. They had clearly coasted at their maximum velocity for as long as possible in order to delay detection until the last moment. Their ETA was less than an hour.

The communal area was transformed by a riot of two- and three-dimensional displays at every conceivable orientation, projecting every imaginable color. Imre kicked through three of them on the way to the center, where Freer and Helwise stood, skimming through the data.

'There's no sign of a matter ram,' Freer said, studying radar and lidar images refreshing every tenth of a second. That was something. A handful of ball bearings dropped before the ships had begun to decelerate would arrive long before the ships themselves, containing enough energy to blow the habitat to pieces.

'I'm a long way from feeling any kind of relief,' said Helwise. 'Are you sure you didn't leave any enemies behind at Mandala 2?'

'No more than usual.' Freer's tone was dry. The consummate professional, he made a point of making as little an impression as possible, except on the battlefield. 'They may have come in quiet, but they're certainly declaring themselves now.'

'This is all we'll get,' said Imre, taking in the information with his arms folded, one leg bracing him against a magnetically fixed chair. 'They're hoping to force a reaction. It's designed to be intimidating, them bearing down on us without knowing what they want.'

'No shit.' Helwise brushed an errant strand of hair out of her face.

'They might want us to break radio silence first. If that's the limit of their intentions, I can live with it. We'd probably be dead already if murder was on their minds.' He thought for a moment. 'How strong are the habitat's defenses, exactly? Could we hold off a direct assault?'

Freer shook his head. 'We could stop them boarding for a while, but eventually they'd get in. To turn them back, we'd need to go out there and engage.'

'And the one ship we have is *The Cauld Lad.*'

'Lots of drones and the like,' said Helwise, 'but they're not going to hurt anyone.'

Imre nodded, keeping the turmoil of his emotions carefully hidden. Ready or not, the time had come to make a decision.

'All right. Get the ship prepped. Then hail them. Tell them we're the survivors of the liner Helwise came here in and ask for ID. Sound nervous, if you can. Let's see what happens when we play by their rules.'

Freer complied. After engaging *The Cauld Lad*'s AI and setting its launch-prep cycle in motion, he brought up a master communications window and broadcast a short message directly at the five approaching ships.

'*Deodati* to incoming vessels: identify and state your intentions. We are not salvage. I repeat, we are not salvage. Please ignore any transmissions to the contrary.'

They waited ten minutes, listening to the crackle of Kuntuzangpo and the long-distance burble of conversations to faint too make out, then tried again.

'Incoming vessels, this is the liner *Deodati*. You may have heard a distress call, but the emergency has been contained. We are in no need of assistance. Thanks for your interest, but we'd appreciate you moving along.'

The five ships were half the distance they had been when a response finally came.

'You're fooling no one, Freer. Get your locks open. We're here for Bergamasc.'

The three of them exchanged glances.

'Do you recognize that voice?' Imre asked Freer.

'Never heard it before.' Freer activated the transmitter again, and broadcast, 'Bergamasc who?'

The response came more quickly. With every minute, the ships drew closer. One of the screens displayed a fuzzy image of their arrowhead formation: five black motes riding forward-pointing jets of fire. Their engines worked on principles very different from the chemical rockets of humanity's earliest ventures into space, but the special effects were not dissimilar.

This time the voice that spoke was very familiar indeed. 'I know you have to try, Al, but you're wasting your time. They know where you are and who's with you. I suggest you stop stalling and hand him over.'

Helwise looked at Freer. 'That's you, isn't it?'

Freer nodded. 'It is.'

'You call yourself Al?'

'Not normally.'

She pursed her lips. 'I don't like this.'

'Neither do I.' Imre pushed himself forward. 'Ask them why they want me – and what you stand to gain by doing as they say. Hel, get those drones you mentioned out of storage but don't launch anything yet. Have them ready to move when I tell you.'

'I think—'

'Just do it.'

She pursed her lips but didn't argue.

'Listen,' Freer broadcast to the approaching ships. 'Say I've got what you want. You're going to have to provide a good reason for me to give it away. What's my motive? Why would I betray a friend?'

The five specks resolved into identical fighters: definitely Vespulas, no decoys. The fighters were much smaller in mass than the habitat, but one of the basic rules of space warfare – writ large and clear on Imre's inherited mind – was that being big and under zero acceleration was a massive disadvantage. Offense was much easier than defense, and the fighters had it in spades.

Helwise nodded surlily when the drones were ready. At precisely the same instant, the other Freer replied.

'I'm not asking you to betray anyone. People are looking for him. Important people, Al. Worry about them, not him. You don't even know if he's real.'

Helwise and Freer looked at Imre. He shook his head, as much in the dark as they were.

'Why wouldn't he be real?' Freer asked.

The response took only a minute. 'We'll fill you in when we dock. Don't stuff us around any more than you have to, for pride's sake. Od knows I understand; no one likes being pushed around. But Imre's a wanted man, and we know he's come here. There's no point dragging it out or getting anyone hurt.'

There was a pause, then: 'Oh, and BB sends her love.'

Freer stiffened and went pale. 'She wouldn't do that. She wouldn't say that. She was either lying or—'

Imre reached out and gripped his arm. 'It's a trap. He used the wrong name; he asked you not to betray anyone; he told you something you knew was false. The rest was just what they wanted to hear.'

'Yes, but who are "they"?' The flesh around Freer's eyes was infused with blood. It was too easy to imagine what his other self's captors had done to force him to lie. Everyone in the Corps had used such techniques themselves, many times.

'Let's not stick around to find out.' Helwise kicked through the virtual displays and headed for the nearest door. 'I'll see you guys at the ship. Don't take too fucking long, will you?'

'We won't.' Imre thought fast, skimming through options until he was certain the one he was following was the optimum. 'Get those drones in motion,' he called after her. 'I want them in the habitat, everywhere! Al, call our visitors and tell them you'll do as they say. Pick an air lock; give them directions; don't make them suspicious.'

Freer's attention narrowed back to the present. 'You're going to let them in?'

'Yes, but we won't be here. The only thing they'll find waiting for them is a nasty surprise.'

Imre brought up the drone master control window and confirmed that Helwise had activated their internal AIs and put them in motion. Simple, reactive machines normally used to widen sensor baselines, they filed in their dozens along the habitat's long corridors like platelets through a human bloodstream. He patched into one of their data feeds and glimpsed the one

next in line, wobbling like a fat top as puffing airjets propelled
it along.

With a series of quick commands, he put their self-defense systems in a state of high readiness. At the flick of a mental switch,
they would go from harmless drifting drones to hair-trigger assassins. As a further measure, he rigged them all to blow if one was
destroyed. The resulting firestorm would play merry havoc with
the habitat's life support and, at the very least, give the visitors a
reason to pause.

Big, slow objects were no good in combat, but they were perfect
for an ambush. Limited ingress, tight corridors, centralized control . . . He felt a rush of adrenaline he hadn't experienced in that
body before. But for the high odds, he might have stayed to see
what happened. At best, they would catch the crew of one fighter
off guard, maybe two. That left three Vespulas to deal with,
making a very close match against the starship.

'You've been here a long time, right?' he asked Freer, as they
hurried from the common area to where Helwise and *The Cauld
Lad* were waiting.

'Long enough.'

'My eyes cross when I so much as look outside. The distortion
gets me every time. They won't be adjusted to it either. We can use
that to our advantage, I'm sure.' He watched Freer closely. 'I want
you at the helm, not Helwise. You understand?'

'You don't entirely trust her.' Freer nodded. 'That's good.'

'It's not that. I don't want her finger on the trigger if we have to
do something you'll regret later. Like killing someone you hold
more allegiance to than you do her, or me.'

Freer kept his eyes forward. 'I understand.'

As they hurried along the last leg to *The Cauld Lad*'s dock,
Imre brought up the external battery command window and put
the habitat's external defenses in a state of readiness. The targets he
allocated weren't the incoming vessels, but the agglomerations of
space junk surrounding the habitat. The graveyard had been
undisturbed since Helwise had crashed through it in the *Deodati*.
The time had come, perhaps, to mix things up a little.

A drone whizzed by like an angry hornet, no larger than his fist. The air lock gaped ahead of them. Imre waved Freer in first.

'Seal us up,' he told the ship, tugging himself from handhold to handhold along the bright blue corridor. His eyes had become accustomed to the gentler tones of the habitat his former self had designed. 'Hel, are we ready to launch?'

Her reply came virtually to his ears from the cockpit. His new body had interfaced seamlessly with the ship's symbolic environment.

'My hand's on the switch and ready to push. Aren't you just a little bit curious as to what you're guilty of?'

'I don't get the feeling they're here to talk.' He reached the ladder leading to the bridge a second after Freer and followed him along it, mindful of the taller man's kicking feet. 'I'm not sure I'd believe anything they had to say, anyway.'

The wraparound screen was full of displays. Many showed the quintet of vessels, their velocities still dropping fast and their courses diverging as they neared the habitat. Front-on they were oval in cross section, but that would soon change as weapons and telemetry vanes extended. Their outlines rippled as in a heat haze, seen through regions of distressed space-time.

Imre pointed at a couple of windows he'd never noticed before. 'What are these systems? I don't recall them from the trip out.'

'While you were busy with the encyclopedia,' said Freer, 'I made a few improvements.'

'Like what, exactly?'

'Weapons, for one. Just in case.' Freer stood next to Helwise. 'We've been around long enough to know that we're not considered threats by anyone. No one came looking for us. You, though, are a wild card. Wherever you go, trouble always follows.'

A window bleeped for attention. Helwise brought it forward through the virtual stack. 'So, now the bastards want to talk.'

'They can want all they like.' Imre opened the habitat's external battery command in the wraparound screen, where the others could see it too. 'You know what I've got in mind. Give me some targets.'

Helwise no longer needed to be asked twice. The view swung and shifted from hulk to hulk. 'That one there. And that one too. It'll fall to pieces with one shot to the bow. See that fat carrier over there, behind the scaffold? It's full of hydrogen. I was saving that for later, if I needed it.'

Imre picked out the targets she selected and locked the habitat's mass and beamer weapons onto them. Projectiles would take longer to hit their targets than a laser, but their effects would be more dramatic. While doing so, he carefully avoided looking at the twisted, shifting backdrop of stars. This wasn't the time to be bamboozled.

'Give them one chance,' said Freer. 'At least let them know they're not welcome.'

'Spoil the surprise?' said Helwise. 'I don't think so.'

'No,' said Imre, sliding the battery screen to one side. 'He's right. Go ahead, Al. They might still think this is your show.'

The Cauld Lad gave Freer an open line to the incoming vessels. 'We don't have to do it like this,' he told them. 'I need reasons, not threats, before I'll hand over anything or anyone.'

The response time was measured in seconds. A different voice spoke, a woman with inflexible vowels: 'Bergamasc is a wanted man. That's all you need to hear. Stand between us and him, and you'll know about it.'

'Well, gee, since you put it so nicely . . .' Freer activated the main air lock by remote. 'Come aboard, by all means.'

'Thank you.' The ships were now so close their speed could be measured in meters per second. 'You're doing the right thing.'

'I have only your word for that.' Freer glanced at Imre, then away. 'I suppose this has something to do with Domgard.'

The response was immediate: 'Your immediate future, Alphin Freer, and the future of the human race, depend on your never saying that name again.'

The five ships diverged like a flock of birds hit by a cannonball.

'Holy shit.' Helwise slapped Freer in the chest. 'What did you say that for? They're on an attack run!'

'They always were.' Imre pushed them apart and instructed the external battery to begin firing. 'Get us ready to move.'

'Couldn't be readier.' Helwise's hands played across *The Cauld Lad*'s contact pads with as much symbolic need as actual. 'Just say the word.'

'Al has the helm. I want you firing at the graveyard.'

If she was surprised, it didn't show. In a dozen windows energy played across the abandoned hulks. Shadows danced as light flared and faded. Clouds of vaporized metal bloomed like mushrooms in fast motion. One particularly fierce explosion left a bright line across Imre's retina. When he looked back, the entire view was moving: the wrecks, the sky, and everything between. What had once been a navigational curiosity suddenly became a serious danger for anyone in the vicinity.

Particularly anyone moving. The five incoming vessels changed course to avoid the worst of it. Telemetry became a hash of noise and ghost signals into which the Vespulas vanished. The battery continued pounding the graveyard until the habitat was surrounded by spinning wreckage. Distant thuds and rattles came through the hull to those inside *The Cauld Lad.* The entire nose of the *Deodati* pinwheeled by, trailing sparks from either jagged end.

'Shall I launch?' asked Freer.

'Not yet. They'll be waiting outside in case we run, all five of them. I want shorter odds than that.'

'I can't get a fix on them,' said Helwise, trawling through masses of raw data. 'They could be anywhere.'

'We know where they want to be,' said Imre. 'They won't keep us waiting long.'

Right on cue, a dark shape slid into view: one of the Vespulas, feigning a tumble. Helwise instantly targeted it.

'Do they think we're idiots?'

Imre held her back. 'Let them think that. Ramp back the barrage, one battery at a time. Make it look like we're running out of ammo.'

'Yes, boss.'

His face froze at the term, and he fought a pointless urge to run. The Vespula rolled by, exposing its flank like a seductive shark. Gradually, fitfully, the pounding of the habitat's defenses fell silent. A full minute passed before—

'One, two, three.' Freer counted off multiple targets appearing in the displays. 'Here they come.'

'Leaving just two outside.' Imre allowed himself to feel relief. The game wasn't over, but its conclusion was now very nearly inevitable. 'Let them dock. Give them enough time to reach the drones. Then let's get the hell out of here.'

Helwise primed the external battery to start firing again the moment *The Cauld Lad* launched. 'Better hope you didn't leave anything behind. We won't be coming back for a while.'

'I can't say I'll miss the place,' said Freer, priming the drives. 'It'll be good to be moving again.'

Imre patted his breast pocket, where the shard of red glass safely rested. He was haunted by the questions that would remain unanswered if they ran: what did these people know about Domgard? Why were they going to so much trouble to find him? How did they know he was here in the first place? For a brief moment, on the brink of explosive motion, he was tempted to surrender just to get those answers, to put an end to the growing uncertainty he felt about his role in the Slow Wave and the fate of humanity. By eluding capture now, he might delay the revelation he so desperately needed.

Perhaps that was a good thing, he told himself. Perhaps the time had arrived to set that mystery aside in exchange for something much more important. Knowing the answers to those questions wouldn't tell him where to go next. He needed to find out where he stood with those he had been closest to in the past – and that meant finding Emlee and putting the Corps back together. That was a much more worthy goal than his obsession with his former self's actions, the wrongs he might have committed in absentia.

Freer blew the dock's external hatch and set *The Cauld Lad* off its leash. Helwise fired the external battery, and the shell of wreckage surrounding the habitat lit up like clouds over a blazing city. Fire and ash and a rain of twisted metal rushed by, making a terrible noise on the hull, then all was distortion and acceleration and liquid stars smeared across the blackness of space.

The fourth and fifth Vespulas appeared in their path with gun-ports blazing. *The Cauld Lad* quaked under the impacts but didn't falter. Sheets of burned hull sloughed away, leaving a wake of matter that looked uncannily like a vapor trail.

Then the Vespulas fell behind them, their trajectories too diver-gent from *The Cauld Lad*'s to correct in time. What fighters gained in maneuverability they lacked in sheer grunt. By the time they brought themselves about, the starship would be well out of range.

Imre checked the course Freer had plotted. He had done exactly as Imre had expected.

'Bring us around Kuntuzangpo,' he said. 'Don't take us straight to Hyperabad. Take us via Di-zang. At least make them think about where we're headed before going for the golden goose.'

Freer nodded. Helwise had no opinion on the subject. She was watching the displays aimed back the way they had come and laying down a trail of hard matter to make rapid pursuit more dan-gerous. The cloud of debris still burned, issuing clouds and jets like the surface of a dirty star. Only two of the Vespulas were vis-ible; the habitat couldn't be seen at all. Imre had no doubt that their attackers could see them as clearly as they could be seen in return. Their escape route would be plotted, projected and – what? Transmitted ahead to more of their kind? It all depended on who they were. Freer had talked about a steady stream of saboteurs and spies passing through Mandala 2 during his tenure there. That spoke of organization and intent. It wasn't inconceivable that the two groups weren't connected.

From Di-zang, they would change course for Chenresi, the sub-ordinate star around which Hyperabad orbited. He would look for Emlee Copas the only place he could. He would commit to her cause, in the absence of his own. They would find Render, if he still lived, and they would rescue him. Then the Corps would be complete.

'You don't know what he's done,' the attackers had said.

At least for now, he thought, he knew what he was doing.

THIS HUMAN CORROSION

Where he treads, the earth is parched!
– Where he breathes, the air is fire!
– Where he feeds, the food is poison!
– Where he turns, his glance is lightning!

Robert Charles Maturin

One relative day away from the Cat's Arse, still accelerating at dozens of gravities, *The Cauld Lad* received a short transmission from the habitat's attackers. It showed Alphin Freer tied with arms outstretched between two bolted crash couches. He had been beaten bloody and seemed barely conscious. There was no sound. He stirred, said something to someone standing out of shot, and spat messily in zero gravity. There was a spike of light, like a flashbulb, and Freer's head jerked back. A fine mist of blood painted the bulkhead behind him a brilliant shocking red.

There the transmission ended.

'I'm sorry, Al,' Imre said. He could think of nothing else to add. They had all lost versions of themselves in combat or accidents. Some had been sacrificed in circumstances not dissimilar to this one. It went with the territory.

'That's okay.' Freer's long, lanky frame bowed, just for a moment, like a tree under heavy wind. 'There's nothing we could have done.'

'No point mourning what you never knew,' said Helwise, with the bare minimum of sympathy.

'Do you really think so?' Imre asked her.

'Sure.'

'I'm wasting my time, in other words – trying to put myself back together?'

'I'm not talking about you, boss. I'm talking about Al. There are enough of him in that skull already. Any more and he might implode.'

Freer straightened. 'How many of me died in that Vespula? How many were in that skull?'

'Don't give me that crap. Would you have traded places with him?'

'Of course not.'

'So you see a difference between this you and that you. Why wouldn't it have been murder, then, if you'd absorbed his memories and got rid of that body? What makes you so fucking special?'

'That's a completely different situation, and you know it. If you really want to discuss the morality of—'

'Not now, you two. Not now.' Imre held up his hands in an effort to quell the argument before it really started. 'I care less about philosophy than getting us to safety. Hel, any sign of pursuit?'

She drummed her fingers against *The Cauld Lad*'s instrumentation panel. 'Three of the five are lagging way behind. No sign of the other two.'

'Will we lose them at Di-zang, Al?'

'I'll bet this life on it.'

'Good. Then there's nothing to worry about – and there won't be for quite a while. Unless you have anything specific to tell me at Absolute, I'm dropping tempo and saving myself the wait. Join me if you want, or I'll see you at the other end.'

With that, he reduced his body's metabolic rate so that a year would last less than a relative day, confident that the ship would bring him up to speed if necessary. He could imagine few circumstances in which that would be the case; the route Freer had plotted took them well away from any known planets, habitats, or shipping lanes. Unless the hypothetical conspirators hunting him had access to unimaginably vast resources – whole governments would have trouble netting a single ship moving at speed through Mandala Supersystem – they would arrive in Hyperabad safely, there to meet a completely new basket of problems.

Helwise and Freer became blurs that swirled and sped about him, arms waving like deranged angels under ambient light that was suddenly bluer and brighter. To their eyes, he would be a statue frozen resolutely in place around which their argument raged. He didn't bother requesting a transcript of their discussion; his fractured autobiography supplied him with enough evidence to indicate that this was a regular occurrence, and one unlikely to be resolved soon.

Helwise was the first to drop tempo and join him. Her blur abruptly slammed to a halt on his left, standing with arms folded and jaw set.

'Our ETA is six hours, relative,' she said in a tone he had come to recognize as provisionally calm. 'Any particular way you'd like to kill the time?'

'I'm not killing anything. Al must have collected a stack of data while he was hunkered down in the Cat's Arse and Mandala 2. I want to know everything he does about Hyperabad.'

'Well, be wary of him. I don't like the way he handled that little scene back there.'

'I hear you, Od damn it.' Freer's motion-smeared form solidified on Imre's right. He was peering closely at one of the displays, adjusting the ship's trim. 'There's no right way to handle scenes like that. At least I don't think there is.'

'For the record, I agree completely,' said Imre, 'but that's not the point. The point is that you two are going to shut the fuck up about it, or I'll ditch you both out the air lock and to the devil with who's in the right or who's in whose head. Get over it in your own ways and your own time. Leave me out of it. All right?'

'Got it,' said Helwise, scowling at Freer. 'You heard the man, or whatever the hell he is. Let's see your data.'

Imre ignored the jab. Freer opened a window in the ship's wrap-around display, and at the same time made the information available directly to them. Bits and bytes flowed like invisible motes between the three people on the bridge. Slowly, a picture of a troubled survivor emerged.

In Imre's day, Hyperabad had been a minor capital of a small empire overshadowed by its neighbors in Mandala Supersystem. The rise of the Alienist Technarchy had barely touched it, and the fall had actually benefited it, since its infrastructure had been critical to the Continuum's rejuvenation of the region. Imre assumed that he had had a part to play in that, although there had been nothing in the Cat's Arse encyclopedia specifically mentioning it, and he didn't remember. The subsequent collapse of the Continuum had left numerous significant regional works unfinished and seen others fall into less beneficent hands. The resulting squabble had somehow ended with Hyperabad on top of a heap of diverse world-states and more than two dozen loosely affiliated habitat governments. A complex bureaucracy comprising several overlapping federations and one more or less integrated military force oversaw the administration of the supersystem – but there were as many opportunities for wriggle room as there were holes to fall through. Kuntuzangpo was one such hole: an entire subsystem of Mandala abandoned simply because it was of no use or threat to anyone. Lawless groups like those that had attacked the habitat – and the Corps itself, since Imre, Helwise, and Freer owed no allegiances to the 'Hypers' – roamed unchecked as a result.

Closer to the centers of power, authority wielded a heavy fist. Corruption and commerce swelled like cancerous twins in Hyperabad's dusty womb. A small, hot world, with 90 percent of its water drawn from aquifers tainted by thousands of cycles of pollution and reclamation, its last official census put the head count at an even billion, Primes and singletons all: no gestalts allowed, thanks to an Alienist Technarchy backlash. Since that census, Freer had picked up news of at least one major population crash that had culled 30 percent of the pre–Slow Wave high. Anyone's guess was as likely to be accurate as to the current head count, but a significant chunk of it clustered in a sprawling, overbuilt capital centered on the base of the 'skyline,' the planet's oldest orbital tower. 'Hyperabad of Hyperabad' was the megacity's official name. Its citizens regarded the city, the world, and the small empire beyond as synonymous.

The Cauld Lad swooped around Di-zang's fiery white orb like a weight on a string, ignoring the prospects of its six rocky worlds and busy industrial complexes. Its elaborate LaGrange constructs possessed a friable, fractal beauty reminiscent of automated processes gone to seed, and Imre wondered if they were inhabited at all. Mandala Supersystem was a garden, feral and beautiful in a very deadly way.

The leg to golden Chenresi passed uneventfully. Two of the five Vespulas had followed them to Di-zang but fallen steadily behind, and no intercept vehicles came out to meet them as *The Cauld Lad* approached its destination. Either there hadn't been enough time to launch an intercept, or the next attempt was going to be less overt. Traffic became denser the closer they approached Hyperabad, and they examined every near pass with all due scrutiny. Makes and classes varied, but all openly dis-played – or at least made the appearance of displaying – their purpose for being in the planet's vicinity. Most were traders or pas-senger vessels; some were on diplomatic missions from elsewhere in the supersystem, escorted by sleek security ships as deadly as poison darts; a handful were refugees, denied landing privileges on Hyperabad itself and orbiting endlessly in an artificial ring, await-ing a second chance. Imre suspected that at least some of these were fronts for security forces, covertly testing incomers or hoping to draw out dissident movements from within the indigenous population.

The Cauld Lad remained resolutely silent except when hailed by government officials. Helwise answered all questions with as much of the truth as they deemed appropriate: they were visitors from out-system; they had no official IDs; they would allow their ship to be searched; they would submit to the laws of Hyperabad as applied to them. There was no reason to buck the system until the system demonstrated its hostility to them, and thus far it had been nothing but officious and abrupt. Imre could live with both.

Governments like this one existed to push people around, thinking that was the only way to keep unrest in check. As long as they let themselves appear to be pushed, and kept their true intentions well out of sight, they would not be bothered.

Whatever their true intentions were . . . Imre had no idea where to start looking for Emlee Copas on a world of half a billion people or more. She had been the Corp's information specialist; with her alongside them, the job might have been manageable. As it was, he, Helwise, and Freer would just have to make do with what talents they had between them. Helwise the covert operative and Freer the sergeant; Imre Bergamasc their ersatz commander.

Their landing permit came with a long list of dos and don'ts plus a selection of ports to put down in. They had requested a ground landing in order to keep *The Cauld Lad* as close as possible, even though such were not the norm on most densely populated worlds. Permission came readily enough, suggesting that a history of mistrust existed regarding the orbital tower networks. They had probably been commandeered or sabotaged in the past, before or after the Slow Wave, leaving more than just physical scars on the planet and its people.

Everywhere Imre looked, he saw evidence of paranoia and aggression. His grief for the Continuum rose rather than faded, for such conditions had been rare in his time. Poverty and political subjugation had been relatively unknown and swiftly eradicated where it arose. The baser aspects of human nature had been carefully pruned or guided into more productive outlets by those like him under the direction of the Forts. Even he, when he had turned on his masters, had been eventually cowed and brought back to heel. How that had happened he still didn't know, exactly. Neither Freer nor Helwise had been present during the fateful conversation with Factotem.

The Cauld Lad adopted a stubby aerobraking configuration on approach. Hyperabad's atmosphere hit them like a hydraulic ram. Back at Tempo Absolute and standing on the bridge with the others, Imre felt a faint vibration trill through the bulkheads. In the displays, the bold, brown sphere of the planet bulged large, dusted with ice at the poles and girdled by a narrow ocean around its southern hemisphere, until its edge became a horizon and the nearest face the ground. Details sprang into sharp relief: sheets of thin cloud; jagged, reddish mountains; geometrically precise roads crossing deserts of pure white; dark clots that were most likely satellite cities or independent settlements, strung out like droplets of dark water on a spider's web.

'Looks about as comely as ever,' muttered Helwise, as the ship's velocity dropped from interplanetary to merely supersonic speed, carving a crack across the sky several kilometers long.

'Don't feel obliged to come with us, then,' Imre told her. 'Someone has to stay with the ship, anyway. That can be your job.'

'Where are you two going?'

'To do a little digging. If Emlee is here and hoping to contact us, she'll have left a trail. It's not going to be easy to find, but it's the best hope we have.'

Helwise said, 'Get us access to the local databases, and I can search from here. It'll give me something to do.'

'That was my very next suggestion.'

'One step ahead of you, boss. This is just like the old times.'

Imre said nothing. He had intimate, if partial, knowledge of many such operations. The connection, however, was still lacking; his actions felt anything but routine. The difference was as acute as that between reading an autobiography and living the life.

The ship rocked as it dropped below the speed of sound. Banking sharply, it lined up for landing at the airport they had chosen, one well connected to the heart of the city. Roads, rail, and maglev transport systems radiated from the port like the rays of a star.

'Apparently I lived in Mandala Supersystem for a while,' Imre thought aloud. 'I might have identities I can still access.'

'It would be unwise to go anywhere near them,' said Freer in a level tone. 'The less attention you draw, the better. You're a wanted man, remember?'

'Lucky I've still got these, then.' He looked down at his breasts, undiminished in size beneath a nondescript outfit of canvas pants, beige flak jacket, and work gloves. A tight-fitting, grease-stained beanie would complete the ensemble when he left the ship. Beneath all of it, he discreetly wore a skin suit for protection from blades and crude projectile weapons. 'Suggest that I pose as your girlfriend, and I'll knock your lights out.'

Freer's expression didn't change. 'You're not my type.'

'After BB,' said Helwise, 'that'd be like cradle-snatching.'

None of them laughed. The moment wasn't about levity. Sometimes conversation existed to fill the silence between key moments in a campaign. This was one of those, Imre thought. The team was ticking over, idling like an engine waiting to be put into gear. Soon enough the time would come to drop the clutch and push the accelerator to the floor.

The Cauld Lad skated on rippling jets toward the bay allocated to it by traffic control. Grapnels reached for it like the mandibles of a giant insect. Half the views on the display became black as the shadowed maw engulfed its prey. A soft boom rolled through the bulkheads, then silence fell. They were at the bottom of Hyperabad's gravity well, with nowhere left to go but down.

The terminal was hot, and it stank. Not in any particular way, and it was certainly no more offensive than the close odor of the Jinc vessel, but it had a particular tang to it that Imre immediately associated with planetfall. The air was less filtered, less specifically tailored to humanity's needs, less safe. It was full of spores and organic chemicals and dust. The lining of his lungs reacted instantly to the soup of irritants, making him cough – just once, but it took him by surprise. Respiratory complaints were unknown to his new body.

Then there were the people, as colorful and diverse as any human population on any colony world. He and Freer had stepped from the egress tube into a broad thoroughfare filled with pedestrians. They were the first strangers he had met since waking up in the clutches of the Jinc, and he felt his eyes grow wide in an automatic and undesired reaction. He suppressed it; people were noticing him back. A woman with hooded eyes smoking a cigarette in a darkened niche. A man wearing a long, red coat flicking through a stack of paper bills. A person of indeterminate sex covered in snakeskin banging two shoes together, raising a cloud of yellow dust. He forced himself to keep his gaze forward and concentrate on something else.

Real gravity tugged at his frame. For the first time, he realized just how much taller than him Freer actually was. Imre had to stretch to keep up with Freer's relaxed, swinging gait. He was overclocking as a matter of course. The slow-motion gait of those at Absolute gave the crowd a surreal edge.

People were still looking at him, and that unnerved him. It wasn't supposed to go that way. Crowds were normally the perfect place to hide. His heart began to work as adrenaline powered through him, ready for a trap to spring. Security had been tight enough to forbid them carrying weapons into the airport. Until they found Emlee or another local munitions source, they would be defenseless.

Then he realized that most of the looks were coming from men.

'Ah, crap,' he muttered.

'What's that?' asked Freer, looking sidewise and down at him, as though from a great height.

'Nothing. Let's find somewhere to stay and get the hell out of sight.'

His companion shrugged. 'What's your hurry? We're not even connected to the local grid yet.'

'How could it take so long?'

Even as they walked the broad thoroughfare, ignoring bright, frenetic advertisements on every visible surface, software agents were exchanging handshakes and setting up protocols between their internal systems and those of the megacity. Hyperabad's symbolic environment was much more sluggish than that of the Jinc vessel or the Cat's Arse habitat. Perhaps that had something to do with the number of individuals accessing the environment. Or perhaps, he thought, it was another sign of how the galaxy had devolved from the pre–Slow Wave heights. Once, such software would have been carefully maintained by Forts or their agents, rewritten as needed and edited when bloat threatened to creep in.

There were no such checks and balances now; Primes and singletons were free to tinker and obfuscate as they willed. Even the
standard systems of identification were unraveling. It had been
disturbingly easy to provide fake names and origins, without only
a token attempt to match their faked DNA to the local database.

But why, he wondered, hadn't new mental networks formed to
replace the old? The Loop wasn't the only way for compound intelligences to connect their disparate parts: the Jinc was proof of
that. Perhaps this unchecked clunkiness was a feature only of
Hyperabad, with its innate prejudice against such advancements.
There might be greater minds forming elsewhere in the galaxy,
even now commencing the long, slow restoration of all that had
been lost.

A darker thought came to him, prompted by the experiences of
his former self: not every gestalt had the best interests of humanity at heart. A disconcerting proportion possessed all the
egalitarianism of a militarized Ebola virus. It had been his job,
once, to keep the galaxy free of such. Perhaps the accrued software
junk of Hyperabad was preferable to the alternative.

Algorithms finally meshed. Virtual windows opened in his
mind, allowing him access to local services. More advertisements
came with them, dancing in the corners of his eye. He ignored
them, too, concentrating on finding vehicle hire, accommodation
and network resources instead – until the glimpse of a shockingly
familiar face tripped him up, almost literally.

'Wait.' He reached out and took Freer's arm. The world around
him faded into the background as he pursued the shocking
glimpse. It eluded him for a second, already dumped into transient
memory by automatic processes occurring just below the conscious level. He retrieved the most recent batch of discarded ads
and rifled through them, glancing at the pictures not the text.

He found it: triangular face, full white hair, pale skin, bright
blue eyes staring right out of the picture as though hypnotizing
the viewer.

Himself.

The advertisement came with text:

The old powers are gone but hope remains.
Reclaim the future.
First Church of the Return.

That was it. No links, no contact details, no explanation.

'I think I see what you're seeing,' said Freer. 'Don't get hung up on it. Keep moving.' His hand was on Imre's arm.

'Yes. Keep moving.' He let himself be tugged along, feeling like a fool to be so poleaxed in public. This wasn't what Himself would have done. He should be calm and calculating. He should partition the shock and deal with it later. He should at least watch the crowd as it flowed by him, ready for an actual attack rather than an assault on his sensibilities.

(Render, standing over a spy who had taken a swipe at him with a molecular knife and actually managed to draw blood before being disarmed and pressed facedown into the mud with one arm held high, so far backward Imre could hear the tendons creak.

'God, save me,' the spy pleaded, as Render placed the muzzle of a very large handgun against the back of his skull.

'There is no God,' the big soldier grunted, 'so pray to me.')

They checked out a ground-hugger from a vehicle station near the terminal exit. Fortunately, Hyperabad hadn't devolved so far as to have reinvented money or capitalism. Imre let Freer take the manual controls and propel them along a steep-walled freeway toward the city center, which towered like a glass-and-steel mesa in the near distance. Aircraft buzzed around it like flies. Chenresi's bright, golden light gleamed sickly off a thousand flat surfaces.

The roar of rubber wheels on tarmac, the rush of air going by, the muted growling of the engine, and the tortured throb of blood through his veins: combined, it made a strange symphony for the city, a theme comprised entirely of noise and anxiety, endless and assaulting on every level. Imre felt caught in the throat of a giant jet engine.

'Maybe that's our clue,' he said. The words seemed to come from someone else, far away. 'From Emlee, I mean.'

'Some clue,' Freer muttered. 'It doesn't lead anywhere.'

Helwise had patched in to the local network and found them. Her disembodied voice came like a ghost's from between the car's two front bucket seats. 'I don't think it's her. She wouldn't be so apocalyptic.'

'Who's to say that isn't part of it? If she thinks someone's onto her, she might be worried about her usual methods giving her away.' He could feel himself reaching for explanations that defused the threat of that serene, confident face. 'The purloined letter, Hel. It's right out in the open. No one would expect it to be a call-ing card.'

'I'm conducting a search as we speak,' Helwise said. 'If this "First Church of the Return" isn't real, then it's an elaborate front – with several outlets, a charter, even a representative on the local government. Their leader is a woman called Zadiq Turin – that's "Mother Turin" to her empty-headed acolytes. There are no pictures of her – none anywhere, which is odd for a cult leader. Just your face on all the church's ads.'

'Bergamosques, anyone?' said Freer.

Imre didn't laugh. 'This woman could be Emlee.'

'She was never that good,' said Helwise.

'She's had plenty of time to practice.'

'Well, yes, Imre, I suppose she has at that. Do you want the address of the nearest congregation? You can go straight there and ask, if you like.' Helwise's tone was dismissive.

Imre rubbed at the stiff bristles of his eyebrows with the thumb and forefinger of his right hand. They were still shorter than he was used to, and he became momentarily obsessed with that small detail. Nothing was as it should be; everything had been dis-lodged from its proper place; his life was a complete and utter debacle.

'It could be a trap,' he said.

'Now you're thinking straight.' Helwise's voice prompted a phantom made of sweat and gunpowder and the rumble of distant guns. 'Stick to the original plan. At least wait until nightfall before jumping at shadows.'

'Sorry, guys. It took me by surprise, triggered a flashback.' He sighed. 'You're right, Hel. This is getting old. Every time I think the lid's screwed down, something new escapes.'

'Are you sure they're memories,' asked Freer, glancing away from the road, 'not fantasies?'

'Am I making them up, do you mean? I know a lot of the pieces don't fit together as neatly as my subconscious would like. It would make sense to create mash-ups to smooth over the rough edges.' He pondered this possibility anew while they took a gradual bend, letting inertia push him into the side of the seat. 'Do either of you remember a long campaign on a water world, with giant blimps and trimarans shooting it out over the one and only piece of dry land? Its name was something like "Anita" or "Anaheim."'

'Anahita,' said Freer, nodding. 'Named after a goddess of water.'

'Never heard of the cow,' said Helwise.

'The fight only ended when we nuked the island so no one could have it. Do you remember that part?'

Imre shook his head. 'Was it my idea?'

'The nuke? Yeah. Not a happy ending, but at least it was an ending. That was the important thing.'

'For the Continuum.'

'What?'

'That was the important thing for the Continuum.'

'Od, yes. It was good for the Anahitans, too. When you say it was a long campaign, you're being generous. We spent the best part of a century trying to untie that knot. A little fallout was nothing compared to the damage they were doing to themselves.' Again Freer's gaze flicked to him. 'Don't tell me you're feeling guilty about it all of a sudden.'

'No, not guilty. I just couldn't remember how it had ended.' He didn't say that he was indeed troubled by the absence of any doubt or remorse in his original's mental legacy. Even if the decision itself was gone, there should have been echoes left behind. There was no memory either of what had been on the island and he was afraid to ask what had been lost. A city? A forest? Nothing at all? 'At least we know that some of my memories are real.'

'Whoop-di-fucking-doo,' said Helwise. 'In the meantime, I've found you boys some digs. Sorry, Imre: boy and girl. The Pilxiel Inn is nothing fancy, but it's central and it has good sight lines. Take the next turnoff and I'll guide you there.'

Freer changed lanes. Imre lent half an ear to Helwise's instructions. The rest of him was thinking about the First Church and its 'old powers,' and wondering who or what 'the Return' referred to. Were they working actively to restore the Continuum or just hoping that someone else was? What else could the First Church be referring to when it talked about reclaiming the future?

He dreaded to think what furor might have erupted had he not deleted the message he'd planned to broadcast to all Hyperabad on his arrival in Mandala Supersystem.

Privately he vowed to look more closely into Zadiq Turin and her enigmatic cult.

The Pilxiel Inn was a hulking, black, rectangular structure composited to look as though it was built of volcanic stone. Sandwiched between a looping steel structure with no windows at all and a tower built entirely out of glass, it seemed to draw shadows to it, as though reluctant to reveal its true face.

'Perfect,' Imre said, as Freer swung the ground-hugger down a ramp to the inn's underground car park. 'But this place does have the connections we need, right?'

'Of course,' said Helwise. 'You're booked under the name "Ravenstone." I've secured you a top-floor suite on the northeast corner. The door will open on the voice prompt "hope remains," so you don't need to register at the desk. There's more than a whiff of gangster chic about this place. No questions, no fuss. The big chains could learn from these guys.'

Helwise's familiar patter put Imre into calmer state of mind. He and Freer left the car behind with nothing on them but the clothes on their backs and heads full of sophisticated espial software. It was much cooler inside the building and smelled of dust and earth, with a faint tang of organic cooking in the background. They found a large metal elevator and rode up to the top floor in silence.

There the doors opened onto a wide, sunlit foyer. Dust particles danced in still air, caught in slanted beams from gold-tinted windows. Imre walked through them, feeling like he was shattering something precious.

The suite was spacious and surprisingly tasteful, given the inn's exterior. Floor-to-ceiling windows lined two walls, with various levels of transparency available. The walls were dead, lifeless things, as befitted an establishment whose clients were likely to possess cognitive and sensory modifications. Low couches and tables broke up the expanse of the common room. Two secondary rooms contained beds large enough for three people to sleep without touching. Only one of those rooms contained a view of the looming city. The other had an old-fashioned en suite bathroom instead.

Imre dialed the windows darker. Even in the midst of sky-scrapers and pollution, the sunlight seemed harsh to his ship-accustomed eyes. Days were long on Hyperabad, and the axial tilt was minimal. There were six hours left until nightfall, then another nineteen until daylight returned.

'This will do,' he said. They had only just arrived, but he was already feeling restless. He accessed the inn's room service menu and ordered a selection of drinks ranging from coffee to liquor, all local and all strong.

'Settling in for the long haul, eh?'

'You said it, Hel. Keep hunting for info on that First Church of the Return while Al and I look for Emlee.'

'You got it.'

He took a seat and leaned back with a sigh. Half a billion people; no certainty that Emlee was on the planet at all; people hunting him on at least one front.

'Just like old times,' he breathed.

Closing his eyes, he fell into the embrace of the city.

There was no easy way. Hacking into transit records and pitting search algorithms through countless images of slight, blond-haired Prime females with green eyes was a first step on a very long mile.

Not knowing if Emlee had kept her hair or eye color or even her Prime status made the exercise more difficult. Imre assumed that at the very least she had changed her name.

Corps scrambling techniques were powerful, but he was reluctant to risk too much. Rather than put keywords into local search engines, where they could be monitored and possibly traced, he downloaded entire databases into isolated caches where he could search them himself. Vast quantities of data moved at light-speed along the city's less-frequented information backbones, appearing and disappearing at his whim. Residential records, traffic infringements, visa applications, vocational postings — he even tried social worker and medical case files, just in case she had popped up as a patient somewhere. As a matter of course, he scanned every legal and military database he could access, expecting at any moment to find her face on an execution order or in a police officer's weapon-discharge report. Genetic records and samples could be easily faked or altered; but he checked them too, just in case any of her distinctive sequences had popped up anywhere.

Nothing. The drinks came, and Freer brought the trolley, left anonymously outside the door, into the room. Imre poured himself an Irish coffee, putting the bottles back exactly as they had been when he'd finished. The mix of alcohol and caffeine set his neurons tingling at their base level, below the enhanced buzz of Continuum technology. As the sunlight angled more obliquely across the room, he increased his tempo until he was overclocking at almost five times Absolute. Transmission delays were becoming annoying. He felt a sudden craving for a steak, rare and bloody — the urge coming to him stark and startling from nowhere. Hunger, however, was like any other biological urge: containable, or at least deferrable, for a time.

Six hours passed like twenty-five. He was exhausted by the time the city lights came on outside. Some had never switched off in the deeper recesses of the canyonlike streets. The night sky was invisible, even the sibling suns of Hyperabad's parent star. The view through the window became multicolored and ever-changing, a far cry from the golden stillness of the afternoon. He altered the glass to let light in but not out. Blinking, flashing, twinkling – the city put on its best face in an attempt to lure him into its gleaming trap.

Freer was getting restless. The tall man paced an L-shaped trajectory back and forth along two sides of the room, his route so well rehearsed that he didn't need to watch for obstacles. He hadn't had any luck either. If Emlee was anywhere on Hyperabad, she was keeping her head determinedly down. Even her former colleagues would have trouble finding her if she didn't want to be found.

The next step, one Imre was reluctant to take without a great deal of forethought, was to be more proactive – to call her forth and lay a trail for her to follow back to them, as he had imagined her doing with the First Church of the Return. That plan might easily backfire if less friendly minds were looking for signs of Imre Bergamasc in the region.

Thinking of the cult, he decided to take a short break and see what Helwise had found.

'Does everything in the galaxy have to be about you?' she asked in an exasperated voice.

'What do you mean?'

'Can't you guess? You're only their prophet and savior, the one they expect to lead them into the Promised Land.'

'Me?'

'Yes, you. That's why your face is on all their posters. How does it feel to be needed?'

He didn't know how to take her revelation, not until he had all the information. 'Go back to the start. Tell me why they're making such a fuss.'

'You said you lived in Mandala Supersystem for a while, before the Slow Wave. Turns out you lived right here on Hyperabad. You made friends; you influenced people. Then the Forts died, and everything went to hell. Hyperabad ground to a halt, effectively quarantined by a transport lockdown. People thought it was local. You went to get help but never came back. These poor saps are still waiting for you. Can you believe that? After all this time, they still think you're going to wave a magic wand and make everything right.'

'That's stupid,' said Freer, listening in while he paced.

'It's so naïve it makes me want to gag. That Turin woman needs a fucking slap.'

'It's a cult,' said Imre, feeling distant from the conversation, as though separated from it by a sheet of thick gauze. 'Faith only works when people don't make sense.'

'The point is that they're wasting their lives waiting for something that'll never come. Unless you're planning on delivering anytime soon, I'd say they're likely to be disappointed.'

'Sure, but why are you so personally affronted? It's not like they're making you join or anything.'

'It's just such a waste,' she said, unconvincingly. 'I suppose it could be worse. They could be worshipping Al, or Render.'

Freer stopped pacing and peered through the window at the street below.

'Someone's casing the inn,' he said.

Imre was at his side in a heartbeat. 'Where?'

'There.' Freer pointed at a man in a tattered grey-and-red jumpsuit leaning against a wall one block over. 'He's been there fifteen minutes. Before him, it was a woman with a trolley three meters to his right. Before her, there was another woman with short black hair. Someone's doing their best to be subtle, but they're definitely watching this building.'

'Hel said this place sees some illegal action. It could be a coincidence.'

'You want to take that risk?' Freer's steel grey gaze slid over him like oil on water.

'Absolutely not. Go down there and find out what you can. No need to be subtle. If they're already watching us, we won't lose anything by being up front.'

'And you?'

'I'm going to check the inn's security system.'

'Already doing it,' said Helwise. 'It's clean.'

'Keep an eye on it anyway,' he said, as Freer wordlessly exited the suite. 'Tell me if you see anything unusual. Elevator movements, power interruptions, data spikes.'

'You got it.'

He walked the perimeter of the room, taking its measure mentally as well as physically. There were too many possibilities
turning in his mind. If the people who had attacked the Cat's
Arse had tracked him to the inn, another attack could be immi-
nent. Sitting still might be foolish. However, running could be
worse, depending on how the attack would come. An assassin
could pick him off in the street more easily than from inside a
sealed room. Better to conserve his energy for when it was needed
than expend it unnecessarily.

Freer appeared in the street below, crossing with long strides
through the traffic to where the watcher stood. When Freer was
within five meters, the man turned and hurried off. Freer broke
into a run. Imre leaned closer to the window as both men disappeared down a lane.

Then he stiffened. There had been no sound, no warning. The
air hadn't shifted. No new odors had reached his nostrils; no shadows stirred in the corner of his eye. Helwise had said nothing to
alert him to danger. Yet he knew someone was standing in the
room behind him.

His mind turned furiously, overclocking at the fastest possible
rate. The man in the street had been a distraction, obviously, a ruse
to get him alone so the job could be done with less risk. One
person could do it – the same someone, presumably, who had cut
or bypassed the inn's data feeds, preventing any alarms or early
warnings.

His spine itched. How had it come to this? How had his cautious
plans been so easily overturned? He pictured a dark figure silhouet-
ted in the doorway, gun in hand, taking aim at his back. There
would be no dodging a close-range shot, if that was to be his fate.

Another certainty penetrated his desperate deliberations: only
one person could have got past Helwise while she was on watch.
And if it really was her . . .

'Don't shoot,' he said, gambling what might have been his last
breath on the hope that his instincts were correct. 'I'm sorry we
didn't come sooner, Emlee.'

He detected a faint indrawn breath at the edge of his hearing.

'Who are you? How do you know my real name?'

'I've always known it.' There was no point answering her first question. No one ever believed him at first. 'We fought together a long time ago.'

'I don't remember you. Al must have told you my name. What are you doing here? Why are you looking for me?'

'You called us. We've come to help you rescue Render.'

'What use are you going to be against Kismet?'

'I don't know what that means,' he said, 'but I don't intend to give up on him so easily.'

'That voice . . .' She performed a silent double take. 'You're Imre Bergamasc.'

'Yes, Emlee.'

With four light footfalls, she was on him. The pistol he had imagined clubbed the back of his head, and he went down, skull ringing. Both hands came up to defend him against a second blow, but it was useless. His mind flared with all the lights of the city and he knew no more.

Pelorus was burning. Evacuating the air had done nothing to stop the slow, terrible combustion that the Fort had ignited. Glowing rot ate more and more of ship's spine with every minute. Before long, the magnificent, ship would be gutted from the inside out, like a tree trunk colonized by white ants, leaving only the living hull behind.

He had to get his people to safety. The crew of the ship first, those who were left. Many had died when the fire broke out in engineering, stripping away the mental contacts and implants that had intimately bonded them to the drives they tended, then carbonizing the flesh itself. Others had been crushed as bulkheads failed and molten metal slumped by the ton through cabins and duty stations. Such a weapon was designed as much to decimate and demoralize as it was to destroy. Many would survive, and they would remember what had happened.

They would remember Bergamasc's miscalculation.

Rage, frustration, and shame filled him.

'We're receiving a hail from the Fort flagship,' said Emlee through the smoke on the bridge. Life support was struggling to cope with the sheer amount of heat and air loss. 'They want to talk.'

'Tell them to go to hell,' said Helwise, dripping blood from the ruin of her arm.

'Ask them what they want first,' Imre said.

'I think they want to discuss the terms of our surrender.'

'Who said anything about surrender?' asked Freer.

Imre knew. The hail would be from Factotem. He would have few options but to follow it up. What came next wouldn't be easy, and there would be no going back, but the sheer lack of an alternative was almost reassuring, in its own way. There was no point second-guessing, no reason to debate. It would be finished. Soon.

He looked around the room, at his companions through many, many conflicts. Didn't they deserve an explanation, at least? Shouldn't he try to convince them first?

He already knew how it would pan out, but he had to make the attempt.

'Tell them we're open to suggestion,' he ordered Emlee. 'That should buy us some time.'

'To fight,' said Render, gripping the stock of a Balzac beamer as though strangling it.

Imre shook his head. 'To talk.'

He waited out the inevitable howl of protest before putting his case forward.

'. . . stupid disguise,' Emlee was saying when he stirred. 'Why just him, Al? Why not you too? You're crazy for moving so openly in public.'

'It's not a disguise,' Imre said, struggling to sit up and failing. His hands were bound tightly behind his back. His ankles were also tied and drawn up against his buttocks. He could barely roll over. The world turned around him. 'It's a mistake.'

Emlee came to stand over him. Her hair was short as he remembered but colored black. Her eyes were different too: brown, not green.

'Don't you move an inch,' she said. 'You're not doing anything until I know exactly what you want.'

'Sorry, boss,' said Freer, coming to join her and towering over them both. 'She did this before I got back from chasing that little weasel. When I went to untie you, she threatened to shoot me.'

'I'd do it too,' she said, hefting the powerful Henschke Sloan pistol she had used to knock him out. 'I'm not joking about this.'

'I never said you were joking.' Imre forced himself to relax into his bonds. They were tight and dug deep when he flexed his muscles. 'You're not the joking type.'

'I don't like being patronized either.' She put a solid boot against his shoulder and rolled his torso so he was looking up at her. 'Is Helwise here too?'

'At the airport.' There was no reason to lie. 'The ship's checked in as the *Turnfalken*. Contact her. She'll back up anything Al's already told you.'

Emlee let him go, and he rolled gratefully back onto his side. His beanie lay on the floor where it had fallen. He rested his cheek on it.

'I've no doubt about that,' she said. 'If you've fooled him, then you've definitely fooled her too. I just don't want her calling in the police or making a scene.'

'What makes you think I'm lying?' he asked her. 'What have I ever done to you?'

Her left hand swooped down and twisted his face up to meet hers. Her breath was as hot as the anger in her eyes. 'It's not just what you did, Imre Bergamasc. It's what you didn't do as well. I don't trust you as far as I can spit.'

'That wasn't me. Al, tell her.'

'I don't know, Imre,' Freer said. 'Your old self left Hel on the *Deodati*, and you might as well have left me at Mandala 2, for all the interest you showed. You reckon you're him. Can't have it both ways.'

Emlee tilted her head in grim satisfaction and shoved Imre back to the floor. Her rage was so alien to Imre that he felt he barely knew her. What had happened to her on Hyperabad? What had he done to make her the way she was?

'I did call you,' she said, returning to the salient point, 'but that was a very long time ago. I don't need your help now. I'll get Render on my own. I know where he's being kept, and I know how to get in there. The last thing I need is a couple of deadweights dragging behind me.'

At that, Freer stood straighter. 'Who're you calling a dead-weight?'

'You're out of touch. You walked in the airport as though you owned the place.'

'We didn't think we'd need protection from you,' Imre said.

She looked down at him, then up at Freer. 'Carry him to your car. We're moving.'

'Where to?'

'Somewhere safer. I had to come out from cover to get you. The Hypers might already be on their way, and I'm not going to sit here like a fool, waiting.'

Freer hesitated.

'Do as she says, Al, while the offer stands. She knows the local scene better than we do.'

'It's not an offer,' she said, glaring at both of them.

'Can it, Emlee,' said Freer, looking weary. 'We get the picture.'

With a grunt, he bent down and hoisted Imre onto his shoulder. The beanie stayed on the floor. Both endured in silence the indignity of being led at gunpoint to the elevator.

'Down there.'

Freer did as Emlee ordered, propelling the ground-hugger off the surface road and into an arterial tunnel. Bright lights swept overhead as she tinkered with chips and wiring under the dash — reprogramming the vehicle's registration data, Imre assumed.

'Tell us what happened to Render,' he said from the backseat, still trussed up like a hog.

'Shut up.'

'We want to help.'

'Then shut up. You're ruining my concentration. If they catch sight of this car on the scopes, we're dead meat.'

'You could do this in your sleep, Emlee. If you're so worried about getting caught, why didn't you move earlier? I think you're trying to frighten us – or keep us off balance.'

'I don't care what you think.'

'We both know that isn't true. Why else would we be here?'

She made an exasperated noise.

'Is this something to do with the First Church of the Return?' he asked, following an instinct.

Her head dipped. 'I don't know what's going on any more. It's all so unbelievably pear-shaped.'

They emerged from the tunnel and reentered the light-speckled ambience of the city. Emlee stuffed a tangle of fine wires back under the dash and issued more instructions for Freer.

'Shouldn't we be blindfolded?' he asked her.

She didn't take the bait. 'We change our rendezvous point every night. Don't think this is going to gain you an advantage.'

She guided them along one-way streets and lanes leading ever deeper into the close congregation of skyscrapers. Imre watched the lights through the side windows, unable to sit up and take in the view properly. He memorized street signs and noted land-marks, just in case he would need them later. He saw no sign of aerial pursuit or ambush.

'How do you know Render's still alive?' he asked.

'That's none of your business.'

'I mean, it's been a long time since you sent that message, telling us he was facing the death penalty. He could have been killed years ago.'

'I said—'

'Yet here you are, all fired up as though he'd been captured yes-terday. Why is that, Emlee? What makes you so certain? Do you have a reason, or are you just desperate to believe in something, even if it's not really anything at all?'

She didn't turn around. She didn't speak, and neither did Freer. Another voice entirely broke the tense silence – a ghastly whisper that seemed to come from the wrong side of the grave.

'Tell my friends, wherever they are,' it said. 'Help me. I'll be waiting for you. This is my nightmare, and you're my solution. I've been expecting you. I'm not asking for a miracle. I've nothing to lose. If I surrender, will you come for me? If I believed – if I forgive—?' The speaker made an awful choking sound. 'I'll believe in you when you come for me. I'll believe in you when the world comes apart. If you come for me . . .'

Silence for a heartbeat, then: 'She scares me. There is no calm in here. I've been waiting for so long now. I've waited years. I've waited all my life for you. I'm so sick with need. I'm trying hard to forgive. But you don't care.' Anger mixed with desperation made the voice louder, yet that only emphasized the tremor, the weakness in every syllable. 'Abandon me. Walk away from me. I don't care. I've seen the guards and the danger. I'm not crawling around, looking for a friend. I'm so sick with pain. I'm trying to hide my scars. I'm talking to you. I'm just trying to survive.

'I am just a voice that no one else will hear.'

The monologue ended with an abrupt click, as though an audio file had been poorly edited.

Freer shifted uncomfortably in the driver's seat. 'Is that really—?'

'Render, yes. I receive files like this every month or so. Anonymously, always. There's no other pattern. The last one came twenty-five days ago.'

'I barely recognize him,' Imre said. 'Who's he talking to?'

'No one. For the sound of his own voice, I think. In the last one he—' She swallowed. 'He's not doing well, anyway, and getting worse. I think they've been trying to Flex him.'

'Who's "they"? The Hypers?'

Her voice hardened. 'I don't have to tell you anything. I don't need you. All I have to do is keep you out of the way until I've got the job done. The worst thing you could do right now is distract me.'

Imre didn't waste his breath arguing. Her mind was so obviously made up on that point that forcing the issue would get them nowhere. There were, however, numerous small battles to engage in before the time came to tackle the war.

'Will you let us talk to Helwise?' he asked. 'She'd probably appreciate that.'

'She can hear us,' Emlee said. 'That's all she needs.'

I'm sure she'd disagree, Imre thought to himself, but so be it.

Freer forced their way through a maze of lanes so narrow the ground-hugger lost a centimeter of girth along the way. The deeper they went, the darker it became and the farther behind them the forest of neon and LCD seemed. Their wheels crunched over drifts of rubbish that might not have been disturbed for decades. Many of the ground-floor windows were permanently opaque, or layered over with graffiti. An ever-present hum of traffic filled every silence, with the occasional human voice rising like birdsong from the urban jungle.

They came, ultimately, to a strange, forgotten space between buildings, one that had somehow managed to avoid the rubbish, the homeless, and the graffiti artists. No windows or doors opened onto it; no light cast a shadow. Yet it was surprisingly expansive, with room for five or more of the ground-huggers. Someone had tiled one wall with a crude depiction of a blue-tinged sunset, now faded by time, as well as the lane they had followed to get there, a narrow crack broad enough for two people promised a second route back to civilization.

There was no one else at the rendezvous point.

'Wait here.' Emlee jumped out and performed a quick survey of the area. She returned empty-handed. 'No note. No sign that it's been compromised.' She exhaled once. 'We wait.'

'Fine,' said Freer, turning off the engine. 'We've got nowhere else to be.'

'If you'd consider loosening the knots,' Imre said, rocking his tightly bound body from side to side, 'I'd be grateful.'

Emlee slipped a knife from under her jacket and reached back.

With three quick slashes, his legs, feet and arms were free. His wrists, however, remained tightly bound.

'Thanks.' He sat up and gratefully flexed his back. He had been in more uncomfortable positions for longer, but that didn't mean he enjoyed it. 'I mean it, Emlee. I am grateful to you for doing that. You didn't have to.'

'Don't be a toady,' she snapped. 'It doesn't suit you.'

He ignored her. 'Listen to me. I want you to hear something.' In a few sentences, he summarized the reality of his situation: re-created from dust on the edge of the galaxy by a god-hunting gestalt; incomplete, so he could never be sure if the memories he had were anything other than plausible re-creations; more ignorant than anyone else on the actions and motives of Himself after the fall of *Pelorus*; mistrusted by his friends and hunted by murderers claiming that he might not be who he thought he was. 'So forgive me if I'm grateful for receiving a simple courtesy. It's more than I've had in my entire life, this time around.'

Her gaze stayed fixedly forward. 'I'm not going to give you any sympathy, if that's what you want. You've had too many lives already and done terrible things in all of them. I don't believe that you are the exception to the rule.'

'You're not being asked to, Emlee. We just came here to help you rescue Render. I don't understand why you won't let us.'

'Because,' she snapped, 'I don't believe you have an altruistic bone in your body.'

'You think I'm going to turn this to my advantage?'

'No. I think you're going to ditch us as soon as you find something more important to do.'

'There's no way I can prove you wrong if you won't let me, is there?'

'I'm under no obligation to give you the opportunity.'

'Okay, but don't damn Al and Helwise with me. At least give them the chance to help Render. He was their friend too.'

'I don't think Render was anyone's friend, really,' said Freer. 'An ally, yes, undoubtedly — but I never got the feeling he cared much about any of us.'

Emlee turned to study him. 'Do you believe that?'

'Are you telling me I shouldn't?'

She sighed and looked down at her lap. Her right hand hefted the weight of the Henschke Sloan she'd kept handy ever since they'd left the Pilxiel Inn.

'Were you lovers?' asked Imre softly.

'Ha.' Her laugh was a bark as contained as a punch to the mouth. 'Now, that I can't imagine. But he was a better friend than any of you three.'

'Come on, Emlee,' Freer encouraged her. 'We've time to kill.'

She hefted the gun again and, talking to it rather than the others in the car, began to tell her story.

'I was stationed here after the Chaos War, picking up the pieces after the Alienist Technarchy. We—'

'Wait.' Freer leaned forward. Someone in a red-and-grey jump-suit had run out of the crack ahead of them and scrambled to a halt directly in front of the ground-hugger.

Emlee raised her handgun, then relaxed. 'That's only Deesticker,' she said. 'The guy you chased away from the inn, Al.'

'Yeah, I recognize him.'

'Wait here,' she said, opening the door and dropping from the car. She and the new arrival talked for a moment, too softly for Imre to make out. The dusty-looking fellow had wispy hair that stuck out around the ears and weathered features. His hands moved quickly and often.

'What are you thinking, boss?' Freer asked him. 'Does this seem as crazy to you as it does to me? Emlee going all commando and cutting us out of the action? It's not right.'

'I'm thinking we're all screwed up, one way or another, and we shouldn't judge her too harshly.' He leaned forward and put his elbows on the back of Emlee's seat. 'Emlee's right. You, me, and Helwise – we've been AWOL for too long. I've been dead; you've been in the Cat's Arse; Hel was in transit on the *Deodati*. Emlee has been deep in the thick of it, tangled up in who-knows-what here in Hyperabad. She'll have seen things we've missed completely. Her perspective is important. We've got to honor her for that.'

'I guess.'

Emlee finished her conversation and hopped back into the car. The man called Deesticker danced lightly through the dust, back into the crack and out of sight.

'Dee says he wasn't followed,' she told them, 'but he doesn't know where the others are either. They should be here by now. He's going to go rustle them up. They might have been delayed.'

'Unavoidably detained,' said Freer, 'like we were.'

'There's a big different between a few hours and a few thousand years.'

'Is that how long it's been?'

Emlee didn't smile.

'Tell me why you're angry,' Imre said.

She sagged back into her seat and picked up from where she had been interrupted.

We were all in Hyperabad at one time or another, not just me: Al, Imre, Helwise, and Render. This wasn't such a backwater back then. People liked us; we'd helped them with the Alienist Technarchy, and they had long memories. The feeling was mutual. I fit in better here than I did elsewhere. Being a Prime is difficult sometimes; people make assumptions. I don't like that.

The system did well under the Forts, before and after the Mad Times. We didn't see many frags moving en masse, as we had in the old days, and their owners kept the grisly details behind closed doors. There were exceptions. Rumors of flesh dumps still circulated: ships and cities, sometimes whole planets left to rot when their uses had run out. They might have been old news, though. It was hard to tell. You know how word used to spread around the Continuum: a hundred thousand years from one side to another; by the time it came back to you, you might not remember saying it even if it bore any resemblance to what you originally said, which was unlikely.

I still hear whispers now, when I hack into the Line: of vast machines carrying out the last orders the Forts gave them before they died; of frags going through the motions by reflex, even though their collective heads have been cut off; of Forts rebuilding themselves piece by piece, in preparation for a counterstrike. Never seen evidence of such myself, and until I do, I won't believe it.

There was something, though, just before the Slow Wave hit: a hint of big things going on in the background. I was tracking signals originating outside the supersystem, looking for meme-line viruses from Old Wilde, when a slice of a message came for you, Imre. I almost didn't notice it, it was so cut up and distorted. But your name was clearly mentioned, so I brought it to your attention.

I don't have the message any more. I erased it, thinking it irrelevant, long ago. I've been bothered by it ever since. One word in particular, endlessly nagging at me:

'Domgard.'

(Imre sat up straighter. He saw Freer do the same.)

'What does that mean?' I asked you.

'It doesn't mean anything,' you said. 'It's just a name.'

'The name of what?'

'The greatest experiment ever undertaken,' you told me, and that was all I would ever get from you on that subject.

But it wasn't the last time I heard the word. After the Slow Wave, everything went crazy. The Hypers decided to restore some of the networks lost in the Slow Wave by building from gestalts up, hoping to create something to fill the gap left by the Forts. It was painful work. I was pulled out of hard-storage – where I'd gone to wait out the worst of it – because they were using the backbones we had put in place after the Chaos War, and they needed my help maintaining them. That was it, at first. I was just a consultant, doing what I could to restore the status quo. As much as I'd disliked the Forts, once, I could see that in some circumstances they were better at doing things we needed – necessary, even. I worked with a cyberneticist called Pam Anders on adapting the backbones to homegrown systems. She was a singleton and keen to reconnect with versions of herself in other systems. A lot of people were like that, orphaned when the Line jammed up and traffic ground to a halt. I sympathized: being

stuck on Hyperabad forever hadn't been part of my original plan
either.

It went well at first. Pam was the right person in the right
place. When the time came to seek volunteers for the next stage of
the reclamation project, she put up her hand. I tried to talk her out
of it. Becoming a Fort isn't like becoming a singleton. They were
going to take her mind apart and give it an entirely new architecture. People have died in the process. She ignored me and proved
my worries unfounded. She took to the processes as though she'd
been born to them, making it from singleton to gestalt and ultimately Graduating into something that did indeed look and think
very much like a Fort. Her tempo slowed; her thoughts grew
deeper, longer. She even took a trick name for dealing with plebs:
Ampersand, an anagram of her old name, and a word that actually
meant something too.

She didn't hold it against me that I'd thought she was doing the
wrong thing. If anything, it brought us closer together. The
Hypers didn't really care about what she was going through; they
just wanted the end result. While she went to work repairing the
communications and data-collection networks so we could look
properly at the damage, she talked to me about how it felt to have
a whole world resting on her shoulders – and in her head too
because she was tapped into every grid in the system by that point.
She became Hyperabad and Hyperabad became her. Sometimes she
could convey how it felt to a Prime like me; sometimes she didn't
even want to try. But she had to talk to someone, and I was it. She
thought of me as a confidante, a friend. She had no one else.

For the first time, I could see what the Forts really were. They
weren't heartless monsters, cold and calculating. They had feelings
so vast we simply didn't see them. They were human too. This one
was, anyway.

For a while, Ampersand was on her own. The attempts to make
others like her failed as often as they succeeded. One or two other
minds limped into being. She helped them, becoming a mother to
them as well as to the planet. Order began to seem possible, finally,
in the midst of bedlam.

Then we were attacked again. I say 'again' because I'm certain the Slow Wave was a weapon. I can't tell you exactly how it worked, but its effects were too specific to be natural. Like a neutron bomb kills the people in a city while leaving the buildings intact, so too did the Slow Wave massacre the Forts alone, and the rest of the galaxy goes on. Why just the Forts? Because it's exactly as you said in *Pelorus*, Imre: they were the big players, the ones who really mattered. With them taken out, humanity is helpless. Vulnerable.

These are the salient facts. (Emlee's brisk, businesslike tone hid emotion Imre couldn't guess at her. Her years as the Corps signals officer had trained her too well in the art of impersonal communications.) It happened over a couple of years. Just like the Slow Wave, no one saw it coming until it was upon us. It was nothing like the original attack, though. This was focused, not indiscriminate: a bullet to the head rather than a neutron bomb. The head in question belonged to Ampersand, and the bullet was an assassin picking her frags off one by one. It looked like a series of accidents at first, then bad luck; then the government suspected internal agitators who saw the proto-Forts as competition or impediment to corruption, or a militant group still disgruntled by the Alienist Technarchy. One minister even raised the possibility of war between Ampersand and the other proto-Forts. Such certainly hadn't been unknown before the Slow Wave. She herself, however, declared that impossible. She wasn't a threat to the others. They were weak things, still finding their feet. Without her helping them, they would've collapsed.

The attack, therefore, had to be coming from the outside. Someone had seen our attempts to rebuild what had been lost and taken steps to stop us in our tracks.

As soon as we realized what was going on, I took myself off technical duties and formed a bodyguard squad. Ampersand had lost eleven frags by then. Only twenty-five remained. A third of her, basically, was gone. She was definitely feeling the bite. I had unlimited resources, but it was a difficult job. I couldn't be everywhere, and we couldn't put all of her in one spot lest she be taken out with a single hit.

('What about us?' asked Freer. 'Where were we?'

Emlee's expression, which had been growing darker through the telling of her story, grew blacker still. 'By the time I came out of hard-storage, I only had Render left. Several versions of you, Al, had come through Hyperabad after the Slow Wave, but you kept merging into one and taking off again, which was no help. Imre was long gone.' Her jaw worked. 'There had been two Helwises at one point, but a shuttle accident had taken out both of them.'

'Are you sure it was an accident?'

'What do you mean?' She frowned. 'That they were murdered?'

'Nothing.' Freer shook his head. 'Go on.')

So I'm on bodyguard detail for one person in twenty-five bodies, doing my best to keep track of the frags as they go from place to place. Even with a gun to her head, Ampersand wouldn't stop working. It was she who connected the Slow Wave with her gradual assassination. She had her collective fingers on the pulse of Hyperabad, and not much got by her.

'There's something odd building,' she told me the last time I saw her. 'This Church of the Return. Have you heard of it?'

I told her the truth: that I hadn't. She explained that it was a new sect rising in the poorer districts of the city. It was just the 'Church of the Return' in those days, no 'First' about it, and there was no mention of you, Imre. It had probably formed in response to the Hypers' attempt to rebuild the Forts.

'It's nice to be appreciated,' Ampersand said, 'but I'm not comfortable with the idea of being worshipped.'

'You won't see me kowtowing in a hurry.'

'I hope not. That's neither needed nor wanted.'

I remember exactly where we had this conversation. We were in the building her original had lived in before Graduating. Once she'd owned a single top-floor apartment; we'd eaten there a couple of times; she'd even cooked. Now all four apartments contained frags – not just hers but some belonging to two of the other proto-Forts the Hypers were building as well. It was a beautiful building set on the edge of the city's inner ring, with a high, curved roof of glass that caught the light of Chenresi every

evening. The southern sky was clear, so you could see the other
suns rising and setting. The walls were covered with real art: nothing electronic or mutable; genuine paintings, sketches, and
hangings from all over the planet. The frags had knocked out
walls where possible, creating an open, accessible space that would
have been noisy if normal people lived there. As it was, the frags
were silent unless they had visitors. They didn't play music or
argue. They came and went, following their own arcane needs.

There were times when I admired the peace of that house too
much. It was so calm and industrious, so untouched by human
chaos.

'What would you do if I said I wanted to join in?' I asked her.

'The Church? I'd think you were insane.'

'No. You and me, as a gestalt.'

'To be honest, I'd think the same thing.'

'Why? I've heard of people joining gestalts — even known a
few, before I moved here. Becoming one would make tracking
you easier because I could live through all your senses at once.
You'd also be better equipped to fight back, with my experience
behind you.'

('I can't believe I'm hearing this,' said Freer, the fingers of his
right hand drumming on the manual steering column. 'You're a
Prime. You don't join gestalts.'

'Why not?' Emlee adjusted the fastenings of her camouflage
top and didn't meet his eye. 'People change.'

'Not you. That'd be like Render taking up origami.'

'Let her continue,' Imre told Freer, sensing Emlee's need to
finish what she had started.)

'It wouldn't be like that, Emlee,' Ampersand told me.

'I thought that was the whole point of forming a gestalt, to
share knowledge around.'

'I mean it wouldn't be that simple. I'm more than a haphazard
assemblage of random parts. I'm me, Pam Anders, multiplied on
a grand scale. More than multiplied: I am expanded exponentially.
To add you to the mix would be like putting salt in a sugar solution. It would ruin the chemistry that is Ampersand and create

someone else, someone who might not function as smoothly or consistently, or might not be willing to cooperate with her fellow citizens quite so well.'

She smiled. Ampersand's frags had such beautiful clear eyes. They were almost colorless. Her skin was as white as chalk, and her jaw looked as though it'd shatter if she so much as coughed. This frag had long, blond hair bound up in a bun; I'd seen others wearing different styles, but I liked this one the best, even as she turned me down.

'Don't you want me?' I asked her.

'You are your own person, Emlee,' she told me, taking my hand in both of hers. 'That's one of the many things that make you who you are: your independence; your clear sense of self. Don't ever turn your back on that. Don't ever be who you aren't. I couldn't bear it. Just because Ampersand can't take you into herself doesn't mean she doesn't like you very much, just the way you are.'

That night, Ampersand's compound was attacked. I was awake; security was tight; Ampersand and the others didn't keep to regular hours, so there was no question of anyone being taken off guard. It made no difference. They came at us from all directions, head-on. One moment it was as quiet as the city ever got. The next it was like being under siege. Windows and walls were blowing in. Half of the frags went down in the opening seconds. Blood was everywhere. This was no subtle, sly assassination. This was a concerted operation with one goal only.

I gathered the frags and took shelter in the heart of the building. We had a weapons stash; we weren't defenseless. Our lines of communication were still open, and we soon learned that the other compounds were also under attack. The Hyper security forces were scrambling, but they were going to be stretched thin. We had to force our attackers back or at least hold them off until help arrived.

We did better than we should've. I was overclocking. Ampersand and the others could see in every direction at once. We were outnumbered, though, and surrounded. Our enemies weren't all human. There were humans out there – to the north, in an armored truck – but the rest were AI drones of some kind, ones I'd never seen before.

They had active camouflage, which made them hard to spot, but when you hit them they took on a kind of shape. They were silver, like mercury, and cannonball-sized.

That's right, Imre. Silver, and deadly. They moved fast around the perimeter. Stick your head out for too long, and they'd laser it right off. They could also sneak through gaps in the masonry and come up from below. I even saw one blow itself up to take out one of Ampersand's frags. Mean.

The seconds were dragging by. As fast as backup was coming, I knew it wasn't going to arrive quickly enough. I tried hacking into the spheres' comms but couldn't get a fix on their signals. Drones are normally noisy, chattering across every available band. These were eerily quiet, like they weren't talking at all. It freaked me out a little, and still does, to be honest.

I thought it was all over when the human contingent moved out from under cover with weapons blazing. One of Ampersand's frags came to stand next to me, the one I liked best. She raised her pistol with her right hand and gripped my shoulder with her left. There was no time to say anything stupid like: if we couldn't live as one, at least we could die as one.

Then I realized that the humans weren't firing at us. They were shooting at the spheres. I stood up and added my fire to theirs, hoping to catch the spheres in a pincer. I didn't know who our unexpected allies were – their uniforms were black and unmarked, their helmet visors impenetrable. It didn't matter. Our defeat suddenly turned into a chance for victory, and I was going to take it with both hands.

The frags joined in, following my lead. The first of the humans leapt our defenses and came straight to me. I can't remember what I said to him; some stupid line about being late to the party, I think.

'Signals Officer Emlee Indira Copas,' he said, pulling me back behind cover, 'we have the situation in hand now. If you come with me, we'll get you to safety.'

'What do you mean, get me to safety? We'll handle this together now you're here.'

'With respect, you don't know what you're dealing with,' he told me. 'The Luminous won't give up without a fight.'

'The who?'

'I'll explain in a moment. Follow me.'

With that, he was up and firing again, clearing a path through the playing field back to the truck he'd come from. There was no reason not to believe him. Whoever or whatever the Luminous were, I figured he was part of some crack team set up to deal with them. I hesitated only a moment before following, laying down a dense covering fire that saw him halfway to safety before the spheres fought back.

Ampersand's frag came with me. I had no choice, really: she was hanging on to me like a limpet. It wasn't until later that I recognized the look on her face as one of fear: mortal fear, for all across Hyperabad her frags were dying, shot down or blown up by the silver spheres — and she was dying with them, bit by bit. One of the other sites was taken out by a small nuke, but I didn't know that then. I had my eyes on the way ahead and the targets all around us. The cavalry might have arrived, but there were still plenty of hostiles to go around.

We made it under cover. I was impressed by the amount of equipment the new arrivals had bought: weapons and surveillance tech; support staff and grunts. There must have been a dozen people under cover and as many again out on the field. They hadn't just happened on our situation; they had been waiting for it.

'Who are you people?' I asked, wondering why I'd never heard of such a group before.

'It doesn't matter who we are.' The leader whistled in a distinctive recall-the-troops way. 'Keep your head down. It'll be over in a moment.'

'Wait.' From behind us, I could hear the sound of explosions and falling masonry. 'The job's not finished yet.'

'It is for us.'

'But Ampersand – the Luminous—'

'They'll sort each other out. You don't need to worry about them any more.'

Nothing could have been further from the truth. Before I could tell him that, however, the frag pushed between us. Her face was ghastly: so pale it looked completely bloodless; its only color was around its eyes and a hot patch on each cheek.

'I recognize you,' she told him through her fear. 'I know who you are. You call yourselves the Barons. Whispers, echoes, rumors – that's all I thought you were. You and Domgard both. But you're real, and you're here. You're here!'

'Too late,' he said. 'The Luminous should never have been drawn into this. We were supposed to intervene before you Graduated, but the traffic embargo kept us out.'

'Yes,' she said. 'Yes. I see that now.'

'Why?' I asked. 'What difference would that have made?'

Both of them turned to me. I felt two years old, trying to understand a conversation between adults.

'You said you'd explain,' I told the man, wanting to grab him by the chest plating and shake the truth out of him.

Ampersand lunged so quickly my eyes barely registered the movement. She had the Baron's pistol in a split second and had turned it on herself in another. The recoil knocked the gun right out of her fingers. The top of her skull exploded. I recoiled as though shot myself. Her body dropped in slow motion, I was overclocking so hard.

'I lied,' the Baron said to me, before her body hit the ground.

I went for him, but at that moment the compound exploded. It went up like a fireworks factory, with lots of pyrotechnics and smoke. The truck shielded me from the worst of it, but I was still blown away like so much rubble. Afterward I saw a metal spike sticking out of the ground like a spear, and a foot lying in the middle of the road with the rest of the body missing. Smoke was everywhere. By the time I staggered to my feet, it was too late. The Barons were gone, the Luminous with them, the Hyper security forces had arrived, and all around the world all of Ampersand was dead.

Emlee sat still for a moment, breathing heavily as though fighting nausea.

'Afterward, I thought I had all the time in the galaxy to agonize over what had happened. I began digging, looking for anything about the Barons or the Luminous. I found nothing at all, which was as compelling evidence of their existence as having one of either in front of me. "Nothing" doesn't exist, as a concept. The galaxy is full of spurious data that pop out of nowhere and disappear as mysteriously. All things are mentioned, unless deleted. Someone was therefore deleting all references to both Luminous and the Barons – and who would do that apart from the conspirators themselves?

'That chain of logic didn't go down very well with the Hypers. They had a bloody circus on their hands. The whole Fort project had been ruined, and they needed something other than shadowy conspiracies to blame. I found evidence that the original assassinations were the work of different people involved in the final conflagration – the Luminous, it seemed, had finished what the Barons had started – but that didn't get anyone off the hook. I didn't realize then just how close to home the Hypers were fishing.'

'A Prime conspiracy,' said Freer. 'You should've seen it coming.'

'I should've, yes, but I had other things on my mind, like trying to avenge my friend. Ampersand was never coming back. It didn't matter who had actually pulled the final trigger. The Luminous and the Barons were equally guilty, and I would bring them to justice.

'Instead,' Emlee said, gripping the stock of her pistol so tightly white showed on her knuckles, 'instead the Hypers went for Render. He had been with some of the frags during the final attack. He had even been injured, and was recovering in hospital, walking off his wounds in slow mo. They took him anyway, dropping him like an animal with a nonlethal dart while he was out one dusk. He managed to get off a warning before they whisked him away, thinking they'd come after me next. They didn't at first, not until I started kicking up a fuss. There had never been a Prime conspiracy to get rid of the new Forts – nothing that would have made a difference, anyway – but the Hypers had their scapegoat, and they weren't letting go of him. That's when I sent out that SOS, in the hope that one of you might hear. I didn't think I had the time to mount a legal challenge, and I knew I couldn't rescue him on my own. When I became too much of a problem, the Hypers took me too and branded me with the same crimes.

'Bad enough that I had watched Ampersand die,' she said. 'Now I was accused of her murder – and, unlike Render, I had no one to stand up for me. I was alone.'

'Hold on a sec.' The drumming of Freer's fingers had started up again. The martial rhythm put Imre on edge. 'If they arrested you too, how come you're here and Render's not? Don't tell me you testified against him—'

'Don't be stupid,' she snapped. 'I'd never do that. I was convicted, just like him, and sent to Kismet to await execution. That's what I was told would happen, anyway. I had interfered with the grand plan to bring back civilization. I was worse than any mere murderer or terrorist. Me and all my so-called conspirators would be made an example of, one by one, so anybody who dared question the regime again would think twice before acting on it. Blah bloody blah.'

'So what happened?' asked Imre, feeling as though he understood her a little better now. 'Did you escape?'

'You don't escape from Kismet,' she said in a flat voice. 'I was set free. Don't ask by whom. I don't know. One minute I'm in confinement, expecting a round through my skull. The next I'm being escorted to a shuttle and brought back here. No explanations, no excuses, no apologies. No pardon, even. Turns out I'm still wanted on a dozen or so charges, which is the main reason I can't show myself in public or go back into hard-storage. What's the point of getting arrested so I can end up in Kismet again, back where I started? I get the feeling someone's playing a game with me, testing me, waiting to see which way I'm going to jump. Regardless, I'll work on springing Render. He's still in there. Those recordings didn't come from nowhere. While he continues to suffer, I have hope.'

'Do you think the person who let you out is the same one who sends those recordings?' Freer asked.

She shrugged. 'Maybe, maybe not.'

'Both of them obviously have some pull with Kismet – and they must both be prepared to go out on a limb for someone like you. One I could believe; two I'd think unlikely.'

'Believe me, I've been following that reasoning along every possible angle. There's only one person I saw in Kismet who wasn't part of the security staff. She breezed through a couple of times to talk to the reprobates. I got the impression she does it fairly regularly.'

'Who?'

'Mother Turin of the First Church. Big woman; wears a full burqua everywhere she goes, so no one has ever seen her face.'

Imre let that sink in for a moment. Again he sensed connections and vectors closing in around them, chains of causality leading him from one unlikely destination to another. Emlee's SOS had led him to Hyperabad, where he had seen his own face on a First Church of the Return advertisement. Now the matriarch of that cult had turned up in the place where Render and Emlee had been held prisoner.

'What exactly is Kismet?' he asked. 'Why's it so difficult to escape?'

'High-security penal habitat,' Emlee said. 'It's—' She stopped and peered through the windscreen.

'What?' asked Freer, doing likewise.

Imre could discern nothing untoward in the city's forgotten space.

'Dee has been gone too long,' she said. 'Helwise, are you seeing any unusual traffic?' Emlee was silent for a moment. 'Of course I don't entirely trust you, but I do still have Imre hostage. Remember that.' She hefted her pistol. 'Al, get us moving. Something's up, and I'm not sitting here to find out what it is.'

The ground-hugger started with an electric growl.

'Let me talk to Helwise,' Imre told Emlee.

'She hears you just fine already.'

He swallowed his frustration. 'I think she should move the ship too. If we've been compromised, so has she. Lose the ship, and we're trapped here.'

Even as he said the words, he thought of the silver sphere in the Jinc vessel and the drones Emlee had called the Luminous. Another connection, one he hadn't had time to process yet. If the silver sphere and the Luminous were one and the same, and if the Luminous were actively hostile to any revival of Forts and the Continuum, how did that connect with him and his rescue from the Jinc? He had once fought against the Forts. Would that be enough to make the Luminous an ally? Was that why one had given him a ship, gratis – even though he had changed his mind after the Mad Times?

Then another thought occurred to him. The people who had come for him at the Cat's Arse – claiming he was a wanted man – had somehow known exactly where he was. There was only one possible way for that information to have leaked. Either Helwise or Freer had called them, or . . .

'No, wait,' he said. 'I take that back. Stay right where you are, Hel. Moving will only confirm that we're suspicious. There's something else I need you to do while you're in dry dock. Go over the ship from stern to tail. Look in every subsystem, every black box. Leave nothing unturned.'

'She wants to know what she's looking for,' Emlee told him.

'Something that isn't showing on the systems we have access to. Something we couldn't see working, even if we were looking for it. Something that's been giving me away ever since I left the Jinc and is still broadcasting now, right under your nose.' He nodded, more certain of it with every second. 'There's a Loop shunt somewhere aboard *The Cauld Lad*. Find it but don't knock it out. Maybe we can use it to our advantage. Okay?'

Freer was staring at him with his hands on the steering wheel, not driving anywhere. The engine hummed with patient restraint. Emlee listened to Helwise's reply, then relayed it to Imre.

'She thinks you're paranoid, but she'll do what you ask.' Emlee nodded approvingly. 'Paranoia is good. It's the only way to see the knives coming.'

'Seeing them is the easy part sometimes,' he said. 'Avoiding them all is much harder.'

She opened her mouth to say something but was interrupted by a light that turned the night into day.

'Get out of the car with your hands on your heads,' boomed a voice from the sky. 'Leave your weapons inside. You have five seconds Absolute to comply.'

Imre overclocked automatically and felt Freer and Emlee doing the same.

'Hypers!' she said. 'Drive!'

Freer pushed the steering column forward. The ground-hugger moved as though through treacle. A rain of energy fire fenced off the lane through which they had come – but that wasn't the direction Freer was headed. Directly ahead loomed the crack between buildings through which Emlee's ally Deesticker had disappeared. It was far too narrow for the ground-hugger.

The muscles of Imre's arms chorused in complaint as he lunged between the bucket seats and pulled Emlee's Henschke Sloan from her hands. His wrists were still tied together, but his tempo was slightly ahead of hers, giving him an advantage. She had time only to open her mouth before he raised the gun and fired two rounds through the car's plastic window. It shattered with a noise like a plank of wood being torn in half.

He jumped as the fenders of the ground-hugger made contact with the sides of the crack. Momentum did the rest. He rolled in a shower of plastic shards through the air, turning with the grace of an underwater ballet dancer between the seats, through the window and out into clear air. Every fiber of his body screamed at the demands placed on it. Overclocking was good for talking and planning, but acrobatics were discouraged.

He landed so hard he thought for a second he might have broken both ankles. Stumble, recover – he didn't fight his reflexes. His hands swung up, holding the gun. Above the ground-hugger – still crunching into the concrete walls – hung an armored vehicle on airjets, engines lowing in an unnaturally deep register. White lights burned red. Orange flashes of weapons fire painted dangerous constellations against the cityscape.

He fired three times, taking out two of the spotlights. Then

Freer and Emlee were out of the car too and running past him, up
the crack. He put two rounds into the hood of the ground-hugger,
aiming for batteries, hydrogen tank, anything volatile. With all
the grace of a nature documentary, the vehicle sprouted a giant,
fiery flower. Finally, he turned and ran.

One crack led to another, and another. He felt like a sentient rat
running through the crevices of the city maze. Threads of blue sky
were pinned overhead between hundreds of meters of parallel
walls. Occasionally, he caught a glimpse of the aerial armored
vehicle, or an AAV very much like it, as they crossed broader thor-
oughfares or relatively open spaces. Beams of light reached for
them from above like insect antennae, flicking and touching, then
fell behind.

Imre was content to run at Emlee's tempo. Sprinting at less
than full stretch gave him a chance to think. She had produced
another pistol from under her jacket. They didn't draw attention to
themselves by firing any further, but it was good to know they had
something to fight with if it came down to that. Three people, one
of them unarmed, against a flying tank and an unknown number
of assailants didn't make good odds. They would be better off
running and going to ground than making a stand and dying.

One thought nagged at him, though.

'They could have killed us,' he said as they weaved down a tight
crevice lined with pipes and plastic crates. 'They had a clear shot
when we were in the ground-hugger. If they wanted us dead, they
would've taken us out then.'

'You think we're of value to them?' Freer asked over his shoulder. He ran with long, loping strides between Imre and Emlee.

'One of us is,' said Emlee from the fore of their small formation.

'All of us or one of us,' said Imre with a flash of irritation, 'the
fact remains: they issued a warning. There's a limit to what they'll
do. That gives us an edge.'

'Because there's no limit to what you'll do,' Emlee said. It wasn't
a question.

'This isn't the right time for an argument on morality,' Freer said to her. 'Are we heading somewhere in particular, or are you just taking us in circles?'

She ducked under a nest of multicolored tubes connecting one building to another like the corpus callosum between two brain hemispheres. 'I always have a bolt-hole ready in the case of disaster. You taught me that, Imre.'

He nodded even though he had no recollection of ever saying such a thing. It struck him as common sense. 'Is Helwise all right?'

'Coming through loud and clear. They've made no move at her end.'

'Good,' he said. 'Tell her to keep the drive warm for a fast dustoff, in case we need it.'

'The drives are more than ready. I had to talk her out of coming for us when you blew the ground-hugger.'

'Thank you,' he said. 'The last thing we need is her violating airspace regulations. Tell her to sit tight and keep looking for that Loop shunt.'

They came to a metal hatch opening onto a stairwell leading down into a building on their right. Emlee checked to make sure no one was observing, then led them down the darkened steps into a musty sublevel, cluttered with rusting metal drums. Sticky, black liquid oozed from the drums, emitting a foul stench. Imre was glad to put the stink behind him.

Emlee guided them through a maze of connected basements and underground car parks. The air was heavy and silent, compressed by the weight of the city above. Their footsteps sounded strangely muffled, as though made by lost things devoured by the vast and ancient earth. Disorientation rolled over Imre in waves, triggered by low sugar levels and fatigue. He would need to reduce his tempo soon or risk physical breakdown. The effort of changing sex was already putting an unwanted strain on his body's resources; he didn't want to trigger a meltdown by pushing it too far.

'We're here,' said Emlee, opening an unmarked door at the end of an unremarkable corridor. 'After you, Mr. and Mrs. Ravenstone.'

The space on the far side was cramped and lined with narrow

shelves. A broom cupboard, was Imre's first thought, and it was in reality little more than that. But it was somewhere to rest, and he slumped gratefully to the floor, breathing heavily at Tempo Absolute.

'Here.' She handed him an energy drink that looked startlingly blue in the drab surroundings. He took it from her, and offered her the pistol in exchange. 'No, hang on to it,' she said. 'Just keep the safety on.'

He did as she asked and swigged gratefully at the drink. Freer sat with his back to the closed door. The shelves contained food, drink, clothes, weapons, and a series of batteries connected to chargers. LEDs glowed at him like the eyes of underground creatures, gathering around him for warmth.

'We should lie low until sunrise,' Emlee said, sitting opposite him, so close their booted ankles touched. Her face was flushed with exertion. 'Perhaps longer.'

'Who were they?' asked Freer.

She shrugged. 'The flier was unmarked so probably not police. Maybe the same guys who attacked you at the Cat's Arse.'

'If that's the case,' Imre said, 'then they've had a change of heart about firing on us. They're also a bigger organization than we thought. They must have access to Q loop technology to follow *The Cauld Lad*. They must have been following you too long enough to know your allies and their movements. Deesticker was probably in their pay, so he gave you away the moment he was sure where you were and that you had us with you.' He shook his head. 'They've been closing on two fronts, and we didn't see them.'

'What's the connection?' she asked.

'You,' said Freer to Imre. 'Hel is right: it all comes back to you.'

'Why?' he asked, genuinely not understanding. 'What did I do that was so awful? I didn't kill Ampersand. That had nothing to do with me.'

Emlee stared at him with pity in her eyes. 'You really don't know?'

'I told you. The last thing I remember is the bridge of *Pelorus*. The ship was burning. We were arguing about surrender.'

'You said you thought we were going about the war completely the wrong way, or something like that.'

He nodded. 'There was an explosion.'

'I was knocked out. Everything's a blank after that. When I woke up, I was off the ship with the other survivors. There weren't many of us. Render was there. You were nowhere to be seen. It took awhile to filter through to us that the deal was done. The argument was over. You'd surrendered on our behalf.'

Imre turned to Freer. 'Is that how it went?'

He shrugged. 'I wasn't there. The Alphin Freer you knew on *Pelorus* died in the explosion.'

Half recollections and secondhand accounts tumbled through Imre's mind like balls in an old-fashioned lottery draw.

'I don't think this has anything to do with *Pelorus*,' said Emlee. 'Everyone loved us here after the Chaos War. Perhaps a little too much. Not even the Mad Times could sour that deal, and what happened after the Slow Wave only clinched it.'

'What did happen?' Freer asked.

She leaned forward and rested her elbows on her knees. The fingers of both hands went into her fake, dark hair and gripped tightly. 'Everyone else was grounded without the Forts in charge. The airports had crashed; the skyline was sealed tight. There were rumors that ships were being shot down if they tried to break orbit. Turns out that was happening in Jampa, not Chenresi, but the effect was the same. People thought the world was ending.

'The Corps' role had always been to maintain the peace, but this was completely beyond us. We were, in fact, making it worse. Factions of the Hyper government were fighting over us, trying to curry favor while at the same time pressuring us to back their particular version of martial law. The guns were out. It was only a matter of time before they started firing.

'That's when you came up with your grand plan, to go get help. Like everything else around then, it was a little crazy. We really needed help, and you said you knew where to get it. We couldn't get out-system in a ship, though, so we had to find another way. That way would be to send a hardcast copy of yourself via the Line. No one had hardcast for thousands of years – and I could see why after the week you had to spend in a scanner, being recorded down to the smallest possible level. But it was supposed to be safe and reliable. Unless the data comprising you was corrupted in transit, you could be rebuilt at the opposite end so you could deliver your plea for help.'

Imre thought of the Drum and the supposed inviolability of the copy he was based on. Nothing was ever completely safe or reliable.

'It made sense at the time,' she went on. 'Don't forget that we didn't really know yet what had happened outside the system. We didn't know that the whole galaxy had been affected. Help could already be on its way, for all we knew.

'So the Hypers backed your plan. The factions stopped fighting. The government gave you everything you needed to punch the transmission through to the nearest Line relay. The publicity machine went into overdrive. Contact with the rest of the Continuum would resume in a matter of years; order would be restored. The knowledge that you'd be out there, firing into the night like a rescue flare, gave everyone hope.

'When transmission day finally arrived, the Hyper president made a speech; you made a speech. Everyone shook hands and toasted to success. No one mentioned the protesters outside, chanting that we didn't need the Forts back, that Hyperabad could rule itself, that this was our last chance to save humanity for the singletons and Primes. I didn't know how this would come back to haunt me later, when they arrested Render.

'The time came to push the button. The press were there, of course. Everyone was watching. You put your hand on the ridiculous switch and smiled for the cameras. You pushed it. All hell broke loose.

'The bomb wasn't as deadly as it could have been, but it was in exactly the right spot, and it had just enough punch to kill a dozen or so people, so its impact was tremendously precise. In one stroke, the most vocal supporters of the plan were killed, including you, the president, and the chief engineer. The equipment was destroyed along with the record of your hardcast. The press caught it all, and the world watched it live. Instead of a brave attempt to reach out for help, the Hypers witnessed a slaughter that would haunt them for centuries. In that instant, Hyperabad knew it was alone for good.

'As we picked through the rubble, however, we discovered something both grim and wonderful. You had seen it coming, Imre, and you had taken steps. The hardcast had actually been broadcast the previous day, just in case of such an attack. The plea for help was propagating across the system even at that moment, traveling at the speed of light toward its ultimate destination.

'When the interim government learned the truth, they kept it from the public in the hope of preventing further trouble from the protesters. I thought that was a mistake, and still do, since the truth was bound to get out eventually.'

'The First Church of the Return,' Imre said with a sinking feeling in his stomach.

'They're kidding themselves,' said Freer in a low drawl. 'They would've had a reply by now, if one was ever going to come. The hardcast must've been corrupted or ignored. It was all for nothing.'

Emlee nodded. 'It was all for nothing, but not for the reason you think. This is where it gets really murky. The identity of the saboteur was never pinned down one hundred percent. In the chaos of forming a new government and quelling unrest, we were all distracted. Someone on the investigative team persisted, however, and arrived at a conclusion that not even she believed entirely. She came to you, me, and Helwise with the information, fearing how the new government might deal with it. When she outlined the case, I could only stare at her at first, thinking she was insane.

'She said, Imre, that you planted the charges yourself, not some volatile terrorist group. You were the saboteur and the murderer. You were the one who had knocked Hyperabad back into a state of fear and unrest. You had done it all in cold blood and left us to pick up the pieces.'

'Why?' asked Imre. 'Why would I do something like that?'

'You didn't share your reasons with us.' Emlee's expression was flinty in the gloom of their bolt-hole. 'I promised the investigator I'd look into it. She didn't want to leave it there – like I would try to protect your reputation by keeping it hush-hush – but I convinced her that I was on her side. Two days later, her body turned up in a ditch outside the city. Her neck had been professionally broken. The evidence was gone. Whoever else she told, they kept it very quiet indeed. Even the most vicious enemies of the First Church have never raised the issue. Al left; Helwise died in that shuttle crash. I might be the only person left who knows the truth – apart from your hardcast, Imre, wherever that is.'

Imre sensed there was something she was hiding. 'You have a theory,' he said to her. 'You wouldn't be telling me this if you didn't think I could help you figure it out.'

'What's to figure out?' she said. 'You ran, and you didn't take us with you. Why? Because of that great experiment you kept so secret, which Ampersand picked up on the Line when she heard about the Barons. I don't know what Domgard was, but it was more important to you than anything going on here. The whole hardcast fiasco was just a means of getting you out to where you wanted to be, which was far from here. You destroyed the equipment so no one else would follow, and yourself so no one would ever suspect the truth. Call me untrusting if you like, but that strikes me as something you'd do if the stakes were high enough.'

'If they were,' he shot back. 'There's no evidence I was involved in any of this.'

'Remember what I overheard in Mandala 2,' said Freer. 'BB called you "the architect of Domgard." She said you'd dropped the ball. You wondered if Domgard was connected to the Slow Wave. What if your great experiment went wrong and killed the Forts by accident?'

'Think about what you're saying, Al. How could I possibly wipe out every Fort in the galaxy by accident?'

'Perhaps this is what the people who chased you out of the Cat's Arse think you're guilty of,' Emlee said. 'Helwise has been filling

me in. This may also explain why you ran after the Slow Wave:
from an uneasy conscience.'

Maybe, Imre thought. Only maybe. 'Until we understand what
Domgard really is, we're groping in the dark. We also need to
know how it's connected to the Luminous and the Barons before
any blame comes back to me.'

'It always comes back to you,' said Freer. 'Best not to fight it.'

'Maybe,' he breathed, feeling as heavy as a planet. 'The traitor of
Pelorus. Wasn't that what BB called me?'

'That's old news, Imre,' said Emlee. 'Anyone who survived the
aftermath of the Slow Wave could see that you had your reasons for
surrendering. The Forts weren't so bad after all.'

A flicker of sadness passed across her features, and Imre knew
she was thinking about Ampersand.

'Let's rest,' he told her. 'We're all tired, and I know I'm not
thinking straight. What did you have in mind for dawn, Emlee?
That's when you said we could think about moving.'

She leaned her head back and rested it against the wall behind
her. 'At noon I should have been on a slowboat heading off-planet
with the others.'

'Well, let's not abandon that plan. Keep our focus tight.
Remember what we're doing here. There's nothing I can do to
change the past. I wasn't even there for most of it. But there's a
whole lot I can do for Render.'

'Spoken like someone who has no idea what Kismet is,' she
said.

'You're right there. Want to fill us in?'

'I'd rather tell you about it than act as a tour guide, but I have
a horrible feeling I'm going to end up doing both . . .'

They spent the rest of the night in a state of restless tension, with
one of them on watch, overclocking at all times, in case they were
discovered. During his off shifts, Imre didn't sleep. He sat awake in
the near darkness, thinking over everything he had learned – about
the fate of the Forts and the Continuum, about Domgard, the
Barons, and the Luminous, and most importantly about himself.

A time line was forming in his mind of the missing period between *Pelorus* and the present, pieced together from the three accounts he had received so far. The argument over surrendering or not had been violently interrupted, leaving Helwise and Freer dead and knocking Emlee unconscious, perhaps Render too. Shortly after that point, Imre's former self had surrendered to the Fort known as Factotem, and the survivors had been evacuated. He himself had disappeared for a time following the surrender, at least in some parts of the galaxy. Emlee implied that he had continuously occupied Mandala Supersystem after the Chaos War, but Helwise hadn't seen him until he reappeared for the Chimeleon operation, apparently perfectly willing to cooperate with the Forts and possessing knowledge of the Loop, suggesting a new intimate relationship with his former bosses. Freer hadn't seen him at all between the Mad Times and the Slow Wave.

At some point in those years, Imre assumed, his original had made the recording that had been stored on the Drum. Taking such a record and being hardcast were different only in the media of transmission between creation and utilization. The Drum, on the one hand, had clearly been intended as a permanent record. The hardcast was only a temporary measure, designed to alleviate the need for a starship to cross the interstellar gulfs.

For a moment, he wondered if he might be the hardcast that the First Church of the Return was waiting for. A casual thought soon unraveled that theory: if he had been, he would have possessed memories of the period between the Mad Times and the Slow Wave, a period about which he knew absolutely nothing.

The arrival of the Slow Wave appeared to have sent his former self into a personal panic. One had abandoned Helwise in mid-journey the moment he learned that the problem was galactic, not local, having spoken earlier of a secret project or mission. Another had concocted an elaborate plan to flee Hyperabad, erasing all chance of anyone following him. An unknown number had come through Mandala 2, seeking answers from BB, an Old-Timer with connections to a lost Fort, and made no effort to regroup with Freer.

Hints of Domgard surfaced in that time, intimately entangled with his own lost history. Emlee detected its name in the Line. BB referred to it. The version of Himself on Hyperabad had described it as 'the greatest experiment ever undertaken.' Details remained nonexistent.

Then there was or were the Luminous – strange assassins competing with a shadowy group called the Barons in the destruction of proto-Forts on Hyperabad, perhaps linking them to the Slow Wave and/or Domgard. Either or both had taken steps to ensure that their existence could never be proved, and perhaps at least one of them was related to the spies and saboteurs cruising the Line that Freer had spoken of, or Helwise's attackers while trying to get into the Cat's Arse. The list of connections was growing fast.

Not long after the Slow Wave, references to Imre Bergamasc grew nebulous or nonexistent, and the First Church became ascendant – clinging to what had been lost and hoping for a glorious restoration. On Hyperabad, he had become a symbol of hope, despite or perhaps because of his continued absence, while for his friends he had come to represent betrayal and abandonment. He wondered gloomily what kind of story Render might tell if they managed to rescue him from his terrible prison.

At the nearest end of the time line, the Drum had been destroyed, and he had emerged from the rubble, new and changed, and still trying to put himself together from the pieces.

You've left me in a terrible mess, he said to Himself. Wherever you are, wherever you've been since the Slow Wave, I hope you're aware of that much. I'm sure you had your reasons; I'm positive you were doing the right thing. It's hard to find those reasons down here in the trenches. Why didn't you leave me a message of some kind? You could've given me a clue: who I can trust, where I should go, what I should be doing. I'm afraid that I'm getting in the way of your grand plan to restore order. What if you're dead, and all my wonderings are irrelevant . . .?

A memory came to him during the night, as subtly insidious as a waking dream. The Corps had not originally been his initiative. He had joined it on leaving his home world's military forces and progressing to mercenary work among the stars. At that point in its history, the Continuum wasn't a new thing, but it remained in a state of constant flux. Pockets of civilization were growing steadily, deepening, diversifying, and adding to the richness of human habitation in the galaxy. As such ventures grew, they inevitably began to overlap. Sometimes this led to feats of cooperation impossible to foresee; other times it led to conflicts on a scale previously unimaginable.

In the middle of a war over a single asteroid between two interstellar empires, each claiming a dozen systems under their flags, the former commanding officer of the Corps died suddenly, killed by the sort of mistake a novice would have been embarrassed to admit to. Khalil Voda had tripped a vacuum mine while inspecting a captured ship. The resulting explosive decompression had sucked her out into space, where the wake of a shuttle had vaporized her before rescue could reach her. It had been a difficult campaign already; losing her was a major blow to all involved.

Imre stepped into her shoes under those fraught circumstances and somehow managed to broker a truce. The details were hazy; they weren't the important part of the memory. What happened afterward had impressed him much more, when a frag representing the Forts had contacted him on the former battlefield and offered him a deal.

The Forts needed agents to work for them, he was told. Humanity was growing more diffuse and diverse every millennium. Works ranged across all scales of time and space. Keeping track of it all, and keeping problems in check, was an unbearably complex task, one the Forts couldn't monitor at all times, just as a human brain couldn't consciously oversee every action of its immune system.

Did Imre Bergamasc and the Corps wish to be involved in the maintenance of the Continuum? If so, he would be given instructions from time to time and left to do as he willed, so long as the objectives were met. Sometimes the tasks might seem incomprehensible; sometimes they might even seem immoral. The important thing to remember was that in the long term it would always work out best for humanity as a whole. That was what the Forts wanted; that's who the Forts were, at the end of the day. In a roomful of people, one counted heads, not nerve cells or intestinal flora; the heads, however, needed every cell 'beneath' them to survive, and they were painfully aware of that fact.

'What do I get out of it?' he remembered asking.

'You?' The frag, to all appearances a man of average height, average build, and unremarkable features, had smiled. 'By pursuing that which we are trying to remove from the galaxy – war, injustice, dissolution – you will experience the very worst humanity has to offer. It is our firm belief that this environment suits some people better than others. Do you not think you'll be more at home in such circles than in the Continuum you strive to uphold?'

Peace did seem a stagnant quality to him, even the dynamic sort of peace to which the Forts aspired. 'I could be tempted,' he said.

'What if I said you've already been doing our work without knowing it? Khalil Voda cooperated with us before she died, and her CO before her.'

'I'd say it makes no difference at all. The Corps is in my hands now. It'll go where I lead.'

'As it should, and as it will. You are under no obligation.' The frag had bowed politely. 'We'll be in touch. Decide then. The choice will always be yours to make.'

In the days following the offer, he had wondered if he really was free to do as he wished. What would happen if he went against the Forts' first order? Would he be replaced – perhaps after suffering an apparently innocent accident as Khalil Voda had? Did he have the courage to put that to the test?

He hadn't. Not for a long while, anyway. He had accepted the first order – a simple diplomatic extraction that paved the way for peace in a complex border skirmish – and the second, and the third. He saw no moral conflict, and the Corps was well compensated with new equipment, privileges, and information for every successful contract. His work for the Forts was sometimes difficult, sometimes simple, and not always possible to penetrate logistically. As time passed, he did indeed begin to take comfort in the thought that he was doing what was best for the Continuum – a simplistic philosophy but one he could not have fallen back on in ordinary mercenary work.

Even such a safety net had proved thin in time. The wars never ceased; the Continuum was ever at conflict. All reassurance was washed away on an endless tide of blood. He began to wonder if the Forts were deliberately provoking dissent among the gestalts, singletons, and Primes in order to reduce their effectiveness as a united force. Once that idea was in his head, it wouldn't go away. Was he, as leader of the Corps, aiding and abetting the subjugation of his own kind? That possibility he found deeply repugnant. In convoluted, secretive conversations with his Fort masters, he found little reassurance.

So: Sol Invictus and the Mad Times; the rebellion; his surrender on the burning *Pelorus.* Betrayal. And then . . .?

He found it difficult to accept that he would simply return to working for the Forts. There had to be something else at stake – Domgard, presumably, whatever that was, either a carrot dangled by the Forts or something unrelated, perhaps even inimical, to them. He couldn't conceive of a morally defensible plan to murder the Forts as a whole – even if they were unjustly dominating the human galaxy, and even if his former self hadn't considered himself a 'decent man.' He couldn't rule it out, however. There might be much more yet to learn about his past.

He thought again of Render and wondered what might lie in that brittle, battle-scarred mind. Unlike Helwise MacPhedron, Emlee Copas, and Alphin Freer, who had joined the Corps after he had taken control, Render had been at his side from the outset. They had saved each other's lives uncountable times, yet Imre knew next to nothing about how Render worked. Thousands of years of personal history lay behind those multicolored eyes. They looked out on a world very different from the one into which he had been born, for Render was an Old-Timer like Bianca Biancotti, perhaps the only Old-Timer left who lived a life of war. Longevity on the battlefield always came at a cost, and Imre could only imagine what it had cost Render.

Rebuilding came at a price too, and Imre would risk more unpleasantness to bring the Corps back together. If Render spurned him, that would create a schism within the group. A fitting symbol, Imre thought, for what was happening in the galaxy at large, and in his mind. If, on the other hand, Render accepted him, that would be a sign of things to come. With the Corps behind him, perhaps the returned Imre Bergamasc could make a positive difference.

During his shift, he tidied the shelves of Emlee's hideout to kill time, putting the cans of food in rows and sorting the ammunition so it would be easier to access. He ran through countless scenarios based on the little he knew about Hyperabad and Kismet, and the rest of Mandala Supersystem. He came to no firm conclusions, but he did dismiss several strategies as patently absurd, direct assault among them. He ran up a list of questions to ask Helwise as soon as Emlee gave him access to her and the ship. He considered which way he would act, depending on whether Helwise found the Loop shunt on the ship or not.

The hours didn't drag. If anything, there weren't enough of them. When his shift ended, he ceased overclocking and resumed Tempo Absolute.

'What would you have done if I'd made a break for it while you slept?' he asked Emlee, whose turn it was to stand duty next.

'Who said I slept?' She looked at the neatly tidied shelves and back at him. 'Don't think I wasn't watching you every second. Don't think I won't keep watching you until I'm sure I can trust you.'

'Do you think you ever will?'

'I guess it's unlikely,' she said, 'considering I never did before.'

His mind replayed the vision of Alphin Freer being executed by the people who had attacked them at the Cat's Arse. It had haunted him for days. He suspected it might haunt him forever until he found out what his former self had done.

'I understand now why you're angry with me,' he said. 'You think I ran to get back to Domgard, which connects me somehow to the Barons. They killed Ampersand, with or without the Luminous. Their guilt is mixed up with mine. I get it.'

'It's not your understanding I want.'

'Then what? An apology won't change anything. I certainly can't bring her back. I want to know who killed Ampersand and the Forts as much as you do. That's all I can offer.'

'Are you sure it wasn't you who killed the Forts?'

'Do you realize what you're asking? Could I possibly have wiped out the galaxy's fittest minds with one sweep of . . .?' He raised his right hand and stared at its slender, feminine fingers. 'The idea is insane. You're insane, and so am I, for contemplating it.'

'But you don't rule it out either.'

'I can't, no.' He sighed. 'I don't suppose it'd help saying that if I'd been there, if you'd asked me to help protect her, I would've done my best to make a difference.'

'No, it doesn't help. You're living in a past I no longer believe in. I thought we were a team, but it turns out we weren't at all. You work through your sins as much as you want. Don't expect me to give you my blessing.'

'We want the same things. Render and the Continuum for two. Why not Ampersand as well?'

She leaned her head against the wall behind her. 'All right. You want to know why I'm really angry? I didn't get a chance to say good-bye. That's what I stewed over all the time I was in Kismet. Everything went down the toilet, and I was left behind to pick up the pieces. Was that fair? Was that all I deserved?'

'I understand,' he said. 'I assume I had a reason for escaping Hyperabad so suddenly, but that doesn't make what I did right. I want you to know that I'm sorry. Really.'

She made a sound that was neither agreement nor dissent, laugh nor sob. Her nostrils flared. 'I was talking about Ampersand.'

'Oh.' He felt his face grow warm in the darkness, remembering that both he and the Fort she loved had killed themselves in front of her.

'I would've died for her,' she said. 'I loved her. I loved a Fort. No, not a Fort. Ampersand was more of a woman, a person, than you'll ever be.'

They said nothing for a long time after that. He was hurt by

Emlee's dismissal of him. She had expressed nothing but anger and loathing ever since he had reappeared in her life. A lot appeared to be his fault, but her plan to rescue Render going awry wasn't one of them. There were limits to how much blame he would accept.

He wondered if Helwise was listening in, and whether she agreed with any of Emlee's sentiments.

'Wake me at dawn,' he said. 'I, for one, am definitely getting some sleep. We're going to need it.'

'You have a plan?'

A possibility had been niggling at the back of his mind for an hour. 'Come morning I will. If no one has any other suggestions, of course.'

'Diplomacy doesn't suit you either, Imre,' she said.

He curled in a corner with his eyes closed and didn't disagree.

THIS PRISON MOON

{I}t is always easier to excite a passion
than a moral feeling.

Robert Charles Maturin

'—the world comes apart.

'I'm so tired. I'm so tired of this. One more time: Where are you? Will you come for me? You owe me, and I need you. I'm not asking you to remember me. Memories are only there to make you bleed.

'Nothing in here but dust. She comes and she goes. This is confusing me again. There's nothing down here but me. I could be dreaming.

'Picture the man when the heartbeat stops. I'll believe in you when the world comes—'

The message conveying Render's latest whispered monologue came an hour after Emlee cracked open the supply cupboard and crept cautiously outside. Imre listened to the broken voice with a growing sense of dread. The words were directed at him. He knew it, even though Render hadn't used his name. When he called for help, there was only one person he expected to come.

The file looped around and around in his mind, as self-devouring as Ouroboros.

'I'll believe in you when the world comes apart.'

'Who's this "she" he keeps going on about?' asked Helwise. Emlee had finally opened comms between *The Cauld Lad* and the others in order to coordinate their movements. They were currently in a crowded marketplace breathing air thick with orange dust. Callers and musicians filled every available frequency with an ever-increasing Babel. Emlee had bought herself breakfast from a pungent stall, but neither Imre nor Freer had felt the need to sample the local wares. The vast assemblage of artisans and their wares was larger than many suburbs and seemed to go forever.

'I don't know who she is,' Emlee told her. 'He talks about her a lot. I'll give you the other audio files to examine in your own time. Maybe you can make sense of them.'

'You think there's sense to be made?' asked Freer, pulling the collar of his combat jacket across his nose and mouth. His grey eyes restlessly scanned the brightly colored crowd. 'I think his mind has finally gone for good. Who could blame him, if everything you say about this place is true?'

Kismet orbited the dead heart of a star called Sakra, in a region of Mandala Supersystem long employed as a military training ground by various indigenous governments. The harsh environment rendered it useless for colonization except by the most extreme of extremophiles, and even they had soon cleared out rather than be mistaken for targets in tactical exercises. Imre doubted that Kismet had always been a prison; even as a powerful deterrent, it wouldn't have justified the efforts and expense someone had gone to to smelt an iron asteroid into a solid steel scaffold as wide across as some cities. Whatever it had once been, that scaffold now supported the numerous tubes and cells of Render's most recent home. Apart from the steel, every external surface was as transparent as air, giving the incarcerated a very clear view of the dead star, around which Kismet orbited in a highly elliptical orbit. The flybys of Sakra during periapsis, Emlee assured them, were terrifying. Imre believed her. Kismet circled the star once every twenty-two hours, moving so quickly that even at apoapsis docking was difficult. To approach a superdense, superradioactive stellar remnant at speed every day, while gripped and shaken by powerful tides, would convey an undeniably powerful lesson in the hostility of the universe.

Imre tried not to think about it too much. He had more immediate concerns.

'Have you had any luck reaching Zadiq Turin?' he asked
Helwise.

'None, fuck it,' she instantly replied. 'There are layers of bureaucracy around her like you wouldn't believe. You'd think the First
Church of the Return was a Catholic enclave for all the fuss they
make about hierarchies and protocol.'

'Keep at it. If we can't get to her, we'll have to look for another
plan.'

'Don't worry. I always get what I want.'

'What about that time in the Siegel Straits?' asked Emlee. 'I
remember you saying that then, too.'

'You must be thinking of someone else. I was never there.'

Imre followed Emlee along a narrow stall, cluttered with
cheap holograms and field effects that batted for his attention
like giant, translucent butterfly wings. His eyes were irresistibly
drawn to the wares on offer, and he found them to be uniformly
cheap and shoddily made: biohack jewelry likely to eat the skin
it clung to; consumer nanotech with an unready, untested look;
data sets with typos on their cases. A new feeling of dread rose up
in him.

'Here we are,' said Emlee, pulling a blue cotton drape back
with one arm and waving him ahead of her into a narrow, white-
lit stall. Imre blinked at the sudden change in ambience. The
interior of the stall was almost clean compared to the outside and
contained little more than a table long enough to hold a person at
full stretch. It took up most of the available space.

'Doesn't look like much,' Imre said.

'Doesn't look like anything at all,' said Freer. 'Are you sure
we're in the right place?'

Emlee nodded. 'Chyro, come out! It's me. I've brought you that
customer I told you about.'

The rear wall folded back, and a small man with a black goatee
and no other visible hair emerged. 'You're not dissatisfied?' he
asked. 'You're sure you don't want me to correct an error?'

'If I did, I would've come back there and dragged you out myself.'

He didn't look entirely reassured. With nervous, darting glances, he took in the three people standing before him. 'Well, good,' he said. 'I'm Chyro Kells. Which one of you wants the service?'

'I do,' said Imre. Chyro Kells was responsible for the genetic patches that had enabled Emlee to dodge discovery for so long. Presumably he had altered her eye and hair color too, and helped her keep in peak Prime condition – unless she had taken on a second genetic tailor to divert attention.

'I presume your brief hasn't changed.' The little surgeon cupped his bearded chin as though weighing it. 'There is no magic wand. Certain repairs are not aided by overclocking and must proceed at a more natural rate. Cosmetic, I can give you what you want in matter of hours, but below the skin . . .' He pulled a thoughtful face, milking what small amount of authority he could from the exchange. 'A week.'

'That's fine,' said Emlee. 'He'll take the contract.'

'In a hurry, are we?'

'Not so much that we wouldn't go elsewhere. Don't push your luck, Chyro.'

'My luck is consistently terrible,' he said. 'Must be all that junk I take – for my back, boys, for my back.'

'Ignore him,' Emlee told them, as Chyro turned around and began extruding workbenches and tools from the previously featureless white walls. 'He's first-rate. The Alienists took him during the Chaos War, screwed his mind up some. He works in exchange for medical data. That's all he lives for. Builds his own equipment so the work can't be traced, you'll either be pleased or terrified to know.'

Imre wasn't sure what to say to that. The surgeon told him to undress. He tried not to look at himself as he did so. The skin of his chest and abdomen was mottled by bruises; stubble had spread across his stomach again. His breasts had only slightly reduced in size since leaving the Cat's Arse, but his clitoris had reached almost an inch long and protruded from the stubble of his pubic hair like a tiny penis. He felt ill defined and awkward, between states. Some people liked it that way; he didn't.

'Please, lie down.'

The table shifted uneasily under him, taking his every measure. He tried to hide his uncertainty, but some of it must have appeared on his face.

'I told you to use the medical suite in the Cat's Arse,' Helwise whispered into his ear. 'You wouldn't listen.'

'I'm not listening to you now, Hel.'

'Outside, please,' Chyro told the others, making shooing motions toward the curtained door. 'I must reduce distractions to a minimum.'

'We won't be far, boss,' said Freer, patting him on the shoulder as they left. 'Scream if you need us.'

'Now.' Chyro fussed about the room, exchanging his white coat for one that looked identical. 'You have two options, my friend. I can decrease your tempo so it'll be over in a moment for you, or I can knock out your neural pathways so you won't feel a thing. Which is your preference?'

Imre considered briefly. The first option was not palatable; he needed to be conscious in case Emlee's backyard surgeon turned out to be untrustworthy. The second unnerved him too, but for reasons less easy to define. Bad enough that his body had the wrong gender and therefore didn't feel like his; bad enough that it was subtly changing with every passing day. To let go of it so absolutely, even for a short time, struck him as dangerous. Without a physical anchor of any kind, would his mind spiral off into a thousand disconnected segments and never reassemble?

He reminded himself that he would still have access to his other senses. He wouldn't be completely removed from the physical world. If worse came to worst, he could always watch what the surgeon was doing for distraction . . .

'I'll take the neural pathways,' he told Chyro.

The surgeon nodded and continued with his preparations. His coat had extruded white tendrils from the sleeves, which ran down his hands and around his fingers. With delicate, staccato movements, Chyro teased those extrusions into numerous exotic shapes, the spirals, needles, hooks, and blades of his craft.

When he was done, he turned to Imre with a smile, and said, 'Turn your head to the right. You might feel some temporary discomfort.'

Imre nodded and did as instructed. The surgeon reached behind him and touched the base of his neck. A glowing thread of agony slid through his skin and into his spine. He stiffened, then relaxed as the pain went away.

'There.' Chyro tilted Imre's head back with the heels of both hands. 'Can you feel anything, anything at all?'

He felt as though he was floating on a cloud of nothingness. 'No,' he said. His voiced was slurred.

'Good. I'll begin. Remember, the changes will only be cosmetic. It'll take a while for the rest of you to catch up. I accept no responsibility for the troubles that'll cause you.'

'We won't be here to accuse you of anything.'

'You're not the first to say that.' Chyro moved lower, and his hands began their grisly work.

Imre's attention wandered. For a while, he talked to Helwise and the others, but their conversations about food and other transient concerns felt far removed from his present circumstances. Eventually he turned them down to a faint whisper, reassuring but not demanding. He went over the details of the plan, but they too seemed irrelevant. Perhaps Chyro had done more than simply shut off the pain, he thought. He felt relaxed for the first time in days. He could have almost fallen asleep.

Needing to remain conscious, he turned to the recordings of Render that Emlee had given him. The melancholy missives could have no soporific effect on him, he was certain. The voice of the missing member of the Corps whispered softly to him as though out of a dream.

'No sleep. Don't let me sleep. I don't want to sleep. There's nowhere to hide in your dreams.

'When I sleep, someone is talking. But it's not conversation. Sounds more like a voice in my head. Sometimes it almost breaks my heart. Sometimes it feels like I could die. I know I'm asleep, but I know this is real. Something is here, in the dark, in the dream. Dark whispers in my head. They whisper "shame." They talk of pain. I've known fear many times but nothing like this.

'I'm so scared I can't breathe. I will do anything – anything, you understand? – just to wake up. She's like death on two legs. I will never sleep alone again.

'Are you afraid, dear listener?'

Imre wondered if Render knew his words were being recorded and sent to Emlee. The question was purely rhetorical. There was no way to know until they got him out of Kismet and asked him. The more Imre heard the more urgent that objective became, despite the occasional protest from Render himself.

'I don't need saving,' began another recording. 'I don't need lies. I don't need heroes. Some heroes! Kiss my arse. I'll give you dead heroes. You were there. You were always there. A shadow of life watching over you, I was cold but not insane. I was young. I was clean. Now my soul eats me alive.

'Some things you can't forget. Some things you can't forgive. I'm too old. I won't forget. I can remember everything: every promise, every lie. I've seen some things I'll remember if I live forever. Forever and a day. She was wrong, and now it's come back to haunt me.

'Memories? I don't need a dead museum and a grudge to feed. I need emotion. Sometimes I remember how to feel again. It hurts, but I'm thinking clearly. I'm still breathing. I don't cry, or forget.

'We are deceived. Valhalla is falling. We all reap what we sow.

'Nothing can help me here.'

It was easy to see why Emlee was so haunted by the messages. The litany of mood swings, as Render oscillated between hope and despair, was both exhausting and deeply moving. Imre didn't know how long Render had been imprisoned, or what exactly had been done to him, but the toll on Render's psyche was terrible, and mounting.

'Here it comes again: that old familiar pain. What am I to do, and where am I to go? I am not myself. This is not my voice. Not my face. Not my life.

'It's all that she knows. Who'd believe she'd be so devious? She said, "You could be here forever." I'm unforgiven, and I have to pay. I hope you forgive me. I'm like a dead man hiding in the dark. So cold. I'm scared to die. A fool in the dark, afraid of the truth. I don't know why I'm afraid. I've never been afraid to face a fear.

'I look at what I've become. My memories, my life, my soul. The things I've seen. The things I've done. I looked inside – a big mistake. All lies, all cold. Here is my small black heart, filled with shame.

'And I know that I can't leave. I cannot be saved. Not by you. Not by God. I can hardly breathe. Sometimes I call out for you, and sometimes I'm afraid. Sometimes I wonder if God laughs at me. I hear His voice when I sleep, here in this room. I wait in the dark, so perfectly cold. I ask for one small mercy. I ask God if He can save me. I beg God for salvation, for an angel, every night.

'He says "It's all too dark."

'I put my fear back in its box. There's no darker place.'

The surgeon worked quickly and with uninterrupted concentration in Imre's abdomen. Despite his determination to stay awake, Imre drifted deeper into a state familiar from long hours of sentry duty. He was aware of the outside world and could react to it in an instant if needed, but his consciousness became dissociated, smeared equally across external and internal worlds. Archetypes from his subconscious stirred, throwing up strange associations and images. Shadowy, formless shapes were to be expected. Creatures with long claws, likewise. None of them frightened him. He drifted almost peacefully until a woman in clerical robes lunged at him out of the darkness with sharp teeth snapping, startling him into full wakefulness.

'Strange,' said Chyro.

'What's that?' he mumbled.

'Something odd. Hmmm. No matter.'

Imre let his eyes drift shut. Render's sorrowful monologues

were drawing to a close. He had missed some during his half sleep.
He didn't doubt that they had filtered down through his mind and
prompted the frightening image at the end. Render's words were
vivid: worlds falling apart, Valhalla falling, bargaining for his
life . . . Imre couldn't decide if he referring was to the Mad Times
or to the Slow Wave – or neither.

'And so it comes to this: death or eternity?'

'I don't like this feeling, like someone haunts me. This is my
future, my one chance. I'd hide in shadows, but the shadows talk
to me. She wants everything. I'm scared to sleep. Does she laugh
at you like she laughs at me?'

There were definitely two people in Render's internal psy-
chodrama. Imre pondered this as the surgeon rolled him onto his
stomach and worked behind him; blood trickled onto the table,
quickly absorbed. The woman tormenting Render warred with the
person he hoped might rescue him, for whom he felt both admir-
ation and anger, love and hate. Could Emlee be the latter, not
Imre as he had assumed? Sad for her if it was. She hadn't forgotten
him; she was doing her level best to get him out of Kismet. That
her efforts were rewarded by these conflicted rants made him
wonder if the messages were intended as taunts by the authorities,
those who had been forced by parties unknown to let her go.

'Do you hear me? Can you hear me fall? Don't let the dark into
me. Like a scar that won't fade, I will be, I'll always be, yours. I'll
be your demon. Shadowman. Call me and I'll run to you. Ask me
and I'd die for you. Let me die for you. Would you like that? I'm
a ghost in the dark, and I'm yours.

'I wonder if at times you ever think of me. I don't suppose you
do. I'm just another old story. Time will help you. Time helps you
forget. Time helps you forget me.

'I'll haunt you. I won't ask for faith or forgiveness. All I need is
a place to hide the pain . . .'

'There.' The surgeon rolled him onto his back and slapped him
on the thigh. Imre felt the slap through nerve endings restored to
full operation. 'All done.'

'Can I—' His vocal cords were rusty. 'Can I sit up?'

'You're not much use to anyone lying there.' Chyro stepped back. Already the tools of his trade were retracting, retreating like light-sensitive worms back into the sleeves of his coat. 'Move carefully at first. It will take you a while to adjust.'

Imre lifted himself onto his elbows. The first thing he noticed was that his breasts were gone. He had a fully masculine chest once more, with smaller nipples and muscles clearly defined. The slight fur on his stomach no longer looked so out of place. Neither did the bruises. His hips were noticeably narrower, but still a shade broad for a man. He presumed that would change further with time. Between his thighs lay penis and testes, hairless and raw-looking with healing blood flow. His whole body tingled from the shock of surgery and a myriad of ongoing repairs.

He went to stand and immediately lost his balance. Resting on the edge of the bed for a moment, he put out a hand to steady himself.

'I told you,' said the surgeon, glancing up from the retraction of his tools. Imre felt those cool, emotionless eyes focus properly on his face for the first time. 'Don't I know you from somewhere?'

'Unlikely,' he said, making a successful second attempt to stand and pulling on his clothes. Pants and flak jacket were baggy until the fabric adjusted around him. Every step was a learning experience, thanks to the new narrowness of his hips.

Not new, he told himself. Old. This was the way the Jinc should have made him from the start. That Chyro now recognized him only confirmed that he had done the right thing.

Freer peered around the flap. 'We heard voices . . .'

'It's done,' Imre said, patting his clothes to make sure nothing had been removed. The pistol Emlee had given him was still in the inside jacket pocket, keyed to his palm print, which it still recognized. She came through the flap after Freer and stood staring at him for a long moment.

'Good work, Chyro,' Emlee eventually said. 'He'll easily pass for himself now.'

'You mean he really is—?'

'Check his DNA if you like. Spread the word. Just give us an hour to get clear; that's all I ask.' Emlee transferred a large amount of data into the surgeon's private banks. 'I've added a little extra for your trouble.'

'A pleasure,' the small man said, covering his awkwardness with a quick bow. 'A genuine pleasure.'

Embarrassed, Imre pulled the hood of his jacket across his face and pushed his way out of the stall and back into the market. They walked in single file, with Imre sandwiched between Emlee and Freer. The sun was high in the sky, the air hotter and even dustier than before.

'You're limping,' Emlee said. 'Are you okay?'

'I'll get over it. Nothing's dropped off yet, anyway.'

'You are anatomically correct, I presume?' Helwise asked from the ship.

'All present and accounted for.' Imre surprised himself with a faint feeling of loss, but he put that down to the stresses of surgery combined with Render's agonized musings. The sensation that he'd been recently kicked in the balls didn't help. 'Any progress with Mother Turin?'

'She's as slippery as soap. You'd think the head of a major religion would take calls saying that her savior is back in town, but no. I'm beginning to wonder if she's deliberately avoiding us.'

'Perhaps she thinks you're a crank.'

'As far as she knows, I'm a rich off-world convert seeking an audience. Profit speaks louder than prophets.'

'Police,' warned Emlee.

Imre looked up to see an armored patrol moving through the crowd, their brassy, domed helmets towering high above the people around them, reminiscent of ancient Norman headgear. Conversation ceased as Emlee led them down another narrow lane, seeking obscurity among the buyers and sellers of Hyperabad's vast and dusty underworld.

'You know what shits me?' asked Freer, when the patrol had fallen behind. 'No one mentions us. We could've at least been disciples, high priests – popes, even. But nothing, like we never mattered.'

'To these guys, we didn't.' Emlee brushed through a series of dangling vines that danced when touched. 'Get used to it.'

'We did matter.' Freer looked genuinely worried. 'Who is she to say we're nobodies?'

'Don't worry. We'll show the bitch eventually,' said Helwise. 'Me, I'd be happy just to get off this dump. Looking at you guys makes me want to take a bath.'

'We're not moving the ship until we have a destination,' Imre reminded her. 'I don't want to provoke the Barons, just in case they do have the Hypers watching you.'

'Yeah, yeah. I know all that. But I'm getting bored arguing with First Church drones and looking for some piece of equipment that might not even exist.'

'Keep at it,' he told her. 'Absence of evidence isn't—'

'Evidence of fuck-all, I know. Just let me get my grizzle on for a bit, then I'll get back to work.'

Imre saw another brassy dome at the end of the lane ahead and drew Emlee's attention to it with a quick tap to her shoulder.

'I see it,' she said. 'That makes two patrols where there are normally none.'

'That slicer friend of yours,' growled Helwise. 'You should go back and cut his tongue out.'

'Not him. The police don't have anything he wants.' Emlee squeezed down a gap between two stalls barely wide enough for her, let alone Freer's broad shoulders. 'I think they're trawling for us, figuring we're likely to come here.'

'They're right,' said Freer. 'So how do we make them think they were wrong?'

'We do exactly what we're doing. We keep moving; we don't let them catch us in their net. If necessary, we head deeper into the city since that's the opposite of what they'll think likely. The last thing we do is make a run for the airport.'

'We wouldn't need to if this bloody priest would take her calls,' Helwise said.

'Don't assume she will,' Imre said. 'We should work on a contingency plan.'

'Separate,' said Emlee. 'Go to ground for a month until things get quiet again. Rendezvous and start again.'

'No,' he told her, certain that he would rather undergo more surgery than wait a month. 'I'm not going into hiding. If I'd wanted to do that, I wouldn't have gone under the knife in the first place. Render has waited long enough. We're going to get him back now.'

'This is why you never got the job done, Emlee,' Helwise said. 'You didn't have a half-finished amnesiac high on hormones at your side.'

Neither Emlee nor Imre responded to the barb.

They circled for what felt like forever through the giant market-place, changing their external garb every hour, from flak jacket to flowing robes and back, with caps, sunshades, and dust-filtering masks completing the various ensembles. Imre's hips ached more with every step, but he didn't order a rest until late in the after-noon, when patrols had been absent for over an hour, and the streets were even more full than before with commuters and bar-gain hunters. Most of them were Primes, as always the lowest socioeconomic class on worlds like Hyperabad, and they main-tained a predictable Tempo Absolute. Every now and again, however, someone weaved through the throngs at speed, provok-ing a chorus of complaints, or stood like a statue on a street corner, watching the tides of humanity ebb and flow.

Emlee chose a bar with an almost invisible entrance, one that served the strongest of the planet's clear, bitter liquors. Imre sank with a sigh into a shaded cane seat at the rear of the bar and felt his abused musculature gratefully rearrange itself. He poured himself a shot of ice-cold liquid and downed it in one.

'That's just fucking cruel,' said Helwise via the grid.

'Cruel nothing,' said Freer. 'You haven't got police breathing down your neck every five minutes.'

'We can't keep this up much longer,' Emlee said. 'No matter how careful we are, we're going to be unlucky eventually. I think it's time to be proactive.'

Imre nodded. 'What do you have in mind?'

'Forget trying to contact the Church directly. That's obviously not going to get us anywhere. Instead, we seed worms to infect every meeting place we can infiltrate. Chat rooms, dating services, newsgroups – whatever. Spread the word everywhere so it'll be impossible to miss. Ads, too. Whatever it takes.'

'What's the message?' asked Helwise.

'That the First Church is a scam and we can prove it. That Mother Turin is a faker and a fraud. That the Forts are never coming back, and you'd be a poor substitute for them.'

'The truth, then,' said Freer. 'I don't think that matters to people like this.'

She shrugged. 'The important thing is that it'll get a reaction. The Church will have to respond somehow. We post a dummy address and filter through the responses until we get what we want.'

'And then?' asked Imre.

'We take the lead right to the top.' She leaned forward over hands folded tightly on the table. 'What do you think?' Her eyes challenged him to disagree.

'I think the principle is sound,' he said, 'but you haven't gone far enough. Does the church have a headquarters in the city?'

'Yes. At the base of the skyline.'

'Good. We're going to find a runner to take something there, a parcel addressed to Zadiq Turin herself. It'll contain a note from you telling her that you have me hostage and that you'll execute me if she doesn't contact us immediately.'

'And then what?'

'She has access to Kismet; you've seen her there yourself. If she can get Render out, you trade him for me. She can't mean me any harm; I'm her savior, after all. After a cooling-off period, I'll slip away and rejoin the rest of you. There's no way it can go wrong.'

'I can think of at least one: why would she believe us? She must get crank mail all the time.'

'None accompanied by pieces of me, I'm sure.'

Freer and Emlee stared at him. He felt Helwise peering through their senses too.

'You're kidding,' she said. It wasn't a question. 'You're not kidding. Which bit are you going to send?'

'I don't know. A finger or a toe; something large enough to get a good match on. It could be faked, but I doubt they'll take the chance. If I am here and being kept against my will, they'll want to know.'

Emlee nodded slowly. He saw in her eyes an entirely different emotion now: excitement, perhaps. Was she pleased that he was going to be physically punished? 'It'll certainly attract attention,' she said. 'We'll have every Church-affiliated police officer on the lookout for us.'

'Not so different from the way things are right now – except we'll know for sure which side they're on.'

'True. So are you thinking of going back to Chyro to get the bit chopped off?'

'I'd be mad even to consider it,' he said. 'Who knows who he's told by now? Besides, my body's still full of pheromones and repair agents. I could do it right here without spilling a drop.'

'Okay. Here.' She slipped her knife under the table into his hands.

'Thanks.' If she thought he might blanch at the last minute, she was mistaken.

'Wait,' said Helwise. 'You only just got your body fixed up, and now you're chopping bits off it? That sounds less like a plan to me than acute body dysphoria. Are you sure this isn't something the Jinc put inside you, screwing with your mind?'

'Who cares about the Jinc?' said Emlee. 'I still think it's worth a shot.'

'You're not really on his side yet,' said Helwise. 'You don't care what happens to him so long as you get Render back okay.'

'What's to care about?' Emlee asked with a flash of annoyance. 'So he loses a finger. Big deal. It'll grow back.'

'Don't do it, Imre. There's bound to be a better way. Al, tell him.'

Freer looked uncomfortable. 'Better, yes. Faster, no.'

'Oh, great. Am I the only person here who thinks this is an extreme overreaction?'

'You aren't here, Hel.' Imre straightened in his seat and brought his left hand palm upward across his lap so his wrist was braced against his stomach. The metal blade felt cool against the knuckle of his little finger. 'We need to do this. I need to do this. Emlee, you might want to get a cloth or something to put it in.'

She nodded once, already ready for him.

There was no point delaying. Wishing only that he had Chyro Kells's ability to switch off his neural pathways, he pressed down with his right hand. Pain as sharp as liquid helium filled his arm, radiating outward from the joint and along his bones, into his skull. He was unable to avoid stiffening; his face became wooden like a mask. His febrile gaze alighted on Emlee's chin and didn't move as he increased the pressure. Singleton flesh was tough, consisting of tissues and fluids bearing only a passing resemblance to actual human flesh. The knife, however, was sharp enough to cut metal, and he was very strong.

Gristle parted. Blood dripped onto his lap. Endorphins gave him a feeling like euphoria as the finger swung free, released from its tendon and joint, as nerveless as a loose button. He concentrated on not cutting too far in order to spare the next knuckle along. His ring finger was slippery. Letting the knife drop between his knees, he brought the remaining fingers of his left hand into a fist and caught the amputated finger in his right.

'Got it.' His voice sounded deeper, hoarser than normal. He fumbled the cloth Emlee handed him. The knife fell with a clatter to the ground. 'Sorry.' There was blood all across his lap and upper thighs. The flow was already easing from the wound. Within seconds, the stain began to fade as his clothes absorbed the spill.

'Od damn,' breathed Freer. The lanky mercenary looked uncharacteristically pale. 'I would've cut it off for you, if you'd asked.'

'He was never going to,' said Emlee with satisfaction. 'This is the guy who blew himself up to keep a secret, remember?'

'I'm sure I'm him now,' Imre said, hearing a distant ringing noise that had nothing to do with sirens or discovery. 'Seal the deal.'

'See?' said Helwise, her voice strident in his ears. 'This had nothing to do with rescuing Render. It's all about proving a point to himself, not to any of us – including the Church and the Barons and whoever else is mixed up in his crazy affairs. We're just spectators – but if we're not careful, we'll end playing the game too.'

'Seal the deal,' Imre repeated. The bar was growing distant and hazy.

'This is no game,' he heard Emlee say. 'He's fighting for his life, I think.'

Then the bar was gone, and he was back on *Pelorus*. The air was full of smoke and ash. His lungs felt caked with it; his eyes stung. Inertial gravity was failing as the Forts' terrible fire ripped through the centrifuge axis. With another mighty explosion, more of the ship dissolved into flame.

He kicked himself along the bucking corridor as fast as he could. A corner loomed. He slammed into the wall, unable to turn in time. Bone crunched in his hip; he ignored the pain. Watching from within and without, like an observer in a dream, he had the time to wonder what was going on. Was this after the argument on the bridge or before? Either way, the new ache in his past self's hip was just one of many he couldn't stop to see to. He had to go faster. They couldn't be far ahead.

Another corner and there they were: Render with Emlee held unconscious in his broad, scarred arms. Imre's first thought – that Render was using her as a shield – struck him as patently absurd. Everyone knew that Render and Emlee were close, despite their differences. If Render had a friend, she was it.

Another explosion shook the ship. The air was getting noticeably warmer.

'Get her out,' Render told him, pushing Emlee toward him. 'Get her out.'

He hesitated. Why? He couldn't understand the uncertainty he felt in his remembered self's mind. Clearly, *Pelorus* was coming down around their ears. Why weren't they running for the bailout pods? Why the sick feeling in his stomach?

There was a gun in his hand – a Balzac beamer, workhorse for Sol Invictus ground troops.

'What's done is done,' Render said, pushing Emlee ahead of him again. 'We must get out of here.'

The moment was leaden, solidifying around him like amber. His heart thudded with terrible certainty, unstoppable, implacable. Why? Why was he still immobile in the face of certain death?

Then Emlee was in his arms. There was blood and bruising about her head, although Render seemed unharmed. Imre held her like a child and turned the two of them about. The nearest air lock was back the way he had come. They would need to hurry if they were to avoid the ship's inevitable destruction.

Render's presence, as heavy as fate itself, followed closely behind. 'Don't ask,' the big soldier said. 'I'm not surprised. There is no longer any normal to me.'

Imre said nothing. His mouth was closed in a straight, grim line. From his memory's memory came the voice of a being called Factotem: 'Seal the deal.' That was all, without explanation. It was enough to make Himself grind his teeth and move even faster.

During his blackout, while Freer watched uneasily from his seat, and Helwise cursed from her distant vantage point, Emlee calmly wrapped the digit in the cloth and wrote a short note to Zadiq Turin. It conveyed everything they had discussed: Imre Bergamasc had returned and would be killed if Turin didn't respond immediately. She bound the note around the finger with a self-sealing plastic sheet and called over the manager of the bar. He told her of a courier service that could be relied on for discretion and speed. A runner came moments later and accepted the contract. Emlee gave him the small parcel and the barest of instructions. The runner left with an assurance that the forged ID number she had given him would be joined by another when the job was confirmed. She would know when Zadiq Turin called the temporary address given at the end of the note.

All this Imre learned when they woke him from his trance and told him they were moving. It wasn't safe to stay in the bar any longer. The runner could be traced back to them if he was interrogated or offered a better deal.

Imre ached all over, from the stump of his missing finger to the holes in his mind that the Jinc had been unable to repair. His body still burned from Chyro's ministrations. Barely had they left the bar when he doubled over, clutching his lower abdomen.

'What now?' Freer hissed, standing close in the busy lane to hide him from view.

He took a deep breath and tried to straighten. The white-hot pain in his groin struck again. 'I think my urethra is rearranging itself,' he said. 'Give me a second. It'll pass.'

'Jesus,' Helwise breathed.

'Police,' said Emlee with the fatalism of a jaded priest.

Imre forced himself to stand. Three brass helmets, limned with attention-getting blue, were shouldering through the crowd. The masses had evolved with night's falling; instead of bargain-seekers and merchants, there were revelers and vice peddlers, prowling or staggering from venue to venue in various stages of intoxication. And thieves, of course, preying on the careless. Music filled the cooling air; aromatic smoke and exotic pheromones tickled the back of his sinuses. Two of Chenresi's sister suns shone brightly across the hazy band of the Milky Way; no other stars were visible.

Imre dropped one shoulder, letting that and the limp he couldn't help give the impression that he was crippled. His hood hung low over his face, casting it in permanent shadow. His right hand rested out of sight, fingers cradling the grip of the pistol Emlee had given him. His brutalized left hand swung free, adding to the illusion he was trying to convey.

Emlee spared him nothing in her efforts to evade detection. They dodged between stalls, along lanes, in and out of crowded squares, through bars. The pain pulsed in hot waves radiating outward from his groin. He had no feeling in his genitals at all, it seemed, except for pain. He wondered if it was possible for his new body to reject the male organs entirely, leaving him shipwrecked on a shore even more uncomfortable than the last. What then, he wondered. Would he attempt to hurry the transition again, supposing he didn't bleed to death or fall afoul of the Hypers, Barons, or whoever else was after him? Was he willing to risk his life in order to become Himself again?

He supposed he was already doing that, by coming to Mandala Supersystem and pursuing his memories, no matter where they might lead him.

More blue-limned brass helmets loomed ahead. Emlee changed tack, heading at a right angle to the line connecting the two patrols. They passed the back of a bar that throbbed with rhythms pitched slightly too high and too fast for Absolute ears. Imre's nose detected a dozen different drugs and their breakdown products. Even in the Continuum, where any conceivable sensation could be accessed at will, people had sought intoxication by interfering chemically, electrically, or cybernetically with their bodies. Sensation wasn't a static thing, not in a biological machine designed to register change in its environment. Unpredictability itself was desirable. Hyperabad wasn't the jungle, or the dangerous plains of Africa, but there was a whiff of the primal to the pursuit of pleasure, even here. Just because people could be gods didn't mean everyone wanted to be.

A third patrol heaved into view ahead. Imre knew then that they were in trouble. 'I presume there's no way we can fight our way out of this,' he said to Emlee, as they took cover in an empty shed.

'Not the three of us, barely armed.' The throb of the nightclub gave her words more gravitas than they needed.

'Okay. Helwise, warm up the drives. We might need a dramatic exit.'

'What about those airspace restrictions?'

'I think we're beyond that now.'

'Right you are, old cock.'

'We should separate,' said Freer, his folded frame closest to the shed's entrance. His eyes didn't leave the path outside. 'Split into two, even three groups. One creates a distraction—'

'No. No one's doing anything like that.' Imre wondered at the strength of his feeling that they should stay together. Freer was making sense; he knew that; but they were already stretched too thin, with Helwise in one place, the rest of them in another, and Render still waiting to be rescued. 'They can't possibly know we're here for sure. Eventually they'll move on.'

Over the thudding of bass drums, a high-pitched whine became audible.

'That's an AAV,' said Emlee, gaze lifting to the dark ceiling. 'Someone's not taking any chances.'

'On one slimy cutter's word?' Helwise sounded skeptical. 'You've been rumbled again, I'd say.'

'How?' Emlee sounded frustrated and angry. 'The only person who knew anything at all was Chyro.'

'That's not true. There's us.'

'Are you saying one of us is a traitor?'

'I'm saying we need to consider the possibility.'

'Be careful where you point the finger,' Emlee said with eyes darkening. 'You're as much a suspect as I am. Who knows who you've been talking to, safe in the ship?'

'There are plenty of fingers to go around, Copas. Broadcasting a distress call is the oldest trick in the book.'

'Enough,' said Imre, his voice raised sufficiently to cut across their growing argument. 'None of us is a traitor. We've just been unlucky. Helwise, is there any sign that you're going to be stopped from launching?'

'None that I can see.'

'Good. Emlee, can you suggest a nearby dust-off point? I want to keep casualties to a minimum.'

She nodded. 'There's a structure called the Granary to the north-east. Its roof would be perfect.'

'Then we'll head there. It'll be easier on my nerves if we keep moving, rather than sitting around waiting for something that might never come.'

Freer nodded once in agreement. 'The way is clear.'

'So let's go.' He waved the mercenary ahead of him and switched his tempo higher. 'Helwise, get in the air. If they're not going to let you launch, we need to know sooner rather than later.'

'You want me to come straight to you?'

'No. Take another heading. Give them something to think about. Stay close, though. We might need you in a hurry.'

'Roger dodger.'

Freer slipped out of the shed and Emlee followed. Imre took a deep breath, shifted his grip on the pistol, and followed.

Ghosts of a thousand campaigns haunted him as they weaved through the tangled streets of the Hyperabadan market. Cat-and-mouse games through steep canyon networks; guerrilla campaigns in ice-rimed city streets; close-combat skirmishes at tempos so overclocked that wars could be won or lost in a second. The dusty, urban nightscape took on a surreal edge. Shuttered stalls and revelers caught up in their own lives swept by, lit by fleeting searchlights from above. Sometimes Imre was unsure precisely which world he inhabited most: Hyperabad or that of his former self. He forced himself to focus on Emlee's narrow-shouldered, muscular back. The shifting, flickering shadows held threats visible only to him.

They crossed a relatively broad thoroughfare one by one, crouched low and moving as quickly as his aching muscles allowed. The air flowed past him like a river of thick soup. The edges of his new flak jacket smoldered. He forced himself to keep moving, to concentrate, to run through the pain. The world contracted around him, became a series of obstacles to be dealt with, then forgotten.

Ahead, a blocky, brick building appeared, looming over the empty stalls and sail-like sunshades. Their destination, he presumed. Somewhere above, among the cornucopia of lights moving in the sky, Helwise was waiting to snatch them to safety. All they had to do was meet her halfway. How hard could that be?

Needles of weapon fire laced the wall at his side. He ducked, following Emlee through an open doorway. Glowing domes, color-shifted to red by his rapid tempo, filled the alleyway behind them. Freer shot out the wall on the other side of the stall they had entered, and the three of them burst back out into the night air. Another shot blew in a door two up, creating an obvious distraction as they took another route away. A forest of streamers and flags caught fire in their wake, ignited by stray shots.

A slow-motion splinter stabbed deep into Imre's thigh. He winced but kept moving, painfully aware that Emlee was lagging behind. If they didn't find cover soon, they would have no choice but to turn and fight. Helwise would have to bring the ship down in the middle of the marketplace, and to hell with the property damage that caused.

Two AAVs slid overhead, their gunners too slow to take advantage of their superior positions. Gunfire raked the stalls and streets, laying down still more smoke and debris. They passed revelers frozen in states of panic, some of them bloodied by shrapnel or direct hits. The market had become an all-out war zone. Imre felt for them, even as the thought of surrender didn't even once cross his mind.

Then, as they neared the eastern side of the Granary, its redbrick wall looming over them like an edifice, Emlee raised a hand. 'I'm getting something,' she said. 'From Zadiq Turin.'

'About bloody time,' Helwise growled. 'Don't keep it to yourself.'

'To the authors of the grisly message delivered to my doorstep this evening,' intoned a rounded, formal voice, 'I say this: why should I negotiate with terrorists?'

'It's a live broadcast,' said Emlee.

'Better answer her,' Imre said.

'Because we have what you want,' she sent back.

'That is not the issue, not when I am told the authorities are close to taking it off you.'

'How does she know that?' asked Freer.

'She's powerful and obviously has friends in law enforcement,' said Emlee to him. 'She could be watching us right now, for all we know.'

'Tell her the goods could easily be damaged,' Imre said. 'This is a volatile situation for all of us. If she wants me back in one piece, she's going to have to talk.'

Emlee passed on the message.

'He's already in two pieces,' came the immediate reply. 'One of them is sitting on my knee at this very moment.'

'Let's not make it three,' Emlee said. 'Or more. I'm not kidding.'

'You sound very serious, my dear girl, and perhaps a trifle too earnest. How can I be sure this isn't a trap? I have enemies too, you know.'

'We're not after you. We want an exchange: Bergamasc for a prisoner in Kismet. I know you have contacts there. If you give us him, we'll give you what you want.'

'There are so many prisoners in Kismet. Which one in particular do you require?'

Emlee gave Render's real name, which Imre had forgotten: Archard Rositano. 'He's been there a long time. He won't be hard to find.'

'Is this the wretch known as Render? He's a special case, never to be released.'

'Everyone in Kismet is a special case, and people do leave.' Emlee's voice was level, but Imre could see the tension in her shoulder blades. 'You'll get him out or never see Imre again.'

'On first-name basis with him, are you? Don't be presumptuous, girl. His affections are not granted so easily.' There was a moment's silence. 'Very well. I can probably give you what you wish, and more into the bargain. Still, it could be a trap. You set the exchange; I'll set the terms. We will meet in Kismet to enact the transaction, or it will not take place. That is my sole condition.'

'You could be trying to trap us in turn,' Emlee said.

'Indeed I could be, but I have something you want too, so we are on equal footing. For each of us the threat is real. Do you accept my terms? Are we agreed?'

'Tell her yes,' Imre said. 'We'll meet her at Kismet in three days.'

'Inform anyone who asks that you're traveling under Diplomatic Privilege 438,' Zadiq Turin instructed them. 'That'll refer any queries back to me and ensure you arrive at Kismet unencumbered. I don't want your cargo damaged. However, the privilege can easily be revoked. If you don't intend to honor your end of the bargain, don't come at all. I can assure you that you'll never leave.'

With that threat, the conversation ended.

'Was that traceable?' asked Freer.

Emlee shook her head. 'Not under these conditions.' They were running parallel to the side of the Granary, looking for an entrance in the sheer, red wall. 'Are you still planning to go ahead with this?'

'All the way,' he said. 'Get us safely onto the ship, and you'll see that you can believe me.'

'A changed man, huh?'

'A man, at least,' said Helwise.

'I'm more worried about getting us off Kismet,' said Freer. 'We could all end up in a cell with Render if this goes badly.'

'We could indeed,' said Imre. 'Do you want to back out?'

Before Freer could answer, the sky above turned to flame and a rain of slow-motion shrapnel began to fall.

'What the hell is going on down there?' asked Helwise. Her voice was barely audible over the thunderous concussions shaking the world.

'Someone's attacking the police.' Imre had rolled for cover under a three-wheeled ground-hugger chained to a rusty lamppost. Molten flakes descended like burning snow to the sidewalk. 'At least one of the AAVs has been taken out, maybe two. It's not you, is it?'

'I'm not the sort to go off half-cocked,' she said. 'That's the guy we're rescuing, remember? I can see the AAVs going down, and I can see at least four firefights happening below. The action isn't far from you, but it seems to be moving away. What I really mean is: why are the police attacking each other?'

A smile of understanding spread across Imre's face. And more besides, he remembered. 'It's her. Mother Turin – she's playing the police force against itself. The faction loyal to her versus the Hypers or the Barons, or whoever most wants us. She's giving us a chance to escape.'

'Then I suggest you take it,' Helwise said. 'It's as hot as a nun's twat up here. Reinforcement's on its way.'

Imre waited a beat to see if the deadly rain was ebbing. It did seem to have slackened off. Favoring the leg with the splinter, he rolled from the car to the shelter of a stall's canvas overhang, pock-marked with bullet burns.

'Okay, people, let's go!'

Emlee and Freer emerged from their own shelters and ran with him down the side of the giant building. Although they were in full view, no one stepped out to intercept them, and no gunfire was aimed in their direction. Flashes of reddish light came and went to their right. The wreckage of one of the AAVs crashed not far away, flinging debris and fire across a surprisingly wide area. A smoke-blackened, domed helmet landed with a clatter in the street behind them. Imre didn't stop to check if it was full or empty.

An arched doorway approached on their left. Emlee led them unhesitatingly inside, where a cavernous storage space greeted them, full of food stalls and offices and hung with vast chandeliers that shook and rattled with every retort. Stairwells snaked to upper levels. They picked one at random and wound their way to the ceiling. A network of girders and scaffolds filled the roof space like the webs of giant metal spiders.

Access to the roof was blocked by a door protected electronically and by a thick metal bolt. Emlee picked the lock and Freer shot the bolt. Smoky night air greeted them on the expansive, flat roof. The Granary seemed much larger than it had on the ground, punctuated only by the occasional exhaust vent and antenna.

'Helwise?' Imre studied the specks moving across the sky. 'Where are you?'

'Right on top of you.' A red dot winked and began to descend.

Imre allowed himself to feel relief. Soon they would be reunited and on their way to rescue Render. That was the most important thing, he reminded himself. The Barons, the Luminous, and his former self could wait; the nature of Domgard and the Slow Wave were irrelevant until he achieved this goal.

His injured thigh throbbed. Blood spread in a growing circle across his pants. Taking off his right glove, he bent over to inspect the wound.

As a result of that slight movement, the shot aimed at him merely clipped his ear. It was still enough, however, to kick his head sideways and drop him dazed to the roof. The world narrowed down to the end of a long, dark tunnel. He saw only dimly what happened next, as Freer and Emlee dropped to a protective crouch over him, firing sustained bursts at the location the sniper had fired from. Sparks flew from another volley, narrowly missing his supine form. He tried to move, but his limbs were distant and vague. Voices boomed like whales, echoing and incomprehensible. He couldn't hear the bark of the guns.

Freer bent over him and, cupping the back of his head, slid him to a less exposed position, while Emlee covered them both. A dark shape slid like oil from one vantage point to another. To the left, he wanted to shout. He's coming around your flank! But Emlee had seen him and sent a fan of lethal energy to cut him off. The shape dodged away.

I recognize him, Imre surprised himself by thinking. I'd know the way my would-be killer moves anywhere.

A blast of fiery air lifted clouds of weightless dust and obscured his vision. *The Cauld Lad* had arrived, black and hostile with spider-eyes flashing in a dozen different colors. Lifters flared, spikes of dangerous heat angled well away from the besieged trio; struts extended for a temporary landing. Emlee waved to Helwise, an ancient gesture meaning: we need help, fast! A hatch opened in the side of the ship, and Helwise's skin-suited figure dropped to the ground. With light, rapid steps she ran to help Freer carry Imre inside.

The sniper emerged from behind a cooling stack, gun flaring. Dust motes disintegrated in showers of tiny sparks like cracks in the world. Freer grunted, hit in the shoulder, and slipped to one knee. Helwise tugged Imre harder, her hands digging into his upper body. The killer was running toward them, all attempt to hide abandoned, clad from sole to scalp in black combat armor, firing as he came. Soft punches struck Imre's body, making him twitch.

He performed the calculations instinctively, as a distraction.

Four against one should have been sufficient to ensure everyone's retreat to safety, including his own, but *The Cauld Lad* was too far away. Two of them were already injured. The assassin appeared to have one objective only, and that was to kill him. Nothing else mattered.

The gun's mouth spat fire in silence. Imre stared at it, waiting for the shot that would end his short life.

It didn't come. Emlee stepped between him and the assassin. She should have been mown down in an instant, but instead the lethal gunfire ceased. Then it was her gun talking, following him as the killer jerked away and tried to make for cover. Too late. The assassin's frontal assault had failed and now he was running away with his back exposed. Shots peppered his armor with miniature explosions. He managed less than five steps before one leg gave way and he sprawled face-forward onto the dusty roof.

Emlee kept her gun trained on the body as Helwise and Freer dragged Imre into *The Cauld Lad*.

Take the body! His mental voice was utterly disconnected from his lips, tongue, and vocal cords. He didn't even think of using the local grid to convey his urgent message. Don't leave it behind! We need it!

Blood had just begun pooling around it as Emlee leapt after him into the ship's bright orange embrace. Lifters burned. Fire ignited the dry air, pushed the body over onto its side. The air lock closed shut on the view. The floor kicked beneath them, and they were away.

Helwise leaned over him, a worried expression on her face.

That was me, he wanted to tell her. Emlee killed me out there. I'm sure of it!

Black despair rose in him as they lifted him and carried him to the medical suite. Freer's hands were bloody, and so were Emlee's. The world turned around him. Had he imagined that flash of familiarity? Could it have been an illusion brought on by the injury he had sustained? Just how badly hurt was he . . .?

He tried not to think about it as the pure white walls of the medical suite enfolded him. The last time he had been there was upon his escape from the Jinc, to heal his broken shoulder. That felt like a million years ago. He was so tired of mysteries and uncertainty, of being fired on and threatened. Perhaps it would have been better to die in the gunsights of the assassin, whoever he had really been.

Helwise glanced at Emlee as Freer cut away his clothes. Her expression mixed concern and suspicion in equal measures.

'Welcome aboard,' she said.

A quartet of Vespulas descended from orbit to intercept them. Imre watched in a state of hazy anxiety as Emlee broadcast the diplomatic privilege Mother Turin had given them. Without further prompting, the patrol broke away and left them alone.

'Do you think he was one of the Barons?' Helwise asked.

Imre blinked up at her. He was lying in a convalescence tube in the medical suite, protected from the ship's powerful thrust by a bath of healing fluids. His many wounds – including the stump on his left hand – had been sealed and cleaned. The cracked skull and concussion he had suffered were no longer considered serious. That left only the psychological injuries to heal.

Helwise had stayed with him, leaving Freer – his relatively minor wound already seen to – and Emlee to fly the ship to safety. She could have flown the ship from the medical suite, just as easily as he viewed their telemetry from his liquid bed, but she assured him she didn't want to.

'Who was?' he asked her.

'The guy who shot you, of course. Could he have been working for the Barons?'

He shook his head. Increasingly the feeling that he had recognized Himself on the roof of the Granary seemed like a fantasy inspired by head trauma. He saw Himself everywhere, in memories and in conversation with his former friends; why not in real life as well? The possibility that it had actually been him, he told himself, was surely remote.

'What makes you think he could have been?' he asked her.

'Well, the Barons saved Emlee when they killed her friend,

the Fort. If she was nothing to them, they would've just let her die with everyone else. Then this guy tonight stopped shooting at you when she got in his line of fire. Doesn't that strike you as odd?'

Odder than he cared to admit. Emlee had been willing to take a bullet for him.

'Perhaps that was just a coincidence,' he offered Helwise. The theory he had briefly entertained he would keep to himself. 'He was probably just another policeman trying to do his job, trying to stop us.'

'Plenty of people have been killed like that before,' she said. 'Don't get hung up on it, if that's what's worrying you.'

He saw an endless parade of victims in his memory: enemy combatants and despots, as well as innocent civilians caught in the melee. He knew the names of some; most were anonymous. It had never bothered him before – perhaps because his utter extinction had never been a possibility. The 'wank-fests,' as Helwise called them, ensured that somewhere in the galaxy part of him was likely to survive, even if a particular version of Himself did not. That had always been a comfort.

Now his former self had effectively disappeared, and someone had blown up the Drum in attempt to erase even that last vestige of him. There was little comfort in such a galaxy. He didn't need to imagine his own self-assassination to be sure of that.

The Cauld Lad left Hyperabad's gravity well at speed, just in case their immunity to pursuit proved short-lived, and powered around Chenresi for the dead star Sakra and its closely orbiting prison. He watched without comment, feeling invisible forces – his own private version of celestial mechanics – tugging him to a dark destiny in that forbidding place.

'I never found it,' Helwise told him later. 'The Loop shunt, I mean – in case you're not keeping up again.'

He had understood her. In fatalistic tones, he told her something he remembered well but which his original self had clearly failed to mention. 'Q looping was essential to the ascendancy of the Forts. It was as essential as the ability to talk is to us – no, even more so: the ability for our neurons to talk to each other. Loop shunts, therefore, weren't something the frags used; it was something they were. Every frag had one inside them, an organ of their bodies just as they were individually organs of their greater minds. Without the shunts, the frags were just dead flesh.'

Helwise nodded, a darkness behind her eyes telling him that she was thinking of the Forts on the *Deodati* and the frags that Himself had killed.

'When I asked you to look for the Loop shunt on *The Cauld Lad*,' he told her, 'I really thought you'd find it; it's the only way we could have been followed. But you didn't find it, and that's when I began to wonder. We were being tracked on the ground as well as in the ship. There's only one place the shunt could be.'

'Inside you,' she said, the darkness deepening.

'Yes. During my reconstruction, Chyro found something odd, something I didn't notice when we were in the Cat's Arse. He didn't tell me what it was, but I think we know now.'

'Did the Jinc do that? Why would they want to track you if they were planning to assimilate you into their happy family?'

He didn't know. 'Perhaps it wasn't the Jinc. Perhaps it was the silver sphere.'

'The Luminous,' she corrected him.

'We don't know for certain they're the same thing.'

'Occam's razor, Imre. Don't multiply entities unnecessarily.'

'They seem to be doing it well enough on their own.'

She was silent for a moment, then asked, 'Do you want us to take the shunt out now?'

'No.' He had been wondering that himself. 'It might even come in handy one day as evidence, or bait.'

'Whatever you say.' She bent down and kissed him on the forehead – a surprisingly tender gesture. 'You look tired. I'll let you rest. Holler if you need anything, okay?'

He nodded and let his eyes shut. He was indeed tired. A long, dreamless sleep would be a blessing for both him and his body.

As Helwise kicked out of the room, however, his thoughts drifted back to Emlee and the Barons. Another coincidence occurred to him: the way the AAV hadn't fired on the ground-hugger while she was inside it. There were assassins on every front, targeting him and the Hypers' new Forts – but not her. What was so special about her? Was there a connection between them and her that he was failing to see? Could the Barons possibly have been the ones to set her free from Kismet?

He drifted asleep with an image of Emlee floating in his mind's eye: on the bridge of *Pelorus*, her jade green eyes alive with anger. A rush of guilt surprised him, carried him down to oblivion. Her hostility was so naked that he couldn't bring himself to suspect her of treachery – or to doubt that he deserved it, somehow.

The dead walked in his dreams, and he walked alone among them.

Kismet from a distance was no more welcoming than Emlee assured them it was on the inside. Looking at the first high-resolution images, Imre was reminded of spores seen through electron microscopes: all prickles and hooks arranged with geometric regularity across a landscape of inverted buttresses and arches. Close examination of its structure revealed regular deformations marching through its metal structure, lengthening and compressing in several directions at once. The tiny dot behind it, blindingly bright in X-rays but almost invisible in other frequencies, was an old, cold stellar remnant eleven kilometers across that weighed one and a half times Hyperabad's primary star, possessed a relatively tiny magnetic field, and had long since swept its orbit empty of gas and rubble. All it had to tug on now was the relatively tiny station, whipping around it like the universe's most terrifying carnival ride.

'Apoapsis is two hours away,' said Freer, studying the station's orbit projected in *The Cauld Lad*'s wraparound display. 'We can be in position if we don't spare the horses.'

Imre nodded, up and mobile but stiff in his muscles from surgery and gunshot wounds. 'Are we the only ships in the vicinity?'

'Two in the dock; a dozen or so in wider orbits. There's at least one military exercise in progress.'

'Hypers?' asked Emlee.

'No. Another Mandalan government – the Consentient Alliance.'

'We'll be a moving target, if they are Barons in disguise,' Imre said, thinking aloud. Should they decide not to dock during apoapsis, they would have to wait almost a full day for the next one. That might make no difference at all to Render, but it could be life or death to them. 'Take us in,' he ordered. 'Watch our backs, though. I don't want anyone sneaking up on us while we're distracted.'

'Gotcha.' Helwise had the helm. She was dressed for combat in inch-thick flexible plate armor that molded to every curve of her form. Her unadorned head and neck looked preposterous protruding from the open collar. Black hair pressed close to her scalp like a helmet.

'Course confirmed,' said the ship in response to her instructions. 'You are entering a region exceeding my design tolerances. Performance may be inhibited.'

'We'll take our chances,' Imre told *The Cauld Lad*, thinking that its warning applied to all of them in different ways. At periapsis, the closest point of Kismet to Sakra, the ship would be moving at over six hundred kilometers per second and experiencing tidal forces of up to eight Earth gravities – hardly insurmountable conditions for a starship, but with a dead star less than a million kilometers away, not trivial either. At such a close distance – had they been orbiting Sol, they would have been skimming its photosphere – the ambient gravity would peak at thirty times Earth normal. 'So long as we don't break orbit at any point other than apoapsis, we'll be fine.'

'Remember what they say about best-laid plans,' said Helwise with an arched eyebrow.

'I'm neither mice nor man,' he said. 'That's why it'll work.'

An automatic system hailed *The Cauld Lad* as it entered a parabolic orbit designed to intersect the station. Addressing the ship by the alias it had used on Hyperabad, the AI warned them that they were entering a restricted and dangerous area. If they approached without authorization, they would be fired upon.

'We're protected by Diplomatic Privilege 438,' Freer replied for the ship. Both Imre and Emlee might have had voiceprints on record, and Helwise was closely watching telemetry. 'Requesting permission to dock.'

'Hold, *Turnfalken.*'

A moment later, a gravelly, female human voice spoke. 'This is Duty Officer Wehr. We weren't expecting you, *Turnfalken*, and you've created something of a conflict. We have only one berth free and another ship docking on a tight schedule just after apoapsis. You can dock, but we'll need you out of the way when the second ship arrives. Anyone aboard will have to stay aboard. That's the best I can offer you. Does it suit?'

Imre nodded. 'Tell her it does. That second ship is almost certainly Mother Turin's.'

'Why doesn't she go first?' asked Helwise, as Freer relayed the order.

'Because she's not here yet,' said Imre.

'I'm not staying with the ship this time. Don't you dare ask me to.'

'I won't. We're going in together. All of us. And we will be armed.'

Freer nodded. 'Wehr and her buddies won't be elite troops. If they were, they certainly wouldn't be working out here.'

'Don't underestimate them,' said Emlee. 'Their numbers aren't huge, but they've kept Render prisoner all this time.'

'You said they strip the inmates down to their balls,' said Helwise. 'No mods, no tempo shifting – just what they need to survive. It'd be like herding cattle – a job for shepherds, not sharpshooters.'

'Criminal cattle from a dozen worlds.' Emlee didn't back down. 'I know we're you're coming from. Don't be fooled. Not everyone who works in a prison is a grunt – just like not everyone in a prison is guilty.'

'We're all guilty of something,' said Freer.

'You have permission to dock,' Wehr told them. 'Warden Goneril will join you in Bay 21.'

'We're not here to meet the warden,' said Freer. 'The people in the ship behind us will fill him in.'

'Everyone meets the warden,' Wehr said in a frosty tone. 'She makes a point of it.' The comms line clicked shut.

'Nice one, dickhead,' said Helwise, nudging Freer with an armored elbow. 'Do you want to get everyone offside before we even arrive?'

Freer ignored her in favor of overseeing the ship's approach maneuvers.

'We'd better get ready,' Imre told Emlee. 'I have to be bound and hooded. You'll need to be obscured too so the warden won't recognize your face.'

'I suggest we're both presented as hostages,' she said. 'There'll be no mistaking us for each other, but it could throw Turin off.'

'That's a good idea, Emlee,' Helwise said, and Freer nodded. Imre agreed too. Leaving *The Cauld Lad* under Helwise and Freer's supervision, Emlee and Imre went to the air lock to don their disguises.

It was a simple matter to modify the ship's black skin suits to look like containment and transfer harnesses, with disguised flaws that would allow them to break free in an instant, if they needed to, and permit data to leak from the exterior through carefully shielded ports. He tried one on first. Thickened black material pressed his elbows tightly to his sides with his forearms twisted awkwardly across his back. A length of flexible plastic joined his ankles, leaving him barely enough slack to walk. Rigid struts up his spine made it difficult to turn. An all-encompassing hood completed the ensemble, flowing up from his shoulders and over his face like a mourner's cowl. For luck, he took the piece of crimson-stained glass he had retrieved from the Cat's Arse and secured it close to his chest.

When the hood slid shut, and he went to move his arms, he found himself absolutely immobile. He wrenched his shoulders to no avail. Nothing but darkness and silence greeted his senses.

Click. 'How do you like that, Imre? Comfortable?'

He forced a lighthearted tone despite sudden claustrophobia. 'It's a little tight across the shoulders, Emlee.'

'Is that too much to endure, after everything you've done?'

'I guess not.'

The pressure didn't relent. He felt her standing close to him. 'I could choke the life out of you, if I wanted to.'

There wasn't the slightest trace of humor in her voice. 'You wouldn't do it.'

'Is that a dare?'

'It's not anything, Emlee.' His muscles found no give at all. 'Quit screwing around and let me go.'

She did something to his suit. It moved without his volition, forcing his knees to bend. His center of gravity dropped. He jerked into a kneeling position at her feet. 'Beg me,' she ordered.

'You're joking.'

'Beg me, or I'll shut off your air.'

'I'm no use to anyone dead –'

'Shut up, Imre.'

He was breathing too quickly. Already he could feel the air in the hood growing stale. He could survive hours without oxygen, but he couldn't fight a sudden tightening of the suit itself. His ribs creaked. Pain flowed in waves across his skull. A fear that he had completely misjudged her flashed through him. What if the Barons had spared her because she was working for them and had never intended other than to betray him the moment she had the chance? He gasped her name.

Then the pressure was gone, and his limbs were released. Air rushed against his face. He fell forward and rolled, gasping, onto his side. Light trickled through pinprick data points, seeming bright to his sensation-starved eyes.

She was a shadow looming over him, shifting in and out of focus. 'On your feet. It's your turn to seal me up. We have to make it look convincing, right?'

He clambered upright, his arms coming free as they had arranged. The sudden reversal of her mood confused him no less than the pounding of blood to parts of his body that hadn't shown life for weeks. Chyro had done more than just hurry along the process of his transformation. He had clearly undone some of the

Jinc's other tinkering as well. Imre hoped Emlee couldn't see the most recent change as he helped her adjust the parameters of her makeshift confinement suit. The plan, he told himself, was what he should be thinking about, nothing else.

His erection mocked him, urgent and novel and mysterious in timing, as he carefully bound her in turn.

The four of them congregated, disguised, in the air lock as the ship came in to dock: two black-clad prisoners, hooded and bound; two guards clad in combat uniforms with no identifiers, sporting visible sidearms at their hips and concealed weapons elsewhere on their persons. Imre fully expected the guards to find most of the weapons. With luck, one or two would slip through the security net. He had no desire to go into the prison as defenseless as he had been on Hyperabad.

The deck shifted restlessly under them as *The Cauld Lad* matched orbits with Kismet. Through the limited view allowed by Imre's hood, he saw the prickled, grey-black surface of the prison grow large before them. One stalk protruded farther than the others: the vacant dock they had been allocated by Duty Officer Wehr. The other stalks — hundreds of them, reaching like silver stalagmites for the cold light of distant stars — were tipped with clusters of transparent bubbles. Each one was a cell, Emlee had explained, large enough for a single person. There were no communications between the cells, no media facilities to speak of, and no shutters to block out the view.

'Pleasant,' said Freer, his voice as dry as a desert on Mercury. 'Which one were you in?'

Emlee didn't acknowledge the question. Her obsidian form stood motionlessly beside Imre, armless, faceless, and powerless. Neither Helwise nor Freer mentioned the exchange in the air lock. He wondered if they had noticed but wasn't going to bring it up himself.

The ship flew itself, with Helwise keeping a close watch on its progress. The dock expanded in the forward view until it dominated the screen. The mechanism was nothing out of the ordinary —

a late addition, Imre assumed, to the station's existing structure, possibly to deal with the increasing demands of the penal system. He wondered if troublemakers and the condemned alike were disposed of in the steep gravity well of the dead star below. Freedom by free fall. He could see the attraction in that, sometimes.

Dock met ship with a boom and a jerk. The floor dropped from beneath him, then settled as grapnels gripped and held tight. *The Cauld Lad* and Kismet were locked together, their orbits one for a brief time. Physical submission to the larger structure came easily, with no sense of resistance. Although the station was in the distant leg of its orbit about the dead star, there was sufficient tidal force to provide an illusion of weight.

Pressures equalized. Electronic handshakes were exchanged. The ship's outer air lock opened to reveal a blank steel wall, which a second later divided into four fanglike sections and slid away.

A short, black-skinned woman stood at the center of the boxy umbilical, dressed in a no-nonsense blue uniform. 'I'm Wehr,' she said shortly. 'Come with me. Stick to the space between the dotted lines.'

She turned on her heel and walked away from them, following a narrow path along the umbilical.

'Do as she says,' said Emlee privately to the three of them. 'Don't stray from the path, or you could be hurt, especially at periapsis.'

'Security?' asked Helwise.

'Tides.'

Freer went first, followed by the 'prisoners,' then Helwise. Imre knew exactly what Emlee meant with his first step. Uneven gravitational forces tugged at him. The floor seemed to be moving under his feet.

The steel doors slammed shut once they had passed through them. Wehr didn't take them far. Bay 21 was a triangular room with seats for ten tucked at an odd tangent to the umbilical. A pocket of gravitational stability, Imre assumed. Wehr turned to face them, her eyes flat and hard.

'You'll need to move your ship,' she told Freer, singling him out, presumably, as the male she had spoken to earlier. His rank had never been clarified.

'When do you expect the second ship?' he asked her, as expressionless as the steel doors.

'In forty minutes.'

'We'll move in thirty-five. Where's the warden? I thought you said she'd be here.'

'I said she'd join you here.' Wehr folded her hands in front of her. They were broad and manicured. She wore a single silver ring on the index finger of her right hand, in the shape of a skull. 'Are these two for us?' she asked, glancing at Emlee and Imre.

'That depends on Mother Turin.'

One eyebrow went up. 'Are you followers?'

'My faith is my business.'

'Or your business is your faith. There's an important distinction.'

'I don't see how it makes any difference to you.'

'To me, none. To the Warden Goneril . . .' Wehr dismissed the problem with a shrug. 'She'll be here in a moment.'

The waiting ate at Freer more corrosively than the banter. 'Doesn't it worry you that we're armed?'

'No. Does it worry you that with a single word from the warden, you will never leave?'

'I told you. We're traveling under diplomatic immunity.'

'That ends here. You're in our territory now. Accidents happen, this close to a dead star. I'd be careful what you say if I were you.'

A hatch hissed open behind her. She looked over her shoulder at the empty doorway, but nothing immediately emerged. What lay beyond was in shadow. Still she didn't move. Imre became conscious of the ambience of the station: a constant susurrus of air overlaid by the soft grating and grinding of the structure as it settled. He could barely imagine the stresses it must undergo throughout its perilous, twenty-two hours orbit around its primary.

What different creatures of iron, he thought, were the Drum and Kismet. One intended to last eternity intact; the other in a constant state of deformation. Which should he aspire to emulate?

A huge figure moved out of the darkness through the open portal and into the room. Imre had to repress the urge to take a step away. The warden was the largest woman he had ever seen, easily two meters tall and broad with it. Her shoulders swayed like the tops of trees in a heavy wind. Her booted feet were like boats. The metal railing shifted beneath her weight. Each step was answered by the station. She looked as though she weighed half a ton, wrapped in a dark blue uniform with silver piping.

Most remarkable of all was her face, which was defined by her cheekbones in the same way that Kismet was defined by Sakra. Her mouth was full, almost sensual, which looked strange on such a large frame. Her scalp was hairless and shone like plastic stretched tight over a cadaver. Her eyes moved with the momentum of worlds, assessing everyone in the room with one heavy sweep.

'Greetings, pilgrims,' she said in a voice that could easily have come from a man's mouth. She stopped next to Wehr and stood with her giant hands behind her back. Imre was glad to see them go. Just looking at them made him feel as though he was being strangled. 'You travel under the flag of the faithful, so welcome, welcome. Has Wehr explained that you need to move your ship?'

'Yes,' said Freer.

'Good, good. Have you visited our facilities before?'

'No.'

'Then allow me to introduce you.' The warden rotated on one heel and returned the way she had come. 'Leave your walking dead behind and follow. Don't stray from the path.'

Freer almost looked at Imre, but he recovered quickly. 'Of course. After you,' he said to Helwise, who strode ahead of him with her hand on her holster. Wehr stayed behind.

'We'll call if we need you,' Imre sent via Corps-encrypted whisper. 'Give us a feed, and we'll see what you see.'

Freer didn't waste bandwidth replying. A window opened in the dark confines of Imre's hood, revealing everything Helwise saw, subtly distorted as though through a fish-eye lens: nothing but more metal so far, in the form of a ramp spiraling around a pillar five meters across. Imre assumed Emlee was receiving it as well. The warden's voice came clearly to them.

'Kismet. It's an appropriate name, don't you think? Those who come here are manifestly caught up in a plan, be it one they're willingly part of or one they've had thrust upon them. Destiny wears many faces, and few are happy to see mine.' They came to a dead end, a curved steel wall that split in two and slid aside when the warden clapped her hands. Revealed was a view across the station's many thornlike spikes. Its resemblance to a seed vanished. Now it was a forest of girders and stanchions reaching ever upward to the stars. Each metal grey 'tree' reached an apex where grapelike glass bubbles clustered in bunches of a dozen or more. Each grape contained a single dark seed.

Separating the guests from the view was little more than a sheet of thick, transparent plastic and a handrail. Freer and Helwise stood on a balcony jutting out over an abyss that seemed bottomless.

'Every one of them a traitor,' said the warden, indicating the nearest cluster of prisoners. 'Every one of them inconvenient, murderous, or indecent. Their old lives end here, in the hope of being born anew.'

Imre thought the word 'hope' desperately inappropriate.

'You believe in reincarnation, then?' asked Freer.

The warden looked askance at him. 'No more than anyone, pilgrim. The only life we have is the one stretching before us. Or behind us, as in the case of some of these poor souls.'

The view suddenly shifted. Imre fought a wave of vertigo as the viewing platform turned around them. He caught a glimpse of the abyss waiting below. Helwise's cry of fear was loud in his ears.

Then she steadied. Freer had caught her by the shoulders and pulled her upright before she could fall. Behind him, the warden's dense eyes glittered.

'You want to watch your balance here,' the warden told them both. 'Lean too far in any direction, and you might fall.'

'It's not falling I'm afraid of,' Helwise said, her voice shaky but firming. 'It's being pushed.'

'We push ourselves. Gravity is nature's way of finishing the job.'

'How about the rest of that tour?' said Freer. 'We don't have long before your next visitor.'

The warden nodded and turned smartly on her heel. Freer shot Helwise a warning look and followed.

There were layers to Kismet just as there were circles in Hell. The most severe and demonstrative punishment was reserved for those in the outermost cells, where exposure to Sakra and its tides was extreme, but there were many other levels in which prisoners were stacked like monkeys awaiting vivisection, each in their own perfectly isolated cell. All that entered was air and gravity. For some, their incarceration was almost comfortable. The knowledge that escape was not possible and that the station could be destroyed if its orbit deviated even slightly was considered punishment enough.

Imre saw only a small proportion of the station through Helwise's eyes. There wasn't time for a full inspection, and he was under no illusions that the warden intended to give them one. Conveyed by maglev bullet capsule and along carefully constrained walkways, they saw no guards, were granted no insight into the station's internal security, and received not the slightest hint as to where the warden herself lived. In or close to the center of gravity, Imre assumed, well away from the worst effects of the tides. There Warden Goneril and her cronies could ride out each twenty-two-hour periapsis in comfort. Perhaps, he thought, she slept. That would be the greatest luxury deprived those in her cruel care.

When they returned to Bay 21, he caught a glimpse of himself: a featureless, black statue standing with feet apart, arms bound tightly behind its back. He experienced a moment's dislocation, finding himself uncertain for a moment where he truly was. There was little to connect him to the body Helwise regarded. His identity had been stripped from it and placed in her skull, bizarrely, impossibly. Who was he, he asked himself, to be so casually passed from body to body like a ball in a primitive game?

The body in black swayed, and he was wrenched back to himself an instant before it fell. Wehr was watching him and Emlee without pause, and had done so while the warden was absent. He steadied himself and tried to radiate nothing but docility, obedience, remorse, impotence.

'It's time to move your ship,' Wehr told Freer.

'Consider it done.' Freer instructed *The Cauld Lad* to break dock and match orbits with the station. 'Thanks for the hospitality.'

'We offer out of necessity as well as generosity,' said the warden. 'We permit no maneuvering beyond an hour either side of apoapsis. The risk of an accident is too high. You're here for the full cycle, now.'

'We understand.' Freer inclined his head in acknowledgment, unfazed. Helwise looked less certain, and Imre could understand that. Until they were overtly threatened, however, there was no sense in causing a scene.

A series of thumps and bumps echoed through the station's metallic structure. Telemetry indicated that *The Cauld Lad* had disengaged and that Mother Turin's ship was lining up to dock. Her vessel was designed to impress, with sweeping flanges and thrusters that shone like tiny suns. The words reclaim the future girdled the ship's belly in royal purple. Its nose was as sharp as a syringe.

A premonition ran through Imre like a sword. Trapped on Kismet for a full orbit with Zadiq Turin . . . What had he been thinking? Did he want to be taken captive by the woman who worshipped him? Did he really think himself capable of saving the human race, as she somehow believed he was? Was he pushing himself into a fate he couldn't escape, and that nature would seal with the certainty of a coffin slamming shut?

More thumps and booms. He wondered if the prisoners could feel the ships coming and going. Did they hope for rescue, as Emlee had been rescued? Did they feel pity for new arrivals? Did those on the outside of the station read the words on Zadiq Turin's flagship and wonder if they had any future at all?

The steel doors opened with a clang. Footsteps echoed along the umbilical: three people, judging by the syncopated rhythms they made. Duty Officer Wehr hadn't gone to meet them. They clearly knew their way around the station and felt perfectly at home.

Imre recognized the priestess as soon as she entered the room. Clad as Emlee had described in a bright, blue robe that covered her from head to foot, she trailed presence like a train. When she stopped in the middle of the bay, it swirled around her like dense smoke, touching the Warden Goneril and Wehr, Helwise and Freer, and the two black-clad prisoners. Two aides walked a step behind her, dressed in cream outfits of multilayered fabrics with crimson stitched around their lapels. Their faces were exposed beneath matching turbans. Each was expressionless and of indeterminate gender. Each wore a simple black broach on their left chest. Mother Turin wore a matching jewel on her left hand.

'Warden Goneril.' Her voice was cultured and resonant with authority. The warden inclined her head in welcome. 'I have come to inquire about the well-being of a particular prisoner.'

'Of course, Mother.' Warden Goneril bowed even more steeply. 'Ask its name, and I will inquire.'

'The one I refer to is the special case: Archard Rositano.'

The warden straightened with a surprised look on her face. 'Mother, you know its condition.'

'Tell me so the others can hear.' For the first time, she acknowledged the existence of Freer and Helwise, motioning economically with her jeweled hand.

'Archard Rositano continues fair,' said the warden. 'Since you last graced us with your presence, it has been moved in accordance with the detainee rotation schedule. Its new cell is identical to the previous. There are no special circumstances to report.'

'That pleases me.' The veil covering the priestess's face moved in and out with every breath. 'Guilt is guilt, but I would hate any harm to come to this one.'

'Of course not, Mother.' The warden bowed again. 'It knew the Awaited. It has a part to play in the Return.'

'What part is that, exactly?' asked Helwise.

'I lack the Mother's wisdom,' the warden told her. 'When the time is upon us, perhaps I will understand. Or—' A hint of asperity crept into the warden's tone. '—if you would allow me an audience with it alone, Mother Turin, I could interrogate it directly—'

'No, Goneril. I've told you: that will never happen. Chip a fingernail, and I'll have your hide.' She turned to Freer. Her invisible eyes seemed to burn through her veil. 'Do you see what you ask of me? This is a prize I will not easily relinquish.'

'I fail to see the problem,' Freer told her. 'The prize we offer you is greater still.'

'So you say, Alphin Freer,' she said, and Imre could hear the smile in her voice. She sounded as though she was talking through a mouthful of shark teeth. 'Yes, I know you. I know why you want the one you call Render. Our motives are not so mysterious, yours and mine, although your methods could use refinement. I insist that you earn the boon you ask. I insist that your claim passes every possible test. One remains that we have not undertaken.'

'What kind of test?'

'Nothing unduly complicated. My prisoner must recognize your prisoner, or there will be no exchange.'

'Exchange?' the warden protested, her eyes dancing from Freer to Mother Turin. 'But by your own order we are bound never to—'

She waved her silent. 'That is my sole condition. I don't think it ungenerous. Without clear and unambiguous recognition, you will never see your friend again – and, dare I say it, you will never leave here alive.'

'I understand.' Freer nodded solemnly. 'You need proof – and so do we. At the moment, we have nothing but the warden's word that Render still breathes. We're not going to think about negotiating without some kind of surety that we aren't wasting our time.'

'All time is wasted,' she said, 'until the Return.'

'I'm sure "the Awaited" wouldn't thank you for wasting any more.'

'Indeed.' Her attention shifted to Emlee. 'Tell me about the second prisoner, first. You offer one and bring two, without explanation. Could she be the one I think she is, the one who escaped?'

'Reading minds is not my specialty,' Freer told her. 'Consider this a sweetener – a sign of our good intentions.'

She sighed. 'Civilization is indeed undone when friends turn upon friends so readily. Warden Goneril, show them what they came to see. I will be in my stateroom. They may call me there when they have reached a decision.'

With that, she flowed past them, out of the room. Her robes hissed like snakes through grass. Her aides followed, silently attentive. When she was gone, the room felt empty.

'As mad as a meat ax,' Helwise said without moving her lips.

'She has her priorities,' Freer corrected her, 'and we have ours.' To the warden he said, 'We'd like an opportunity to confer after we've seen the "special case." Do you have somewhere private we can retire to?'

'Of course.' The warden seemed unsettled by the audience with Mother Turin and newly wary of her visitors as a result. Questions hovered about her, begging to be voiced. 'Duty Officer Wehr will direct you there.'

Then she was gone, following Zadiq Turin with rapid, heavy steps.

Wehr was startled in turn by her superior's sudden departure. 'We have a conference room on level eight,' she said, 'that will suit your needs, I'm sure.'

'Thank you.'

She said nothing else as she guided them via capsule and a series of narrow corridors through a bird's nest of reinforcing girders deep into the station's interior. Biometric sensors examined her at every juncture and doors opened only as she approached. Still they saw no guards. Strange gravity tugged at them everywhere they went. There was no clear sense of falling, just restlessness as the distance between them and Sakra rapidly contracted. An hour had passed since their arrival – almost 10 percent of the distance from periapsis to apoapsis. Any discomposure they felt now was only going to get worse.

When they were safely ensconced within a broad, circular space
with reinforced walls supporting a low, domed ceiling, Wehr
brought up a holographic display. 'This is the best I can offer you,'
she said. 'A passive feed from the cell containing the special case
you asked about.' No mention of exchanging anything, Imre
noted. Wehr was playing it safe on uncertain terrain. 'The biometric data is current. I can give it to you raw if you like, but you
will not be granted access yourself. The warden wouldn't want me
to go that far, I think.'

'I understand,' said Freer. 'Let's see it.'

A pinkish, egg-shaped image appeared in the center of the
room. Render was curled in a fetal position with his head tilted
sideways, floating at an angle to the floor. His massive, scarred
body appeared intact; his muscle mass was still considerable. Dark
hair covered much of his skin; that on his head was matted and had
pulled free from his scalp in places.

His lips were moving.

'What's he saying?' asked Helwise. 'I can't hear.'

Wehr motioned and sound came up.

'. . . sick and no one can cure me . . .' Render's voice exactly
matched that in the transmission Emlee had received the day they
had left Hyperabad. '. . . blind and no one can see me . . .'

Imre sensed Emlee beside him, physically shaking in her skin
suit. She had said nothing since entering Kismet. He could only
guess at what memories the experience was bringing back to her.

'Can we talk to him?' Helwise asked.

Wehr shook her head. 'The warden wouldn't allow that.'

'I'll bet,' Helwise said privately to the others. 'I think this solves
who the mysterious "she" is. That ugly thug has been breaking her
own high priest's orders and trying to make him talk.'

'Render would never crack,' said Freer.

'Only because he's already so broken it'd be hard to notice the
difference.'

'What's been done to him?' Freer asked the duty officer.
'Imprisonment alone wouldn't do this.'

'He was Flexed on arrival,' she said. 'That's standard for all political activists. The objective is to rehabilitate even the most hardened of criminals.' Her voice was mechanical and her explanation unconvincing. No doubt she was retreating to a stock-standard answer in order to gain time. 'His behavior didn't modify the way we would have liked. It seemed to make him worse, if anything. His brain was already too plastic. When Mother Turin took an interest in him, she asked that the treatment be stopped.'

'If they've hurt him—' Emlee whispered in a soft, choked voice via the Corps protocols. 'I'll kill them all.'

'Let's get him out of there first,' Imre told her. 'Then we can decide what needs to be done about it.'

'. . . lost and no one can find me . . .'

'Shut it off,' said Helwise. 'I've heard enough.'

Wehr did as instructed. 'You are satisfied of his identity?'

'Yes.'

Relief greeted the admission, but it was short-lived. A long, slow complaint rolled through the structure, reminding everyone that its harrowing journey around Sakra was only beginning.

'I'll leave you here,' said Wehr. 'You can ask for Mother Turin by name, and the communicator will connect you.'

'Can we move about?' asked Freer.

'Not until I or the warden returns.' Some of her abrasiveness had gone. Imre couldn't decide if it was the sight of Render, the hints as to their business with Mother Turin, or duties elsewhere calling. 'If your intentions are honorable, I see no reason for concern.'

The room's door slid open and closed as she passed through, leaving the four of them behind. Freer tested it by walking within range of the biosensors. It stayed tightly shut.

'What do you reckon?' asked Helwise via Corps protocols. 'Are we going to be honorable or not?'

'We go through with it,' said Imre. 'We have no choice. There's no doubt Render's here; they didn't have time to prepare a fake as convincing as that. There's no reason to worry about me.'

'Unless Mother Turin prefers the picture without you in it.' Helwise paced restlessly around the room's perimeter. 'Remember what they say about prophets and honor.'

'That's a chance I'm prepared to take.'

'So we offer the exchange, give you for Render – and Emlee too, if we need to.' Freer went over the details with methodical calm. 'If all goes well, we sit out the orbit and leave when the station reaches apoapsis. We go back to the Cat's Arse and wait for you there. Right?'

'Right. As soon as I find out what the hell she wants, I'll get away as soon as I can.'

'You've got no interest in being her god?' Emlee asked.

'I'm having enough trouble being me right now,' he told her with absolute candor. 'I don't think I'm in much shape to save the galaxy.'

'I'm not sure I believe you. But that's your decision, I guess.'

'Okay.' Freer nodded and looked down at the floor. Imre could practically hear him running through the plan one more time to make sure nothing had been forgotten. 'I'll call her and get things moving.'

Imre let himself sag into his rigid containment suit as Freer discussed the details with Mother Turin. He felt profoundly weary and dreaded the hours to come. A three-way holographic discussion ensued when Duty Officer Wehr came on the line to discuss Render's release from his cell. It wasn't going to happen immediately. One hundred minutes Absolute, they decided in the end. In that time, Render would be brought to the conference room and come face-to-face with Imre Bergamasc. If Render recognized him, the exchange would proceed.

'What about the sweetener?' asked Freer, as the final arrangements fell into place.

'If the one you call Render recognizes Imre Bergamasc,' Mother Turin said, 'I will have no further interest in her. Emlee Copas has effectively slipped Kismet's noose.'

'You're still saying "if,"' Helwise said. 'You've tested his DNA. You know who we are. What doubt can you still have?'

'The sample could have been grown from a tiny portion of the original – one of many originals that once existed. It could have been grown from a corpse. The man in the suit could be surgically altered to look like him. That's why I have kept your friend alive: because he is the only litmus test I have.'

'Why do you think you've needed it?' asked Emlee speaking from inside her hood. 'Why hasn't your so-called savior come back to of his own accord?'

The blue-shrouded image of Mother Turin shifted uneasily in the three-dimensional image. 'He has enemies,' she said. 'People such as yourselves, who hold grudges beyond reason, for instance. He interceded for us and paid the price.'

'Imre surrendered to the Forts,' said Freer. 'Is that what you mean by intercession?'

'His actions went beyond surrender. He stood between the great ones and us in order to forge a balance between the two. The responsibility for the war was placed on his shoulders. He bore the burden of our multitudes and spoke for us among the mighty few. If anyone can save the galaxy from our rapacious ways, it will be him.' Her head rose slightly, emphasizing the proud nose beneath the veil. 'It has to be him.'

Freer nodded. 'Okay, I get it. He's the best option you have. Well, here he is.' He indicated Imre's containment suit. 'He's not much of a savior like this, Od knows. He certainly didn't do much for us. Are you sure you still want him?'

'More than you can possibly imagine.' The line clicked shut between them, and Wehr disconnected too.

Helwise crossed to help Emlee disengage from her suit. 'What the hell are you trying to do?' she asked Freer. 'Make her change her mind?'

'Just testing the water. Speaking of which . . .' The mercenary performed three star-jumps in quick succession. 'We're falling at around 10g and rotating with residual angular momentum. I'm guessing the station will be tidally locked for the flyby. Emlee?'

'That's right. Expect some attitude adjustment as we get closer. It makes for a bumpy ride. Maybe they'll sound a warning, but I wouldn't know about that. I've never sat it out from this privileged position.'

Imre watched enviously as Emlee's head appeared. She looked

flushed, sweaty, and relieved to be free as the suit shrank back to its normal dimensions. He wished he too could stretch his arms and see more than what came through his metaphorical pinhole, but they couldn't take the chance that Wehr wasn't watching. He had to maintain the guise of a prisoner for a couple of hours more.

Helwise was restless too. She checked *The Cauld Lad* every five minutes to make sure it was holding steady with respect to Kismet. There had been no deviations from its orbit, and nothing had interfered with it.

'You know,' she said, 'this might just actually go to plan.'

'Well, you've jinxed us now,' said Emlee. 'If we don't make it out the other side alive, I'll personally blame you.'

'That makes a change,' said Imre.

'Don't get used to it.' Emlee cast him a warning look, and the banter ceased.

Time passed. Ambient noise levels increased steadily as the station approached its primary. Metal joints shifted back and forth; beams flexed and twisted; molecular welds creaked. Sometimes it seemed to Imre that with every aggrieved groan the station was voicing the despair of its tenants. It, like them, was trapped in a terrible cycle of peril and respite. How long until metal fatigue manifested physically as well as psychically? Would Kismet crumble into pieces or explode? He could feel the imminence of its inevitable rupturing but couldn't tell what form it might take.

'Don't you worry,' said Helwise, coming to stand with him. 'We won't let anything happen to you.'

That wasn't what he was worried about. If Chyro hadn't done his job right, if Render, who knew him best, failed to recognize the reconstructed Imre Bergamasc, that would leave all of them in a difficult predicament. While it might under ordinary conditions have been possible to extract from the interior of such a station, periapsis was no place for a firefight.

'I wanted to bring us all together,' he told her. 'I wanted everything to be the way it used to be.'

'I know,' she said. She leaned against a wall and put her hands in her pockets. Her long, lithe form wilted. 'No one can blame you for that. But that's not the way it's going to be. The Forts are gone. We're out of a job. Whatever caused the Slow Wave is still out there, waiting to be dealt with. It's a different galaxy now. You have to move on. The sooner you do that, the better for all of us.'

'What do I move on to?'

'You tell me, Imre, when you've worked it out.' She put a hand on his shoulder. He felt her touch as a distant, light pressure. 'I'm still looking.'

He felt a strong urge to hold her, then. Nothing more. But he couldn't move his arms in the straitjacket of his confinement suit, and he wasn't going to ask to be released, lest that be interpreted as a sign of betrayal. He could only take what comfort he could from her presence nearby, while it was offered.

'Did something happen between you and Emlee down in the air lock?' she asked.

'No.' He was certain that this was the truth. Between them, nothing; within him, something he still couldn't fathom. 'She's tougher than she used to be.'

'Yes. It's hard to believe, isn't it? Our little girl has grown up.'

He had forgotten until then the difference between their ages and Emlee's. He and Helwise had been born thousands of years Absolute before her. Primes usually didn't live as long as singletons, unless they spent a lot of time in hard-storage or were deemed useful by the Forts.

'What's she become, Hel? What are we all?'

'Don't even ask that question, Imre. Existential bollocks only gets you killed. We do what we must to survive. It's really that simple.' She leaned farther into him, pressing her warm flesh against the cold black of his suit. 'Remember that, and you'll be a lot happier. I promise you.'

They were standing that way when the door to the conference room slid open. Mother Turin breezed in, with her attendants behind her. The warden came close behind, feet ringing on the unsteady deck.

'You're early,' said Freer, moving to confront her.

'It took less time to decant him than expected.' Wehr brought up the rear, pushing a convalescence tube ahead of her. Visible through its transparent plastic hood was Render, lying in a grotesque posture midway between fetal and straight. His hands were pulled up tightly to his chest, with fingers in claws. His head strained backward as though he were trying to see something behind him. His eyes were closed.

Emlee took a step forward, her hands clutched together. One of Mother Turin's aides blocked her path.

'No closer,' said the woman in blue. Wehr wheeled Render into the middle of the room, then left him there. Mother Turin waved Imre forward. 'Drop the mask,' she said. 'Let's see what lies within.'

Helwise did the honors, dismantling the protocols of the containment suit from the neck up. Imre blinked as direct light and fresh air struck him. For the first time he saw Kismet and its occupants with his own eyes: Mother Turin and Warden Goneril, staring at him with cautious awe; Duty Officer Wehr hovering protectively over the convalescence tube, her eyes averted; the iron grey walls and the stink of metal.

And Render. Render clad only in a gauzy undersuit, damp as though from heavy exertion.

A shock of memory ricocheted through him. He barely heard the station grumble in sympathy as a series of rapid-fire, painfully vivid recollections flashed across his mind. Render dropping into combat with weapons blazing; Render moving through a crowd like an icebreaker; Render the scarred Old-Timer, subject to strange moods and insights; Render the man caught by the beauty of a sunset over a blood-soaked battlefield.

Render on *Pelorus* saying, 'Don't ask. Don't be surprised.'

Imre came back to himself with a jolt. Render's eyes were open and locked fast on his.

'Who am I?' Imre asked. 'Can you hear me? Tell me who I am.'

'Open the tube,' said Mother Turin.

'He can hear well enough with it closed,' said Wehr.

'Open the tube, damn you. Let there be no excuses.' The priest-ess's veil shivered. Her voice had a wavering timbre that hadn't been there before. 'We need to be absolutely certain.'

'Do as she says,' Goneril snapped.

Wehr made no visible motion toward the tube. Its hood retracted with a sigh. The stink of decay filled the room.

'Render.' Imre moved as close as he dared. 'Render. It's me, Imre. Say something.'

Render blinked once. He inhaled, judderingly, as though he hadn't breathed for millennia. 'I don't believe it,' he whispered.

'Believe it,' Imre said. 'We came for you. We never abandoned you.'

'I don't believe,' Render repeated, 'in you.'

An indrawn breath might have come from Emlee. Imre ignored it. 'What's not to believe? I'm standing right in front of you.'

'Don't tell me lies.'

'I'm not lying, Render.'

'No more lies. I don't need lies.'

'Listen to me, Render. These people are going to let you go if you can tell them who I am.'

Render's bloodshot gaze roamed the room, then returned to him. One iris was murkily blue, the other green. 'What happens to her?'

'The warden won't be able to hurt you any more.'

'I never—' blustered Warden Goneril, but Mother Turin waved her silent.

'She wants everything.'

Render had said those words in one of his monologues. Imre hastened to reassure him. 'I'm here to save you. Emlee's here too, and the others. All you have to do is confirm who I am.'

'So few of us left . . .' Render's eyes drifted shut. His tongue touched his lips, then withdrew. 'Who are you? Forget who you are. I remember, but I don't care. Burn if you want to. Burn the whole world down. Who am I to criticize?'

'Just tell them I'm Imre Bergamasc, Render. Tell them, and you're free to do whatever you want.'

'A glorious lie.'

'It's no lie. It's the truth.'

'My savior. He lies to you and deceives.'

Imre wanted to throw himself on Render to bunch his fists in his undershirt and shake the truth out of him. 'I'm no one's savior. I'm just me – back from the dead and pissed off. Everything fell apart while I was gone. That's not my fault – and it's not my responsibility to fix it, either. I'm just a man. I'm tired. I'm Imre Bergamasc, and if you don't tell them that, Render, they'll kill us all.'

Render's eyes opened a crack.

'You are you,' he said in a weary, defeated tone. 'You are.'

'I'm Imre Bergamasc? Is that what you're saying?' He would not let himself feel relief. Not yet, not when everything rested on the deliberations of a damaged mind.

'Look at me. Look at you. Look down into the face of God. You are.'

Imre turned away, unable to look at the others. Mother Turin was watching with her blue-gloved hands clasped tightly in front of her, as though praying.

'Is that enough?' he asked her. 'Do you believe him?'

For a terrible moment, he didn't know what she would say. If she denied his identity, he would have no choice but to throw himself on Render's mercy again. If she did accept the mumbled concession of a man whose mind was clearly in pieces, he would be taken from the others, perhaps never to see them again.

A thunderous convulsion shook the station.

'Do I believe?' she said, as the sound died away. 'Yes, I have seen enough.' Her hands unclenched and fell to her sides. 'Warden Goneril, I have found what I have been looking for. You may release the prisoner into our guests' custody.'

The warden wasn't looking at Render. Her eyes flicked from Imre to Mother Turin and back again. 'He's really—? You say that he is—?'

'Do not question me,' she snapped. 'Just do as I tell you. Hand the prisoner over and return to your duties. My long work here is finished. We have done well, you and I. You should be proud.'

The warden beamed, but uncertainty remained. Imre saw it in the snappiness of her orders to Wehr, as control of the convalescence tube was handed over to Helwise and the others. Emlee's face was a mask of self-control. She, like Imre, wasn't allowing any emotion free rein until everything was over.

'What do you want us to do with Imre?' said Freer. 'I'll open the suit all the way, if you like.'

'No,' said the priestess. 'He will remain as he is. You may have convinced me of his identity, but his motives remain unclear. We have much to discuss, he and I.'

With a swoosh of robes, she turned and headed for the door. Imre assumed that he was to follow, and went to do so.

Render reached out and grabbed him as he went by. The ancient, scarred fingers were powerfully strong. They dragged Imre down, closer, so that Render could whisper in his ear.

'I like your lies.'

The fingers loosened, and Imre staggered free.

Mother Turin's identical acolytes ushered him to the door. Powerless, he could only look behind him as they shepherded him away. Freer bent over Render, examining him. Emlee hung back, as though hardly believing what had transpired. Only Helwise watched him leave, her frown lines deeply etched.

The door shut behind him, and they were gone.

Mother Turin said nothing as they traveled deeper into the station than he had gone before, forgoing bullet capsules for stairs and ramps. Under the circumstances, he could appreciate the necessity for that. The restlessness of the walls, ceilings, and floors worsened as the ambient gravity of the dead star only increased. Kismet rocked and swayed in the grip of an invisible giant's fist. If a maglev track slipped or broke while they were in transit, they would be instantly killed. He was very careful to stay within the lines.

Her stateroom was one of four leading off like leaves of a clover from an atrium decorated in copper and platinum. Delicate engravings ornamented every surface. In the heart of the station,

Imre felt as removed from reality as was possible. The four doors —
one of which led to the warden's stateroom, he was certain — could
have belonged to a luxury liner from a dozen worlds. The stench of
iron was absent, replaced by air as fresh as any Imre had smelled in
his life.

He tried calling the others but received nothing at all in reply.
There was simply too much metal between him and them — or so
he hoped.

'Wait here,' Mother Turin told her acolytes. They took up positions on either side of her doorway, which slid open as she
approached. 'Come,' she said to Imre, not waiting to see if he obeyed.

He followed her into an expansive suite containing a desk that
appeared to be made out real wood. Everything was made of
curves, from the arc of the desk to a round bed at the far end of the
room. A crescent bar occupied one corner. Muted artworks hung in
circular frames on all four walls. A disk motif in browns and greys
repeated itself on the carpet.

'Stand there,' Mother Turin told him, pointing imperiously at a
spot in the center of the room. The lapis lazuli of her robes clashed
with the warm colors around her, an electric jewel in a world of
timber.

Despite her claim that they had much to discuss, she had done
nothing but order him from place to place since leaving the conference room. Her reticence made him nervous. She had been
seeking him for more years than he cared to think of. She had
taken a religion venerating the Forts and turned it around to focus
on his disappearance from Hyperabad. Wouldn't she have questions, accusations, entreaties?

While he stood uncomfortably in the center of her stateroom,
she walked behind her desk, opened a drawer, and took something out of it. She slipped it under her robes before he could see
what it was.

The station growled in a low, metal voice.

'So what happens now?' he asked the woman who would be his
priestess. 'You've got what you wanted. What do you expect me to
do for you?'

She came back round the table to stand in front of him. This was the closest he had ever been to her. His nostrils twitched at a strong scent of sandalwood. He searched her veil for any sign of what lay beneath, but her emotions were contained once more. She could have been a faceless robot for all he could tell.

'Your friends abandoned you,' she said. 'That must make you angry.'

He didn't know how it made him feel, if he was honest with himself. The plan was for the separation to be temporary, but it didn't have to be. 'They say I abandoned them a long time ago. I suppose that makes us even.'

'Does "even" satisfy you?'

'It's not a question of satisfaction.'

'Our sense of justice demands to be satisfied. Do you believe that justice has been properly meted out? Has your guilt been assuaged?'

He supposed it did make him feel better for having thrown himself into the lion's den. Mother Turin could kill him or deify him, as she preferred; he was entirely in her hands. She could even let him go, and he would leave lighter for it, having cast off some of the karma bequeathed to him by his former self. There was little to be angry for, the way he saw it.

'I should tell you where I came from,' he said. 'The notion of what I feel guilty for is not a simple one.'

'It doesn't matter,' she said. 'You're here. You're alive. I knew you would be. I always knew you'd return.'

'I'm not a savior. I'm not part of your church. I didn't even know it existed until a few days ago.'

'That doesn't matter either.' She waved his objection away with a swipe of one blue sleeve. 'The Church is irrelevant now. I've got what I wanted.'

'Irrelevant?' She was standing close enough to make him feel uncomfortable. He swayed under the influence of strange gravity. 'What exactly do you want?'

'Survival.' Mother Turin reached under her robes and produced a short length of blue cloth. 'Close your eyes.'

He did so, and she tied the blindfold tightly around his head. He was plunged into darkness again. He held himself still as she accessed the protocols of his containment suit and loosened his bindings. His arms shifted, slid free. He breathed deeply, filling his lungs with air. He took a step backward.

'Don't make any sudden moves,' she said in a hard voice, 'or I'll shoot you where you stand.'

He froze, hearing the promise in her whiplash tone more clearly than any words. Cloth slithered against cloth. He felt the air move across his cheeks and lips.

'Faith is a complicated thing,' she said. 'We only need it when things are going wrong. The Forts could have been gods once, but they made sure we were kept happy, provided we played by the rules. Those who broke the rules were punished. Maybe the punished had their own gods to call on when things went badly, gods they prayed to for help toward the end. I don't think faith did them any good, because their gods weren't real. The only hope they had was imaginary, and that's worse than none at all.'

'If you really believe that,' he asked, 'then why the charade on Hyperabad?' He could hear her moving but couldn't decipher the sounds. 'False hope is all you've offered your followers.'

'Not necessarily. The Forts may bounce back. Your call for help may yet pay off. Don't you think that a possibility?'

He thought of everything he had seen and learned since leaving the Jinc: Forts unraveled, the Continuum in tatters, the hair-thin threads of the Line breaking, the collapse of civilizations and the end of peace. 'No, he said. 'I can't see that as a possibility. The only chance we have is to do it ourselves, to stop waiting for someone to swoop down from on high and save us. The longer we sit on our hands, the harder it'll be. Eventually it will be impossible. And then—'

He stopped, unable to voice the thought. If the Forts didn't return – if the Barons and the Luminous and whoever else were always out there, ready to lop off any budding replacement of the old order – then humanity would remain a teeming, unruly mob filling the galaxy to the brim. Wars would spark and spread on a scale never seen before. Like a hurricane building up speed across an ocean, there would be nothing to stop them. Life would never be completely extinguished, for somewhere small pockets of civilization would always survive. But there would be no return to the glory days of the Continuum. They were gone forever. Humanity in its present form was not fit to rule the galaxy.

'Someone killed the Forts,' he said, feeling the certainty of it in his bones. 'They're still around, and we have to counterattack. We have to find out who the murderers are and stop them from doing any more damage to us. We have to find out how to hurt them.'

'To get even?' she asked, becoming still.

'No,' he said, realizing then that he had been speaking like his old self. That wasn't what he wanted. 'This isn't about retaliation or justice. It's about fixing what was broken. It's about remembering the dead. The Forts would expect better of us, and I think that's worth aspiring to.'

'Are you sure you don't want to be a savior, Imre Bergamasc?'

He didn't answer that.

Mother Turin took a step closer and slipped off his blindfold so he could see her face.

'Kiss me, lover,' said Helwise MacPhedron, 'or I'll break your arm.'

She was naked as well as unmasked. The floor was strewn with strips of bright blue cloth. He reeled physically and mentally, recognizing only then her scent beneath the sandalwood and hearing her voice behind the disguise. He went back a step, and another.

'You!' he exclaimed. 'All the time?'

'All the time,' she said, with gloating in her eyes.

'From the founding of the Church – no, from when I disappeared—?'

She nodded, coming after him.

'Do you believe any of it?'

'Do you?' She was suddenly so close he could see golden flecks in her eyes. 'Who gives a fuck about the galaxy's salvation when we can have our own right here?'

He found it suddenly difficult to breathe. His original suspicions about the First Church were well-founded, but he had been completely wrong about who was behind it. Helwise, not Emlee. It must have been she who let Emlee go in order to widen the net, she who killed the investigator who stumbled across the truth about his 'suicide.' 'All to draw me here.'

'Something like that.'

The back of his thighs hit the desk. He had run out of room to retreat.

'Don't worry about it now,' she said with the heat of her body all along his. 'Talking is the last thing on my mind.'

'The others—'

'Won't be going anywhere until apoapsis. We're all stuck here until then, so we might as well make the best of it. Let's ride it out together, you and I, and leave the revelations until after.'

Gravitational eddies pulled at him. The vibration through the deck reached a distinctly higher pitch. Now, finally, he felt as though he was hurtling to his destruction. Helmetless, chuteless, hopeless, he plunged in unfettered free fall down through the thickening atmosphere of his fate.

Savagely, angrily, he kissed her on the lips. Her mouth was already open, and her tongue thrust into his with startling force. His body responded with hammering pulse and desire rising. Weeks of repressed libido burst in him as though Sakra's ashes had caught a spark and ignited all at once. Helwise gripped his arms and pushed him back against the desk. His suit peeled away at her touch, exposing his flesh. The hairs on his chest were white and short. She tore her mouth from his and bit his nipple with sharp teeth. The stained-glass memento fell unnoticed to the floor.

When he was naked, he picked her up by the armpits so she could wrap her legs around him. Together they moved to the bed. He relished her wetness and his rigidity. Clumsy, impatient, he felt as though he was losing a virginity he had long since forgotten. His urgent need startled even her. Once inside her, he climaxed almost immediately, and cried out for the force of it, overwhelmed by a feeling that was more pain than pleasure. A fleeting concern that some of Chyro's hasty work might have come undone vanished into the avalanche of sensation. For an eternity, he didn't think at all.

They lay together, side by side, while he recovered. He hadn't injured himself. Quite the opposite: he felt fully functional for the first time, as though the orgasm had jump-started nerve endings and functions left dormant too long. His skin tingled all over. Every part of him was aware with heightened sensitivity to her: the taste of her mouth, the smell of her sex, the pulse in her neck, the sound of her voice.

'I was afraid of scaring you away,' she said. 'You hadn't returned willingly. You had to have another reason to come, something to attract your interest. Your ego was always your weak point.' A smile flickered across her lips, then vanished. 'Also, I was wary of attracting unwanted attention. You understand that, right?'

Imre told her what he had seen at the Cat's Arse: her other self hunted and a squadron of Vespulas coming after him. Extremes of caution seemed eminently justified in the new and dangerous galaxy.

'Not everyone thinks the servants of the Forts worthy of veneration,' she said. 'We certainly didn't, back in the Mad Times.'

'Whose side would we be on now?' he wondered. 'The First Church or the Barons?'

'The who?'

He explained what he knew of the mysterious group trying to get its hands on him. He didn't mention the Luminous or the Loop shunt that might be inside him. One revelation at a time, he told himself. There would be other opportunities he was certain. Helwise, in her role as Mother Turin, had influence on Hyperabad. She had kept the police at bay during their escape from the market; she had allowed them into the very heart of Kismet, where Render had been imprisoned; she had followers in the tens of thousands, waiting on her every word. What couldn't he do now, with her behind him?

A shadow fell across the bright future he imagined, a shadow in the form of a body burned black in the fire of a hasty takeoff. He remembered Emlee standing in front of him, ready to protect him with her own flesh. Helwise traced the fading circles of scars on his body, asking him where they had come from. He couldn't answer. There were no words, and soon it was too loud to talk with lips and throat, the only way that seemed natural to him in bed.

They made love as the station shook around them. Explosive attitude jets kicked in, sending powerful shock waves echoing through the metal structure. It sounded like someone pounding the bulkhead behind him like a drum. Tides reached their invisible tendrils even into the heart of the station itself, lifting thin streamers of dust into the air. Helwise sneezed while he went down on her, gripping him momentarily in the vise of her thighs. She rode him to a second orgasm with long, black hair whipping slowly around her, tugged this way and that. He gripped her waist and held on.

Periapsis, when it came, was a nightmare of noise and violence. The bed shook, and the sound of iron drums became an endless tattoo, deafening him to all but the most urgent thought. He clung tight to the bed, and Helwise clung to him in turn, bent over him with unnatural flexibility, her spine curved in a graceful, near-mathematical arc. He kissed her with his eyes closed, holding the moment tight in his mind, where it would remain forever, the epitome of their relationship so far: sex, violence, and deceit in perfect measure. The future might be brief or eternal. Caught between the two possibilities, he was unable to summon a care either way.

Then it all went wrong.

His eyes shot open at a pinprick pain in his upper arm. A tiny dome of blood shook free of his skin and tumbled in an accelerating arc past his head. Someone had shot him. He tried to sit upright and failed – dazed by the tides, he thought at first – and fell onto his side. Helwise was already moving, more used to the vagaries of Kismet than he. But it wasn't just gravity and inertia making his head swim and his body heavy. Something new was coursing through his bloodstream: a drug of some kind, fired into him from across the room.

He tried to increase his tempo, but a disconnect had formed between his thoughts and his actions. He lay on the bed as limp as a fish. Drug-muffled drumming provided a surreal counterpoint to what he saw next. A dark shape slid across his vision from the stateroom's entrance, firing in slow motion. He tried to follow it, but his eyes wouldn't track. Helwise rose to meet it halfway, knocking the gun away with a stiff-toed kick to the wrist. A shout of anger from her throat filled her room as the fight accelerated into a blur and passed beyond his comprehension.

It ended with horrifying suddenness, as such fights inevitably did. A spray of blood splashed hotly across him. Something heavy thudded to the bed beside him. Helwise was suddenly standing over him with a knife in her hand, breathing heavily. A primal light burned in her eyes. She tipped back her head and shook the sweat-soaked hair from her face. Her teeth gleamed like a predator's.

'What—?'

'Don't try to talk,' she said over the station's racket. 'The drug will wear off in a moment. I just needed to keep you out of the way.'

'Who—?'

She crouched over him and rolled him onto his back. With easy sensuality, she straddled his hips. 'I can't believe you fucked her instead of me.'

For a second he thought she meant Emlee, in the air lock. He opened his mouth to protest his innocence. Then it occurred to him that she was dressed in black body armor, not naked as she had been a moment ago.

He managed to tilt his head minutely to one side. Another Helwise lay on the bed beside him, sprawled with life emptied out of a ragged cut to the throat. The sheets were sodden with red and stank of a very different form of iron.

'I took her by surprise,' the Helwise atop him said. The satisfaction in her voice was horrible to hear. 'While you two were dicking around, we were fighting for our lives. She sent her goons for us half an hour after you left, and the station fired on *The Cauld Lad*, knocked it out of orbit. They never intended to let all of us go unharmed, not ever. Luckily, I got the jump on her. She obviously thought I wouldn't figure out that because our bodies are identical, hers and mine, the biometric data works for me as well as her. That gave me everything in the station, handed to me on a fucking plate. There wasn't much time to come up with a plan, what with apoapsis on its way and the guns already firing, but we did what we could. I was right about guards here; they're no match for us. The drug I hit you with comes from a station stun gun. I took it off the warden herself. She's crazy, you know. More faithful than her faithless leader – and torn up inside about the prisoners slipping through her fingers. That wasn't the deal as she understood it. She wasn't going to let Emlee and Render go without a fight. The internal conflict was killing her. She just about popped a vein when I triggered a lockdown.'

'My God,' he said, only then piecing the clues together. Helwise fighting a woman in combat armor in the graveyard around the Cat's Arse ('my normal, charming self'); Emlee's account of two versions of Helwise dying in a suspicious accident; Freer's subtle hints. It fit together too well. Even before the Slow Wave, singletons dealt with their multiplicate natures their own particular ways. Gathering semiregularly to swap memories, as Imre's former self had done, was just one of many methods of maintaining a continuous sense of identity across many bodies and great distances. Now, though, with the Continuum gone, singletons had to find new ways to survive in a galaxy beset by failing communications and unreliable transport. Freer absorbed his various selves into one, gradually accruing all his worldly experience into a single body, or trying to, while Helwise—

He could barely bring himself to think of it.

'You're killing yourself,' he said, forcing out the words. 'One by one. Everywhere you go. That's your solution.'

'I'm one of a kind,' she said with grim satisfaction, 'and that's me. Accept no substitutes.'

She bent down to kiss him. His arms were still frozen. He couldn't push her off. All he could do was turn his face away.

She straightened, hurt in her eyes. 'What's this? You'll fuck her but not me? Do you see a difference between us that I can't?'

'She hasn't murdered herself.'

'Really? Don't you bet on it. Look at her private files when you have a moment. You'll find out that she's killed more than I ever have. What do you think this setup was really all about? It wasn't about you. It was about flushing other versions of me out of the woodwork so she could kill them. I got lucky; I had you along for the ride. That distracted her, forced a mistake. Don't think she would've retired once she had you aboard. I guarantee she would've used you to bring in even more for the slaughter, just like she used Emlee and Render. It's what I'd do.'

He believed her.

'That's who Render was talking about,' he said. 'The "she" tormenting him. It wasn't the warden; it was you. What did Render say in one of his rants? "Who'd believe she'd be so devious?" He guessed. She could only have been you – Mother Turin – her. I should have known you'd be capable of something like this.'

Helwise glared. 'Are you judging me, Imre Bergamasc?'

He stared up at her, willing his body to throw her from him. The most he could coax from his hands was a weak twitch.

'Yes,' he said.

She spat on his face. 'How dare you – you of all people?'

'Get off me.'

'No.' Her strong hands found his throat, but not to strangle him, as he initially feared. With a powerful jerk, she tugged him into a sitting position so their faces almost touched. 'You still need me. You won't get through that door without my say-so, let alone off the station. I could kill you now and let the others think the real Mother Turin did you in – and me with you. I could walk off Kismet into my own little empire and pick up where she left off, all the better for knowing your sorry corpse had been ejected from an air lock.'

'You won't,' he said without flinching. 'You're capable of it. I

know that now. I think I've always suspected it. But you won't do
it because you need me, too. The warden will figure it out eventually; give her a reason to be suspicious, and she'll find a way to
take your biometric data out of the security system. If you don't
walk out of this room with me at your side, dressed as Zadiq
Turin, whose face she has never seen, she'll know something's
wrong – and you'll be stuck here forever, or worse. How well do
you think the warden will react to the news that you've killed the
high priest of her religion?'

A protracted rumble shook the bed. The stresses on Kismet
were beginning to fade, but they were still powerful enough to
silence even the bitterest argument.

Helwise bared her teeth and pushed him back onto the mattress.

'We need each other,' she said. 'I can live with that.'

'There's a big difference between need and want.'

For a moment, he thought she might hit him, or stab him
through the heart just to spite him. Her skin went very white and
her eyes seemed to retreat into her head. She looked more like her
corpse than the corpse itself, cooling beside him in a puddle of her
own blood.

Instead of killing him, she upped her tempo and left in a furi-
ous, blue blur, taking the Mother Turin robes with her. The double
whoosh of the door opening and closing was accompanied by a
protracted cacophony of metal on metal. He let his head sink back
onto the mattress. His side was wet with spilled blood. The stateroom had become a slaughterhouse. His plan had worked on every
point: Render was safe, and there was no doubt about that; with
Helwise's help, they would be able to escape unharmed, together.
However, any triumph he might have felt was tarnished by
Helwise's crime. How many of her had died at her hand since the
Continuum fell? He had personally witnessed two such murders in
a matter of days. There might have been hundreds. All that blood
shed; all that experience lost . . .

The dead stare of the corpse rebuked him. He couldn't bear to
look at it. In Helwise's eyes, she hadn't committed a crime at all.
We do what we must to survive, she had told him before handing

him over to her other self. Remember that, and you'll be a lot happier. I promise you.

Once he would have found the outcome satisfactory. He was sure of it. Perhaps he would have been happy. That was the worst realization of all. He wasn't, so where did that leave him? Was he growing as a person – or understanding, finally, that he was a different person altogether? Remembering the strange nights he had spent in the Jinc ship as they searched the fringes of the galaxy for evidence of a long-absent god, he closed his eyes and prayed silently to Himself for insight.

THAT TACITURN
AND INVISIBLE GOD

Alas! in what moment of success do we not feel
a sensation of terror!

Robert Charles Maturin

A trio of unmarked ships awaited Kismet as it ascended from the dead star, its iron skeleton intact despite all fears to the contrary and its pitiful cargo newly shaken. Shedding velocity with every hour, it tumbled toward a rendezvous neither it nor its occupants could avoid.

'Barons,' said Emlee, studying the telemetry from the mahogany bridge of the First Church flagship, *Memento Mori.* Two hours earlier, Helwise had walked aboard her other self's ship with the poise of a queen and calmly taken it over. Warden Goneril had escorted her with ingratiating but subdued pomp, a cloud of indecision trailing her like a ghostly veil. Imre didn't know how much the warden had guessed about the short-lived revolution that had taken place aboard the prison. Wehr watched with sharp eyes from behind her superior's shoulder as all of them were described as honored guests and invited to return at a moment's notice.

'What are those fuckers doing here?' asked Helwise, dressed in the robes of her predecessor but with the veil tugged back, exposing her face. The ships' crew – a half dozen of the identical acolytes, loosely knitted into a short-range gestalt – had followed Goneril and Wehr off the bridge and been banned from returning indefinitely. 'Did they follow you?' she asked Imre with clipped tones.

He could only presume so, but he would assume no guilt for this new development. 'If I had any control over the Loop shunt inside me, I would stop it. But I don't.'

'Chyro found it once. He can find it again and cut it out.'

'That's a decision for the future,' he said, absently rubbing the stump of his missing finger. He had halted its regrowth for reasons he was still unraveling. 'Let's concentrate on right now.'

'They're not making any threats,' said Emlee. 'They'd be stupid take us on out here, with so many witnesses.'

'Maybe they just want to talk,' said Freer, studying the display with keen eyes.

'If they made any fucking sound at all,' said Helwise, 'that would be progress.'

No comment came from Kismet. *Memento Mori* was clearly on its own. After being fired on by Kismet's cannon, *The Cauld Lad* had tumbled away shortly after periapsis and vanished in a hail of X-rays, the latest victim of the hungry stellar remnant. Its demise struck Imre harder than expected. *The Cauld Lad* had been his sole companion for much of his journey, bland but unquestioningly reliable.

'Does this ship have weapons?' Imre asked.

'Armed to the teeth,' its new mistress said with satisfaction.

Of course, he told himself, thinking of the piece of stained glass he had carried into Kismet, now resting in two pieces in a pocket of his skin suit. He thought of Freer asking without any emotion at all, when Helwise unveiled herself on the *Memento Mori*'s bridge, 'Which one are you?' He thought of the corpse presented to Warden Goneril as evidence that the rogue element in her guests had been contained. There was a tidiness, a symmetry, to the way things had turned out that appealed to part of him — even as a greater part recoiled in revulsion from where he stood now.

Everyone was looking at him.

Sometimes, he thought, you can't choose your friends. Your enemies, however, are a different matter altogether.

'Prep us for combat. I want us free of the dock as soon it's safe —

sooner, if that'll take them by surprise. Don't wait for them to make a move. We jump them first chance we get.'

They went immediately to work, a team in deed if not in spirit. Fate forged strange alloys from even the most familiar of metals.

There was, however, one ingredient missing.

'What about you, Render?' he asked, diverting his attention from the preparations for battle to the ship's medical suite, where Render's scarred body and tangled mind were undergoing careful rehabilitation. A botched Flexing could leave permanent damage on even a healthy psyche. 'Is there anything you'd like to offer?'

'Old face, new sound.'

'What's that?'

'Dreams are cruel. Everybody's infected.' Render lay straight on his back in the convalescence tube with his large-knuckled fists folded over his lap. His eyes stared nowhere. Old scars on his freshly depilated scalp gleamed in the harsh light. But for the voice, he might have been a particularly ugly corpse. 'This game turns me cold.'

'I don't understand. I'm not going to surrender, if that's what you mean. Or are you telling me you want to pull the plug——?'

'No. I feel so tired and I feel so helpless. Sometimes I could scream. But I'm thinking clearly. I don't look for love that I don't need.'

'That's good.' And it was. Imre hated the thought that they had gone to so much trouble to rescue someone with no interest in living. 'So what are you trying to tell me?'

Render sighed but gave it another go. 'Nothing's forever. Can you feel it? Something's coming. The new god of panic. The change disturbs me. But you don't have to play. You're every-body's friend. That's okay. Well, maybe. I'll stand by your side. I'll forget who you are. I want to believe. This is a new kind of cure.'

Imre fought a sudden flood of emotion similar to the one he had experienced for *The Cauld Lad*. Sentimentality was dangerous. He needed to remain cold in the face of the Barons. But he could hear the effort in Render's voice as he reaffirmed his allegiance in his strange, convoluted way. Imre could only imagine what it cost.

'What did I do?' he asked. 'How did I betray you?'

The reply took a long time coming. Render's chest hardly seemed to be moving, but he definitely breathed. 'Wrong place, wrong time. You learn quick or you learn nothing. No one has to know I was there.'

Before Imre could ask Render what that meant, the ship lurched underneath him and launched itself toward the waiting trio of ships. The purely cosmetic needle at its nose retracted. A cluster of spiky weapons extruded in its place. He upped his tempo so time seemed to drag. The stars wheeled in slow motion. Kismet receded with painful tardiness. G forces from the dead star pulled at them, urging him to turn around and follow *The Cauld Lad* to oblivion.

The Vespulas fanned out in response, their drives brightly flaring against the sun-pocked starscape of Mandala Supersystem.

'We're receiving a transmission,' said Emlee.

'Put it on the display.'

'It's audio only.'

'Then let's hear it.'

'Stand down, Imre Bergamasc,' said a voice over the bridge speakers. Its clipped, compressed tones hinted at vocal masking. 'We haven't come to fight you, this time.'

'Why are you here, then?' he responded. 'Give us an answer, or you'll have to fight us anyway.'

'I've come to give you a message.'

'We're two minutes from engaging. Can you fit it in before then?'

'You need to stay away from Domgard,' the voice said. 'That's all I have to tell you, although perhaps you'd like to hear more.'

Imre stared at the display showing the trio of ships diverging at speed. If they were going to attack, they would have changed course by now in order to close on *Memento Mori* from three sides.

'Who are you?' he asked.

'If you don't already know, then the answer won't mean anything to you. I've told you what you need to hear. Will you hear the rest out or not?'

He closed his eyes and raised a hand. He stood that way for

almost a relative minute, weighing every variable he could think of. Opportunities versus traps; misinformation versus truth. Then he gestured affirmatively at Helwise.

She just looked at him. 'What?'

'Do as he says.'

'I would if I could understand a word he's saying.'

'What?' He looked around the bridge. Emlee and Freer stared back at him with the same puzzlement in their eyes. 'Put the attack on hold,' he said, thinking, What now? 'Just do it.'

Helwise cooled the drive but didn't kill it. The ship coasted on momentum, ready to roar into life at a second's notice.

'We're getting visual,' said Emlee with a worried look.

A new window flickered to life in the display. It showed the interior of a Vespula cockpit with its lights dimmed. The pilot wore a flight helmet with the visor down. His or her face was impossible to discern through the shadows.

'All right,' Imre said. 'I'll give you five minutes at this tempo. First up, you're going to tell me how they can't understand what you're saying but I can.'

'I'm using the Aldobrand Cipher, of course.'

'Should that mean something to me?'

'It certainly should. During the Mad Times, you kept a journal. To prevent its contents ever getting into the Forts' hands, you invented a code so densely personalized that no one could understand it, not even your fellow members in the Corps. That code was the Aldobrand Cipher.'

'How did you get your hands on it?'

'One of us is a fool, Imre Bergamasc. Don't make the mistake of thinking it's me.'

He felt his face turn red. It wasn't his fault that he had no memory of where the cipher had come from. He hadn't even been aware that he was translating it, correcting its divergence from everyday speech as easily as he could translate machine code. The ability to do so was clearly ingrained in him, a gift salvaged from the wreckage of the Drum, a gift he hadn't even known he had.

'I didn't ask to be insulted,' he said.

'And I don't know what kind of game you're playing. Understand something very important, if you understand anything. You're in great danger. Everywhere you turn, enemies are gathering against you – some because of who you are, but appear not to be; others because of who you appear to be, but aren't. That uncertainty makes you dangerous. You are a threat to people who would like to see any uncertainty eliminated.'

'A threat how? I don't understand how I could be this important to anyone.'

'There's a war going on you can't see. As in any war, there are rules of engagement, and you aren't following them. Are you bluffing or ignorant? Or are you a fake intent on stirring up trouble? Any of those is a cause for great concern.'

'I know about the Forts on Hyperabad,' he said, trying to demonstrate that he wasn't completely in the dark. 'Several were killed there after the Slow Wave. I presume you're with the Barons.'

'No, but their work is important.'

'So whose side are you on?'

'My own. Listen to me, Imre Bergamasc.' The shadowy figure in the display leaned closer. 'We monitor the Line, as many do. It contains echoes of events long past and intimations of what's to come. That's where we learned of your resurrection. We don't know where you came from or why, but we do know that we're not the only people looking for you. We got lucky and found you first. The Loop shunt confirmed it was you, but your behavior was not consistent. We approached you, tested your reactions. You can defend yourself. That's good. But it's only a matter of time before someone comes whom you won't be able to fight.'

'Why?' Imre asked. He leaned over the bridge's instrumentation panels, his attention focused so absolutely on the image on the screen that he didn't see the others, didn't notice *Memento Mori*'s course shifting as gravity tugged it, didn't register the continued dispersal of the three Vespulas. 'How does the Luminous fit in? And the Slow Wave? Did any of the Forts survive? You have to tell me. I have to know. If it has anything to do with why I was murdered—'

He stopped there, breathing heavily and hanging his head. What did it matter how the Drum had been destroyed when the entire galaxy was at stake?

'Who said you were murdered?' asked the shadowy figure.

'It doesn't matter.'

'Of course it matters. Why do you think I'm here? You should remember. That you don't makes me suspicious. Yet you seem to be who you say are. If you weren't, Mother Turin would have seen right through you, and the Aldobrand Cipher would've defeated you.' The figure sat back in its seat. 'What's the explanation?'

'My memory is damaged.' That wasn't the whole of it, but it would do for now.

'How badly?'

'I don't remember anything after the end of the Mad Times.'

'Nothing at all?'

'There are gaps, particularly on *Pelorus*.' Arguing with the others, helping Render and Emlee escape. Fractures in his mind. 'I don't remember surrendering.'

'That's because you didn't. What makes you think you did?'

'That's what everyone tells me I did.'

'You should know better than to believe what everyone says. Don't be a fool, man. There's always a deeper truth.'

'And that is?'

'That you are not,' said the shadowy figure, 'a decent man.'

The words were a trigger for memories buried deeper inside him than any other. Imre found himself plunged back to the day in question. Repressed sensation assailed him: smoke, flashing lights, urgent ululations from the dying ship, and the taste of blood in his mouth. There were so many memories missing; there would always be more holes than substance. But the skeleton of those moments was almost enough as he exhumed what he had tried so hard to forget.

His original reconstruction had been half-right. The ship had been burning; he and the others had been arguing. Then the Forts had requested a meeting to discuss the terms of their surrender, Helwise had assumed. He had thought differently, having met the Fort called Factotem years earlier and talked about the need for change. The only hope he could entertain lay in that statement.

'Whatever it takes to get us out of this,' he had said, 'isn't that worth pursuing?'

He met Factotem's frag in the belly of a ship so strange and wondrous that he retained only hints of it now. Their conversation was brief and to the point. The Forts would dominate the galaxy no matter what happened. There was no fighting that fact. Until a new form of humanity emerged, superior even to the Forts, it would always be that way. The only point of disagreement was on how the Forts interacted with the rest of humanity. They could guide and shape to ensure relative calm between the vast numbers of singletons, gestalts, and Primes inhabiting the galaxy; they could fight when unrest broke out at their intervention; they could seek new ways when the old ones failed to work.

'It's getting crowded in here,' said Factotem in a memory Imre had not been able to access before. 'Your numbers are growing, and as a result governance is becoming increasingly difficult. We expected the flash point you call the Mad Times long before it came, and your role in it too. The Corps would maintain the balance, then it would turn against us. There was nothing we could do about it. We anticipated this moment, too. Our projections strongly indicated that you would be here now, talking to me.'

'You made this happen?'

'No.' The frag stood in a forest of crystal glowing all the colors of the rainbow – or so it seemed to Imre, looking back on it through a very foggy lens.

'You didn't stop it,' he said.

'We couldn't have stopped it. It's a natural function of humanity: to expand and spread, to create and multiply networks. We are an expression of that function; so is war. We have tried to encourage one at the expense of the other, but there are only so many imbalances we can correct. Breeding programs and genocide are quick and brutal fixes only. So much of humanity that is beautiful and strange would be lost if we resorted to such measures.'

'So what are you suggesting?' he asked. 'That we're forcing your hand? That if we don't back down or calm down of our own accord, you'll slaughter us?'

'No. There is an alternative. There might even be a precedent. We are thinking in the long term, Imre Bergamasc. You must remember that. The juncture we have reached today will seal the destiny of all humanity, not just the Forts. You are invited to join us in that great venture. Are you interested?'

He remembered thinking: yes. Yes, to save his friends, and to save humanity from a bloody conflict they couldn't possibly win. They had tried and failed. There was honor in that.

But what was he being offered? What role was he being asked to play?

The memory consuming him wasn't about the deal so much as what came next.

He had returned to *Pelorus* with Factotem's words ringing in his ears. 'Seal the deal.' The others wouldn't go along with the plan. He was certain of that. 'If you do this, you're as much a traitor to the human race as they are.' Freer had been referring to merely talking to the Forts. Anything else would be abomination.

The ship was burning. An atmosphere of carbonized ash surrounded it like a black halo. He slipped aboard unnoticed and set charges around the bridge. The traumatized security system didn't question his actions. He triggered the explosives unimpeded.

Emlee Copas was unconscious when he walked onto the bridge. Helwise was on the floor, with Freer bending over her. Render stood alone in the center and was the first to see him. The big soldier's face turned to stone. He knew, instantly. Imre raised his Balzac beamer, fired once and missed. The others were already moving. Freer had a weapon out and was shouting something as he brought it to bear. Imre shot him in the chest. Helwise screamed and leapt, reaching for him with her uninjured arm. Two rounds caught her in midflight but didn't deflect her momentum. Her corpse burned him when it hit, he was overclocking so fast. He went down hard, losing valuable seconds.

By the time he regained his feet, Render was gone, and so was

Emlee. There was only one way they could have left the bridge. Cursing under his breath, he followed.

The smoke-filled corridors of *Pelorus*. He had already seen this. Turning a corner and finding Render clutching Emlee protectively to his chest.

'Get her out,' the big soldier had said. 'What's done is done.'

A change of heart. Imre let them live. Emlee hadn't seen anything. And Render—

'No one has to know I was there.'

Thus the deal was sealed, and sealed again. His former self had killed Helwise and Freer in cold blood because they were singletons and existed elsewhere; they would live on, no matter what happened to those two particular versions. Instead of killing Emlee, he had knocked her out so she wouldn't witness his betrayal and need to be silenced. Render was an Old-Timer with hundreds of thousands of years behind him; killing him would be like razing Earth to the bedrock, a crime that would far outweigh anything else Imre had done. Render seemed to understand. In his own, strange way he had put the incident behind him and moved on: to saving Emlee, to getting off the ship, to living. Imre would trust Render with his secret because he had no choice.

(In the present, Imre thought of the Barons and how, three times, they had acted to spare Emlee Copas's life. At the Cat's Arse habitat, they had been perfectly happy to fire on singletons, and him. Could their sense of honor be so congruent with his – and mean nothing?)

Later, on a rescue ship, Imre's former self had doubted. Removed from his friends, from his new conspirators and former masters, from the urgency of the situation, he had felt uncertainty. What had he done? He had done everything his friends had accused him of: betrayed the cause, betrayed them, and betrayed himself. What did that make him? Strangely, the uncertainty had fueled an equal and opposite reaction: a certainty that he was attaining a new stage in his development as a person, as a political figure, as a player in the affairs of the galaxy. Forts Graduated by crossing a threshold of complexity unobtainable by 'lesser' humanity. He felt as though he too had reached a similar juncture, one from which he could not easily turn back.

(Imre thought of the Loop shunt in his body. It wasn't an addition added by the Jinc or the silver sphere. It was part of him – part of the version of him that had laid down his meeting with Factotem, deal intact, along with all the rest of his memories onto the Drum's endless spiral.)

Not a decent man at all, Imre knew now, or at least not entirely a man. He saw in an entirely new light his former self's personal panic after the Slow Wave, the abandonment of colleagues, the desperation to be elsewhere at any cost – and the secrecy with which he had made his plans. After *Pelorus*, he had been more Fort than man – perhaps a hybrid of both, since he had weathered the cutting of the Loop with his sanity reasonably intact. But the truth remained. He hadn't just surrendered. He had gone over to the other side. That fact more than any other he had tried to hide from his friends – and even, ultimately, from himself.

Imre felt like vomiting. Helwise and Freer murdered to keep that secret. He would have fired on Render too, he was sure, but for the fait accompli Render had handed him. Everywhere he looked he saw dead bodies, freshly exhumed but in various states of decay. Ghosts crowded him – people, events, and decisions past. He couldn't avoid them. They hung around his neck with the weight of an albatross.

Someone was shaking him. He raised his head. The bridge of *Memento Mori* crept back over him as though scales had fallen from his eyes. Emlee had her hand on his shoulder. The voice was talking in the language only the two of them could understand.

'. . . to live provided you abide by the rules of engagement,' the figure was saying. 'I understand now why you're not behaving the way we expected; it's not your fault you don't know what's going on. Until you decide which side you're on, however, you will remain at considerable risk. Trying to build a Fort will provoke retaliation. Trying to use a Loop shunt, including the one inside you, likewise. There are too many mistakes you can make. You may not survive long enough to come to any decision.'

Imre wasn't really listening. 'I know who you are,' he said, brushing Emlee away. 'More to the point, what you are.'

'It doesn't matter,' said the figure impatiently. 'What I'm telling you is the important thing. Stay away from Domgard. Go anywhere else but Hyperabad, since your cover is blown there now. Be careful. You'll know how to contact us when you work out what you want. I can't promise we'll take you in, but that is an option.'

'I know exactly what I want,' he said, surprising himself with the certainty in his voice. 'I don't need to think about it.'

'That is?'

'I have a second chance. When the Jinc brought me back, they were pursuing their own agenda. But they did bring me back, and I'm not going to waste what they've given me. I can undo the damage. I can right what's gone wrong.'

The figure laughed. 'With the galaxy? That's a bigger job than you can possibly imagine.'

'I'm not talking about the galaxy. Not yet. I'm talking about me. Everything I did in the past isn't what I'd do now. I want — yes, I want to be a better person than I was. If that means turning my back on everything you're hinting at, so be it. I'll find my own way.'

'The chances are you'll only find yourself as lost as you are now.'

'At least I'll be lost following my own trail, not yours.'

'Don't be so sure you know who I am, Imre Bergamasc. That could be a fatal mistake.'

Helwise waved a hand in front of his face, breaking his near-hypnotic focus on the display. 'I said, are you seeing this? The ships are changing course. They're going to get away if we don't do something about it now. This is your last chance to change your mind.'

Imre blinked and shifted his gaze. As she had said, two of the three Vespulas were coming around to join the third, which was thrusting away into free space. *Memento Mori* too had deviated from its original course, following the parabola dictated by the laws of gravitation back toward the dead star. The distance between it and the three ships was rapidly increasing.

'I see it,' he said. 'What's the problem? They're not attacking us. We're not attacking them. We're going to go our separate ways, for now.'

'Are you sure about this?'

'Yes. I'm sure.'

She turned to the ship's maintenance. Freer did the same, happy to be given orders to follow. His inner feelings on the matter were carefully hidden. Only Emlee watched as Imre turned his attention back to the screen.

'Leave us alone,' he said to the unwelcome ghost. 'I think we've said enough to each other.'

'Let me ask you something first. Did you say that the Jinc brought you back?'

'That's right. What of them?'

'You've just told me where you came from. I remember that repository on the edge of the galaxy. As a matter of fact, I ordered its destruction.'

Imre closed his eyes. 'Why?'

'To dispose of the evidence, of course. It should never have existed in the first place. If you don't know that by now, you'll soon work it out. Good-bye, Imre Bergamasc.'

The display window closed at the same time a small packet of data arrived on the same channel. Imre cautiously scanned it. The file was a simple audio recording containing no known viruses or trojans. He considered hitting 'erase' without opening it, unwilling to accept a gift that he doubted would come cheaply.

Emlee was still watching him, no doubt wondering what all the fuss was about.

The tiniest mental gesture opened the recording. It began with a second of deep, no-signal hiss: the music of stars in their trillions, burning brightly in the dark. Then a familiar, genderless voice half-buried in static began to speak.

'You were old when the universe was young,' it said, loudly enough to fill the bridge. 'The evidence of your existence spans the arch of the heavens. You are the creator and the destroyer. Heed the prayer we commit to the void.'

Imre's fingers clenched tight around themselves, digging his nails into his palms. He would recognize the voice of the Jinc, fifth ganglion of the Noh exploratory arm, anywhere.

'Your emissary is gone,' the Jinc went on. 'We were blessed but found unworthy. You gave us evidence, and we did not recognize it. For that we are deeply penitent. A prophet and an angel were in our midst, but our eyes did not open until your name was spoken and our mind was cleared of all other thoughts.'

Startling in its clarity came Imre's own voice from the speakers, crying a single word – 'Luminous!' – as he had summoned the help of the silver sphere. The Jinc employed it now as a talisman to invoke the deity it worshipped, whose name Imre had until that moment not known.

Helwise and Freer added their stares to Emlee's as the voice prayed on.

'The one who called you was found and is now lost. Your angel has departed. We beseech you, our God, to shine your light upon us once more. Illuminate our sacred path that we may know the road toward you. Hear our words, and grace us with an answer. We are patient. We sift the darkness for your guidance with rapturous hearts. We dedicate our quest to you and to your mighty works. You are master over all levels of creation. Your seed created us, and your wrath destroys us. We worship you in your absence.'

There the file ended.

He bowed his head, understanding that although the message had not been intended for anyone's ears, it had been intercepted and its significance noted.

Freer was thinking along the same lines. 'That was you?' He nodded. 'I guess the Barons recognized your voiceprint. That's how they knew you were back.'

'Pretty easy from there,' added Helwise, 'to look for you 'round here.'

'Did they tell you anything,' asked Emlee, 'about what the Luminous was? I'm not going to accept that it's actually a god.'

Imre shook his head, dragging his thoughts back from the far-off horizon of his speculations. 'I asked, but – but he changed the subject. There's a war, apparently. He told us to stay out of it. To forget about the Forts, Domgard, and Q loop technology. To keep our heads down or lose them altogether.' He felt a thunderhead of anger building in him that hadn't been there before. This was different from Helwise and her other selves; it went beyond the Jinc getting his gender wrong and trying to absorb him into it; it eclipsed the First Church of the Return and its attempt to turn him into a messiah.

But it wouldn't have existed without those things. Each was part of the solution, as well as the problem. The road he glimpsed would be long and hard, but it would be good for a change to move forward without constantly glancing behind him, trying to second-guess the man who had destroyed his own backup because the small moment of doubt he had experienced after *Pelorus* would incriminate him if it were ever discovered.

'We're going to Hyperabad,' he said. 'We're going to pay a visit to Chyro Kells and offer him a job as my personal surgeon — because I think every savior should have one, don't you?' He began to pace. 'The first thing he's going to do is cut the Loop shunt out of me. The second thing he's going to do is turn me into a Prime. Being a singleton hasn't done me any good. I don't want to have anything to do with the rest of me. I'm going to be myself, and feel beholden to no one else.' He took a deep breath, feeling a chorus of memories rising up in complaint at that decision. He ignored them and concentrated on the stump of his missing finger, the one palpable part of his body that truly belonged to him. 'Once I've done that, we're going to Earth.'

'What?' asked Helwise, looking as though he'd taken complete and utter leave of his senses. 'Why there, of all places?'

'Because it's anarchy out here,' he said, 'and the time has come to put things in order. Time to stop waiting around for the Forts to come back and fix the Continuum. Time to make a new beginning, back where it all started. Are you with me?'

Freer nodded, as Imre had known he would. 'All the way.'

'Do you intend to look for the Luminous as we go?' asked Emlee more cautiously. 'I still owe them for what they did to Ampersand.'

'What people see on the surface,' Imre promised her, 'will hide all manner of things. Finding Domgard, the Luminous and the people behind the Slow Wave — if they aren't one and the same thing — is a priority.'

'Then I'll back you,' she said with her eyes locked on his, 'if Render will.'

'I won't kneel down,' said the big soldier from the medical suite. 'I won't praise your name.'

'I'll never ask you to,' Imre told him. 'The same goes for all of you.'

'Well, it's somewhere to go,' said Render.

That was as close to an unequivocal 'yes' as Imre was going to get.

Last of all, he turned to Helwise, who stood with her blue-robed arms folded on the far side of the bridge.

'I'm with Render on this,' she said with a guarded expression on her face. 'I'm happy to kick some arse, but don't expect me to kiss yours.'

'You'll never be a slave to anyone but yourself, Helwise.'

He caught a flicker of hurt in her dark eyes, but it was quickly hidden. 'All right, then,' she said. 'What are we waiting for? Let's get out of this joint and go make some noise.'

'My sentiments exactly,' said Freer with a sloppy salute at the iron station. 'Farewell, Kismet. May you and Warden Goneril be happy forever.'

'I'll be happy when we leave this whole system behind us,' said Emlee, looking weary. 'It's been a long haul.'

'Fade to scenes of violence,' said Render. 'Let the fun begin.'

Empty words, Imre thought, and empty promises. He let his attention wander to the display window showing the trio of ships receding into the starscape.

Under Helwise's command, *Memento Mori*'s drives surged and began the long, hard climb out of the dead star's gravity well.

Map of the Milky Way

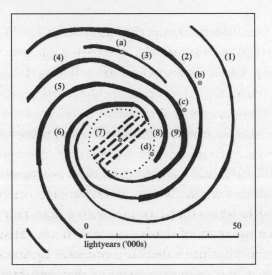

lightyears ('000s)

1. Outer Arm
2. Perseus Arm
3. Local Arm
4. Carina Arm
5. Crux Arm
6. Norma Arm
7. Bar
8. Scutum Arm
9. Sagittarius Arm

a) Sol
b) Chimeleon
c) Mandala Supersystem
d) Morwedd

Appendix A: Absolute Calendar

Subjective time (like humanity) is a flexible thing. While Primes perceive the ticking of seconds in much the same way humans did before leaving Earth, overclockers may live hours or days in a minute, and Forts regard the passing of a year Absolute as a lazy afternoon. Everyone dances to a different beat, as governed by convenience, necessity, or local regulation. (The common rule of thumb, that the relative tempos of Primes, singletons, and Forts matches their usual environments of planets, interstellar space, and the galaxy as a whole, doesn't always apply.) For this reason – combined with light-speed transmission lags and relativistic effects – keeping track of dates is very difficult. Historians may despair that the Absolute Calendar is observed by few and adhered to by none, but life for most citizens of the Continuum proceeds happily enough. The hypothetical clock counting the beats of Universal Time ticks on, regardless.

Following is a list of important dates in the Absolute Calendar, accurate to the nearest thousand years. 'C' is employed as an abbreviation for 'Century,' so 'the twentieth century' becomes 'C20.' Similarly with 'M' and 'Millennium.' As the Absolute Calendar nears its first million mark, no other simplification has emerged.

C20 — Archard Rositano and Bianca Biancotti born
C30–M30 — Great Human Expansion
M50 — Continuum defined
M100 — Mandala Supersystem discovered and settled
M150 (approx.) — Milky Way settled from end to end
M220 — Fort domination complete
M250 — Corps founded
M349 — Imre Bergamasc joins the Corps

M402 — Chaos War

M443 — Anahita Campaign

M550–722 — Mad Times

M777 — Morwedd Campaign

M790 — Chimeleon Campaign

M820 — Slow Wave epicenter

M830 — Slow Wave hits Morwedd

M840 — Slow Wave hits Hyperabad

M850 — Slow Wave hits Sol

M862 — Slow Wave hits Chimeleon

M844+ — Battle of the Lines

M864+ — Hyperabad government dominant in Mandala Supersystem

M861 – Hyperabad proto-Fort experiment

M861 – Foundation of the First Church of the Return

M870 – Slow Wave finishes

M878 – Drum reconstructed

M879 – 'now'

Appendix B: Glossary

Absolute: see Tempo.

Alienist Technarchy: A regime founded on principles of radical rationalism and technological expansion; major aggressor in the Chaos War; destroyed by Imre Bergamasc in a Corps Campaign during the 402nd Millennium.

Continuum: The term by which the sum of human civilization is usually referred, from the 50th Millennium on; includes all civilizations within the Milky Way, and some efforts at expansion beyond.

Corps: Mercenary force founded in the 250th Millennium that proved influential in the Mad Times due to its intimate dealings with the Forts, against which the Corps's then leader, Imre Bergamasc, defiantly turned. Last known members are: Imre Bergamasc (commander), Emlee Copas (signals), Alphin Freer (resources), Helwise MacPhedron (intelligence), and Archard Rositano (combat specialist).

Frag: A Fort component, resembling a Prime or singleton but possessing little true individuality; frags may be separated by light-years yet firmly connected by Q loop technology to its parent mind; Forts regard frags as functionally expendable, but may display affection to particular frags in the same way that Primes keep pets or look after their hair.

Fort: see Tempo.

Hyperabad: Capital of the Hyperabadan regime; also a planet orbiting the star Chenresi; also the regime of the same name, which has come to dominate Mandala Supersystem after the 864th Millennium.

Jinc: Component of the gestalt commonly referred to as the Noh; one of seven similar components that function as far-sensing organs on the fringes of the Milky Way, searching for the source of life in the galaxy, which is presumed to be of exogenic origin.

Line: Common term for individual legs of the vast electromagnetic telecommunications web spanning the Milky Way.

Loop / Loop shunt: see Q loop.

Mad Times: Major conflict spanning 550th to 722nd Millennia in which non-Fort human civilizations revolted against the Milky Way's effective rulers; ended with the defection of Imre Bergamasc during the Battle of *Pelorus*.

Mandala Supersystem: One of three similar, possibly artificial, multiple star systems in the Milky Way consisting of one central, massive star orbited by several smaller stars, each with their own planetary systems. The eight companion stars in this particular supersystem are: Akasagarbha, Chenresi, Chugai Zhang, Di-Zang, Jampa, Kuntuzangpo, Manjushri, and Sakra.

Old-Timer: Common term for a living individual born during the 20th Century; usually refers to those who have lived continuously, in one form or another, since their births.

Overclocking: see Tempo.

Pelorus: Flagship of the Sol Invictus movement; destroyed at the climax of the conflict known as the Mad Times.

Prime: Common term for an individual whose identity and values closely conform to those of Old-Time humans, particularly those of the twentieth century, when the first Old-Timers were born; most Primes function as a matter of principle at Tempo Absolute.

Q loop: Means of communication employed by Forts to enable long-distance, untraceable communication between component frags and each other; loop shunts are devices requiring little power and possessing extremely high signal/noise characteristics.

Singleton: Common term for an individual that is neither a component in a gestalt nor a true Prime; it is common practice in the Continuum to possess several singleton copies that exchange, merge, or overlap memories at regular intervals throughout an extended life; tempo is flexible among singletons, ranging from very fast to near-Fort states of existence.

Sol Invictus: Name of the dominant anti-Fort movement during the Mad Times; founded on the planet of Uraniborg, whose sun was destroyed during the early stages of that extended conflict in an attempt to crush the movement.

Tempo: Usual term employed to describe the perception of time at varying rates. 'Tempo Absolute' refers to time as experienced by Primes and Old-Time humanity and is widely held as a default referent; 'overclocking' is the practice of fitting more seconds than one into a single second Absolute, thereby experiencing time at an increased rate; the most evolved human individuals, known as Forts, experience time at an extremely slow tempo, with individual relative seconds sometimes spanning centuries.

Vespula: Common brand of interstellar fighter employed extensively during the Mad Times; millions remain in active service, scattered across all arms of the Milky Way.

Appendix C: 'My Confession'

Use the word 'gothic' and one of two associations spring to mind: gothic literature (pick your own definition) or gothic music (ditto). The former is, arguably, the easiest to reference in a space opera novel, since they belong in the same medium, but it struck me as unfair to ignore the other completely. Music inspires me as much as literature, particularly when setting the mood for my daily writing sessions. Who better to reference, when combining science fiction and gothic concerns, than seminal electronic musician Gary Numan?

The choice seems obvious to me. A postpunk Philip K. Dick regarded as a founding father of synth-pop, Gary Numan obsessed in the early 1980s about such universal subjects as religion, sex, heartbreak, and the inevitable dystopia. He used science-fictional imagery without embarrassment. He even sounded a bit like a robot at times – but one whose heart had broken, with more humanity than the more processed vocalists whose descendants we hear today. His relevance continues: across thirty years and almost as many albums, his unique brand of music has evolved with the world and is currently undergoing a mainstream revival.

I joked, once, that I would use his lyrics in a novel – to pay tribute to him, and also to bring the influence full circle. The words of Ballard, Dick, and Ellison clearly influenced Numan; so too would Numan's words influence mine. The joke became more serious the more I thought about it. His professional philosophy was in full accord with my desires: in his song 'My Confession,' he sings of his willingness to 'steal anything in sight or sound.' Surely it would be possible, someday. Surely.

This book is the culmination of many years of wishing and a great deal of recent hard work. The character of Render takes his nickname from the Numan song 'I am Render.' He is my creation, but he speaks with the words of Gary Numan – every one of them, from the most banal of everyday phrases to the most complex internal monologue. Why would Render do this? Perhaps he, like me, was a fan in his long-buried youth. Perhaps he found the legacy of a kindred spirit locked away in a dusty archive and adopted the affectation as a tribute. Perhaps Render is tapping into the same depersonalized melancholia that Numan was accessing almost a million years earlier. Or perhaps it's just a fluke. Pick your own reason.

I owe a debt of thanks for this wonderful opportunity to Gary Numan himself and to his manager, Tony Webb. Cat Walker and Melinda Mondrala at Universal, Steve Farnaby, and Richard Churchward also played important roles. See the end of this Appendix for lists of Gary Numan albums referenced in this novel (the first list) and songs quoted from (the second).

For different reasons, I would like to thank Lou Anders, Danny Baror, Ginjer Buchanan, Richard Curtis, Tim Holman, Darren Nash, Robin Potanin, Chris Roberson, Jonathan Strahan, Scott Westerfeld, Kim Wilkins, Stephen Wilson, and the wonderful Amanda Nettelbeck. I would lastly like to thank Garth Nix for inviting me to dinner at Melbourne's Flower Drum restaurant, during which meal this novel was born. I'm sure I was the only one who noticed.

Albums: *Berserker* (1984), *Dance* (1981), *Exile* (1997), *I, Assassin* (1982), *Jagged* (2006), *Machine + Soul* (1992), *Metal Rhythm* (1988), *Outland* (1990), *Pure* (2000), *Replicas* (1979), *Sacrifice* (1994), *Strange Charm* (1986), *Telekon* (1980), *The Fury* (1985), *Warriors* (1983).

'A Child with the Ghost,' 'A Prayer for the Unborn,' 'A Question of Faith,' 'An AlienCure,' 'Before You Hate It,' 'Bleed,' 'Blind,' 'Breathe in Emotion,' 'Call Out the Dogs,' 'Change Your Mind,' 'Cold Metal Rhythm,' 'Confession,' 'Creatures,' 'Cry,' 'Cry, the Clock Said,' 'Dark,' 'Deadliner,' 'Desire,' 'Devious,' 'Devotion,'

'Emotion,' 'Exhibition,' 'Exile,' 'Face to Face/Letters,' 'Fold,' 'Haunted,' 'Heart,' 'Here Am I,' 'Hunger,' 'I Can't Breathe,' 'I Can't Stop,' 'I Don't Believe,' 'I Still Remember,' 'I Wonder,' 'Icehouse,' 'I'm an Agent,' 'In a Dark Place,' 'Innocence Bleeding,' 'Jagged,' 'Listen to my Voice,' 'Love and Napalm,' 'Love is Like Clock Law,' 'Love Isolation,' 'Machine & Soul,' 'Magic,' 'Melt,' 'Miracles,' 'Moral,' 'My Brother's Time,' 'My Dying Machine,' 'My Fascination,' 'Night Talk,' 'Nightlife,' 'Outland,' 'Play Like God,' 'Poetry and Power,' 'Poison,' 'Pressure,' 'Prophecy,' 'Respect,' 'Rip it Up,' 'Rip,' 'Rumour,' 'Scar,' 'Shame,' 'Sister Surprise,' 'Slave,' 'Slowcar to China,' 'Some New Game,' 'Strange Charm,' 'The Angel Wars,' 'The God Film,' 'The Image Is,' 'The Joy Circuit,' 'The Need,' 'The Rhythm of the Evening,' 'The Seed of a Lie,' 'The Skin Game,' 'The Tick Tock Man,' 'This is Emotion,' 'This is New Love,' 'This Prison Moon,' 'This Wreckage,' 'Torn,' 'Tread Careful,' 'Tricks,' 'Turn off the World,' 'Unknown and Hostile,' 'Voix,' 'War Games,' 'Warriors,' 'We Are Glass,' 'We Take Mystery (To Bed),' 'Whisper of Truth,' 'Whisper,' 'You Walk In My Soul.'

'Do You Need the Service?'

'You Are In My Vision'

New York Times-bestselling author **Sean Williams** live in Adelaide. He is the author of over sixty published short stories and eighteen novels, including the Book of the Change and (with Shane Dix) the bestselling Evergence and Orphans trilogies. He has co-written three books in the Star Wars: New Jedi Order series and is a multiple recipient of both the Ditmar & Aurealis Awards. For a change of pace, he likes to DJ and cook curries.

Find out more about Sean Williams and other Orbit authors by registering for the free monthly newsletter at www.orbitbooks.net